THE COUNTRY YOU

Liverpool Science Fiction Texts and Studies

Editor
David Seed
University of Liverpool

Editorial Board

MARK BOULD
University of the West of England

VERONICA HOLLINGER
Trent University

ROB LATHAM
University of Iowa

ROGER LUCKHURST
Birkbeck College, University of London

PATRICK PARRINDER
University of Reading

ANDY SAWYER
University of Liverpool

1. Robert Crossley *Olaf Stapledon: Speaking for the Future*
2. David Seed (ed.) *Anticipations: Essays on Early Science Fiction and its Precursors*
3. Jane L. Donawerth and Carol A. Kolmerten (eds) *Utopian and Science Fiction by Women: Worlds of Difference*
4. Brian W. Aldiss *The Detached Retina: Aspects of SF and Fantasy*
5. Carol Farley Kessler *Charlotte Perkins Gilman: Her Progress Toward Utopia, with Selected Writings*
6. Patrick Parrinder *Shadows of the Future: H. G. Wells, Science Fiction and Prophecy*
7. I. F. Clarke (ed.) *The Tale of the Next Great War, 1871–1914: Fictions of Future Warfare and of Battles Still-to-Come*
8. Joseph Conrad and Ford Madox Ford *The Inheritors*
9. Qingyun Wu *Female Rule in Chinese and English Literary Utopias*
10. John Clute *Look at the Evidence: Essays and Reviews*
11. Roger Luckhurst *'The Angle Between Two Walls': The Fiction of J. G. Ballard*
12. I. F. Clarke (ed.) *The Great War with Germany, 1890–1914: Fiction and Fantasies of the War-to-come*
13. Franz Rottensteiner (ed.) *View from Another Shore: European Science Fiction*
14. Val Gough and Jill Rudd (eds) *A Very Different Story: Studies in the Fiction of Charlotte Perkins Gilman*
15. Gary Westfahl *The Mechanics of Wonder: The Creation of the Idea of Science Fiction*
16. Gwyneth Jones *Deconstructing the Starships*
17. Patrick Parrinder (ed.) *Learning from Other Worlds: Estrangement, Cognition and the Politics of Science Fiction and Utopia*
18. Jeanne Cortiel *Demand My Writing: Joanna Russ, Feminism, Science Fiction*
19. Chris Ferns *Narrating Utopia: Ideology, Gender, Form in Utopian Literature*
20. E. J. Smyth (ed.) *Jules Verne: New Directions*
21. Andy Sawyer and David Seed (eds) *Speaking Science Fiction: Dialogues and Interpretations*
22. Inez van der Spek *Alien Plots: Female Subjectivity and the Divine in the Light of James Tiptree's 'A Momentary Taste of Being'*
23. S. T. Joshi *Ramsey Campbell and Modern Horror Fiction*
24. Mike Ashley *The Time Machines: The Story of the Science-Fiction Pulp Magazines from the Beginning to 1950*
25. Warren G. Rochelle *Communities of the Heart: The Rhetoric of Myth in the Fiction of Ursula K. Le Guin*
26. S. T. Joshi *A Dreamer and a Visionary: H. P. Lovecraft in His Time*
27. Christopher Palmer *Philip K. Dick: Exhilaration and Terror of the Postmodern*
28. Charles E. Gannon *Rumors of War and Infernal Machines: Technomilitary Agenda-setting in American and British Speculative Fiction*
29. Peter Wright *Attending Daedalus: Gene Wolfe, Artifice and the Reader*
30. Mike Ashley *Transformations: The Story of the Science-Fiction Magazines from 1950 to 1970*
31. Joanna Russ *The Country You Have Never Seen: Essays and Reviews*
32. Robert Philmus *Visions and Re-Visions: (Re)Constructing Science Fiction*
33. Gene Wolf (edited and introduced by Peter Wright) *Shadows of the New Sun: Wolfe on Writing/Writers on Wolfe*
34. Mike Ashley *Gateways to Forever: The Story of the Science-Fiction Magazine from 1970–1980*

THE COUNTRY
YOU HAVE NEVER SEEN

Essays and Reviews

JOANNA RUSS

Liverpool University Press

First published 2007 by
Liverpool University Press
4 Cambridge Street
Liverpool L69 7ZU

Copyright © 2007 Joanna Russ

The right of Joanna Russ to be identified as the author of this work has been asserted by her in accordance with the Copyright, Design and Patents Act 1988.

All rights reserved. No part of this book may be reproduced, stored in a retrieval system, or transmitted, in any form or by any means, electronic, mechanical, photocopying, recording, or otherwise, without the prior written permission of the publisher.

British Library Cataloguing-in-Publication data
A British Library CIP record is available

ISBN 978-0-85323-859-1 cased
978-0-85323-869-0 limp

Typeset by XL Publishing Services Ltd, Tiverton
Printed and bound by CPI Group (UK) Ltd, Croydon, CR0 4YY

Contents

Reviews 1

Essays 191

Letters 247

Index of Books and Authors Reviewed 299

Reviews

The Magazine of Fantasy and Science Fiction, December 1966

Strange Signposts, An Anthology of the Fantastic. Ed. Roger Elwood and Sam Moskowitz (Holt Rinehart and Winston, 1966, 319 pp., $5.50)

Strange Signposts is a bottom-of-the barrel anthology. There are Big Names in it, but don't be tempted: most of them are represented by bad stories, or excerpts from novels, or unfinished works. Mary Shelley's "story," for instance, is an extremely disjointed 21-page condensation of an entire novel, freed from any "extraneous dialogue, description or other unnecessary exposition." They're lucky she's dead. H. G. Wells is represented by a very early story – unfinished – and Edgar Rice Burroughs by a very late one – unfinished. There is an unusually silly excerpt from a novel by Jules Verne (which you can probably find in its entirety if you want to), and an excerpt from a boy's book that describes a helicopter (and then goes on much too long), and early pieces by Arthur C. Clarke and Robert Bloch that I sincerely hope are their worst. Two other Big Names are included: Lovecraft ("The Whisperer in Darkness") and Nathaniel Hawthorne ("Rappacini's Daughter"). The former is available in a paperback collection of Lovecraft's from Arkham House and the latter – how could they have the face to include it? – is available just about everywhere; there is no excuse for including it in anything again except a textbook. There are three naive stories from writers of the '30s, one so-so nineteenth-century piece by Edgar Allan Poe that is two parts tedious philosophizing and politicizing and one part real fun. (This story *should* be in the book and this one they should have cut.) Mr. Elwood's Introduction thoughtfully synopsizes most of the stories, apparently without the slightest suspicion that he is letting out Hawthorne's whole secret and ruining Lovecraft's very slow, very effective build-up of suspense. Lucky they're both dead, too.

 A collection of obscure stories by Big Names might be worth it; or one of unfindable stories or out-of-print works or previously uncollected writers (I believe someone has just issued "The King in Yellow" in paperback and a fairly expensive paperback collection of Lefanu); or even of historical curiosities like Frank Reade's helicopter (if they're tolerable) but this is none of them. It is not even a collection of predictions, as the introduction suggests: Bloch's story is sheer fantasy, Burroughs' certainly the same and Hawthorne's hardly more. This is one of that damned flood of anthologies that do nothing but cheapen the market, exasperate reviewers and disappoint all but the most unsophisticated readers.

The Magazine of Fantasy and Science Fiction, **October 1967**

The Warriors of the Day. James Blish (Lancer, 60¢). *Stealer of Souls* and *Stormbringer.* Michael Moorcock (Lancer, 60¢)

What is James Blish doing writing a book like *The Warriors of Day*? Mr. Blish is a writer of excellent qualities: intelligence, logic, complexity, precision, wide knowledge, intellectual rigor (and vigor) and a natural preference for exact and telling detail. *Warriors of Day* is a bastard sword-and-sorcery *cum* science fiction novel which resembles nothing so much as a mulligan stew (a little bit of everything with explanations thrown in mostly *ex post facto*) and it provides a beautiful display of all of Mr. Blish's defects. Swashbuckling demands a certain suspension of the critical sense and an inability to make exact comparisons, neither of which qualities Mr. Blish can acquire any more than he can cut off his own head. He is a speculative realist trying to write a romantic novel; he cannot write it and he will not give it up, so he goes on and on, clashing gears and grinding (my) teeth. Let me give an example. When the hero, early in the story, walks from earth into another world – in a sub-arctic forest – *at night* – Mr. Blish conveys the strangeness of this experience by comparing it to a sudden passage from the Kodiak forest path to – Times Square. This is a good, functional comparison and it is absolutely anti-evocative. It is dead wrong. And the man does it again. And again. Flowers in the strange world look like daisies but are "cornflower blue" with an undertone of "electric green." A beast resembles something "in the Berlin zoo." The motionlessness of a forest "could have been measured with a micrometer … a still photograph." And so on. When the novel grows exotic or fantastic the style becomes unbelievably sloppy and stereotyped ("ragged men hawked portions of green liquor cupped in transparent skins") and the word "wrong" is repeated innumerable times in a half-desperate, half-annoyed effort to create a sense of the Strangeness Of It All.

About the characterization I will only say that beyond Mr. Blish's hero you cannot go; he has no romantic insides because Mr. Blish is not able to create that sort of character, and he has no realistic insides because they would blow the rest of the book skyhigh; the result is an emotionless, invulnerable superman who is not even believable as a stereotype and whom Mr. Blish instinctively makes detestable except when the action grows too silly to be credible at all.

I would not execrate *Warriors of Day* so much if I did not know what James Blish can do when his heart is really in it. Either the typewriter wrote this book, with Mr. Blish's contribution nothing but occasional pieces of sharp observation and a profound air of disgust, or there is an Anti-Blish hidden in the real Blish's gray matter, and that is a serious business indeed.

In Michael Moorcock's *Stealer of Souls* and *Stormbringer* the work and the writer are entirely at one. Vividly colored, sensuously evocative but always a little vague, impressively single-minded and written with the utter conviction that is probably the indispensable element in this genre, Mr. Moorcock's sword-and-sorcery romances are near the top of the mark. I must add, though, for the benefit of those who came to sword-and-sorcery through writers like Fritz Leiber or Jack Vance, that Mr. Moorcock's romances are also entirely innocent of either the slightest trace of humor or what might tactfully be called the common operations of intelligence. Elric, the protagonist, is a Byronic hero and nothing else: cynicism, suffering, pride and loneliness, with devastating weakness paradoxically linked to evil, unhuman strength. This kind of thing crumbles the moment it allows you to think, but Mr. Moorcock never makes the mistake of giving you anything to think about; there is no real geography here, no real morality, no real characters and hardly even any real weather. All is dissolved in a fiery emotional mist. *Stormbringer*, a complete novel, suffers much more from the necessity of sustaining all this than does *Stealer of Souls*, which is a collection of shorter pieces. Moreover, *Stormbringer* has to make explicit the morality implicit in its predecessor, and this morality – stupefyingly simple as it necessarily is – does excite the critical faculty just a little and so threatens to weaken the romance. Also, Moorcockian orthography tends to have a cumulatively unsettling effect. I swallowed Myyrrhn, Imrryr, Yyrkoon, h'Haarshanns and D'a'rputna, but when I came to the monster Quaolnargn, who "would answer to this name *if called*" (italics mine), I began to speculate whether Mr. Moorcock was Welsh, whether he was *very* Welsh, whether he had ever written for the Goon Show and so on and so on, quite against the purposes of Elric, last Prince of Melnibone. The verse-spells, too, are awful and should be cut. And "reed" should be "rede" throughout.

Otherwise, for those who like this sort of thing, this is the sort of thing they will like very much. Myself, I find James Blish's sense of fact a hundred times more exciting – even in a bad book – than all Mr. Moorcock's cloud-capp'd towers and gorgeous palaces. These are splendid but ultimately boring while fact is never either; fact is suggestive, various, complex and free – in short, it's fact – and this is the stuff with which writers like Mr. Blish are trying, however erratically or imperfectly, to deal.

The Magazine of Fantasy and Science Fiction, January 1968

Lord of Light. Roger Zelazny (Doubleday, $14.95). *The Mind Parasites.* Colin Wilson (Arkham House, $4.00).

Roger Zelazny has been working at the problem of plotting a novel for some time now. *This Immortal* had no real plot; *Dream Master* was essentially an expanded novella. In his latest book, *Lord of Light*,[1] he combines seven episodes – some splendid, some merely very good – into what is not quite a whole novel.

Lord of Light draws on classical Indian culture to recreate it on a future colony of vanished Earth, where the first settlers (who deliberately made up the culture after the Earthly model) play the roles of the gods and goddesses of the Hindu pantheon, relying on their mutant psi powers and considerable scientific gadgetry. Reincarnation is a reality, for personalities are now transferred from body to artificially grown body, and the demon Rakasha of Hindu legend is the original, energy-based life of the planet: protean, immortal, and inimical to humankind. A banished god, Siddhartha, Binder of Demons, and then (as a deliberate move against his former colleagues and in imitation of Earthly history) a reviver of Buddhism with himself as the Bodhisattva, sets out to fight the heavenly Establishment and thus bring back technical progress to the mass of mankind. At the end of the book, Heaven (a geographically locatable city) is on its way to ruin, and the hero – who has been many people in many bodies, for the story spans generations – vanishes in the mysterious manner typical of his religious and mythological prototypes.

None of the above gives more than a slight idea of the brilliance of *Lord of Light*, of the manner in which the mimicked Hindu culture is both splendidly described and splendidly explained in the purest science fiction terms; Zelazny can write like the Ramayana while discussing incendiary grenades or the flush toilet. He can also recount events in Heaven in colloquialisms that would embarrass every god and goddess in it, and rightly so. There is even a physicist's equivalent of Nirvana in something like a visible Van Allen belt. The two worlds never conflict; they are always at one, and that is a triumph.

1 Two sections of *Lord of Light* appeared in *F&SF*: "Dawn," April 1967 and "Death and the Executioner," June 1967.

But the book is still not a whole. Behind the gorgeously colored, woven screen of the foreground there are glimpses of something else: the personal stories of these inhabitants of Heaven, the actual colonization, the effect upon human beings of immortality and the Aspects and Attributes of the super-human, a real conflict of philosophies and attitudes. In one sense it's a tribute to the book that these begin to seem, after a while, more real than the episodic adventures of the foreground. But they also begin to seem more interesting, and when that happens the foreground – although not exactly dull – becomes irrelevant. The beginning of *Lord of Light* promises much more than the book ever delivers. Kali, the goddess of destruction, on whom a great deal of motivation and plot depend, turns out on close view to be neither particularly interesting nor particularly believable; the great final battle with Heaven is disappointing and even annoying because none of the personal or philosophical issues raised in the course of the book is really settled. The mechanics of the plot are satisfied; that's all. Behind the exciting surface movement of the book is a tale of outsiders fighting entrenched insiders and the story of X who loves Y who loves Z who knows better. But Sam/Siddhartha/Buddha never rises above the personal adventurousness of a kind of combative instinct, and Kali, who is as beautiful as rain-clouds, whose feet are covered with blood, and who wears a necklace made from the skulls of her children, whom she has slain (in the original mythology), is only a tepidly conventional bitch without even the force to be genuinely destructive, let alone the "disfiguring and degenerative disease" that Sam calls her.

Will Zelazny ever write the inside stories of his stories? Can he?

Colin Wilson has produced, and Arkham House has published "a 'Lovecraft novel'" entitled *The Mind Parasites*. Devotees of HPL will be disappointed, however, and so will everybody else; the Outsider's latest is not in the Lovecraft tradition but in the Boy's Life Gee Whiz tradition and ought to be called "Tom Swift and the Tsathogguans." It is one of the worst books I have ever read and very enjoyable, but then I did not have to pay for it. An example:

> He [the President of the United States] asked how we proposed to stop the war.
> "First of all, President, [sic] we want you to get on to the central television agency and announce that you will be appearing in six hours' time to make an announcement that concerns the whole world."
> "And you can tell me what it is?"
> "I'm not yet sure. But I think it will concern the moon."

I have an announcement to make too. It concerns a severe letter to August Derleth (who seems to have suggested this book, possibly out of exasperation), a gallon of kerosene, a match, a certain 222-page home-cooked romance, and a copy of *The Shadow Over Innsmouth* to relax with afterwards. Howard Phillips, you never looked better.

The Magazine of Fantasy and Science Fiction, July 1968

The Best of the Best. Ed. Judith Merril (Delacorte, $6.50). *Ashes, Ashes.* René Barjavel, trans. Damon Knight (Doubleday, $3.95). *A Torrent of Faces.* James Blish and Norman L. Knight (Doubleday, $4.95)

The Best of the Best is a collection of stories chosen by the editor from her previous anthologies, *The Year's Best S-F*, from 1955 to 1960. At about the fifth story, the Merrilian bent of these twenty-nine tales becomes clear – they are human, "poignant," chosen for feeling and not for gimmickry or detachable ideas. The hard sciences are conspicuously absent. So is philosophy, despite the editor's introduction. At best this leads to stories like J. G. Ballard's "Prima Belladonna," the first of his Vermilion Sands stories I ever read. Is it the first ever published? When it appeared in the second annual *Best* anthology this story seemed cryptic, but it vindicates Miss Merril's judgment retrospectively. It's not only full-bodied and perfectly clear; it's probably one of the earliest future-society-taken-for-granted-instead-of-explained stories and it still manages to look futuristic and fresh. Human feeling and literary finish were also good guides in selecting the star of the collection, Gummitch the superkitten (!), who returns in "Space-Time for Springers" by Fritz Leiber. The less I say about this story the less I will slobber over the page and make a nut of myself. There are also two by Carol Emshwiller, Avram Davidson's "Golem," and an early (?) Cordwainer Smith ("No, No. Not Rogov!") which is only half mad, and Damon Knight's "Stranger Station." These are all first-rate stories and so are many of the others. But.

The editor's taste for "the human factor" – or a retrospective interest in New Thing writers like Ballard and Emshwiller – or perhaps a reaction against too much hardware in the field (both now and back then) – has made *The Best of the Best* a surprisingly monotonous book. The stories are good, but the tone is somehow the same all through. In her introduction the editor notes that science fiction is "a field which degenerates ... readily into mere adventure story." In avoiding "mere adventure story," Miss Merril sometimes chooses stories that degenerate into mere something-else. Walter Miller's "Hoofer," for example, need not have been done as s-f at all. It's a re-doing of a good old American cliché, The Man Trapped by Marriage, and it isn't nearly as good as (say) Tennessee Williams' "Moony's Kid Don't Cry." Isaac Asimov's "Dreaming Is a Private Thing" is really about the movies. A story like Clifford Simak's "Death in the House" is moving, but it's sixth in the book; by the time one gets to Theodore Cogswell's "You Know Willie" (next to last) a certain feeling of repetition has begun to creep in. And a story like Fritz Leiber's "Mariana" is too close to untransformed fantasy.

Of course you needn't read all twenty-nine stories at one go, as I did. One of the best things about *The Best* is that it is fat, the way anthologies used to be in the fifties. You could lose yourself in one for weeks. It's a good book to give to people who think they don't like "science fiction.' If you read it yourself and start longing for missile trajectories and DNA, you can buy another sort of anthology and dip into the two alternately, like a Chinese dinner. If you haven't been following the annual Merril *Bests*, then by all means buy *The Best of the Best* and gnaw your way through it solo.

Ashes, Ashes, translated by Damon Knight from the French of René Barjavel, was originally published in France in 1943. Why on earth wasn't it translated twenty years ago? Why on earth didn't Doubleday pick something more recent? There's a certain *frisson* in reading about French cardboard people instead of American cardboard people, and the satire of future French society is pleasant for the first fifty pages. But once the book gets serious the fun vanishes. The novel is anti-technological and reactionary, the characters' adventures are trite by now, and the Utopia at the end is interesting only as pure cliché. Those passionately fond of High Camp may enjoy this, though even they will boggle at some teeny impossibilities in the text. Like the spontaneous generation of cholera microbes, for instance. The translator has apparently enjoyed himself (when he could) and has happily left the style of the novel French instead of trying to Americanize it. For example: "The most beautiful of these statues ... represented Intelligence. She opened her arms ... as if wishing to press to her breasts, each a meter in radius, all these men whom she had inspired." If only she had inspired Barjavel to stick to satire or Doubleday to stick to sense!

A Torrent of Faces is written by James Blish and Norman L. Knight. This makes for difficulty in constructing a compound name – it comes out either Blight or Knish, which is unfair to the book. Let's settle on B & K. The novel is a picture of Utopia in the twenty-eighth century; the earth supports one thousand billion people in reasonable comfort and contentment until natural disaster destroys the world society. The technical details of feeding and housing such vast numbers are the most fascinating things in the book; the many air views of cities, reefs, oceans, and "biological preserves" are superb. The authors' preface mentions "pages of calculations ... drawings and diagrams [and] about thirty thousand words of notes" going back to 1948. One can believe it. The shapes and sizes of cities, methods of food processing, family conventions, strange hotels, air travel, artificially bred mermen ("Tritons"), sewage disposal, et cetera – these are all beautifully presented. But the people are completely unreal. They aren't simply conventional or inconsistent or carelessly written. They are *pretexts* (most of the dialogue is expository), and their human reactions are flatly unbelievable. People in the mass are fine (a family convention in a "disaster city" is the best part of the book), but individual people don't even have the reality that comes from a strongly felt stereotype. It's as if everything human in the book was conceived in a movie long shot and then half-heartedly turned into a close-up. There are no overtones in the people or the social system. Etiquette, travel, leisure, habits, attitudes are presented as isolated facts, one at a time. They have been figured out logically but never felt as a whole. For example, there are two bloodless romances, one interracial (between human and Triton), but neither generates as much tension as a decision about whether to have a cup of coffee or not. There is also a psychotic member of the world government whose scheming isn't even necessary to the plot. There are times when *A Torrent of Faces* reads like a particularly antiseptic juvenile.

What happened? Maybe those years of notes and diagrams have something to do with it. This Utopia is so full *as a place* that there is no room for the people. The individual Tritons are clean in body and mind, like Boy Scouts or Sidney Poitier's recent roles, but *all mermen* (we are told) are inveterate shutterbugs. The latter is real. Disasters are real. Statistics are real. Slime culture is real. The most dramatic scene in the book concerns a large capsule of gallium and a lightly alloyed magnesium baffle. The most memorable character is an asteroid called Flavia. Why should the human beings be there at all? I would've been ten times as pleased with a fictional history or fictional textbook. The material is fascinating in itself. Why follow the *same* silly characters all through? There's a great deal to enjoy in the book but it's mixed with a lot of bland, exasperating lifelessness. Here's a Triton calming his hysterical Dryland sweetheart: "There are some facts about Tritons that you don't know, and they will almost certainly change your outlook when you do." And here is the panicky end of the Jones convention: "... a surf of Joneses was already out on the roof of the city. He could see several amoeboid batches of them, dim and sad in their drooping finery, clumping together like slime molds on the flyport's staging apron; but most of them were invisible, masked by the trees ... A falling star, so immense that it might have been a falling sun, was streaking with preternatural slowness over the city, lighting the whole landscape with a garish blue-white glare."

There's plenty of both. Take your choice.

The Magazine of Fantasy and Science Fiction, December 1968

Black Easter. James Blish (Doubleday, $3.95). *The Final Programme*. Michael Moorcock (Avon, 60c). *The Still Small Voice of Trumpets*. Lloyd Biggle (Doubleday, $4.50). *The Doomsday Men*. Kenneth Bulmer (Doubleday, $4.50). *Flesh*. Philip José Farmer (Doubleday, $3.95)

In the field of science fiction or fantasy, morality – when it enters a books at all – is almost always either thoughtlessly liberal (you can't judge other cultures) or thoughtlessly illiberal (strong men must rule) or just plain thoughtless (killing people is bad). James Blish has taken thought and has written a novel called *Black Easter*. This book is about nothing less than the problem of Evil, and it is brilliant. Says Yeats: "If God is good he is not God. If God is God he is not good,"[1] a dilemma for which there have been many solutions. Blish chooses a heretical solution, the Manichean, and pushes

---

1 So I think, but can't find it. *Author's note*: The verse above is part of *Job*, a play written by Archibald MacLeish. Eric Bentley (somewhere) calls the play "a portentous magnum of chloroform." I agree.

it to its logical outcome. If God is omnipotent and benevolent, why does Evil exist? And if God is not omnipotent, if Evil has any kind of positive existence, what may not happen? To go any further would give away part of the book that a reader ought to have to himself; plot, in this book, is the very embodiment of the theme and not merely a diversionary tactic. It is as beautifully worked, as thorough and as complete a cul-de-sac as I have seen in a long time. Blish's gift for relentless, technical detail is at its best here – more than that, his gift for portraying people who are passionately fond of logic, knowledge, and technical detail. His equation of black magic with science is no accident; it was Levi-Strauss (I believe) who called magic a primitive form of science. And the motives here are the same. In an author's note, the author states that "the vast majority" of "novels, poems and plays about magic and witchcraft ... classify without exception as either romantic or playful ... I have never seen one which dealt with what real sorcery actually had to be like if it existed." *Black Easter* is not in the least romantic, nor is it, God forbid, playful; in a world of such pedantic religion and legalistic metaphysics, it is indeed better to curse God and die.

This horrifying novel may sound too special, as I have described it, but the nerve it hits is in all of us. Westerners are all unconscious Manicheans; perhaps most people everywhere are. One has only to remember the common reaction to Eichmann's trial ("a fiend in human form" as if the soul and the crimes must somehow match *in essence*), or the usual reactions of people to political opponents, to see that most of us believe – somewhere, somehow – that Evil and Good both have a substantive being apart from the historically accidental, particular acts that people do. Good and Evil are conceived as nouns, not adjectives.

What one might call the orthodox Problem of Evil (how can an omnipotent God permit it?) is a special case of a more general Problem of Evil that exists in a widespread secular form, particularly in this country. It is a conception of Good and Evil that severely handicaps Good, and is perfectly exemplified by the commonplace, "Good guys finish last." Good is here conceived as restraint, inaction, *adhering to the rules* by not allowing oneself to do X, Y or Z. Evil is the freedom to break the rules and do as one pleases. *Black Easter* embodies this idea also. The "black" magician of the book is free (within the limits of his craft) to commit whatever atrocities he wishes; the "white" magician is constrained not to meddle, *not even to pray for the failure of the other's schemes*. A man not hampered by Good would have shot the "black" magician in the back, and a good thing, too. For the results of a self-limiting Good confronting an Evil which does not limit itself would be altogether horrible without the intervention of a benevolent Deity – and that is where *Black Easter* turns on the reader and bites him in the jugular, so to speak. It's the theme of *High Noon*, which got out of its dilemma by changing the terms of the argument at the last moment. Blish does not let you off so easily.

The book is dedicated to the memory of C. S. Lewis, which I find odd. Not only does it knock *That Hideous Strength* into a cocked hat; Lewis is more than a bit of a Manichean himself, and *Black Easter*, if not a *reductio ad absurdum* of the Manichean view, is at least a *reductio ad nauseam*. To put it another way, to C. S. Lewis the question, "What does it feel like to be a demon?" is a conceivable question, while to Blish it is not. *Black Easter* emphasizes the hideous boredom, the nothingness, the inhumanness of Evil again and again. These are not qualities that can reside in a human breast, and Blish does not try for a subjective view of his demons. They remain, like avalanches or firestorms, outside the possibility of human comprehension, though not human horror.

The Problem of Evil – how to combat it if one isn't allowed its freedom – is unanswerable within those terms. Eastern cosmologies which do not feature a Creation separate from the Creator do not have the religious problem; and any philosophy which subordinates the struggle of Good against Evil to other matters does not encounter the secular version. If what is important in life is to understand and share suffering (Buddhism, in part) or to become part of the transcendental (Taoism in its original form), then Good vs. Evil simply does not matter. Indeed, Lao Tzu is supposed to have admonished Confucius that "All this talk of goodness and duty ... unnerves and irritates the hearer; nothing, indeed, could be more destructive of his inner tranquillity."[2] When what matters is one's inner "unmixedness," goodness and duty are irrelevant.

And indeed, the only solution for the Problem of Evil is to get outside the terms of the problem. This is in fact what is happening. In Shaw's *Misalliance*, one character says to another, who demands "justice":

> A modest sort of demand isn't it? Nobody ever had it since the world began ... Well, you've come to the wrong shop for it: you'll get no justice here: we don't keep it. Human nature is what we stock.

When people begin talking this way, when one hears the word "values" more often than "morals," when books are published with titles like *Life Against Death*, it is a sign that Good and Evil are being redefined. This is happening both in the churches and in secular life. Interested readers may try the early chapters of Sartre's *Saint Genet* for a radical critique of traditional ideas about Evil and a radical redefinition of Evil.

---

2 Arthur Waley, *Three Ways of Thought in Ancient China* (Doubleday Anchor Books, 1956), p. 14.

Black Easter is in itself a sign of this change. It is not only about an Armageddon; it is also part of one. There is no room for me to mention the superb things in this bare, powerful, immensely suggestive book. I will adduce only a few: the "white" magician's ironically innocent worryings about the very problems the book embodies; a good magician, "Father Anselm, a brusque engineer type who specialized in unclouding the minds of politicians"; the extraordinarily un-angelic Celestial Princes, one of whom vanishes with a roar; and best of all, Satan's "petulant bass voice, at once deep and mannered, like a homosexual actor's."

It's a stunning book.

"Beyond Good and Evil" might be the subtitle of Michael Moorcock's *The Final Programme*, another book about Armageddon, but it is one that has abandoned all the usual concerns for something that is beautiful and strangely moving but very hard to describe. Moorcock dedicates his book to (among others) "the Beatles, who are pointing the way through," and the novel can be best pictured by analogy with their music. The book is not "savagely satirical," as the blurb says, or "horribly funny." Rather it shows, like Beatles music, the use of pastiche as an artistic principle. All the shopworn chichés are here: monster computers, mad scientists, incest in the mode of Byron *and* Poe, people who live on pills and candy, mod clothes, expensive cars, James Bond weapons, hermaphroditism, crowd-mindlessness; you name it, the book's got it. But these things are not the subject of the book. They parade through it like blank-faced mannequins in a fashion show. They are simple, flat, brightly colored objects that Moorcock is using to make patterns about Something Else, like the Beatles song that consists almost entirely of the words, "You say goodbye/And I say hello." There is the same avoidance of dynamics: in one case always using the voice *mezzo-forte*, in the other pacing each scene so that suspense or development are entirely eliminated. There is the same deliberate flatness of tone, the same balancing just this side of satire, the same absence of emotional expressiveness that becomes – somehow – a positive force.

If I tell you that fully one-third of the novel is given over to describing people's clothes, you will laugh at me; yet it's true. And if I say that the central character's motives change constantly and have nothing to do with the plot, you'll be put off; but that's true, too. And if I add that the plot itself is made up of dead-ends, inconsistencies, irrelevancies and unexplained events, and that all this is beautiful, exciting, and moving, you won't believe me. But it's true.

Moorcock has apparently decided to treat characters and plot on an equal footing with every other element of the book; the result is a kind of literary Cubism: a shifting, unstable, shallow foreground in which every element is constantly entering into new associations with every other element.

It is very pleasant to be able to review *Programme* and *Black Easter* at the same time. Both are impressive achievements. *Black Easter* has luckily been released as general fiction by Doubleday; unhappily *Programme* (which should have been given the same treatment) has been put out as science fiction, which it is not. To call it fantasy would be inaccurate also; let me just close by noting that the only sticky patch in it is a discussion that almost deviates into sense (pp. 109–111), that the cover is abominable, and that the jacket blurbs are, as usual, totally misleading.

After such heights, it's hard to come down to the run-of-the-mill. Lloyd Biggle's *The Still Small Voice of Trumpets* is a good example of a bad trend – the short story blown up into a novel. I remember the short story as a small, graceful solution to a small, graceful problem. The transition to novel length has necessitated a great deal of padding, which shows. There are a few interesting points about music and a plot that is silly and hard to follow, not that such a feat is absolutely necessary. The book is innocuous and mildly analgesic, which is (I suppose) what this sort of book is for. It has the kind of respectable cover that Michael Moorcock's book should have had.

The Doomsday Men by Kenneth Bulmer is more pretentious and fails in proportion. There are sinful orgies (well, sort of) and thrill-killing and a general air of dissolute city living that recalls innumerable detective movies in which the hero Cleans Up City Hall. There is an interesting gadget, a device by which one person can read another's memories right after the second person's death, but Bulmer does not explore what such a gadget would imply about the state of medicine and psychology (at least) or what such advanced science would mean for sociology, city planning, and the whole state of society. It's another case of extrapolating only one aspect of the present and ignoring everything else. There is a stream-of-consciousness page (called in its entirety "Chapter Five") which should have been not only cut out but also burned. The writing generally tends to get pretty bad in moments of stress. For example:

> Thickly, Durlston spoke, the words dropping like curdled blood. "It's a radio trigger! And they're not going to have the chance to set it off! The Shield is there to protect me – me!" ... he could not control the spittle that dribbled from the corner of his lax mouth – but his forefinger tightened on the trigger – tightened – the narrow red creases disappeared from the knuckle – the blood flowed away – the whiteness of marbled death showed – (p. 201)

The plot ends with a sudden leap into the incredible, a real breach of contract between reader and writer.

Philip José Farmer's *Flesh* is "a revised and expanded version of a novel by the same name first published by Galaxy Publishing Corp." The original copyright is 1960. It is my uninformed, outsider's opinion that the revision and expansion have been minimal and that the book might have been very good if more time had been spent on it. It is a satire (part of the time), an adventure story (part of the time), a celebration of primal appetites (ditto) and a primitive society created out of whole cloth along the lines of Frazer's *Golden Bough* (likewise). Farmer seems never to have settled on a consistent attitude toward his material; none of the versions of the book listed above manages to mesh with any of the others. Most promising but worst achieved is the celebration of primal appetites (eating and sex) – arch when it should be coarse and coyly evasive when it should be specific. The book keeps heading into erotic scenes and shying off at the last minute. And some very unpretty things lie under the "comic" surface: mass castration, death by rape, and the ripping apart of children, to name a few. The book gives the impression of a naturally austere, cultivated and somewhat morbid sensibility trying to portray Rabelaisian simplicity and heartiness with all the forced go of an unhappy conventioneer. There are vivid flashes of imagination that no one but Philip Farmer could even come near, but even so, it isn't a good book. It does his reputation a particular disservice because it could have been one. Readers especially interested in Farmer can simply consider it early Farmer and read it as such. Others will probably wish it were less uneven and confused.

The Magazine of Fantasy and Science Fiction, April 1969

Pavane. Keith Roberts (Doubleday, $4.95). *The Age of the Pussyfoot*. Frederik Pohl (Trident, $4.95). *The Santaroga Barrier* (Berkley, 75¢). *Transplant*. Margaret Jones (Stein and Day, $5.95). *Omar*. Wilfrid Blunt (Doubleday, $3.95).

Unlike the little girl with the curl, science fiction is usually neither very, very good nor very, very horrid. Moreover, as it has in other fields, the vocabulary of praise has become so overblown that a simple "good" means, more often than not, "don't bother," while "brilliant – magnificent – unequalled" means only that the book in question won't kill you.

A good book from Doubleday is *Pavane* by Keith Roberts, about whom a reader ought to know more than is provided on the dust jacket. Keith Roberts is an Englishman and was associate editor with *Science Fantasy*, but what Doubleday does not mention – and what I do not therefore know – is whether *Pavane* is Mr. Roberts' first book or not. There are weaknesses and limitations in the book that mean little if the writer is simply inexperienced but a good deal more if he's not; and there is a fine imagination that would be a respectable achievement for an experienced writer, but is a much greater promise for a beginner.

Pavane is an alternate-universe book: in 1588 Queen Elizabeth I was assassinated; therefore Spain conquered England, Protestantism was destroyed in Northern Europe, and Europe and the New World remained under the control of a repressive Church. Mr. Roberts does not make the mistake of confounding the sixteenth century with the twelfth, or of seeing a slowly developing society as static; one of the best ideas in the book is that technological progress, although slowed down, has not disappeared. Twentieth-century England has steam locomotives (eighty horsepower), a middle class, the typewriter (a rare luxury), Zeiss binoculars, primitive radio, and a social system that is not just an excuse for romance, sadism, or adventurous nonsense. The author's feeling for historical period is impressive, perhaps not in every technological detail (internal combustion, yes; nylons, no) but certainly in his unshakable assumption that leather clothes and porridge do not an idiot make, and in the extraordinary, half-expressed melancholy of a society that became static *after* the Renaissance. It is a kind of Paradise Lost.

The alternate-universe story is subject to a particular weakness: the pleasure of feeling morally daring, of being "ahead" of a purposely benighted society. Mr. Roberts doesn't entirely avoid this. In general, though, his weaknesses (and he has them) only mar details here and there; they don't cut deep enough to hurt the story. *Pavane* is a real, detailed, self-contained world, affecting and convincing. To an Englishman who is familiar with every town, every road, every seacoast, every forest (or vanished forest) in the book, it must be a poignant novel indeed.

Moreover, Keith Roberts is a real writer. By this I mean that he dwells on things for their own sakes, that he doesn't conceive of the details of his book as merely a means to get from point A to point B with as little sweat as possible (and with some superficially attractive tinsel thrown in). One feels that he would discard his plot instantly if the characters and the world decided to develop in some other direction; it is this risk that makes a book live. This is worth mentioning in a field that seems to conceive "good writing" (or "style") as either an irritating distraction or a mysterious gift before which we ought to be simultaneously awed and a little contemptuous. Style is respect for real life. The characters in *Pavane* have visions – real visions – of things like fairies – real fairies – and the visions turn out to be true. I don't approve of or find likely the view that we are only instruments of a Higher Purpose, but Keith Roberts believes it. He does not believe it polemically, which would kill it; he presents it poetically, as a real experience. *Pavane* has the suggestive power science fiction so often lacks; the most important points in the book are not the most important points of the plot, and at its best, the novel has that lyrical meaning that is so easy to feel and so hard to explain. "Do not grieve for the deaths of stones," says a father to his son (p. 278), and here is an adolescent fisher girl, of minor importance to the plot but of major importance to herself:

> Sometimes then the headlands would seem to sway gently and roll like the sea, dizzying. Becky would squat and rub her arms and shiver, wait for the spells to pass and worry about death ... (p. 102)

Frederik Pohl's *The Age of the Pussyfoot* is likely to suffer in this review, not because I think it bad, but because there is not much inspiring to say about its goodness. The book has one rare quality, what might be called Not Shoving Your Nose In It; Mr. Pohl assumes a certain intelligence in his readers and forbears giving them careful analyses of his future world when a glancing detail will do. It is good, for a change, to be treated as an adult by an adult. The book is intelligent, quite funny, stuffed full of charming things, fast-moving and decently predictive; it is probably better than 99 percent of everything else written in the field this year. Mr. Pohl has points to make and he makes them, sometimes gracefully, sometimes with genuine wit, a few times a little awkwardly (but I'm willing to blame his editors). You may even forget, while you are reading the book, that the book is dead.

Perhaps this shouldn't be held against the author. Satire always suffers (or gains) from the intrusive author, and what may be at fault here is that the author isn't intrusive enough; one of the pleasantest moments in the book (one feels a positive glow of affection for Mr. Pohl) is the last two sentences, in which the author sticks his head through the page and waves at you. *Pussyfoot* is polished, professional, straightforward, and all on the surface. It even has detachable ideas in it, about which you can argue afterward. (Some people will think this makes the book profound, though to my mind what makes a book profound is the undetachability of its ideas – you spend much time trying to define them before you even reach the stage of being able to argue about them.) *Pussyfoot* is one of the best disposable books I have seen in a long time and good enough so that I wish Mr. Pohl had let himself go all the way. One example: at the end of Chapter 16 is a grim version of Goldilocks that turns from melodramatic horror to earnest school lesson to dramatic performance. For a moment something follows the laws of its own quirky nature, and that damned plot can wait.

The novel seems to me to have had more impact at its magazine publication in 1965 than it does today, the penalty of writing topical, i.e. disposable novels. There are few flaws once you accept the major premise that the book is comfortably dead: Mr. Pohl suggests in his Afterword that the book ought to be set one century in the future and not several, and he is right. There is also an unexplained difficulty with the indoctrination of the hero, Forrester, who has died in our age and is revived in the future. (Why do science-fiction authors always call characters by their last names?) If he has learned the – presumably – changed language, why is it so hard to teach him the elementary facts of social life? Readers will also note that, although people may be frozen and unfrozen at will, though we may travel to Sirius, men will still earn more money than women and that free enterprise and the suburban housewife will go on forever.

Frank Herbert is an interesting writer, or perhaps I should say an interesting phenomenon, for both *Dune* and *The Santaroga Barrier* are not first-rate books, but carefully worked up third-rate ones. The exhaustive care with which the working up is done deserves praise, but many a reader of *Dune* has thought himself responding to the profundity of an elemental vision of life when what really got him was a combination of reckless exoticism, flamboyantly impossible social conditions, sheer thoroughness, and what I can most politely call megalomania. *The Santaroga Barrier*, while not a good book, has the quality that amateur acting companies sometimes achieve: a kind of evenness, so that while nothing is really good or striking, nothing shows anything else up. *Dune* fans will be disappointed.

Santaroga is the story of a "consciousness fuel" (a consciousness-expanding drug) seen from a conservative point of view. That is, the drug has created a conservative, yet dangerous, community – the author makes his drug quite unlike LSD, on purpose. The book is full of nineteenth-century hotel lobbies, thirty-year-old cars, waitresses, crusty doctors – what might be called American Nostalgic. The oddity of the novel is in marrying this kind of "Spartan" community (Mr. Herbert's description) to a consciousness-expanding drug. What power the novel has is the power of exhaustive detail; there is, for example, so much food in the book (usually the community's cheese, which is sometimes tangy and sometimes smooth and sometimes rich and sometime all three at once) that you read it after dinner at your peril. The food is not described well, but it is there in heaps; similarly the people, though they do pages and pages of accurately commonplace things, are pure cardboard, and the hero's psychedelic experiences compel me to assume that Mr. Herbert has neither experience in the field nor imagination enough to fake it. Here is the hero, thinking about his sweetheart and another character:

> *Jenny*, he thought. *Jenny ... Jenny ...* (p. 16) ... *Jenny ... Jenny ...* (same page, five paragraphs later.) Dasein moved down the steps. Piaget ... Piaget ... (p. 65) ... a fiery pain through his shoulder. Piaget ... Piaget ... (p. 66)

After a good deal of unnecessary mystification and travelling into the Santaroga Valley and out of the Santaroga Valley, for no apparent reason except to rack up pages, the novel ends where a good novel would begin. There are interesting glimpses of behind-the-scenes Santaroga, which Mr. Herbert does not develop. The book has the doubtful virtue of persuading you on every page that although nothing worthwhile is happening at present, something surely will if you only go on reading. It also has the air of treating its materials seriously, although the problems it broaches are never explored or elaborated on. What is reality? Are socially shared delusions normal? Don't ask Mr. Herbert. Interested parties can read *Synthajoy*, a book with the same plot (psychological entrapment) and exactly the same twist at the end, to see how even a flawed novel can attempt to provide answers to questions and not just display the questions triumphantly on the last page but one.

When the British are bad, they are awful. *Transplant* by Margaret Jones is about a dying painter who has his head cut off and stuck on someone else's body, and this other guy likes sex, see, but this poor ascetic guy just wants to paint and he's abnormal because he likes it and his wife won't even look at him because she thinks he's dead, so –

Actually the book is far less coherent than the above. As far as I can make out, it's about adultery and consequent guilt feelings, or poetic justice (the painter's paintings are thrown into a river by the tart he's keeping just for brutish sex), but the medical – not to say, scientific – not to say, simply, logical – fallacies in the book beggar description. Miss Jones can write convincing, realistic, single scenes, but she cannot make them add up to anything, so that the utter idiocy of the whole proceeding becomes apparent only gradually. She ought to get out of science fiction and write ordinary novels; there is a lot of gritty, nasty, sordid, dull, English (?) life (?) in the book, including a view of sex that makes the worst American squalor look glamorous. After her third or fourth novel, Miss Jones might be able to manage a whole book and it might even be worth reading, but publishing *Transplant* is stupid at best, and at worst, downright insulting.

Omar by Wilfrid Blunt is "A fantasy for animal lovers." It is pleasant, charming and slight. It is a fantasy in the old-fashioned sense (say, talking badgers) and if your sugar tolerance is low, stay away. I liked it.

The Magazine of Fantasy and Science Fiction, August 1969

The Sword Swallower. Ron Goulart (Doubleday, $4.50). *The Phoenix and the Mirror*. Avram Davidson (Doubleday, $4.95). *Small Changes*. Hal Clement (Doubleday, $4.95). *The Best SF Stories from New Worlds #2*. Poul Anderson (Berkley, 60¢). *7 Conquests*. Poul Anderson (Macmillan, $4.95)

Southern California wackiness consists not only of odd-ball phenomena but also in the attitude you take toward them; more than matter-of-factness or casual acceptance, it's simply the lack of realization that anything odd is going on. Ron Goulart is the only science fiction writer I know about who writes from this point of view – in fact, he hardly seems to write from any other – and *The Sword Swallower* is a running fire of dead-pan jokes of this peculiarly Forest Lawn kind. (The back jacket says Mr. Goulart spent his first twenty years in Berkeley, so maybe it's just California.) The tone of the novel resembles that of Mr. Goulart's Max Kearny stories and the plot (to speak heavy-handedly of what doesn't, after all, matter much in a comedy like this) sprawls and straggles over a planet-wide cemetery which is complete with ten-story neon wreaths, The Eternal Sleep Coffee Shop, etc. Through this world of mad monologists travels a tired, realistic, decent, unsurprisable government agent who has been hybridized with Plastic Man. It is a world of flower children, leftists, rightists, retired Wing Commanders, geriatric hotelees, incompetent girl spies, protest singers, tomb-robbers and other all-too-credibles. A shorter version of the novel was first published in this magazine in 1967; it was funny then and is funny now, although it spirals out of control once in a while and the constant whimsy tends to dematerialize not only the action (which hardly matters) but also the characters and situations. Like mad Ophelia, the book turns all to favor and to prettiness. Sometimes the essential innocence of the characters is refreshing, but sometimes Mr. Goulart looks like a man who has wandered observantly through Gehenna and decided it would make a great place for a wienie stand. The self-righteous and vicious young, the callous old, middle-aged liberals with massive guilt complexes, ineffectual innocents, rigidified right wingers – if this were a serious book, the hero would have killed himself on the last page, only the reader would have anticipated him.

As it is, the whimsy is unflagging (or relentless, depending on your taste), detail proliferates insanely, and the plot serves well enough, though there are important weak points (e.g. would you send someone you *know* can change appearance at will out into a fake jungle to be hunted?) I found it a very funny book. For example:

> "I guess you spies get a lot," said Alberto ... "The way you're always working with these girl agents ... Some of these girl agents aren't exactly zoftig but even a wisp of a girl agent is okay now and then if you want to change your luck. Sure, you get cooped up with a slender girl spy you can get just as horny as if it was a nice hefty broad. I figure."

Sometimes you get cooped up with a slender, insane Goulart novel and it's okay too.

Avram Davidson's *The Phoenix and the Mirror* is an oddly dragging, sometimes fascinating book that ought to be a classic romance and is not. Mr. Davidson has created an entirely new never-world, that of Vergilian Rome as seen in medieval legends, a "backward projection of medievalism" in which the ancient world becomes half Dark Ages and wholly strange, and Vergil not a poet but a sorcerer. The background is extremely well realized, so much so that I doubt whether one reader in twenty will recognize the amount of research that has gone into it – I doubt if I recognize this myself. The novel is not simply an all-out fantasy world or an excuse for adventures; the magic in it is developed with awesome logic, and one of the climaxes of the book concerns the making of a mirror – constructing a furnace, crushing the ore, making the crucibles, and so on. Either you follow this patiently or you deserve to be shut up in a television set and forced to read *Marvel* comics until your brain turns to oatmeal. There are wonderful details: the mineral kingdom alone includes the terebolim, the male and female firestones, whose mating produces an unquenchable conflagration, and the petromorphs, whose stony and venomous jaws love to crunch the coals of fires. Except for the hunting scene, which seems to have been introduced merely to show off too much medieval lore, none of this stuff is dull and most of it is first-rate. But something has gone wrong.

I thought at first to look for the difficulty in the characters, and these are indeed types – the Beautiful Maiden, the Bluff Friend, the Ambitious Bitch, the Gentle Monster, the Loyal Gutter Urchin – but typing has never been a bad thing in itself. In fact, the characters in the novel are not only vividly conceived, but also almost always there is an extra twist – realistic or paradoxical or suddenly matter-of-fact – that makes them real people. It is all the more distressing to see these real people somehow forced into the role of puppets and made to populate a book that drags in spite of its splendid exoticism and the solidity of its background.

Perhaps the problem is in the plot. The book does not really have a plot, that is, an action in which self-motivated characters come into conflict with each other or something else through the pursuit of things they really want. What it has instead is an *intrigue* that never quite comes off (sometimes developments are too slow, sometimes too fast, often just arbitrary) and an intrigue needs a *diabolus ex machina*. One of the characters is pressed into service for this and is promptly ruined, although she has all sorts of potential (as do the others) for doing other things, if only it weren't for that damned plot. Mr. Davidson gives glimpses of the characters, looking remarkably lifelike; and then episodes of exotic action or description; and then the characters again, still looking lifelike but now subtly out of place; and each time the characters reappear they are more out of place. The denouement is like one of Dickens' worst novels, where you find out at the end that people have all sorts of complicated relationships with each other and wonder why you should care or bother. The logical solution is not a dramatic solution, and what ought to have prepared for it, not only *looked* like an excrescence before; it still is one.

Perhaps Mr. Davidson is trying to imitate the stylization-cum-actuality of medieval romances, but his characters are much too real for this arbitrary playing around with their emotions. For example (the worst), the hero, having gotten half-way into a mystery – through a gimmick – must now have a motive to get all the way in. So he falls in love at first sight with the Beautiful Maiden, glimpsed in the magic mirror. A Vergil who got into his adventure through curiosity, or professional pride, or desire for money, would be much easier to take. The realism of the book does not jibe with many of the plot machinations. For one thing, there is some very modern Monday-morning quarterbacking about science (sort of!), music, and poetry. There is also an intelligence at work here, a modern, skeptical, cool, rather tired mind which is far more interesting than the ostensible romance of the main action.

The novel appeared in serial form, badly shredded, several years ago. Those who were puzzled by it then certainly ought to read it now. If it were a worse book, it would be more unified, but it would also be a worse book, and a half a loaf can be very welcome, even when it's frustrating, as this is.

Small Changes by Hal Clement, *The Best SF Stories from New Worlds #2* and *7 Conquests* by Poul Anderson are as different as short-story collections can possibly be.

"Old-fashioned" is a derogatory term nowadays, but it is the best single word for *Small Changes* – with the emphasis on "fashioned." Mr. Clement's world is that of *homo faber* and within its confines the stories are nearly flawless. All but one of the nine tales have been published before and are probably familiar to readers of the magazines. Without exception they are leisurely, extremely carefully done, and ingenious. Mr. Clement is in love with the laws of basic physics, and they are in love with him right back; in no other set of stories that I remember do the words "angular momentum" carry quite so much of a thrill. Mr. Clement's scientific ingenuity and accuracy have been praised before, but I would like to point out also that his thorough, careful, somewhat pedestrian style restores the astonishment to extremes of heat and cold, and that two stories ("Halo" and "The Foundling Stars") are fascinated by huge, slow-living, low-temperature organisms whose eyeblink (if they had eyes) would consume most of a human lifetime. Five of the nine stories are sort-of detective tales but Mr. Clement does not ask you to outguess him, nor does he play on suspense of the Omigod-I'm-dying or heave-and-sweat school. In "Uncommon Sense" (my favorite) he even telegraphs the ending – the hero survived – so that a reader can forget the *what* and concentrate on the *how*, which is amply rewarding.

REVIEWS

Mr. Clement's world is certainly limited (hardly anything in these stories could exist in non-s.f. terms), but it's well worth the limitations. The characters are remarkably sane, calm people; there is a convention in science fiction of calling characters by their last names, and in this book alone (of all those I've read) does that convention seem entirely natural and appropriate. In "Trojan Fall" and "Fireproof" Mr. Clement uses central characters who are outside his range – a criminal and a spy – and the stories suffer accordingly. The other tales are slow to get started, exhaustive in detail, very quiet, almost completely devoid of social or psychological interest, and sometimes devoid of plot except for the will-this-factory-run sort. When people talk about "pure" science fiction of the "good old days," this is what they mean. Unluckily the good old days saw as little of this as we do; luckily Hal Clement is around now.

At least a week should intervene between reading Hal Clement and *New Worlds #2*, or the reader will be in danger of getting the cosmic bends. Not only is this grab-bag made up half of non-s.f.; what there is, is in another universe. What is most striking about the stories as a group is their sleaziness – not only their accidental sleaziness, but also a deliberate and systematic use of pastiche, fragmentation, little bits from popular magazines, and a sort of interested shuffling of avant-garde devices which are themselves parodies or derivatives of other straight writing. Some of this book is very good and some of it is awful, but none of it is solid.

Among the stories are three conventional and not particularly good s.f. stories based on ideas that, to put it politely, have lost their bloom: "The Transfinite Choice," "The Total Experience Kick," and "The Singular Quest of Martin Borg." There is an absolute howler called "The Countenance." On the deliberately sleazy side is an essence-of-Ballard story ("You: Coma: Marilyn Monroe") in which J. G. Ballard strips the Ballardian props down to the bare minimum and sets them drifting moodily past each other without even a pretext at continuity. Brian Aldiss's "Another Little Boy" creates a world similar to that of Michael Moorcock's *The Final Programme* (although more intelligibly), the common modern fantasy of an amoral, polymorphous-perverse existence in which death, although it exists, is either not really painful – to oneself – or not bothered about. "The Pleasure Garden of Felipe Sagittarius," in which the astute may discover an even stronger resemblance to *The Final Programme*, is another of the same breed, though to my taste a more evocative and less obvious piece. There are two decent science fiction stories by John Sladek and Kit Reed, both parodic, and three excellent non-stories by Tom Disch, also parodic, which contain such gems of non-information as "When the ship sank, with all hands on deck, the captain went down with it. And so on." In short, the usual characteristics of avant-garde writing outside science fiction. What vexes people who don't like this sort of thing seems to be that although the stories are not exactly meant to be funny, they are nonetheless stuffed full of the traditional devices of comedy: repetition, mechanism, discontinuity, incongruity, surprise, exaggeration, lack of explanation and general bizarrerie. I don't mind this kind of work's being bizarre (which it is) or incomprehensible (which it is only sometimes) or sleep-walker-cruel (which I rather like). What bothers me is that this kind of writing is basically parasitic on "straight" writing and hence very quickly exhausted. It is also best when it is shortest. The last story in the book, Roger Zelazny's "For a Breath I Tarry" is another kettle of fish. It works by sheer surface razzle-dazzle, as I suspect all Mr. Zelazny's writing does. It is a very silly and totally irresistible tale in which God, Satan, Adam, Eve and the Ancient Mariner all appear under impenetrable pseudonyms, disguised as computers. It triumphantly manages all the mythical significance, the quasi-religious larger-than-lifeness that Mr. Zelazny has been trying to put into everything else lately (or was it before?) If the story hasn't done so already, it will undoubtedly win the Hugo, the Nebula, the Comet, the Nova, the Pebble, and everything else anybody chooses to toss at it.

7 Conquests is a collection of seven previously published stories by Poul Anderson about war (some indirectly so), and there is a succinct and sensible Foreword on the matter which is very welcome in an age of shrill unanimity on the Left and a scarcity of brains on the Right. Let me make it clear from the outset that I don't like adventure stories or war stories per se. It seems to me that they are severely limited forms; that is, one laser duel is like another laser duel and one chase like another chase, unless you pull a Hatchplot[1] and set your characters to chasing each other over Mount Rushmore and shooting their lasers while hanging by their toes from Teddy Roosevelt's eyebrows. The book includes a good deal of material that sneaked in while the author was asleep ("Lois, she of the fire-colored hair and violet eyes") and some that could appear outside science fiction with almost no alteration ("The trouble is these critters won't know about Carl Bailey, who collected antique jazz tapes, and played a rough game of poker, and had D.S.M. and a gimpy leg from rescuing three boys whose patroller crashed on Venus.") The stories are fast and hard but they are often jerry-built, the bad material apparently coming in when Mr. Anderson has certain givens to set up and doesn't care how he does it. The curious result is that many of these stories – though they are all thoughtful and most

---

1   *MAD* magazine's name for Hitchcock.

pack a genuine emotional punch – *start out* as if they were going to be the worst sort of schlock. "Wildcat," one of the best and a picture of the Jurassic that I won't easily forget, begins as if it were going to be pure cliché: rough, tough, womanless men in an isolated jungle. It ends as something altogether different. The book is full of flat and conventional people who exist for the sake of the plot and not the other way round. They ought not to be more real but less so; there is no reason to learn about the psychological complexities of a man when it's the situation he's in that matters. And when Mr. Anderson reaches for images of the good life he somehow comes up with things that are frankly incredible. I wouldn't worry this point if the stories were bad, but when the author turns (with apparent relief) from the manly men and the lady with the violet hair and fire-colored eyes, he can be pointed, poignant, careful, wise, even funny – "License" casually mentions the American Freebooters' Laborunion and the Criminal Industries Organization, for one. And he recognizes, understands, and takes into account experiences that the authors in the *New Worlds* don't even know exist. Anyone who thinks I am talking about simple-minded patrioteering ought to read "Kings Who Die," a story that leads you right into a patriotic mess and leaves you there. One comparison: *Conquests* is a grim, low-keyed, joyless, sometimes dreary book (not first-rate Anderson) which stuck with me and made me think – surprisingly, when you consider some of those cardboard personages. Zelazny's "For a Breath I Tarry" is an emotional orgy that made me cry, but I didn't respect the story for making me cry or like myself the better for it.

7 *Conquests* also contains "Cold Victory," "Inside Straight," "Details," and "Strange Bedfellows."

The Magazine of Fantasy and Science Fiction, September 1969

The Prometheus Project: Mankind's Search for Long-Range Goals. Gerald Feinberg (Doubleday, $4.95). *Let the Fire Fall.* Kate Wilhelm (Doubleday, $4.95). *World's Best Science Fiction: 1968* (Ace, 60¢). *The Last Starship from Earth.* John Boyd (Berkley, 75¢). *The Da Vinci Machine.* Earl Conrad (Fleet Press, $5.95)

Of the making of many books there is no end. And they are all published, too. And the people cried out, saying: Give us a sign, we would have a sign. So Doubleday gave them a sign.

Virtual immortality, space travel, the extension of consciousness, artificial intelligence – topics like these have been explored in science fiction for years. *The Prometheus Project: Mankind's Search for Long-Range Goals* by Gerald Feinberg adds nothing to the exploration but an appalling naiveté. *Prometheus* is a stupid book, stupid beyond description, shallow beyond bearing, and as devoid of subtlety as it is of logic. To say that Dr. Feinberg is not equal to his subject is nothing; none of us is equal to the question of whether mankind ought to have conscious, long-range goals and what these ought to be, but some of us at least are troubled by the doubts that intelligence brings. Some of us at least have an inkling of the difficulties involved, let alone the agonizing choices one would have to make, let alone the problems of even defining the subject. *Prometheus* is sillier than the worst Flying Saucer scare book; it is written on the village-atheist level and riddled with inconsistencies; and Dr. Feinberg's attempt to keep moral considerations out of his discussion only exposes him to the oldest and most vicious of ethical fallacies. For example (p. 166):

> ... modifications ... may involve ... psychological conditioning of future generations ... Yet to be raised in any society is to be conditioned into certain beliefs and forms of behavior. In most cases the conditioning is done unconsciously, and the beliefs are tacit. I do not think that any new moral principle is established if we do the conditioning consciously ... It is a question of what the principles that are instilled ... are to be, and it would seem that the freely chosen goals of the human race are worthy candidates.

In other words, if what is done *inadvertently*, or *out of necessity* (as much social conditioning is), or *to the smallest possible degree* is morally right, then what is done *knowingly, gratuitously*, and *as completely as possible* is also morally right. And the end justifies the means. A few more gems:

On p. 69, intelligence is defined as the ability to answer questions, a definition that would fit any automatic telephone switchboard; by p. 77, intelligence has somehow become synonymous with consciousness. On p. 107, "there is no external standard for ethical statements" while on p. 126, "we should not ... feel any qualms about introducing ethical principles for determining human actions *other* than the arbitrary preferences that people alive at one time have ..." (italics mine). On p. 154, Dr. Feinberg defends his own pet goal, the extension of consciousness, by simple assertion: "Consciousness is the most precious thing man possesses." On p. 64, a particular course of action is condemned because it would undo "the slow growth of unity in mankind," while on p. 134, "man is anything we call one." On p. 83, the possibility is raised that virtual immortality might make people more afraid of death than they are now, but Dr. Feinberg says he doesn't think so. No evidence is given. On p. 161, the book considers whether we know enough about "our own mental lives, the sources of our motivations, and the conditions that would lead to happiness" to formulate long-range goals for the entire human race, and comes to the staggering conclusion that "these problems are less important if we are trying to make statements about groups of men because the individual factors tend to average out." Anyway, "In any situation human beings must plan and act on the basis of the best information they have." (The Feinberg version of *Why not put beans up your nose?*) In Chapter VI we leave reality altogether; there is going to be a world-wide publicity campaign, discussion groups, and finally a consensus of the human race as to what its long-range goals should be, a process that will take from twenty to fifty years. There will also be a Prometheus Coordinating Agency, or PCA, about which Dr. Feinberg (he is a Physics Professor at Columbia) fusses for several pages.

Odd John is not a book I approve of, morally speaking, but after reading *Prometheus* I know what drove Stapledon to write it.

It is a pleasure to get back to science fiction, especially to a book that shows uncommon intelligence, like Kate Wilhelm's *Let the Fire Fall*. The novel is not as good as her best short stories – none of her novels have been – but it has many good qualities and some that are rare in science fiction.

For one thing, the novel disregards commonplace pulp form completely, and with no ill effects. For another, it is brimful of the details of ordinary life – too full almost, for the people and places take on a liveliness beyond that necessary to the plot. At times this is confusing, but more often it's delightful – real people, recognizable people whose lives twist and shift, whose motives change, whose most commonplace decisions have unexpected effects. The book is written in a style Henry James once (in another context) called "feminine"; that is, the accents never fall where you expect them to, the "big" events are over in a flash or are revealed obliquely, and the novel always presses on to something else. It's uncommonly like life and often compelling. Kate Wilhelm has begun to experiment with style in a way I like, introducing herself here and there, making lists of things, and generally turning from the straight path of virtue to say things when she wants to and not when she "ought" to. There is the odd matter-of-factness of real life, and the book is a real novel, a considerable achievement in a field in which the adjustment of story to detachable ideas is a perennial problem. And it's a pleasure to read a novel in which childbirth and family life are described by someone who knows about them.

However, the book's virtues often kept me reading when I had intellectual objections. For example, the characters in the book change their minds quite a lot, sometimes very confusingly, especially the young evangelist whose career provides the motive power for the plot. I could not always follow what was going on, but the characters could, and I found myself believing in them willy-nilly. Also, the book – although set some ten years in the future – seems to me to occur quite definitely ten or fifteen years in the past, although this may only mean I'm a provincial New Yorker not acquainted with the "normal," decent-American, small-town people Kate Wilhelm is writing about. The novel employs that conflict of science with a fundamentalist and revivalist religion so dear to the hearts of science-fiction writers: the book traces the career of a sort of Billy Graham (Obie Cox) and the kind of social changes caused by his Voice of God Church. It seems to me that this theme, a beloved paranoia of ours, is not credible, that the great twentieth-century wars of religion have been wars of political ideology, and that any catastrophic repressions likely to occur in the future will be political in name and nature and not in any way identifiably religious (except for their intolerance).[1] Scientism is our besetting vice, and without some great disaster (like atomic war) we are unlikely to persecute science, or even decently restrain it. The book reviewed just before this one is a case in point.

That croggle aside (and a few pieces of dead wood, like a riot on page 120ff that I haven't yet straightened out), *Fire* is a believable and exciting book. Here is one of the main characters:

> Dee Dee sang in the choir and bought the Pill from a college friend. Dee Dee had read all of DeSade, had turned on twice with pot, smoked a pack a day, and could drink three martinis and still drive ... She

1 Author's note: Oops.

sang in a sweet soprano: "I will follow, follow all the way." She opened her mouth for the high notes, but didn't try to reach them. Only the choirmaster suspected, and he never had been able to pin down the exact source of the reduced volume when the notes got up there.

The Wilhelm baddies are better than the goodies, and this one has a career worthy of her.

World's Best Science Fiction: 1968 is an excellent anthology, packed with fine stuff, and with the special virtue of including many good stories originally published outside the science fiction magazines: Poul Anderson's "Kyrie," Brian Aldiss's "The Worm That Flies," and Terry Carr's "The Dance of the Changer and the Three" from *The Farthest Reaches*; Kurt Vonegqut's "Welcome to the Monkey House" and Damon Knight's "Masks," both from *Playboy*; and three from Britain – Colin Kapp's "The Cloudbuilders," Fritz Leiber's "The Square Root of Brain," and Samuel Delany's "Time Considered as a Helix of Semi-Precious Stones." The last two are not only superb, but also eligible for any kind of award, please note (first publication in this country).

Picking favorites here would result in my naming almost everything in the table of contents; a few stories are weak but none is bad and most range from good to – well, you decide. Robert Sheckley has a story about a city that's a Jewish mother; Burt Filer (a newcomer) has a first-rate story about time-travel with a beautiful twist at the end; Fred Saberhagen re-tells the story of Orpheus and Eurydice with *another* beautiful twist at the end; and Katharine MacLean has a realistic, detailed, impressive story about telepathy.

I am convinced – for the duration of this paragraph – that the short story is the proper form for science fiction, always was, always will be. I particularly liked "Backtracked," "Kyrie," "The Worm That Flies," "Masks," "Time Considered etc.," "The Dance of the Changer and the Three" and "The Square Root of Brain." Buy it, read it, and find out which ones you like best.

It is not really a crime to write *The Last Starship from Earth* (by John Boyd) but why *publish* it? Why *re-publish* it? I would guess from much in the book that the author is a very, very young man, and if he wants to go on writing science fiction novels, I for one will not poison his coffee, because the third or fourth try might be readable. But duty is duty, and I hereby publicly state that *The Last Starship from Earth* is incoherent, bumbling, enthusiastic, pretentious, ineffably silly, and – to put it kindly – immature in the extreme. Berkley has no right to foist this amateurishness on the public. It is no favor to Mr. Boyd to expose him to this sort of public shredding and no favor to the public to convince them that science fiction is even worse than they always thought it was. In time Mr. Boyd may learn what a plot is (he thinks he can tie up 175 pages of loose ends in a few paragraphs) and what men, women, and society are like. But he must also learn something about science ("It was several microseconds before the aesthetics of her motion intruded on his consideration of its mathematics"), something about practical observation ("her voice dropped an octave"), and something about style ("it was the first time in his life he had ever heard of a female professional not in a house of recreation volunteer so titillating a witticism from behind such a titivating facade"). I forgive Mr. Boyd the anguish his novel caused me and hope he will eventually forgive me the anguish this review may cause him, but for Berkley there is no forgiveness. Only reform. *Don't do it again.*

The Da Vinci Machine by Earl Conrad is an interesting and promising collection of short stories by a writer new to the field. Subtitled "Tales of the Population Explosion," the book is a gaggle of satirical fantasies in which the science is purposely absurd. Mr. Conrad doesn't seem to have gained full control of the short-story form yet, and although the tales are literate and sometimes funny, his false-naive, "throw-away" manner leads to many stories coming on strong only to fade away after the beginning. The stories suffer from being presented in a collection, as they are all alike and the one manner gets monotonous; the best of these could have appeared to advantage in the science fiction magazines. The style is Lafferty-and-water, and often good.

The Magazine of Fantasy and Science Fiction, January 1970

The Day of the Dolphin. Robert Merle (Simon and Schuster, $5.95). *Bug Jack Barron.* Norman Spinrad (Avon, 95¢). *Emphyrio.* Jack Vance (Doubleday, $4.95). *Best SF: 1968.* Eds. Harry Harrison and Brian Aldiss (Putnam's, $4.95). *The Empty People.* K. M. O'Donnell (Lancer 75¢)

All books ought to be masterpieces. The author may choose his genre, his subject, his characters, and everything else, but his book ought to be a masterpiece (major or minor) and failing that, it ought to be good, and failing *that*, it at least ought to show some sign that it was written by a human being.

Robert Merle, Prix Goncourt winner and author of *The Day of the Dolphin* may be a word-mill for all I know; the book is pure commodity, written by the yard to be bought by the yard. Out of 320 pages the author uses more than fifty to establish that there are dolphins, that they are intelligent, and that these facts interest the U.S. Government. Knowing the temper of his readers (whose delicate mental balance can be upset by the least sign of intelligence or originality) M. Merle introduces scores of characters to talk about dolphins and scores of others to listen to them; and when that runs out, the hero's lab assistants spend two hundred more pages (dear God) quarreling about each other's utterly stereotyped sexual proclivities without, unfortunately, ever doing anything even remotely indecent. I have been heard to complain that there is not enough characterization in science fiction, but I hereby repent in tears and blood. If characters have to be introduced to do utilitarian things in books – like turning on electric lights – I far and away prefer the lightweight, portable, flexible cardboard cutouts that science fiction writers are so fond of to M. Merle's well-rounded, "realistic," ponderous, wooden dummies. The characters are supposed to be Americans, but they are all French, including two ex-Vassar girls with uvular r's[1] (ah, those languorous Poughkeepsie summers!) and the plot proper starts on page 200. Everybody talks about the Vietnam war as if he had just heard of it. If the book had been cut by two-thirds, the material about the dolphins kept and the rest sketched in as lightly as possible, this could have been a bearable novel, for M. Merle's dolphins are interesting and likeable characters. It's the old story: a teeny dollop of idea mixed with vast amounts

---

[1] Your uvula is the dingus that hangs down in front of your tonsils. An uvular r is a liquid, trilled r, quite impossible in English.

of ultraconventional sludge. Do not be alarmed, nervous readers. Even though the story is about dolphins, it will not hurt you, it is not really science fiction, it is full of recognizable things straight from novel-land, and nothing is real. M. Merle writes like this, by the way, it is very modish and experimental, it is called "run-on sentences," she flung herself on the bed, I will kill all publishers, she thought.

I sometimes wonder if these vast, content-less, commercial megatheres are not the last degenerate descendants of the nineteenth-century realistic novel – dinosaurs, so to speak, whose great grandpa is *War and Peace*, the panoramic effect of which they try to imitate by sheer size, that being the only thing about realism they can remember.

Only half commodity is *Bug Jack Barron* by Norman Spinrad, the other six or seven halves being Spinrad, word-wooze, exasperation, show biz, screaming, and loss of control (the book does everything to excess). Reading it is like trying to fix a watch with a jackhammer. It is a genuinely offensive book – that is, it climbs up off your lap, pulls your ears, breathes in your face, and tries determinedly to punch you in the nose. It has unmistakably been written by a human being, but it is a bad book, partly because it is an imitation Big Fat Success Novel and partly (I suspect) because the author is not in control of his material, but is in the process of being smothered by it.

BJB is written in a breathlessly baroque style like M. Merle's, except for the obscenities. Everybody talks like everybody else (including the villain, who is supposed to be twenty years older than the hero and from a completely different social background). Nor only that, they all *think* in the same style and the book is *narrated* in that style; except for a few passages about the hero's ex-wife, there is no rest from the strident, insistent Johnny-one-note, always-on-the-same-level intensity. If a character picks up an ashtray, that ashtray will have as many verbal rosettes on it as a suicide, or a murder, or any really important thing, and so will the cigarette ashes that drop in it. Many scenes which are moving or charming on their first appearance (like the love scenes, and they *are* love scenes) are considerably less so when they are used as set-pieces the third or fourth time round. I think also that a novel of political intrigue ought to have an intelligible intrigue in it, and after a third reading I still cannot tell who is doing what to whom and why (most of the uncertainty revolves around Sara Westerfeld, Barron's ex-wife). Moreover there ought to be a real villain in it, and Benedict Howards (the mad millionaire of the book) is not even a stereotype but only a villain-shaped hole crammed with super-high-gear prose (no commas even) which somehow misses making anything of him at all, not even a conventional gesture.

Algis Budrys has noted that *BJB* moves in and out of the symbolic, and I suspect that's what's wrong. This is one way of not being in control of your material. Passionately, illogically, and spasmodically the book puts forward certain moral ideas which I propose to treat seriously, as they are neither trivial nor frivolously presented. They might be summarized as follows: (1) Everybody adores power, especially women. (2) Death is worse than anything. (3) Since nobody lives up to conventional moral standards, nobody has any standards. (4) Everyone can be bought. Now I agree with the last of these, but with none of the others, the offensive words being "everybody," "anything," and "any." If death is worse than anything, people ought not to risk their lives or commit suicide, but they do both – very often, in fact. And (beyond the needs of self-protection) some people adore power, some do not, some are afraid of it, some are sober about it, some don't know anything about it, and so forth. As for number three, it is only the first stage of disillusionment and a big mistake in practical affairs; there are the things people believe and the things they think they ought to believe, and the latter are usually the more destructive. I agree with Jack Barron's "Big Secret" (it is really the most open of all secrets) – i.e. that every man has his price. To have your price means that you can be pleased, that you have needs you must satisfy, that you can be hurt and therefore coerced, in short that you are a human being and not an invulnerable superman. But the subject takes too long; George Bernard Shaw's *Major Barbara* and the preface thereto are recommended reading. With Shaw, I would say that every man's having his price, far from being a scandal or a moral horror, is an indispensable condition for any kind of human society and that it is ridiculous to despise people for what is obviously as necessary and natural a part of them as their arms and legs. The real question about a man's price is not whether he has one but how high it is and in what coin it must be paid. People who cannot be bought by anything (pleasure, happiness, creation, others' happiness, life, freedom) have a name. They are call fanatics. Also recommended is Erich Fromm's distinction between self-aggrandizement, self-abasement, and self-love.

In fact, *BJB* is not about power at all – the conflict in the book never gets beyond lines like "Nobody crosses Benedict Howards!" or "Nobody owns Jack Barron!" which would be downright silly in the context of a real fight. The book is really about seduction, glamor, corruption, mana, magical essences – in short, *vanity*. One thing Mr. Spinrad understands inside out is entertainment as an industry and the fantasies bred by celebrity; *BJB* is a hall of mirrors. There is only one real character in the novel and the others stand around him in adoring attitudes; even the villain is there only to serve as an enlarging mirror – if Jack can take on *Benedict Howards*, what a giant-killer he must be! I think this is why Howards is so unreal, and why nobody in the book is ever genuinely cruel or genuinely cold, just as nobody is ever sad, or quiet, or kind. Howards' "paranoia" (the author ought to look that word up) is self-obsession, just as Jack Barron (who would be intolerable in real life) is endlessly self-obsessed and incapable of seeing any other character in the book as real, just as the author shows over and over – perhaps without meaning to make so much of it here – the paradox of celebrity and fake power. The rock star who makes thousands of girls scream is surely a god, but the girls would not be there if they did not want to scream; nothing is being done to them, since they are doing it to themselves. This is the subject Spinrad can write about. But power as money, anonymous power, legal power, real competition, compromise, coercion, the weighing of real risks, the power to make people do what they really don't want to do – these are quite outside the scope of the novel. A character in *Death of a Salesman* tells Willy Loman, "My son doesn't have to be well-liked because he has something to sell," and these are the cruelest lines in the play. They are also the most hard-headed. They have more to do with power than anything in Norman Spinrad's romantic, half-innocent, youthfully bouncy, exasperatingly schlocky and ultimately silly book.

Measured against the preceding works, Jack Vance's *Emphyrio* like a star i' the darkest night sticks fiery off indeed. Mr. Vance has written a fine book. It is very strange to glance back from this eerie, transparent cockleshell of a novel, so much stronger than it seems (it's made entirely of forcefields) and so much faster than you'd think (it's faster-than-light and has a reactionless drive), to see the chrome-finned Cadillac of *Bug Jack Barron* fighting to keep to ninety on the curves, and still further back, Robert Merle's version of the Merrimac wallowing badly in heavy seas and finally capsizing.

Science fiction, like all literature, usually tries to make the strange familiar, but Mr. Vance makes the familiar strange. One would swear he had read Bert Brecht and decided to produce a novel that would be one extended *Verfremdungseffekt*.[2] He does it, too. Reading *Emphyrio* is like looking at the world through the wrong end of a telescope – I don't mean that everything is small but that in some indescribable way everything is *set at a distance*, and this combination of strange things seeming familiar and familiar things suddenly becoming strange is the oddest and the finest in the world. The cover artist (who understands this) has put a homey,

2 Usually translated as "alienation effect." It might be better rendered (as Brecht has done) as distancing, or the framing effect, or the effect you get by putting something in quotation marks.

commonplace kitchen next to a set of ruined Corinthian columns, and the odd thing is that the two obviously belong together. The first chapter of the book is misleading, for *Emphyrio* is not an adventure story but a *bildungsroman*[3] that describes a perfect curve from beginning to end. It is very slight on the surface, cool and quiet throughout, without any of the sourness of *Eyes of the Overworld*. Mr. Vance's novel about the seven demon princes suffered from a mismatching of plot and mood, but here the story and the people are entirely at one. I really cannot do it justice. Mr. Vance knows about childhood, grief, love, social structure, idealism, and loss, but none of these breaks the perfect surface of the book; everything is cool, funny, and recognizable while at the same time everything is melancholy, real, and indescribably strange. There are veins of pure gold. The seven-year-old hero, after seeing a puppet play, "had come to suspect that the puppets were stolen children, whipped until they acted and danced with exact precision: an idea investing the performance with a horrid fascination." Or "I watched a Damaran walk; it walked with *soft* feet, as if its feet hurt" (italics mine). Except for the very beginning (which might easily have been omitted) the tone is perfectly controlled. What is one to say of a puppet play the title of which is "Virtuous Fidelity to an Ideal Is the Certain Highroad to Financial Independence"? Or of an author whose ear is so sure that among names like Ambroy, Undle, and Foelgher, he can serenely place a district called Riverside Park? Others grunt and heave to sweat out sophomoric diatribes against organized religion; Mr. Vance merely produces a Temple Leaper who asks the hero's father severely whether he has lately leapt to the glory of Finuka. Even the "happy" ending of the book is curiously abrupt and somehow sad; what remains is not the euphoria of a successful revolution but the memory of two boys watching the sunset from Dunkum's heights and dreaming of riches, the exact and effortless taking-apart of a whole social system, the old puppeteer (his puppets are living creatures) who says, "The years come fast. Some morning they'll find me lying stark, with the puppets climbing over me, peering in my mouth, tweaking my ears ..."

Best SF: 1968 edited by Harry Harrison and Brian Aldiss is a fair mixed bag of stories framed by an Introduction and Afterword that indirectly – and unfortunately – lead one to expect more from the stories than they manage to give. The book does a great service to readers by reprinting four reviews of *2001*: Lester del Rey's, Samuel Delany's, Ed Emshwiller's, and Leon Stover's. The book is moderately funny, moderately interesting, and, well

---

3   A novel of the formation of a character, or the process of passing from childhood to adulthood, making oneself into a person.

– moderately everything. It's hard to know what to say about a collection in which nothing is particularly good but nothing is bad. One of Brian Aldiss's psychedelic-war stories is here, well done, although I have begun to have had enough of the whole series; there is also a story by a new writer, David Masson, which presents two fascinating ideas but fails to connect them fictionally: mood-weather ("Insecure, rather sad feeling today and tomorrow, followed by short-lived griefs") and "poiks," areas that have become mosaics of different eras, geographically contiguous, into which people can get lost. I found "Final War" by K. M. O'Donnell quite good, and the collection will certainly be worth getting when it appears in paperback. It leans toward the obvious and toward stories which have one good, clear, conventional idea: Asimov's "Segregationist" (robots), Kit Reed's "Golden Acres" (old-age homes), Stephen Goldin's "Sweet Dreams, Melissa" (computer psychology) and two technical puzzles, Mack Reynolds' "Criminal in Utopia" and Bob Shaw's "Appointment on Prila" (the first solves its problem; the second only pulls a rabbit out of a hat). There's also a sprinkling of the falsely profound, though I ought to admit that Robert Sheckley's story, "Budget Planet," is out of its proper context, and that I have been told it is not only funny but also subtle in Mr. Sheckley's novel, from which it has been untimely ripped. Perhaps it's because I was brought up with no religion at all that I detest the science fiction tropism toward re-writing Christianity from what one might call the village-atheist point of view. Although "Budget Planet" and Fritz Leiber's "One Station on the Way" are colorful and active enough, there seems to me to be no point in flogging dead fundamentalist doctrines so late in the day.[4] That alone is not enough point for a story. Bert Silverberg's "To the Dark Star" hangs a lot of bizarrerie on a very slender thread; it seems oddly gratuitous, as if the author had finished the story before he decided what its theme was. There is also a well-written story by John D. MacDonald, but its subject (the man who hallucinates days of life at the moment of death) has been public property for some time, e.g. "The Occurrence at Owl Creek Bridge" and "Mr. Arcularis."

K. M. O'Donnell's *The Empty People* is a well-written book which I do not understand at all. As far as I can tell, what seem to be the lives or fantasies of various people are really the hallucinations of a man whose brain cancer has been removed by heroic surgery and whose brain has been, so to speak,

[4] A gorgeous instance of the falsely profound is an irresistible story, probably written tongue-in-cheek (I'm afraid I don't remember the author), in which a group of space explorers find out that the universe is really the effluent of a huge flush toilet. For reasons unknown to me, one kills himself, several go mad, and the one character left sits around brooding about The Horror Of It All.

re-wired. The book is the universe inside his skull; three characters have been captured by aliens (a situation deliberately derived from trashy s.f.) and are put to different tasks. One waits; one pursues; one flees. There are constant promises that the metaphysical mysteries raised throughout will be cleared up at the end and the meaning of the insistent symbolism finally revealed, but the only thing that happens is that the cancer patient dies. Mr. O'Donnell may be using his plot as an excuse for disconnected fantasies, or he may not have mastered his method yet, or it may be a method I cannot understand. The book has the air of being something that was either cut after it was written or that never got itself properly written in the first place. I remain baffled.

The Magazine of Fantasy and Science Fiction, July 1970

The Ship Who Sang. Anne McCaffrey (Walker, $4.95). *Satan's World*. Poul Anderson (Doubleday, $4.95). *Report on Probability A*. Brian W. Aldiss (Doubleday, $4.50). *I Sing the Body Electric*. Ray Bradbury (Knopf, $6.95)

Professionally speaking, Anne McCaffrey is just a pup, as those who wish to read *The Ship Who Sang* can verify for themselves. As late as 1966[1] Miss McCaffrey was indulging in plenty of slipper-worryings, barkings-at-nothing, and enthusiastic fallings-over-own feet. For me one of the pleasures of reading *Ship* is watching it progress from some rather awful gaucheries through the middling treatment of middling ideas to the two final sections in which the author at last begins to dramatize scenes with ease and some polish. But readers are not critics and may not find the eager awkwardness of the beginning as appealing as I do. It tickled me, for example, to hear a character remark gravely, "Such an A Caruso would

[1] The date of magazine publication of the novel's second and third episodes. The first was published in 1961, the fourth and fifth in 1969, and the final episode appears only in the novel.

have given the rest of his notes to sing," or to find that the heroine's first mission (she is a cyborg built into a spaceship) is to rush a vaccine to "a distant system plagued with a virulent spore disease," while her second leads to a tangle with "a minor but vicious narcotic ring in the Lesser Magellanics." Miss McCaffrey is infested with gremlins. My favorite in the whole book is the statement (on page 56) that "A second enormous stride forward in propagating the race of man occurred when a male sperm was scientifically united with female ova," a pronouncement that blends the impossible with the ineffable. It's true that these whoppers do not occur in the last third of the novel, but all the same, somebody (God, the author, Walker, the author's children) should have rewritten the first three episodes so that all the parts might be equally readable – and equally sensible.

For example, we are told that Helva, the heroine, is born deformed but that she spends her first three months enjoying "the usual routine of the infant." Anyone not *internally* deformed would be better off with prosthetics than with Helva's all-enveloping metal "shell"; moreover, Miss McCaffrey later insists that shell-people do not sleep, which is impossible, and that her heroine has "no pain reflexes" – by itself a better reason for shell-life than lack of limbs. There is considerable description of the technology used to keep shell-people in their metal bodies, a long explanation of how Helva can sing, and many references to special conditioning, but some very important things are never explained. For one, an education that allows Helva to see her first normal human being at the age of fourteen does not seem practical for someone who will be spending much of her life working with human partners. I am also confused as to how a shell-person who has a microphone *in* or *at* her throat can produce consonants; Helva's voice is "instrumental rather than vocal" but the details are not clear. Most important, we are told that Helva is a deliberately dwarfed *but whole* woman. Leaving aside for a moment the problem of what happens to hair, fingernails, eyelashes, eyebrows, and dandruff inside a shell-person's nutrient bath, I find myself very curious about the one question the author never answers: is Helva sexually mature? We know she's sterile, but what about her ductless glands? If she is indeed a sexually mature woman, encapsulating her in a metal shell strikes me as a form of refined torture and I do not think we are supposed to imagine that Central Worlds is that callous. On the other hand, she falls in love with her first "brawn" (human partner), as do other brain ships in the novel – one even tries to commit suicide for love. Perhaps shell-life agrees with women better than it does with men; at any rate, the few male cyborgs in the novel are presented as fussy, complaining types with over-inflected voices. I would also like to know what life without olfactory or tactile sensations does to the human psyche (compare Fritz Leiber's *The Silver Eggheads*). And why *does* Helva lack these?

REVIEWS

Couldn't those areas of the brain be turned to good account in reading gauges or sensing meteor swarms or whatever else one has to do to run a spaceship? (See Samuel Delany's *Nova*.) At one point in the book the heroine briefly inhabits an alien body; one would think such an experience would be either devastating or addicting, but not much is made of it.

All these confusions seem to me to be the result of a lack of rewriting. In its last episode, when the book really picks up, when people lose their mechanically explanatory voices and start yelling at each other, when Helva finds her second love, a short, blunt-mannered, vain, fake-hard-boiled guy who's a bit of a dandy, *Ship* turns into quite a good thing. Even at its silliest the book has a contagious joyfulness. An added pleasure: people's motives are usually connected with love or family feeling, a respite from the war, commerce, and rivalry of the usual space romance. Write more of the same sort, say I.

But alas, what happens when you do? *Satan's World* by Poul Anderson is one of what James Blish calls a template series – *Trader to the Stars* appeared in 1964, and although *World* may be the second in the series or the fifteenth (I am ignorant thereof), something unpleasant has happened to the template in between, and that something is weariness.

Poul Anderson can write rings around Anne McCaffrey and he makes an interesting and in places fascinating and moving book out of material she would cover (scratchily) in four pages. But he doesn't enjoy it. There is, in *World*, a sense of sourness, of things gone stale and wrong. The characters' personalities have declined into mannerisms, and the mannerisms into tics. Adzel, who should be serene, is merely smug; Chee Lan, who should be explosive, is irritated and irritating; and David Falkayn, who began (if I remember correctly) as a charming mixture of eagerness and youthful cynicism, has become a cad when the author bothers to make him a character at all. Even Nicholas van Rijn, whose scrambled English remains amusing and sometimes brilliant, is more often just a greedy, lecherous, dirty-old-man.

Mr. Anderson has never minded jerry-building his stories, although he usually keeps the jerry-building in the beginning (the least worst place) and uses it, as here, to force-feed the reader as quickly as possible with the standard background of the standard characters and the few givens the story needs. There is a girl, I swear to God, clad in "a few wisps of iridescent cloth," who remarks that "none of us girls has travelled past Jupiter" and is described by the hero as "sophisticated." Characters lecture each other on what both of them already know. There is a line separating Anderson the Good from Anderson the Awful which Anderson the Author crosses with apparent unconcern, at one moment giving his hero "an animal alertness developed in countries for which man was never meant" and in the next describing a chief secretary "who was of a warrior caste in a tigerish species *and thus required to be without fear*" (italics mine). Or "four and a half meters of dragon following on tiptoe."

As one would expect of a series, the best things are the new ones made up for the occasion. The scenery is grand and the aliens are fine, although Mr. Anderson's aliens always seem to be violently belligerent no matter what kind of planet they live on or what sort of creatures they are: flying carnivores (a recent magazine series), freak herbivores (this book), or feline beings with women's faces (a past story). There are scattered remarks that are very provocative and insufficiently discussed, my favorite being "Vegetarian sophonts do not have purer souls than omnivores and carnivores. But their sins are different." Mr. Anderson also presents some apologetics for the Polesotechnic League (which apparently has not yet found out that a conspiracy in restraint of trade, as the technical term has it, pays more than competition) and remarks about government, evolution ("ruthlessly selective"), and the biological basis of personality which make me burst with impatience to refute them. There is one comment about "private war" that makes me long to send the author a copy of *The Oresteia* and Hobbes' *Leviathan*, postage due. Mr. Anderson should write prefaces, like Shaw's.

It is rude to make nasty noises about half-loaves to someone who must, after all, make a living from the stuff, but I would like to take this opportunity to register a personal *hwyl* on the subject of what Anderson the formalist has done to Anderson the artist. The novels he *could* write! The novels he *won't* write! If this goes on much longer, I shall burn my copy of *Three Hearts and Three Lions* and expire amid the ashes. And it would not be so bad if the man were not – intermittently – so very, very good.

I think Poul Anderson sees the world as an unhappy place of much vulnerability and little splendor and that he ought to say so. One of the striking things about *World* (and this is usual lately with this author) is that the book's evocations of joy, strength, and freedom fall very flat indeed. At one point Adzel reminisces about:

> the wide prairies of Zatlakh, earthquake hoofbeats, wind whooping off mountains ghost-blue above the great horizon! After dark, fires beneath a shaken aurora; the old songs, the old dances, the old kinship that runs deeper than blood itself.

David Falkayn has a similar passage:

> Hikes through the woods; swims in the surf ... a slab of black bread and cheese, a bottle of some wine, shared one night with the dearest little tart ...

In short, when asked to invoke the joy of life, the author carries on like the Scand of Minneapolis (to use William Atheling, Jr.'s phrase), while the book's descriptions of misery, failure, weakness, and pain, especially emotional pain, are considerably more convincing. One wrests from life, with great effort, a kind of bleak, minimal happiness – this is the unspoken message of the novel. There are no equals in this story and no love, although space adventure does not automatically preclude either (cf. Miss McCaffrey's romance). There is a conventional, stylized camaraderie between shipmates Falkayn, Adzel, and Chee: otherwise everything in this world is seen as a question of hierarchy, or perhaps it would be better to say a question of dominance – one of the horrors in the story is "Brain-scrub," the taking over of one's very personality, and I think it no accident that such complete control of one person over another is spoken of as a rape. Nor is it a matter of chance that the heroine-victim, Thea (the only fully developed new character in the book, aside from the aliens), is seen as tragically vulnerable, vulnerable through her feelings, responsive, affectionate (not only to her master but also to van Rijn *and* Falkayn *and* someone who is actually an employee), and far more interesting than the successful characters. If only the weak can feel, only the weak are real. Success anaesthetizes and isolates.

As I said, I think this is Anderson the Somber trying to surface. He also had a hand in creating the horrifying sexual relationships in the novel: Chee Lan's open contempt for her lover; van Rijn and his whores (I really cannot remain polite about this); Falkayn's cheerful exploitation of his simp of a calendar girl, and hers of him; and – to top it off – Thea's tragic adoration of her raging alien master.

Not that I think the author should stop this. He should go to the limit with it. Mr. Anderson has written in a fanzine column about what he called the "fascist" virtues and cited as one of them *an awareness of the tragic*, that is, an awareness of irremediable failure. I wish he would let this virtue into his work in its real form, not in the form of grim glory or ersatz Byronism (common forms in heroic romance). He has done it before, as in "Kyrie," a very interesting short story published in one of the *Orbit* collections. I also remember an adventure story in which the aliens (warlike, as usual) had beautiful "muliebrile" (i.e. womanish) faces and strange aesthetic/erotic overtones, in which the Garden of War was a disturbing and disturbingly lovely place, a story far more interesting, both artistically and dramatically, than the usual space-opera set-up, however smoothly and professionally done and however spectacular the scenery (Mr. Anderson, as usual, is very good at this).

World is a book made almost completely out of overstory: conscious, controlled, craftsmanlike, economical, ultimately irritating. I wish Mr.

Anderson would stop controlling things so hard, would allow more breathing space for the understory, and let us see the results.

Brian W. Aldiss's *Report on Probability A* is a Robbe-Grillet novel with Harold Pinter conversations that has somehow bemused Doubleday into printing it as science fiction. Part One is entitled "G Who Waits" and the last two lines of the book are "She waited" and "He waited." In between *you* wait. There is an epigraph from Goethe which sums up the novel, "Do not, I beg you, look for anything behind phenomena. They are themselves their own lesson." *Report* is a false-narrative, a book full of narrative cues that raise expectations only to thwart them. The prose is purposely meandering, sometimes funny ("A pigeon called X"). There are hints of a mystery that remains unresolved, one hundred and ninety pages of clear, beautifully written prose which slowly builds up to a perfectly controlled, low-keyed lyricism, and a great deal of repetition. Most of the book deals with the objects in and around a certain house and the quiddity thereof; the following is typical:

> Below the door was a stone step. This stone step had two features, one permanent, one temporary. The permanent feature stood on the right, the temporary feature stood on the left. The permanent feature was a shoe scraper of ornamental ironwork, the two ends of which curved upwards like dragons' heads; through the telescope's circle of vision, it was impossible to determine if they were intended to represent dragons' heads. (p. 76)

I admire everything about the novel except its length. Matter organized in the lyrical, not the narrative, mode cannot be sustained for this long. *Report* would have made a brilliant novelette, but as a novel it is sheer self-indulgence. I had to work very hard to get through it all and would on no account read it again.

Ray Bradbury does everything wrong. Anne McCaffrey can sing better; Poul Anderson can think him under the table; and compared with Brian Aldiss, he is as a little child. To him old people are merely children, in fact *everybody* is a child; he prefers imitative magic to science (which he does not understand); his morality is purely conventional (when it exists at all); his sentiment slops over into sentimentality; he repeats himself inexcusably; he makes art and public figures into idols; and there is no writer I despise more when I measure my mind against his, as George Bernard Shaw once said of Shakespeare.

Mr. Bradbury has put out a new collection of stories, *I Sing the Body Electric*. It is third-rate Bradbury, mostly. It is silly. It totally perverts the quotation from Whitman which it uses in its title. It is very good. Much has been made of Bradbury's lyricism, but no one (I think) has stressed the extraordinary *economy* of his style. He presents almost everything either in lyrical catalogue or dramatically, and while the lyrical catalogues sometimes fall flat, the dramatic dialogue hardly ever does. This gives his world tremendous immediate presence; "Show, don't tell," might be the frontispiece for any of his books. Or "Do many things *simultaneously*" (which is the real secret). Near the end of "The Kilimanjaro Device" the narrator says:

> I had the car up to ninety.
> We both yelled like boys.
> After that I didn't know anything.

The one thing Mr. Bradbury has going for him as content is an extremely fine understanding of a certain kind of childish or child-like emotion – the girl who was afraid to swing on a swing after her mother died because she knew it would break, in "The Kilimanjaro Device" the narrator's careful avoidance of Hemingway's name, the ancient lady who is selfishly delighted that her long-dead fiancé is really dead. And who else would talk of the summer air as "the summer swoons"?

In the book are two science-fiction stories, both refugees from *The Martian Chronicles* (as it were), a sprinkling of realistic stories with the smell, if not the content, of fantasy, a very bad poem, three very funny, charming and slick Irish stories, an uncharacteristically realistic story about incest, a gorgeous paean to beautiful, ageless Mother ("The Electric Grandma"), and several previously un-reprinted fantasies: "The Women," "Tomorrow's Child" (the blue pyramid baby), "The Tombling Day," and "Downwind from Gettysburg." Bradbury-haters will insist that these stories, like all his others, are about nothing. The truth is that his voice varies little and there *is* little in his stories – hence the effect of something spun gleaming out of nothing. Art can exist without encyclopedic knowledge, sophisticated morality, philosophy, political thought, scientific opinion, reflection, breadth, variety, and a lot of other good things. What else can I say? Mr. Bradbury strikes me as a writer on the same level as Poe, the kind of writer people will still be reading, still downgrading, still praising, a century from now. Damon Knight's *In Search of Wonder* (Advent Press, Chicago, 1967) says all I want to say and says it better. See Chapter 10, friends.

Still vibrating gently from the effects of the electric book, I quote Auden:

> Time that is intolerant
> Of the brave and innocent,
> And indifferent in a week
> To a beautiful physique,
> Worships language and forgives
> Everyone by whom it lives ...

Doubters please note the exact meaning of that last line.

The Magazine of Fantasy and Science Fiction, February 1971

This Perfect Day. Ira Levin (Random House, $6.95). *The Simultaneous Man*. Ralph Blum (Atlantic-Little Brown, $5.95). *The Dark Symphony*. Dean R. Koontz (Lancer, 75¢). *Sea Horse in the Sky*. Edmund Cooper (Putnam's, $4.95)

> *Madame X* presents, in an intensified form, a common problem of movie interpretation. Children sometimes interpret movies in terms of what they see on the screen, and the adults with them often try to explain what they are *supposed* to see, so that the children will be able to follow the plot ... In general, the wider the gap, the less the connection the movie has with art or talent or any forms of honesty ...
> Pauline Kael, *Kiss Kiss Bang Bang* (Bantam, 1969), p. 150

> Stage life is artificially simple and well understood by the masses; but it is very stale; its feeling is conventional; it is totally unsuggestive of thought because all its conclusions are foregone ... Real life, on the other hand, is so ill understood, even by its clearest observers, that no sort of consistency is discoverable in it; there is no "natural justice" corresponding to that simple and pleasant concept, "poetic justice"; and, as a whole, it is unthinkable. But, on the other hand, it is credible, stimulating, suggestive, various, free from creeds and systems – in short, it is real.
> George Bernard Shaw, "A Dramatic Realist to His Critics,"
> *The New Review*, London, July 1984

Ira Levin, the author of *Rosemary's Baby*, has written a science fiction novel called *Son of Brave New World* – sorry, I mean *This Perfect Day* – which is 309 pages long. It has a pretty cover and there are a lot of characters in it. It is a tidy and comfy book, smooth as Crisco from beginning to end, and if I sound unduly nasty, please keep in mind that I am not after Ira Levin in particular. I wish to shoot down a whole class of bad, bad writing and to do that, one might as well take a shot at one of the best examples, if rottenness can be said to have a best and a worst. "All its conclusions are foregone," says Shaw, above, and when you say that, you have said what is (to my mind) more morally damning than anything about implausibility or awkwardness or lack of skill. *This Perfect Day* makes science fiction written by science fiction writers look amazingly eccentric; I never realized what a freaky bunch we are, or what a strong impression of real, individual minds at work one gets from even the worst science fiction. I might add that a bad book written by a human being is infinitely preferable to a "perfect" book apparently written by a sales chart.

Mr. Levin's pale monster of a novel takes the saccharine, passive, affectless, drugged world of Huxley and reduces it to very weak tea indeed. For some reason, "our Ford" and "our Freud" (Huxley's witty and compact comment on us) are changed to Marx, Christ, and two other persons whose significance or cultural contribution is never explained. The society is coercive in a saccharine, "unselfish," very modern way – what the devil has Marx to do with this kind of togetherness? The blandness of the hero's experience is evoked very well at first, but when he manages to duck his required drugs and starts "coming alive" (the name of the second part out of four of the novel), the prose remains exactly the same, and the character's perceptions remain exactly the same. It is all very sensible, very detailed, and very thorough, but there is not the slightest intensity, the slightest vividness of characterization, the slightest trace of dramatic climax, the slightest exploration of the moral and social problems raised by such a society (or the slightest offering of alternatives), nor is anything in the book genuinely or vividly visualized. *This Perfect Day* (like *Gone With the Wind*) gives the impression that a truly momentous climax is brewing just around the corner – only read on, read on, and before you know it, you're in the end papers. There are no low points, but there are no high points, either; in fact there are no points at all, and you can put the book down and pick it up anywhere.

How many times can one take apart a commercial mechanism? Readers are timid, so the book is very slow; readers want value for money, so the book is very long; readers have no background, so the book avoids explaining anything technical; readers are not literate, so the style is simple; readers like sex but are conservative, so the sex is mild. Readers (you, dear reader) are stupid, so the hero's final "sophistication" barely approaches that of the feeblest member of the audience. Mr. Levin has made up or found (it really doesn't matter; in science fiction ideas are free because what really matters can't be patented) some of the God-awfullest clichés of our poor field – the women in this society have *no breasts*, for example (does he have any idea of the hormonal manipulations necessary for this?) except for the heroine, of course (!) and you know the hero is a *throwback* (ha ha) because he has one green eye and one brown eye. This is a crude sort of genetic determinism to find in a book that's trying to be a paean to individuality – but never mind; read Pauline Kael (above) and you'll understand. There is, of course, the usual reward for good morality, i.e. good sex (a liberal cliché if there ever was one; I'm tempted to write it Goodsex, like Orwell), and naturally there is nary a whisper as to what sort of social system is to replace the bad one. Mr. Levin doesn't want to be moral; he only wants to be pious.

In *Brave New World*, Huxley's loyalties are divided and hence there is some inner drama; Huxley is interested in real life and hence there are real people. But why go on? *This Perfect Day* is readable only in the way that the kind of movie Pauline Kael talks about is seeable – in terms of what we know we are supposed to see, not what is really there.

This is a lot of animus to direct against a fat, smooth, harmless bestseller (you may say), but I have become convinced that these fat pets are genuinely vicious en masse, and that the habit of lazily accepting "supposed to be" for "is" is responsible for a lot worse things than a few hours in a hammock with Ira Levin's latest. Let me quote Algis Budrys in the December 1968 issue of *Galaxy*:

> Characterization and motivation in commercial writing ... [are] there in predigested form, or if not the fact itself, then its inevitable consequences. In order to hit fast with it, get it done and get out, you and the reader both simplify ... "I know better, but ... for entertainment's sake I'll go along with *their* belief." ... But implicit in this blithe surrender is an acknowledgement, right there at the heart of the process, that the process is of no consequence.

Certainly minor matters can be of little consequence; Poul Anderson (as I've had occasion to mention before) jerry-builds the beginnings of his stories. But *This Perfect Day* is jerry-built all through, and like *Rosemary's Baby*, *pretends* to mull over deep moral problems. It is a thoroughly complacent book. Other readers (stupid readers, not like all of you who are proving your wisdom by reading me) will come up to us at parties and actually want to talk about the moral problems posed by *This Perfect Day* –

as though there were any! This is the kind of habit we laugh at when it involves only books; but go read the recent collection of writings done by children in Harlem schools, where it involves human lives, and then look long and hard at the title of the collection: *The Way It Spozed To Be*.

Ralph Blum, author of *The Simultaneous Man*, may be suffering from Levin's Disease, but then again he may just be inexperienced. The book jacket promises that "This Book Is Based On Fact" and I suppose it is: people do spend most of their lives opening file folders and then shutting them, looking at desks, looking away from desks, drinking drinks, drumming their fingers, lighting cigarettes, going from this place to that place, being aware of the rooms they're in, driving in automobiles, drying their hands, washing their hands, turning lights on, turning them off, and so on. But they really ought not to spend whole novels doing almost nothing else. What the book jacket meant, I suspect, is that the brainwashing described in the novel is actually being practiced by our government. If Mr. Blum has the slightest evidence that anything like that is going on, he ought to go directly to *Evergreen Review, The Realist, Life, The NY Times*, and any and all underground publications he can find and holler cop as loud as he possibly can. To put such stuff in a bad novel is foolish and cowardly. But there I go again – actually trying to believe the story, as if it were a real construct that existed. Technically *The Simultaneous Man* is very bad – Mr. Blum uses the worst point of view imaginable for his material – that of the omniscient author – and his story bucks badly: seemingly endless exposition followed by a spurt of plot, another huge chunk of exposition and another spurt of plot, *und so weiter*. There are lots of characters one never gets to know, and a description of a brain operation which fails completely to convey the moral horror of what is being done. I tried to separate relevant from irrelevant detail only to decide that all the detail was irrelevant – the book is full of irritating bits like "He was aware of a pulse in his left temple" which seem to be indices of emotion, but which somehow never succeed in making clear just what sort of emotion. There are also bits of material that are peculiarly scattered, sentences in which a reader is asked to visualize material without the proper background or is given the background in the second part of the sentence when he needs it in the first. An example:

> Through the scrub-room window, they could see into the green-tiled operating room where Art Ballard, already gowned, was filling a syringe. (p. 13)

This exasperating, jump-about stuff is all through *The Simultaneous Man*.

I suspect that like most big publishing houses making their first venture into science fiction, Atlantic-Little Brown simply lost all judgment and assumed that anything would do, just as a famous colleague of mine at Cornell once expressed astonishment at my knowing any science. "When you need a scientific explanation in one of those stories, you just make it up, don't you?" he said. The science in Mr. Blum's book is not only inaccurate but also stupefyingly inconsistent; he's as bad as A. E. Van Vogt but without the charm. *The Simultaneous Man* is about faking memory; the way this is done is to question subject A while A is under drugs (the perfect drug for this purpose having been discovered), then have a troupe of actors re-enact A's life. Their re-enactments are filmed. Subject B, his own memories having been surgically eradicated, is then "fed" the film of A's memories at very high speed while he (Subject B) is under the same perfect drug. Subject B then becomes a duplicate of Subject A. Mr. Blum doesn't seem to have considered the time it would take a troupe of real actors to re-enact *thirty-odd years* of a man's life (even allowing for time spent during sleep) or the lack of all senses except sight and hearing. For a long time science fiction has assumed that the only way to transfer memories is through direct electrical patterning and this still seems to me inherently much more sensible, despite the fact that both methods are now impossible. Halfway through *The Simultaneous Man*, Mr. Blum's A and B go into telepathic contact – this is neither explained nor used as part of the plot. B apparently falls apart because he does not match his memories physically (he is black, A is white), but there are also suggestions that the presence of the original "pulls" at the twin like "a magnet" – we never find out the real cause.

Apparently the visual/auditory tape is played to the subject during a kind of enforced catatonia, but in the novel A watches B's eyes *during* input – so just where is the input put in? If it's direct electrical stimulation of the brain, then I go back to my original objection.

There is a young lady put in the novel for the hero, A, to have Goodsex with but who seems otherwise totally unnecessary. She is a surprising character, however: "Her face was amazing: still buoying Lehebokov on the outgoing tide of her thoughts, her mind was shifting to Horne and he felt the drag and rush of feeling" (p. 226).

The book jacket tells us that the author's parents "were movie people" and that *The Simultaneous Man* is his second book. I'll hazard a guess and say that Mr. Blum does not know the first thing about writing fiction, that he is trying to write a film or TV script without realizing it, and that he is an intelligent man whose idea of writing fiction is to put down everything in the characters' field of vision – and that is no idea at all.

All this, mind you, is directed at the publisher, not at the writer. A publishing house which goes into s.f. without some experienced person on its staff is heading for trouble: either incoherent drek or slick blandness. A few hints of government nasties and a lot of file cabinets and tiled floors do not a novel make; nor does one old idea and lots of padding. Nor are the usual rules of consistency, economy, good writing, and good sense suspended in our field because "you just make that stuff up."

On page 115 of *The Simultaneous Man* there is a beautiful translation of a poem by Alexander Blok. I take it this is Mr. Blum's (no credit is given otherwise). Anybody who can write those curiously Brechtian stanzas ought not to waste his time producing mimic novels. Starve or teach like the rest of us.

The Dark Symphony by Dean R. Koontz is a silly, ritualistic adventure story of Rebellious Hero in Repressive Society. There is no pretense about the book; all is as economical, ridiculous, and flamboyant as can be. It will probably be morally corrupting to adolescents who take it seriously, but it is so stripped-down an example of its kind that I can't imagine anyone taking it seriously. There are as few scenes in the book as is compatible with the plot's moving at all: Hero in Arena (with background of Bad Society), Hero with Rebellious Mutants, Revolution, Hero Beating Up Non-Revolutionary Best Friend, Hero and Heroine Escaping to New Land. It is rather silly and lurid ("bloodlust in every cell") but it is unpretentious and quirky, and it has all the glomph of the stories we told ourselves when we were twelve. It also has a Women's Lib heroine, ta-rah! (well, sort of). There is one good idea: Manbats (known as bat-men to other writers). Mind you, it's only bearable in comparison with *This Perfect Day* and *The Simultaneous Man*, but it's unabashed trash and will do to prop up a table leg.

Sea Horse in the Sky by Edmund Cooper has surprisingly pleasant, understated characters in a thoroughly impossible frame; I suspect the book was never thought through or rewritten. The Desert Island ploy is one of the easiest to set up in literature and one of the hardest to resolve: sixteen people wake up in front of a hotel on a strange world; there is food and water and a road that leads nowhere; who – or what – is conducting an experiment? Mr. Cooper's people are interesting and his alien "stage-set" (for several groups of quasi-humans are being kept in this way) convincingly blank and eerie. The trouble with this sort of thing is that the resolution of the mystery (whose experiment and for what purpose) has to be a humdinger, and Mr. Cooper had nothing plausible or even moving to hand, so he brings the curtain down on one of the flattest denouements of all time. It is neither impressive nor plausible, and what's worse, it is in no way a dramatic resolution of what's gone before. It's simply arbitrary and it completely spoils the novel.

Otherwise there is a charming Stone Age couple, the good sense and matter-of-factness of the other characters, and a certain low-keyed good humor. As Mr. Cooper has set up his plot, however, the end must justify the preceding mystification, and the end here is just nothing.

The Magazine of Fantasy and Science Fiction, April 1971

The Bed Sitting Room. Richard Lester (movie). *First Flights to the Moon*. Ed. Hal Clement (Doubleday, no price). *SF: Author's Choice 2* (Berkley, 75¢). *One Step from Earth*. Harry Harrison (Macmillan, $5.95). *The Cube Root of Uncertainty* (Macmillan, $5.95). *Time Rogue*. Leo P. Kelley (Lancer, 75¢). *Operation Ares*. Gene Wolfe (Berkley, 75¢)

Movies don't belong in a book review, but Baird Searles (our new film reviewer) will probably never have a chance to see Richard Lester's fine science fiction film, *The Bed Sitting Room*, and I want to call readers' attention to it. The film was released some time ago and seems to have died so quietly that no one I know even heard about it. I saw it last summer only by accident.

The Bed Sitting Room (we would say "one-room apartment") is a familiar story of England ravaged by the Bomb, but the world of the film has suffered a weird shift into the ultraviolet, so that the familiar incidents one would expect are represented not by themselves, but by absurdities that are only half metaphorical. Plague? Sir Ralph Richardson not only fears that he will turn into a bed-sitting room, but actually does so (in an unfashionable part of London). There are the young lovers – Rita Tushingham, seventeen months pregnant, who announces herself as "Penelope, the celebrated fiancée," and complains to her lover, Alan, that they really ought not to eat Dad, who has been metamorphosed first into an intelligent parrot and then into a barbecued chicken. The perversion (a gentleman who has spent a decade in a bomb shelter after shooting his wife and mother-in-law as they tried to get in) is of a kind that would astonish Krafft-Ebing. In a very British clinging to business-as-usual, a Mrs. Ethel Noakes (the nearest to the throne) has become Queen; at the end of the film everyone sings:

> God save Mrs. Ethel Noakes,
> God save Mrs. Ethel Noakes,
> God save Mrs. Ethelnoakes.
> (Then they add her address.)

Mrs. Noakes appears, royally dressed and mounted on a horse under an arch made of junked refrigerators; radiation is declared unnecessary and despair un-British, the sky turns blue, the grass springs up, Penelope's monster-baby turns to a real baby; and it is declared that everything is now hotsy-totsy. My favorite is the young man who appears in a dirigible (it's weighted by the dangling chassis of a Volvo) and announces: "Times of crisis and social instability often produce new leaders. Here I am, so watch it."

The audience I was with (like the critics, apparently) could not make up its mind whether *The Bed Sitting Room* was a Laff Riot or a Stark Drama; it is, of course, neither. The film moves slowly, almost pastorally, amid the eerie beauty of an industrial ash-heap: mountain ranges of shoes, valleys of bright yellow or vermilion mud, deserts of trash, the rusty skeleton of an old car-wash at which men congregate, drinking the dirty water as if the place were a bar. It is absurd, sad, surrealistically beautiful, and very, very frightening. It is the *Goon Show* gone sad. (There are many *Goon Show* actors in evidence.) A straight story of atomic devastation would not affect us by now, but this weird, skewed collection of absurdities goes right to the heart. I think the original commercial failure of the film was due to people's (and critics') not picking up the science fiction cues (which are obvious to anybody in the field) and so not knowing how to take the film. Will the Kindly Editor forward this column to whoever owns the rights to *The Bed Sitting Room? Publicized as science fiction* (to a college audience for starters), the movie would attract the audience it needs. You might very well have a commercial success on your hands. The film is already an artistic success.

In my last column I noted that writers new to science fiction often produce God-awful books. Luckily movie directors new to the field, like Richard Lester, often produce films as good as *The Bed Sitting Room*.

Anthologies seem to be growing introductions lately, clone-fashion; the worse the stories, the longer (and more burbly) the introductions. This is called "padding." Doubleday's *First Flights to the Moon* is an extremely slight collection of reprints eked out by an awful lot of commentary. Except for

Larry Niven's fine "Wrong Way Street" and Mr. Clement's comment on A. Bertram Chandler's "Critical Angle," *First Flights to the Moon* is nothing but an exploitation of the moon shot. It simply should not have been done.

Harry Harrison's *SF: Author's Choice 2* also suffers from fat-between-the-stories. It may be interesting to fans or other authors to see what s.f. writers pick as their own favorite tales, but the result is an uneven collection. More than that, it is an encouragement to silly self-indulgence; people ought to be interested in our work, not in us. I too am pathetically grateful for the chance to peek out from behind the typewriter, but unless the introductions are little stories in themselves (as in Harlan Ellison's *Dangerous Visions*) there is really no excuse for them. The stories – bad as some of them are – are better than the authors' comments on their typewriters, their wallpaper, the fact that they are modestly proud of the story, the fact that it isn't well known, or their clichés about writing, criticism, the unconscious, and the Creative Process.

To stick to the stories: the collection is a mixed, uneven, moderately interesting grab-bag, second-rate (and mostly second-hand), but readable. There are four good stories in it: Alfred Bester's "Fondly Fahrenheit," Robert Silverberg's "To See the Invisible Man," Brian Aldiss's "Auto-Ancestral Fracture," and Hal Clement's "Proof." Mr. Clement's story is a triumph of sheer conception over naiveté (it was first published in 1942), and Mr. Aldiss's is a mannered, pretentious, "literary" tale of the Acid-Head War. Much of the static description in "Fracture" is really fine – e.g., the moviemaker's swimming pool overgrown with water hyacinth – but Mr. Aldiss does not seem able to handle action in this way, and there are poems scattered through the tale that, even in context, are just plain awful. Writers ought not to indulge themselves by smuggling bad verse into their stories; take your chances with the little magazines like a man.

Harry Harrison's *One Step from Earth* is a collection of nine stories bound together loosely (and not altogether truthfully) by the idea of matter transmission. There is another hypertrophied introduction, hypertrophied in this case because it has nothing to do with the stories; in fact, the matter transmitter described in the introduction is of the kind used in only one of the nine. Two of the tales don't really need matter transmission at all. The stories are routine, unoriginal, mildly interesting, and readable.

Robert Silverberg's *The Cube Root of Uncertainty* is a collection of twelve stories: six Old Silverberg (before 1967) and six New Silverberg. Old Silverberg is an idiot ("But it takes all sorts to make a continuum," he philosophically decided), but New Silverberg is something else: a highly colored, gloomy, melodramatic, morally allegorical writer who luxuriates in lush description and has a real love of calamity. Six such tales are not worth the price of the hardcover book, but the paperback will probably be out soon. I find myself in real trouble in evaluating New Silverberg. I don't like his feverishness or his intense, mad romanticism, and I suspect Mr. Silverberg (as Old Silverberg, the extremely self-conscious and clever hack) needs some time to get out of his system all the sophomoric dark doom that most of us – far less technically expert – dealt with during our apprenticeships. The book contains the famous "Passengers," "To the Dark Star," "Neighbor," and "Halfway House." "Sundance," the best of the lot, achieves a playing with reality that is often aimed at in science fiction but seldom realized. Mr. Silverberg gets better and better. His recent serial in *Galaxy*, *Downward to the Earth*, is a genuine novel that needs no apologies (except perhaps for the very end – why are science fiction writers so obsessed with turning into the Messiah?) The future seems bright for an author who can write in his Introduction (excusable because it's funny, the first use I have seen Mr. Silverberg make in print of his really extraordinary wit): "The newspapers teem with the horrors that smite us: the swerving auto, the collapsing bridge, the ptomaine in the vichyssoise, the fishhook in the filet of sole … But … the gorgeous worst is yet to come."

How is one to criticize a book written by two authors? Two minds were involved in the creation of *Time Rogue* by Leo P. Kelley. Both may have been the author's, for all I know, but whoever created the extraordinarily good characters in this book cannot possibly have created the truly idiotic frame of the plot, nor can the writer whose characters talk real, living, modern American (a rarity in science fiction) have written the following account of a black revolutionary's disillusionment:

> He witnessed with sadness the fact that corruption was common to men of every color. The leaders of the revolution he had helped to create – those who came after his own death – still called for equality of all but practiced a subtle inequality that favored only themselves. Monies intended for the relief of distress, whose names were hunger and want, found their way to steel vaults in foreign countries while obsequious accountants hired by the revolutionary leaders wrote false figures on command into impressive audit reports. (p. 144)

Such are the thoughts of the character who has previously spoken like this:

> "And black, I say brothers, is where it's at! *Black*! Do you know what black means? It means beauty. It means we are a people of color and

I would remind you all that most of the peoples of this world are also people of color." (p. 46)

Mind one is responsible for a wonderful child chess-genius named Barry, who daydreams that he'd like to be "a real King and have a castle and ladies-in-waiting all over his court and hey, a jester! He'd have a jester with a three-pronged cap with bells on the ends that jingled when he hopped about and told dirty stories to make everybody laugh" (p. 31). Barry also informs the company at one point that he knows worse words than "ass" (p. 79):

> "*Hooee!*" Barry cried, grinning. "I've heard a lot worse. I've used worse words myself too. I could use words that would stand your hair on end."

I am also inexpressibly grateful to mind one for providing a middle-aged lady scientist who is neither a castrating bitch nor an obsessively frustrated virgin, but a real woman whose love and guilt for a long-dead sister (killed in a concentration camp) is the mainspring of her character.

Mind two writes like this:

> When they were all on their feet and facing the Sergeant, they began to realize with immense relief that Caleb had at last forsaken them. They knew that the mechanism that had been Leda had been returned to the time from which she had come and they were aware that the murder the Sergeant had come to investigate could never be proven. Even if Leda's body had been left in their own time, they would have insisted that it was not they but the one named Caleb who had killed her. (p. 178)

Mind one is writing a psychological novel disguised as science fiction. Mind two provides a science fiction frame which must be read to be disbelieved, but even this is shot through with inconsistencies and discontinuities. One never quite finds out what the dickens the entity from the future (Caleb) wants to *do* with the seven contemporary characters, or why Caleb had to be driven mad, or why the dickens the computer sent after Caleb is a beautiful sexless girl (!), or why the seven contemporary characters can't be murdered in a perfectly ordinary way, like hitting them over the head with rocks. Even the reader's sympathy is shifted, from the Rebel Against the Cyborg Establishment (Caleb) at the beginning of the novel to the Establishment (Leda) at the end. Nothing makes any sense.

What is ominous about *Time Rogue* is that Lancer seems to make a habit of either finding or creating these cripples. In January of 1970 I reviewed K. M. O'Donnell's *The Empty People*, also put out by Lancer; there is a distinct similarity of style and mood between Mr. O'Donnell's novel and *Time Rogue*. Perhaps it's only the effect of incoherence interspersed with very good writing. Or is K. M. O'Donnell really Leo P. Kelley? Or does Lancer print only schizophrenic authors? Both books look like novels that were quite good until somebody or something got hold of them – whether a wicked part of the author's own personality or a Creative Editor, I don't know. Whatever it is, it ought to be stopped. The good parts of *Time Rogue* (that is, most of the book) are far too good to be messed up, and as the book stands, that is exactly what it is – not a bad book, but an inexplicable mess. Messes win no prizes and make nobody's reputation; books do.

Operation Ares by Gene Wolfe is going to do the author's reputation a disservice someday. I know what Mr. Wolfe can do when he sets his mind to it; *Ares* is far below his best. It is a convincing, quiet, low-keyed, intelligent book which somehow fades out into nothing. The characters are surprisingly decent; time after time there are touches of good observation and well-textured realism, but in the end Mr. Wolfe doesn't really seem to care. The book uses an interesting technique of presenting things obliquely; big events happen offstage, and often the explanations of events will be given long after the events themselves – I don't mean that this is mystification but that the significance of many things only becomes apparent long afterwards. One of the best things in the novel is its intense concentration on the present moment – time after time one swallows stereotypes without realizing that's what they are (the rational, naive Martians, the emergency government that can only harass and annoy, the fear of scientific "heterodoxy"). But all in all, the novel is a failure, shadowy and inconclusive. Books like this are generally called "promising," but by the time you read this review, Mr. Wolfe will be as far above *Operation Ares* as *Ares* is above the worst science fiction hack-work.

The Village Voice, **September 9, 1971**

Never draw pentagrams in the bathroom

The Satanists. Ed. Peter Haining (Taplinger, $5.95). *The Complete Book of Magic and Witchcraft.* Kathryn Paulsen (Signet, 95¢). *Practical Candle Burning.* Raymond Buckland (Llewellyn, no price). *Diary of a Witch.* Sybil Leek (Signet, 75¢). *Master Guide to Psychism.* Harriet A. Boswell (Lancer, 95¢). *Here, Mr. Splitfoot.* Robert Somerlott (Viking, $7.50)

Evil is dead. Split reason from emotion, Good from Evil; empty out your own experience, abandon it; convince yourself that Evil has a substantive, Manichean existence, that real excitement, real romance, real intensity, real pleasure, are always *elsewhere*. The literature of Evil and Satanism is a literature of alienation.

In Peter Haining's *The Satanists* there are: "evil and perversion ... creeping insidiousness ... a growing evil ... bestial ... debase ... in the most sickening ways ... barbaric acts ... notorious ... their dark secrets ... known perverts ... dance abandonedly in the nude ... diabolical acts of sacrilege ... terrible rituals ... the ultimate in degeneracy ..." (pp. 14–18). What a wonderful promise!

Good and evil, reason and emotion, deferred gratification and the immediate moment – the splits we make in our experience try to heal themselves while we go on acting as if they existed. Satanism is an essentialism. In this stale but hopeful mental underground Alice Kyteler is still a witch (Montague Summers, undated), "Jewish sorcerers" ride again, and the Goddess of Reason is "adored by the Revolutionaries and Parisian satanists." Somebody, somewhere, is having a really jolly wicked time.

Like other essentialists, Haining is allergic to history – almost nothing in the collection is dated because, of course, it did not *happen*: it is *always happening*. We are dealing with Sacred Time. the undated, unsupported garbage of the two Introductions leads to a conventional collection of horror stories, with two science-fictional specimens (paranoid rather than Satanist). None is as good as Arthur Machen at his best, or as personal, but there is the same beglamored sexuality, the same abundance of the gross or unclean (toads, flies, fat flesh – often linked to male homosexuality), the same archaic literalism, the same simple-minded religion, the same delight in the archaic and exotic – in short, the return of the repressed.

E. F. Benson's "Sanctuary" locates real life in what is tittery and/or disgusting. Algernon Blackwood's "Ancient Sorceries" in sexuality and the romantically archaic, H. P. Lovecraft's "The Festival" in the revolting and terrifying, Dennis Wheatley's "The Black Magician" in Benson's territory, and August Derleth's "Watcher from the Sky" in a bad imitation of Lovecraft. Cleve Cartmill's "No News Today" and Robert Bloch's "Spawn of the Dark One" are modern stories, the former celebrating paranoia (the truth is dangerous and contagious and now you, the reader, have caught it), the latter, violence (motorcycle gangs are really demons). Real life as violence and persecution is our formula for the split and just as useless as the old one – no amount of carrying violence or paranoia to their extremes can disgust us with them – this is *celebration*.

Margaret Irwin's "The Book" is the only non-Manichean story; evil here is an *illusion*, a pathological mental state, and worst of all a rejection of love. This is very modern, although the story is not. (Female culture triumphs again.) The tracing of the progressive pathology is well done, as is the kind of cheerless unpleasure the protagonist has let himself in for.

There is a piece of prose by Aleister Crowley which tells how to crucify a frog; what is striking is not its blasphemy but the lengths to which nostalgic humanity will go to mythologize natural objects. One catches a frog ("in silence"), keeps it in a chest, lets it out ("with many acts of homage"), keeps it tethered ("in apparent liberty"), speaks to it, makes promises to it, "arrests" it, talks to it some more, then crucifies it, stabs it, takes it down (talking all the while), and cooks and eats the legs (still talking). The idiocy of the procedure is really extraordinary. For example, what would the frog think of it?

Lovecraft's story is good Lovecraft (for those whose taste runs that way) and Blackwood's builds up a delicately lovely atmosphere only to throw all atmosphere away for the traditionally crude ending. "Sanctuary" and "The Black Magician" are full of fat evil men, and flies. Bloch and Hartmill are not at their best. As Summers says, "On occasion the devil preached a sort of sermon, but he spoke in a low gruff voice and it was *hard to hear what he was saying*" (italics mine).

Kathryn Paulsen's *Complete Book of Magic and Witchcraft* is sloppy and unbothered by footnotes, but it has a bibliography, and sources for some of its material. The appendices do without. The book seems to be an adapted Ph.D. thesis with footnotes removed, i.e. the historical section seems detailed but unsupported by any evidence. We are in the same wonderfully cozy world in which everything has a Significant Inside, and the trivia of daily life reveal magic correspondences with just about everything.

Ms. Paulsen equivocates about the truth of the stuff, but it is all very colorful and detailed. There are some charming medieval anecdotes (e.g.

a Scottish schoolmaster tried a love-charm on a pupil's sister and got a heifer instead). It's personal in scale – fertility, contraception, illness, visions, luck, etc. – and one talisman "to know the secrets of war". (The section on astrology and the Tarot is much more concerned with public events.) Many of the ingredients in the Paulsen recipes are hard to get – or even recognize – and, as the author notes, "the Pentagon, which likely would be unresponsive to ancient formulae, would rise in obedience to a carefully developed modern ceremony."

Raymond Buckland's *Practical Candle Burning* is sub-titled 'Spells and Rituals for Every Purpose'. A very ethical writer (only two out of 31 spells are even mildly destructive), Dr. Buckland is concerned solely with personal matters – e.g. To Overcome a Bad Habit, To Heal an Unhappy Marriage, and so on. Spells come in two forms: the "Christian Version" and the "Old Religion version", the latter being either Bucklandian free verse or odd bits of poetry I can't place (one seems to be a translation from the Greek), and the former, mashed Biblical verses, e.g. "I trusted also in the Lord; slide therefore shall not I." The 23rd Psalm (deformed) is used several times. Dr. Buckland is angry at those who want to practice evil magic and makes their use of it next to impossible; you too can make a "Hand of Glory" – *if* you "take the right or left hand of a felon who is hanging from a gibbet beside a highway ..." Dr. Buckland is "director of the only Museum of Witchcraft and Magic in the United States" (unlocated, page v) and "a reviewer of witchcraft books for this country's largest occult magazine" (unnamed, page v). Dr. Buckland has opened a new field for poets – "the most effective words would be spontaneous ones from your heart."

Sybil Leek's *Diary of a Witch* is a chatty, glowy success story of the most banal kind, with the usual sloppiness and vagueness. None of these books except Somerlott's has the slightest idea about what public events or personages are important or why, e.g. "Philosophers such as Plato, Aristotle, Hume, Kant, have all been influenced by reincarnation." Anonymous persons abound: "It is no coincidence that *many psychologists* are beginning to study astrology" (italics mine). Mrs. Leek defines "retrograde" without reference to astronomy. "African leaders," "Persian ladies," and a descendant of Catherine the Great come to see her, although "Enlightenment ... is not easy to live with in a world that derides beautiful things and thinks only in terms of material needs." She gets into awful hot water trying to reconcile astrology and free will, and is apparently unaware that anyone else has ever thought about the problem before.

Except for the possibly significant facts that her childhood home was matriarchal (she makes a similar point about witchcraft), that she luckily did not spend much time in school, and was therefore able to go her own way, Mrs. Leek's personal life does not fare much better in the book. There is the period of trial obligatory in this sort of memoir (her landlord cancels her lease in the New Forest), the piety ("she must personally strive to outbalance evil with good"), the profundities ("all scientific experiments have a positive and negative aspect – for example, the splitting of the atom"), the various incidents of precognition or healing, all small-scale and all involving anonymous persons, and in general the minutiae of a life whose meaning has vanished in print, like a piece of seaweed taken out of the ocean.

There are hints of a romantic youth (reading Shakespeare in the New Forest with the gypsies), a colorful family, and one piece of wit: her schoolmistress says, "The bathroom is *not* the place to draw pentagrams; it worries the maids." H. G. Wells came to visit, and Aleister Crowley, who is interestingly described as an unhappy and arrogant Romantic artist. Perhaps even bad writers can express some of the fragrance of childhood, or perhaps there is something about the occult that flattens and deconcretizes actual historical incidents.

In Harriet A. Boswell's *Master Guide to Psychism* everything is true: telepathy, ESP auras, sensitivity, tea-leaf reading, physical mediumship, apports, precognition and premonition, telekinesis, table tilting, automatic writing, reincarnation, astral projection, possession, psychometry, psychic photography, and the fourth dimension. You can also talk to plants. Ms. Boswell receives "beautifully worded philosophy" through her Ouija board, such as, "There is no night so dark that God's love cannot light it, no burden so heavy that His strength will not ease it, and no error so grave that His grace cannot forgive." "Eminent names" such as "authors, lecturers, scientists, theologians, and so on" are serious psychic investigators. Well-known authors like Victor Hugo, Goethe, Sardou, Charles Linton, and Mrs. Lenore Piper wrote their books by automatic writing. Some of "the great people" who believed in reincarnation were Plato, Aristotle, Voltaire (!), Carlyle, Walt Whitman, Thomas Edison, Henry Ford, and Luther Burbank.

Ms. Boswell finds an alien (sans aura) at a friend's house (p. 72). If you look at yourself in the mirror until your eyes blur, you will see your aura (p. 59). There are lots of accurate ancient predictions on record (p. 77). Put a *very* dim red light under people's faces in a dark room and you will see traces of their past incarnations (p. 135).

Unnamed places and anonymous cases abound. As in magic, everything has a marvelous and significant Inside, but at least magic concretizes itself in physical objects or words; *here* is a world in which nothing and everything can be proved, in which everything has somehow been reduced to trivia, like daydreams or reveries separated from the daydreamer whose concrete experience gives them life. Again, *life, is elsewhere* – we are back in an apolitical, acultural, static, trivial world of essences.

Robert Somerlott has written a dry, ironic, tired, well-researched history of modern occultism, i.e., the nineteenth and twentieth centuries. Ladies predominate in *Here, Mr. Splitfoot*, there is a bibliography, an index, and a wealth of facts, but no real notes. Those who want such information will like it, but who the dickens will pay $7.50 for it? Mr Somerlott finds some of his material incredible, some of it possible. He works hard.

The Magazine of Fantasy and Science Fiction, **November 1971**

The Dialectic of Sex. Shulamith Firestone (Bantam, $1.25). *Abyss*. Kate Wilhelm (Doubleday, $4.95). *The Light Fantastic*. Ed. Harry Harrison (Scribner's, $5.95). *Partners in Wonder*. Harlan Ellison (collaborations with various authors) (Walker, $8.95). *The Day After Judgment*. James Blish (Doubleday, $4.95)

It's long been a truism of our field that science fiction is better at gadgets than people. Unfortunately the truism is also a truth. Our social extrapolation is pretty much in the state technical extrapolation used to be – one change projected into the future without the (necessarily) accompanying changes in everything else. Even the supposed innovations in social structure almost always turn out to be regressive – e.g. Heinlein's family system in *Moon is a Harsh Mistress* is a patriarchal, patrilocal "stem" family very like those of the middle ages, with the added feature of *droit du seigneur* for the men (in order of seniority). None of this is new.

The most exciting social extrapolation around nowadays can be found in *The Dialectic of Sex* by Shulamith Firestone. You will have a hard time with this book if you believe that Capitalism is God's Way or that Manly

Competition is the Law of the Universe – but then you can go back to reading *The Skylark of Valeron* or whatever and forget about the real future. Firestone is a radical, a feminist, a Marxist (or rather, a thinker who has absorbed both Marx and Freud) and the author of a tough, difficult, analytic, fascinating book. In her extrapolated future:

> There will be no distinction between the political and the personal.
> There will be no split between sex and emotion.
> The dichotomy of emotion vs. reason will vanish.
> The technological and the aesthetic will merge. High art will disappear. In fact, culture as we know it will vanish, to be replaced by serious play and direct satisfaction.
> Childhood, a fairly recent invention, will vanish.
> The family will "die" – that is, the parental role will be diffused to everybody, just as the "feminine" role will be diffused to everybody.
> Children will be compensated by society for their physical weakness and their inexperience.
> Artificial reproduction will be available as an option (it is very close to being possible right now).
> Racial caste arises from the paradigm of caste embodied in the family; with the creation of an androgynous world, racism will disappear. The psychology of power, whose source is the biological family, will disappear.
> There will be no distinction between child society and adult society, male cultural experience and female cultural experience; in fact, sexuality will become polymorphous-perverse, thus taking the compulsiveness out of it and uniting it with all love and all play.

There is a good short history of the woman's suffrage movement, a fine analysis of the connection between opposition to population control and the chauvinism of the private family ("private bid for immortality"), a good explanation of scientific schizophrenia and Snow's two cultures, a short history of childhood (which began only a few centuries ago), and some fascinating alternatives to the family which recall much of Samuel Delany's fiction. To say, for example, that children are oppressed as a class seems absurd, but consider:

> Children must be living embodiments of happiness ... it is every parent's duty to give his child a childhood to remember ... This is the Golden Age that the child will remember when he grows up ... "minors" under the law without civil rights, the property of an arbitrary set of parents ... economic dependence ... It is clear that the myth of childhood happiness flourishes so wildly not because it

satisfies the needs of children but because it satisfies the needs of adults ... (pp. 93–95)

Within a century, she says, if we don't blow ourselves up.

The two novellas that make up Kate Wilhelm's *Abyss* are flawed, the first ("The Plastic Abyss") because it attempts more than most successes and the second ("Stranger in the House") because of Wilhelm's entirely original set of virtues and defects.

As George Orwell has pointed out, most human "worlds" are not represented in art at all, for to be a member of such a world demands that one not be an artist. Orwell's example is Kipling, who managed somehow to become a full member of colonial Anglo-Indian society *and yet* keep enough of an antithetical self alive to report well on that same society. Not only to describe but also to embody in oneself a world-view that leaves no room for art takes quite a lot of doing.

Kate Wilhelm is an escapee from the feminine mystique. As Shulamith Firestone points out, women and men live in different cultures though neither group knows it – men consider the male experience to be the only reality, and so do women, who therefore distort and deny their own experience. Until recently we have had of the female experience only versions sentimentalized and distorted in the service of self-glorification and the status quo. Good women artists have generally had atypical experiences; as a friend of mine put it, they've brought themselves up as men, since "man"– in the general view – was the equivalent of "human."[1] Like Kipling, Kate Wilhelm manages to be both an artist and the voice of an experience *that is defined by its not having a voice*. To find a voice one must move out of this culture and yet stay in it; Wilhelm almost does this. "The Plastic Abyss" is the eerie fusion of women's-magazine "reality" and real reality, as if sentimental pictures had suddenly begun to move and speak. There is a tall, glamorous, hard, patronizing husband in "The Plastic Abyss" who is breathtakingly close to the Ideal Husband of bad fiction; there is the Sweet, Ideal, Passive Wife of romance who almost makes it into artistic definition; and there is the magnificently irresponsible playing-around with reality only possible to those who don't have the conventional stake in it and are therefore wise enough not to believe in it. Still, there are vestiges of un-ironic cardboard. The heroine of "Plastic Abyss" says she "should go back to work, back to writing articles, to traveling, prying, learning" although it is perfectly clear from her character that she has never done any of those things; the heroine of "Stranger" has a "fashion" job that

---

1 E.g. myself and Anne McCaffrey.

is never made real to her or anybody else. There is a stepdaughter in "Plastic" who (we are told) will do better than the heroine, although her situation is in no way different. There is a Nice Young Painter who is something of a nebbish but otherwise rather sketchily realized. There is a patronizing Good Old Man who is as much of a sexist as the Bad Husband, though Wilhelm doesn't think so. The Bad Husband is put down by the Good Old Man and The Real Scientist, not by his wife, who remains passive and dependent throughout. She escapes from her dependency, her childishness and her husband only by jumping clean out of reality. She then finds out that she's the one who's controlling everybody else. "Stranger" is more conventional and easier to follow, although again the women (and the young people) are more alert to what's going on than the men and readier to believe in what is real but strange. Wilhelm gets her second heroine's husband out of the way by giving him a bad heart medically; the husband of "Plastic Abyss" has a bad heart humanly. I was struck in both novellas by what seemed to me the unearned adulation given to both women, but I wonder if this simply reflects our not being used to feminine protagonists who are involved in real activity. Most male protagonists in s.f. are glorified (or unrealized) in exactly the same way. It seems to be an occupational hazard. "Plastic Abyss" is much farther along the road to realized Wilhelm than "Stranger," which dates from 1967. Both stories use rhythms of narrative quite unlike those of slick fiction; the earlier tale proceeds jerkily through some awful bloopers ("When the planet had been discovered, Earth year 1896, Gron year 14,395, the excitement on Gron had been rampant") to a very moving ending; Wilhelm – luckily for her – has art but no conventional craft. Some of the writing is fine ("Gary's pale hair and the doctor's thin face side by side like a Dali distortion, facets of the same thing, and that thing not what she had always called man before"), some of it oddly unnecessary ("She had knocked over her wineglass, and sherry was spreading across the *glossy* surface of the table," italics mine).

Knowing my radical Feminist tendencies, the Kindly Editor sent me only good books (by men) this month. Harry Harrison's *The Light Fantastic*, subtitled "Science Fiction Classics from the Mainstream," is a fine, if partly an obvious, collection and reminds one what definitive treatment of a theme *can* be – from the last phrase of Anthony Burgess's "The Muse" ("not blotting a line") to the hand of God knocking on the woman's sleazy soul in C. S. Lewis's "The Shoddy Lands": "It was in some curious way, soft; 'soft as wool and sharp as death', soft but unendurably heavy, as if at each blow some enormous hand fell on the outside of the Shoddy Sky and covered it completely. And with that knocking came a voice at whose sound my bones turned to water: 'Child, child, child, let me in before the night comes'" (p. 213).

I have some quibbles: Leo Szilard's charming but slight "The Mark Gable Foundation;" Gerald Kersh's "The Unsafe Deposit Box," with its large, logical hole; Kingsley Amis's "Something Strange," a good early example of a theme that is somewhat too familiar by now; and the too-thin "The Door" by E. B. White (1939). There remain: "Sold to Satan" by Mark Twain, Graham Greene's "The End of the Party", Borges' "The Circular Ruins," "The Shout" by Robert Graves, E. M. Forster's "The Machine Stops," John Cheever's "The Enormous Radio" and that splendid tale of Kipling's, "The Finest Story in the World." There is an extremely good introduction by James Blish. All in all, a fine collection.

On page 297 of Harlan Ellison's *Partners in Wonder* is a William Rotsler drawing of King Kong on top of the Empire State building, holding a squidgy little Fay Wray in his fist. Only her head is visible. Someone down on the sidewalk is screaming, "Trip him, Fay, trip him!" For me the cherry-and-whipped-cream of Ellison's anthologies is this quality in his introductions, for example, "*Base canard* is the bottom duck in a beachside pyramid of athletic French ducks" or "If trolley cars had wings, would elephants have overhead runners?" Through the whole book runs the strangest sweetness of triumphant, loving absurdity, of mind taking off into the wild blue.

Ellison is hung up on words and the small details of existence, just as an artist should be. "Countenances" he writes; "(conteni? contenubim?)" Ellison's mode, in both reportage and fiction, is hyperbole – in dramatic terms, *extremity* – so that he is always operating either on the absurd or the desperate edge of experience. *Partners* is a very good collection and would be a good collection even without the introductory material; to say that most of the stories don't exist on the same level as the best of the introductions is hardly dispraise; in fact, some of the former are first-rate. Moreover (and this is rare in anthologies) they reinforce one another, so that the book benefits from the cumulative effect. The newest stories are better, the best of them being, to my mind, the Ellison/Sheckley "I See a Man Sitting on a Chair and the Chair Is Biting His Leg," which seems much more coherent in this setting than in *F & SF*, where it was previously published; Ellison's "Prowler in the City at the Edge of the World" which is at the top of the collection; the fierce and sentiment-full "Song the Zombie Sang" (Ellison and Silverberg); and the Ellison/Zelazny "Come to Me Not in Winter's White," a lyrical fairy tale (no pun intended) haunted by the ghost of a banal triangle – as every once in a while the skeletons of Zelazny's own stories show through the flesh. There is tremendous motion in all of these – Ellison's contribution, insofar as I can figure it – which is not far, for the stories are all seamless, except for Ellison/Laumer's "Street Scene" in which the patchwork-quilt effect is deliberate and quite funny. Other collaborations include "Brillo" with Ben Bova;

Robert Bloch's "A Toy for Juliette" (which sparked Ellison's "Prowler"); "Up Christopher to Madness" with Avram Davidson, which may contain too much Damon Runyon but which I found a pleasant romp; "The Kong Papers," which is a delightful fribble drawn by Bill Rotsler and worded (?) by Ellison; and with A. E. Van Vogt a surprisingly vivid treatment of a familiar theme in "The Human Operators." The Ellison/Delany collaboration, "The Power of the Nail," does not quite come together nor does the scattered "Runesmith" with Theodore Sturgeon (besides, sf writers ought to resist the temptation to make their heroes turn into The Messiah). Others – quite at the level of most sf anthologies – are collaborations with Joe L. Hensley (1962), Henry Slesar (1959), and Algis Burdrys (1957).

James Blish continues his exploration of ethics, theology, and medieval magic in *The Day After Judgment*. The book is a sequel to Armageddon, which ended the earlier *Black Easter*, and attempts to answer the question: After the death of God, what? The condensation is as fine as ever, the morality as stringent, and the keen, dry, exhilarating atmosphere of Blish's intellectuality is a pleasure of the first order. Everything in the book is as distinct and clear as an object painted by Giotto. The very syntax is brilliant and the characterization as solid as outside analysis can make it – take a look at General Willis McKnight's encounter with the image of Satanachia and his subsequent insanity (later he decides that the demon prince is something worse; i.e. Fu Manchu) or the gem of bad reasoning in which Jack Ginsberg blames God for the end of the world. Blish is in his element here, and even his limitations work for him. *The Day After Judgment* (with *Black Easter*, for they should be read together) is – if I'm not mistaken – close to being a masterpiece. It's my uninstructed impression that relative financial independence has allowed Blish to write more idiosyncratically than he ever did before, about themes he knows may not interest large numbers of readers. Both books, like Blish's beautiful *Doctor Mirabilis*, are absolutely *sui generis*. *Judgment*'s solution of the problem of evil is less overwhelmingly dramatic than the catastrophe of *Black Easter*, probably unavoidably so. I find the masque-like Miltonics at the end both *crabb'd* and *pedantique* but am willing to allow that the author had reasons I do not see. The magic is as fine as ever, particularly the means by which the characters rendezvous in the last chapter: airplanes, transvection, and ecstatic trance-levitation. Hell is "an incombustible Alexandrian library of ... evasions," in Ware's ruined palazzo "the window panes were out, and the ceiling dripped; the floor was invisible under fallen plaster, broken glass and anonymous dirt; and in the *gabinetto* the toilet was pumping continuously as though trying to flush away the world."

We're lucky to have the book.

The Shape of Utopia: Studies in a Literary Genre. Robert C. Elliott (University of Chicago Press, 1970, 158pp., $6.50). *Into the Unknown: The Evolution of Science Fiction from Francis Godwin to H. G. Wells*. Robert M. Philmus (University of California Press, 1970, 174pp., $6.95)

Science fiction is receiving more academic attention than it used to, a species of kindness that may turn out to be the equivalent of being nibbled to death by ducks. For reasons nobody seems to understand, voyages to the moon fascinate academicians, as does anything written before 1800, or satire, or Utopian fiction – in short, anything that avoids the fecundity and speculative wildness of twentieth-century science fiction. It is probably a question of what's manageable, but unfortunately voyages to the moon tend to be the oldest (often the dullest) kind of science fiction, and Utopian romances are not only secondary in the contemporary *oeuvre*, they are relatively unimportant.

Robert C. Elliott's *The Shape of Utopia* is a scattered collection of pleasant, modest, clearly written essays, none of which treats its subject with any complexity. There is much in the book that is just, much that turns into truism if you look at it twice, and not really enough to tie the essays together into one volume. Much is stated without being explored or fully described; much is mentioned or proposed without being done. For example, Elliott twice brings up a rather important topic – what's the relation of the teller of these tales to the author, of More to "More" (in More's *Utopia*), or Coverdale to Hawthorne (*Blithedale Romance*)? What did More think of communism, for example? One must, says Elliott, avoid "a priori judgments and listen ... to the voices as they speak"; but if one does, he concludes:

> I think it very doubtful that we can ever know what he, in his many conflicting roles of philosopher, moralist, religious polemicist, man of great affairs – what this man "really" believed about communism. Of Thomas More, author of *Utopia*, we can speak with confidence. The idea attracted him strongly ... Utopia argues for the ideal of communism by the best test available: More has given to Raphael Hythloday all the good lines. Thus the shape of *Utopia* is finished off, enigmatically but firmly ... (pp. 47f)

But in the middle of this, the relation of "More" to More gets lost.

Throughout, Elliott promises more than he delivers. There is, for example, the connection between satire and Utopia, which Elliott calls genetic, but which seems to me to be somewhat forced; there is the topic of the distribution of negative and positive elements in Utopian fiction which is never explored at length or much used as an analytical tool; there is the question of why satires and Utopias are so often framed by "an encounter between a satirist and an adversary" (p. 23) which is not answered; there is the fascinating suggestion that the proper mode of Utopian fiction is *lyric* ("the idyll as Schiller describes it," p. 107), an idea which unfortunately remains unelaborated and unexplored.

In short, there are scattered insights all through (like Elliott's definition of "anti-Utopia," the modern nightmare of the bad place which is bad *because it is somebody else's ghastly Utopia*, typically the Grand Inquisitor's). But the insights are not bound into any coherent theory, nor does most of the book go beyond descriptive detail. The last three studies, "The Fear of Utopia," "Aesthetics of Utopia," and "Anti-Anti-Utopia" do constitute more of a connected argument, as well as marking the historical change from "longing" to "possibility" – a lovely distinction Elliott mentions only once (p. 85) and promptly drops for ever. "The Fear of Utopia" centers on the fear of progress (due to a perceived incompatibility between freedom and happiness); "Anti-Anti-Utopia" deals with the contemporary reaction against this fear in favor of happy unfreedom; and "Aesthetics of Utopia" deals largely with the aesthetic flaws of Utopian fiction, which Elliott suspects are inherent in the genre.

All the above are adequate and what one might call minimally intelligent, but I don't find in them anything out of the commonplace – perhaps the penalty of the author's ignoring modern science fiction, or R. D. Laing, or Wittgenstein, or critics like Samuel Delany[1] (criticism of modern science fiction is squirrelled away in ghetto periodicals, like so much else about the genre). In connection with Hawthorne, Elliott picks up "idea-as-hero" ("'background' takes on independent life," p. 83), connecting it with the historical novel but ignoring its vast importance for science fiction – the variety of ways in which modern science fiction handles this problem might be prescriptive for Utopian fiction. As in science fiction, the technical problem of exposition takes up the bulk of the book, "the central element" as Elliott calls it, one which has "baffled even the best writers" (p. 109). Elliott seems to waver between perceiving Utopian fiction as *sui generis*, not

---

1 See, for example, "About Five Thousand One Hundred and Seventy Five Words," in *Extrapolation* (newsletter of the Conference on Science Fiction of the MLA), ed. Thomas Clareson, College of Wooster, Wooster, Ohio, May 1969, Vol. X, No. 2.

to be judged by the same standards as other fiction (pp. 110ff), and the view that this is precisely what's wrong with it – it's a "bastard form," it's inescapably thin (p. 116), it cannot tolerate fully developed characters (pp. 116, 121) and so on. There is also "the ancient and notorious problem of depicting the good" (p. 117). "Health," says Elliott, quoting Swift, "is but one thing and has been always the same" (p. 117). Whether the good is in itself "stupefyingly boring" (p. 119) or whether "we lack ... conventions for depicting man in a happy state" (p. 120), Utopian fiction seems to be committed to dullness. Moreover, it may be possible (this ties in with "Fear of Utopia") that "happiness ... cannot accommodate instability" (p. 125) and that Utopia is incompatible with art, an incompatibility that retroactively blights Utopian fiction (to be fair, Elliott doesn't say this).

I'm afraid I find the discussion rather routine. Certainly the aesthetics of didactic romance will differ from those of literature with more commitment to mimesis and – as in science fiction, which is also a didactic and non-mimetic kind of romance (at least by intention) – the intellectual/moral content must function aesthetically.[2] But it's not nearly enough just to say that Utopian fiction is a bastard form and therefore difficult. I also think it's a mistake to conceive of the aesthetic problem as one of expressing lyric matter in narrative-dramatic form. Brecht and Shaw have both dealt with the problem of the aesthetics of didacticism. Non-Utopian science fiction seems to be developing all sorts of ways of dealing with lyric (or "static" material), which Utopian novelists might well imitate. After all, finding out is itself a process, and perception is an act. Samuel Delany believes that in modern fiction the center of narrative interest has switched from the passions to the perceptions;[3] if this is true, it might well rescue Utopian fiction. And it's possible to see the irruption of the lyric mode into prose narrative as typical of what has been called the post-realistic novel.

Talking of Utopian fiction (or science fiction) inevitably involves one in all sorts of extra-literary speculations. It seems to me that Elliott's extra-literary armory is pretty meager and that his discussion of freedom vs. happiness ("The Fear of Utopia" and "Anti-Anti-Utopia") suffers thereby. Only at the very end does the last essay attain to considerable complexity. "Huxley," says Elliott, "has no command of the *celebratory* style" (p. 152, italics mine); "the Palanese have created a society in which it is not a *profa-*

---

2 I am indebted to Alexei Panshin, science fiction novelist and author of *Heinlein in Dimension* (Advent Press, Chicago, 1967), the first full-dress study of any writer in the field. See his series of theoretical essays printed in *Galaxy* monthly during 1971.

3 Samuel Delany, in conversation.

nation to be happy" (p. 153, italics mine). Elliott seizes in both those significant words more complication than he ever allows himself in his explicit discussion of the issues. Again: "But whereas the Grand Inquisitor demands *a great act of abnegation* from those who would be of his party, Skinner offers us a lollipop" (p. 153, italics mine). Happy unfreedom as an act of abnegation seems to me an extraordinary insight into what is really going on under our fallacious reasoning about happiness vs. freedom.

On the other hand, in the body of the essay Elliott seems to accept without much demur the idea that freedom always leads to unhappiness, that happiness is substance, not process, that harmony does not admit of idiosyncrasy, that equilibrium is always static and never dynamic. These are not only routine; they're wrong. When existentialists start writing Utopias, when perception is commonly seen as a dynamic process (and so on and so on) we can step out of Elliott's double-bind without trouble – double-binds (as R. D. Laing says) can't be solved in their own terms; one can only get out of the terms.

I suppose the book is a good introduction to Utopian fiction, and it claims neither to be a history of the genre nor a treatment of the ideologies of various Utopian novels. It is a mine of scattered questions and bibliographical references. But much is unoriginal and much of the analysis has been surpassed elsewhere, sometimes in very unlikely places. I find it not enough, as Ivan the Terrible said after the boyars had their heads chopped off; he had something nicer in mind: more boyars' heads. More boyars' heads follow.

Robert M. Philmus's *Into the Unknown* is almost as hard to review as it was to read. Professor Philmus's sources are unimpeachable, he is stuffed to the gills with obscure erudition, he has read more than anyone could reasonably be expected to read in ten lifetimes; but what good is all this when it is embodied in language that only God can understand? More than that, Professor Philmus's logic at times defies me (or anybody else, I think); he seems to make literary points by a process of knocking down straw men – that is, he mentions A, brings in B by a process of sheer association (thus implying sub rosa that A and B are similar), finds that they are *not* similar – behold, a point! But they never were; they were only associated *via* some middle term chosen almost arbitrarily. An example:

> To appreciate the nature of the antlike Selenites and their highly organized society in *The First Men in the Moon*, it is relevant to compare them with what in some respects they are not – the conquering ants of Wells' short story, "The Empire of the Ants" – and thereby to determine what in *The First Men* is mythically new for Wells. (p. 144)

What is "mythically new" is that the conquering ants are unorganized and sinister, whereas the "Antlike Selenites" are specialized, social, intelligent, and benevolent – i.e. there is no similarity between the two except Wells' use of the term "antlike." No further conclusions are drawn. Here's another, from a discussion of Capek's play *R.U.R.*

> They [the humans] eventually find that they can no longer control the situation that they have brought about and are as caught up in the mechanical logic of events as the "robots" over whom they are supposed to have mastery. The entrepreneurs in *R.U.R.*, Rossum's successors, thus face essentially the same predicament as the people in the mechanized subterranean world of E. M. Forster's *The Machine Stops*. "Year by year [the machine] was served with increased efficiency and decreased intelligence. The better a man knew his own duties upon it, the less he understood the duties of his neighbor, and in all the world there was not one who understood the monster as a whole." (p. 157)

The "mechanical logic of events" here is a robot revolution – in fact the "logic of events" is precisely given as *not* mechanical; it is the robots' becoming emotional and "human" which causes the revolution. Furthermore, this revolution is hardly the "same predicament" as that of *The Machine Stops*. In Forster's story the machine breaks down because nobody knows how to repair it; in Capek's play the downtrodden robots revolt and take over the world. I do not see what is "essentially the same" here, except that people and machinery are involved in both stories.

Perhaps the manuscript for the book underwent drastic condensation or rewriting. English sentences usually have internal signposts that tell you where the sentence is going logically and syntactically, but in Philmus's prose, as in a country at war, all the signposts have been turned wrong-way-to, to deceive the enemy. Here are some results:

> These works satirically dramatize accepted ideas and ideals, reducing them to near absurdity by depicting their consequences as cosmic principles or demonstrating their partiality by embodying as myth "the opposite idea." (p. 27)

> But beyond their reliance on explicit scientific explanations or the (usually implicit) metaphors of natural philosophy, some of these voyages can serve as rudimentary examples of how, by extending the range and detail of human experience and enlarging and multiplying the concepts that order that experience, science can influence the form of the fantasy. (p. 52)

REVIEWS 73

> But by perceiving right away the reality that the fiction displaces, one discounts the fact the Gulliver insists his *Travels* is a record of what he has actually seen and undergone. (p. 5)

> To say that there is a kind of logic operative in *L'Autre Monde* – principally a logic of association – and that the mostly explicit arguments set forth in Dyrcona's voyage to the moon prepare for, and help to elucidate, their allegorical counterparts in the voyage to the sun does not contradict the view that *L'Autre Monde* is satiric fantasy. (p. 130)

There is sense under this awful stuff. Professor Philmus works hard to show that science fiction is *about* something and that writers read their predecessors' works. He recognizes that science fiction is not simply fantasy (p. vii), that it deals with metaphors turned into literal realities (the "displacement" he speaks of, I think) and that it is connected with the scientific thought of its period. He does not get beyond describing rather obvious similarities between works and considers so many different ones that none can be treated in detail; he usually has room only for a re-telling of the story and a few generalizations. The scattered essays have been given beginnings and endings that attempt to hook them onto each other, usually unsuccessfully. There is good – and new – material here for a theory of science fiction ("the mythic displacement of 'existing circumstances' and tendencies as they are projected into the dimension of 'prophecy,'" p. 78) but the style is so barbarous, the construction so haphazard, and the arguments so exceedingly hard to follow, that one might as well give up.

There is accurate and evasive praise from Isaac Asimov printed on the cover.

The Magazine of Fantasy and Science Fiction, December 1972

Moderan. David R. Bunch (Avon, 75¢). *The Falling Astronauts.* Barry N. Malzberg (Ace, 75¢). *In the Pocket and Other SF Stories* and *Gather in the Hall of the Planets.* K. M. O'Donnell (Ace double, 75¢). *Humanity Prime.* Bruce McAllister (Ace, 95¢). *The Committed Men.* M. John Harrison (Doubleday, $4.95). *Pig World.* Charles W. Runyon (Doubleday, $4.95). *Can You Feel Anything When I Do This?* Robert Shackley (Doubleday, $4.95)

We all know that Reason is superior to Emotion. (After all, look where it's got us.) And that souls ride inside bodies, like people inside Edsels, right? And that Edsels often break down, leaving us to cry like Saint Paul, Who will deliver me from the body of this death? I have actually met engineers who told me (in all sincerity) that they lived their lives according to the dictates of Reason, and when I got them enraged – which is easy to do – they told me I was irrational. In *Love and Will* Rollo May describes a patient of his, a chemist, who had invented the perfect daydream erection: a metal pipe extending from his brain directly through his penis. The rest of his body was irrelevant.

There has to be a division of labor here, since it is not so easy to throw away your fleshliness, your vulnerability, your emotions, your mortality, your passivity, and your knowledge that you are an object in a world of objects (try falling downstairs). Thus we find Man the Rational and Woman the Emotional, Man the Soul and Woman the Carnal, Man the Active and Woman the Passive, Man as Humanity and Woman as Nature, Man as Strong and Woman as Weak, Man as Tool-maker and Woman as Man-admirer, Man as Political and Woman as Home-oriented. Every man deserves the freedom to have his own abortion. Man bears his young alive. Man is the only animal who menstruates.

David Bunch, a loud, crude good poet, has come up with *Moderan*, a half-novel, half-collection-of-stories about what it is like to live out the male mystique. Mind and body could not be more split. If you are really somebody in Moderan, you are 97 percent new-steel and only 3 percent flesh; you spend your time as the master of a Stronghold (which runs itself anyway) playing war games with other Strongholds, thinking Deep Thoughts in your hip-snuggle chair (it is kind of hard to walk, somehow, if you're new-metal) and perhaps delectating your aesthetic sensibilities with the tin flowers that pop up through the metal-covered floor of the world at the touch of a button, or noticing the change of seasons by changes in the color of the sky (they rotate the sky very punctually in Moderan). True, there are problems; as Mr. Bunch notes:

> ... it was envisaged that a few outstanding, special wives might be "replaced" and allowed to share the Stronghold forever-life ... there were, on science grounds, long and bitterly contested debates as to whether any female of the species would be strong enough to stand that nine-months' battery of the "replacement" operations. Finally, in a spirit of benevolent bravado and what-the-hell charity and choice, the panel, all men, and all great new-metal scientists ... and all, so it chanced, bachelors, said ... (p. 62)

Terrified Stronghold Masters receive letters beginning *"Greetings"* (this is a very funny book) but as the narrator says, "Moderan was man country," and the wives end up in a high-walled, maximum-security prison called White Witch Valley.

Death has been licked at last. Stronghold Masters never die, although Strongholds fall. There are robot mistresses with "blue eyes, blue-bulb blue and like small glass globes sliced carefully." Armed with Wump Bombs, "high, shrieking wreck-wrecks," Honest Jakes, walking doll-bombs, and White Witch rockets, there is safety indeed.

So of course the inhabitants of Moderan are terrified over and over and over again. They spend eternity in fear.

The author knows what he's about. There are sly references to Mailer and Hemingway upon the arrival of the new-metal mistress in her carton and excelsior (she later flees the hero, apparently out of boredom), penis-machines that batter down the earth at the beginning of the book ("huge black cylinders swung spinning between gigantic thighs and calves of metal") so that new-metal can cover the earth from pole to pole, with no soft spots. There is even soul power (pp. 229ff) and the hero's very familiar pique when – at the end of the book – he unleashes his great, final bomb, the Grandy Wump, only to find that everybody else has got one, too:

> Not only had they stolen my secret, but vile, vile to the last and plotting, apparently they had installed detective devices to steal my moment of firing! (p. 229)

Part II, "Everyday Life in Moderan," seems to be made up of earlier stories; it is not perfectly integrated with Parts I and III.[1] Note: of all the

---

1 Credits for individual stories go back to 1959.

flesh-bums still alive in Moderan, the only genuinely willful, hating-loving, human is a four-year-old girl:

> It was in Jingle-Bell weather that Little Sister came across the white yard, the snow between her toes all gray and packed and starting to ball up like the beginnings of two snowmen. For clothing she had nothing, her tiny rump sticking out red-cold and blue-cold, and her little jewel knees white almost as bones. (p. 166)

Five-year-old Little Brother spends his time weight-lifting and thinking about rockets, jets, and space. He will grow up to live out his new-metal immortality in impoverishment and terror, as does everyone else in this beautiful, "dense" (don't read too much at once), and vividly fantastic book. But as Father says, "could one ever think too much about rockets and jets and space?" (p. 170).

The protagonist of Barry Malzberg's *The Falling Astronauts* knows you can. He has gone mad doing so. The real name of the game is depersonalization. Like Rollo May's patient, Mr. Malzberg's astronaut can only copulate with his wife if he imagines them both to be machines; and again, the only character in the book who knows something is wrong is the wife, although she cannot quite explain what it is. What is astonishing about this novel is not that the protagonist (the point-of-view character) is mad, *but that everyone else is, too*. It is eerie to listen to a mad madman being interviewed by a "sane" madman in a world where any pretense to "rationality" is the maddest thing of all. Mr. Malzberg uses (and perceives) NASA as Big Government, the quintessential split between emotion and reason. In the lucidity of his own insanity, the hero says quite sensibly, on the last page but one:

> "It won't work, don't you see? It won't work. It's just too late and all meant to be this way because this is the way you wanted it. This is what you built and you're just going to have to take the full consequences ..." (p. 190)

The consequences are the end of the world.

The Falling Astronauts resembles "Still-life" in Harlan Ellison's *Again, Dangerous Visions*. (I am glad to announce, for the sake of clearing up my own confusion, that Barry Malzberg *is* K. M. O'Donnell.) The theme benefits from the comparative roominess of the novel, but the book also seems to become somewhat repetitive, as if Mr. Malzberg suffered from that curse of all freelance writers: lack of time. (Not time to write, but most importantly, time to think or just do nothing.) Nevertheless *The Falling Astronauts* is a good book.

REVIEWS 77

Also cursed with silly jackets and sillier blurbs are two other good books by O'Donnell-Malzberg: *In the Pocket and Other SF Stories* and *Gather in the Hall of the Planets* (one Ace double, a bargain). Without anybody's noticing it – except Theodore Sturgeon, in a recent review – Mr. Malzberg has sneaked up on us as a fine writer. The Ace double also suffers from some unevenness, in parts sloppy, in parts poignant, sometimes brilliant, though not as finished as *Astronauts*. *Planets* is the better half (it's about a science fiction convention in 1974). I especially liked ice-cubes "whisking" down a woman's dress like "silvery fish."

Humanity Prime is Bruce McAllister's first novel and a promising one, although a good deal of the story does not cohere scientifically. Mr. McAllister seems to have worked in the way least common in s.f. – that is, the experience of the strange world/strange people came first and the scientific rationale later. I assume this because the local color of Mr. McAllister's water-dwelling humans is very well rendered, as is their Siciliana *mamma* who has become a cyborg and watches over her aquatic *bambini* from a grounded satellite. What Mr. McAllister has done is to take s.f. clichés – e.g. the warlike lizard people, the "inborn" yearning of the adapted humans for dry land, the development of new senses underwater, the eternal partnership of Man and Dog (both now aquatic!) – and try to recreate them as genuinely realized experiences. However, the re-vitalizing (or contradicting) of the clichés *plus* the exposition of these entirely through dramatic development lead to some awful holes in the book's logic. Gianna (we are told) has gone crazy because the technicians who made her a cyborg forgot to provide her with REM sleep – surely a very elementary error. (My own theory is that anybody with a "maternal drive" of 9.99 is already crazy.) Moreover, the Man–Dog business really does not move out of cliché; I kept hoping that those funny, hairy creatures who kept trying to play with the mer-people were man's best friend, the noble cat, but no go. And the reproductive system Mr. McAllister has given his people is *awful*. He seems to have been carried away by his successes with telepathy into inventing a method of telepathic copulation, in which the males project a mental image of a legged fish (the longing for dry land, see?) to the females, who thereupon *fertilize themselves*, since they carry both testes and ovaries inside their own bodies. This method of reproduction not only throws away the enormous advantages of sexual reproduction (constant hybridization); it loses even the advantages of asexual reproduction, since we do not have endless repetition of a single individual (as in budding) but what is far worse, *a constant re-shuffling of the genetic material of one person* – in which much hereditary material is bound to get lost for good, by sheer chance. Genetic drift would be very fast in such a group of creatures, and probably lethal. The end of the novel gives us only one Eve, a sure recipe for disaster. There is no reason for this mess. After all, even fish reproduce sexually. There is still less reason for chaste monogamy – or for that matter, heterosexuality. Mr. McAllister has just not thought the whole business through. The real subject of *Humanity Prime* is mer-life and telepathic consciousness; the mer-dogs, the reptile Cromanths, the whole reproductive mess, and even the cyborg (entertaining as she is) could be dispensed with. I hope Mr. McAllister's next book is less encumbered with traditional material.

The Committed Men by M. John Harrison stops where most American novels would begin. It is the British ending the world again; after the Bomb comes the usual Character Consumed by Guilt (I never figured out for what), the Odd Communities, the Plagues, the Realist, the Madmen, and the Dreary Pilgrimage through the Rubble. Finally the characters make contact with some exceedingly interesting "mutants" (specially bred by the Government, actually), and there the book ends. The final confrontation with the mutants is especially fine – a weird, parodic version of the Queen of Faerie of old English ballads – but except for an enigmatic character named Nick Bruton (who resembles Michael Moorcock's Jerry Cornelius) most of this is very much a twice-told tale. It is good writing thrown away. The psychological subtleties of dreary suffering, accurate as they were, only bored me. *Committed Men* is Mr. Harrison's first novel; I hope that he and Mr. McAllister both learn to cut the cackle and get to the 'osses. They are both good writers.

In an article entitled "Thea and I" published in *Entropy Negative #3*, a fan magazine put out in Vancouver, Ursula Le Guin said that Charles W. Runyon's *Pig World* made her feel a little sick. I suppose you have to take the book more seriously than I am capable of doing for that. An ineffably silly blend of infantile Marxism, cardboard revolutionaries who carefully summarize their positions to each other, a hero named *Marvin*, for God's sake, who is radicalized *in one evening*, total vagueness as to anybody's ideology or political orientation, and a story that takes half the book to quit summarizing and start dramatizing itself – this is *Pig World*. There are tremenjus chunks of mysterious exposition about what's happening in West Somaliland, Siberia, and points all over. There's oodles of play-money, which the revolutionaries live on like James Bond. There is a hugeous power machine (Sex, Money, Power, and Megalomania = Revolution!) At the end the hero shoots the villain on Main Street, and the Eternal Feminine tells the hero he's betrayed the revolution by succumbing to Power and forgetting Love – I mean I think so or Mr. Runyon thinks so, but only God knows and She won't tell. *Pig World* may become a curio on other grounds, though: every woman in it has pubes, breasts, buttocks, and sometimes even a navel! I tend to take these things for granted, but Mr. Runyon (despite his three children and wife, all mentioned in the blurb) has apparently never gotten over that first shock of peeking into the girls' locker room. So we start with Dominique, the mini-skirted sexpot who awards herself in bed to good revolutionaries: "Since she wore the medallions of her sex right out in front, he decided to take her on those terms" (p. 17). (Where should she wear them, on her head?) Dominique's mother, Marie, has breasts (p. 30) and buttocks (p. 32). Faye has breasts and buttocks (p. 40). And a navel (p. 61). Teej has breasts (p. 120) and pubic hair (surprise! p. 123). More breasts on p. 149 (Big Yoni), breasts, belly, and "bush" (p. 158), two sets of breasts and pubis (p. 160), more breasts (p. 181), breasts and pubic hair (p. 176) and a nipple-less, vagina-less goddess (p. 214). The weirdity of all this is that almost all the anatomy is described in the most un-erotic moments, when the women are dying, wounded, fighting, or doing very ordinary things, like driving cars or saying hello. There is one real copulation in the book and that is a memory; naturally there is no anatomy involved, but only the usual overblown imagery of the vague-and-inflated school.

> He had felt the first tremors inside her chest and heard the moan rising up inside her throat. A strangled cry escaped into the room, then the sound burst out like a tiger released from its cage; he was hammered, clawed, ripped, squeezed, and finally annihilated, by her passion. (p. 124)

Alas, the hero survives for duller doings. I myself am writing a novel about a revolution, in which all the males are characterized as follows:

> He was a medium-sized man with round buttocks and lumpy testicles, one longer than the other. They swayed as he walked. Sometimes they swayed freely. His penis hung down in front. I decided to take him on those terms.

Can You Feel Anything When I Do This? is a collection of Robert Shackley's short stories, very polished, sometimes funny, but mostly haunted by other people's themes or ways of thinking (e.g. James Sallis, Brian Aldiss, Jorge Luis Borges). Many of the tales are slight and conventional. Mr. Shackley is at his best when he's comic; "The Petrified World" is really original; "Cordle" is quite funny, and "Tripout" ditto. A pleasant book.

The Magazine of Fantasy and Science Fiction, February 1973

Pandora's Planet. Christopher Anvil (Doubleday, $5.95). *The Light That Never Was.* Lloyd Biggle (Doubleday, $4.95). *Midsummer Century.* James Blish (Doubleday, $4.95). *Beyond Apollo.* Barry Malzberg (Random House, $5.95). *What Entropy Means To Me.* George Alec Effinger (Doubleday, $4.95)

Outsiders mean bad and stupid things when they say "science fiction," but sometimes the bad and stupid things are unfortunately accurate. In the 1930s even the most simple-minded tale written for bright, white, male, conventional fourteen-year-olds had some shock and novelty value (because of its context), but the same thing written and published in the 1970s is another kettle of Venusian fishoids. (Some day s.f. writers will stop tacking "oid" onto nouns. We may even stop having our characters drink coffee under other names like Anne McCaffrey's "klah.")

Pandora's Planet by Christopher Anvil turns on one naive joke: that we are smarter than the aliens who invade us. Human chauvinism seems fairly harmless – after all, how many giant ants have been demonstrating for civil rights lately? – but *Pandora* does not really include all humans. If "America" is geography and "Amerika" the radical-left nightmare, then *Pandora* is pure *Amurrica* – women, children, non-whites, non-Americans, homosexuals, the poor, even the genuinely religious, need not apply. Even the invading aliens (to judge from the book's detail) are white, male, American, middle-class, and middle-aged. A fan writer recently characterized one type of s.f. fan as The Galactic Square. *Pandora's Planet* is written for The Galactic Square. If we lived in a sensuous, emotional, erotically permissive, egalitarian, heterogeneous, more-or-less matriarchy, Mr. Anvil's novel would be a stunning piece of speculation. I've been kind to routine s.f. in the past, but *Pandora* doesn't have the energy or luridness that can make s.f. stereotypes minimally interesting. The central joke isn't even new; a fine story written in the 1950s from the viewpoint of a human con-man ends with the aliens being sold the Brooklyn Bridge. And then one has to put up with *Pandora*'s conviction that intelligence means only technical or military ingenuity, with emphasis on the latter (Einstein would not be at home here), that all humans have IQs of 130 or above, that a *deus ex machina* is a good way to end a dramatic conflict (the book has two of them), and that Communism and Fascism are silly-simple decals. The only funny episode in the novel is one in which the alien hero undergoes a spell of deep depression brought on by watching TV.

James Blish once spotted a bad flaw typical of certain s.f. – the smeerp business. That is, if you have rabbits in a story and want to make the story s.f., you change "rabbits" to "smeerps" and there you are.[1] *Pandora*'s details are often Smeerps: "What we are giving you is no perfumed hammock of sweet flowers" (bed of roses, p. 74), "iron road" for railroad (*chemin-de-fer*, p. 86), a Huntley-Brinkley newscast (pp. 147–48) and so on. It is all racist, sexist, antiseptic, and good-humored, and The Galactic Square would love it. The best (or worst) *frisson* comes early, on p. 22:

> "We can't help it!" sobbed several voices in unison, "they're smarter than we are."

I can't help it, either.

Lloyd Biggle must be writing for the same audience, for although *The Light That Never Was* is more completely dramatized than *Pandora* and more colorful, it's just as bad. There is the same failure in dramatic resolution (a "plague" of hatred on two dozen worlds demands more of a cause than a single, mad, unscrupulous – and dull – millionaire), the same Smeerps ("wrranels" instead of oxen or horses, "revs" instead of parties, "lumeno console" instead of piano-playing or card games, and so on). The book's message seems to be that one ought to consider unhuman sophonts ("animaloids") one's brothers; that is why a horse-like sophont, the one individualized alien in the book, is told "there, there, old fellow" and patted on the neck. (The oppressed "animaloids" are all totally noble, unselfish, and peaceful, of course.) *Light* is ostensibly about artists, but the novel's view of them is pure Hollywood; to Mr. Biggle artists apparently mean painters and painters mean nobody after the Impressionists. In *Light* art dealers recognize masterpieces after "one brief look" (p. 14), some subjects are artistic and some aren't (p. 19), painters refer to each other as "X, the artist" instead of "X, the abstract-impressionist" (or whatever, p. 33), and paintings *become* masterpieces once they're officially recognized (p. 107). Part of the plot turns on the sudden conversion of dozens of hacks into real artists when they find new subject matter (i.e. scenes) to paint (p. 190). Not only has Mr. Biggle not invented a science-fiction version of painting; he does not seem to know or care about the last ninety years of Western painting. For example, there is a lot of talk about finding the best natural light to paint in – you would not know from the novel that most contemporary painters use artificial light.

1 William Atheling, Jr. (James Blish), *The Issue at Hand*, Advent Publishers, Chicago, 1964, p. 92.

There are women in the book, although the most important of them says "Posh!" and is called a "minx" and a "wanton." The men are just as bad. Mr. Biggle has an occasionally ghastly way with words: on p. 22 someone's memory "was still *replete* with what he had seen," on p. 45 someone else is "not certain *whom* the public might be," on the same page "it was the most unusual city they had ever seen, *but* it was also the most memorable," on p. 73 everyone is "enthused," on p. 122 "She loved to eat but ... *despised* the lozenges that followed overindulgence." On p. 63 someone "pointed a finger *impalingly*" and on p. 66 someone is followed by "children ... *mouthing* shrill taunts" (italics all mine). It is also a very small planet; the head of the secret police finds things out by hanging around the spaceport and listening to the tourists talk (p. 92), apparently not having any staff who can do it for him.

It's narsty to beat up on authors who are probably starving to death on turnip soup but critics ought to be honest. Both books are juveniles, though not so labeled, both books are awful, and I wouldn't want any juvenile to read either of them.

James Blish's *Midsummer Century* is like the old proverb: if we had some ham, we could make some ham and eggs, if we had some eggs. There is something strangely gratuitous about it. Mr. Blish's powers as a writer of single scenes are as keen as ever and *Century* is crammed with ingenious ideas, but to my mind the book just doesn't cohere. It was Mr. Blish who invented the term "intensively recomplicated plot," and *Midsummer Century* has what is surely the most intensively recomplicated plot in existence; what's more, the plot turns are explained or rationalized after they happen, an unsettling procedure at best. I thought for a while there was too much material in the book (although a kind of epic, spanning many years, it is only 106 pages long); then I decided that the trouble lay in the point-of-view character, one Martels, a twentieth-century scientist flung forward in time to the 250th century. He is vividly and economically characterized in the book's first eight pages, but after that he might be anybody, or rather nobody, for he has not a single human reaction. (There is one emotional moment on p. 26 which is pure stereotype.) His character is quite irrelevant to his situation. He seems, in fact, to be irrelevant to the book except as a plot device; Mr. Blish's future tropical world of re-tribalized humanity, sentient Birds, a disembodied brain, and small colonies of scientifically oriented people living at the South Pole could get along much better without its twentieth-century visitor. (The book resembles Jack Vance's dying earth.) It might – without Martels – be possible to set up dramatic givens and then follow them. As the book stands now, there is no way to make dramatic sense of it – that is, the givens themselves are perpetually changing and in some places judgments seem to be made without any evidence. After a while it begins to seem as if *every* episode is being resolved arbitrarily, or at least each episode is resolved on the basis of knowledge neither reader nor protagonist possessed *until that moment*. Although *Century* is not exactly self-contradictory, it might as well be.

I suspect that Mr. Blish has a coherent intellectual or thematic scheme for the novel (perhaps his subject is consciousness itself), but the dramatic conflict in the novel is quite disjunct from the thematic pattern. The world of the book is vivid and strange, but there is some flaw in construction that makes reading *Century* genuinely exasperating – just when you think you've got hold of the puzzle, the author changes the terms on you. If only we could have plunged into the consciousness of some native of the world and then stayed there for four or five hundred pages! As it is, Mr. Blish packs a full-scale Bird/Human war into four paragraphs, treats "juganity" and the Platonic model of consciousness as if he had explained them (which he hasn't), and wrenches his plot back and forth like a zigzag ride at a fun fair. Perhaps *Century* is the first stab into new territory for Mr. Blish, a sketchy vision of something that may become an important new part of the Blishian canon. I remain confused.

Barry Malzberg's *Beyond Apollo* fulfills the promise of his earlier novel, *The Falling Astronauts* (Ace). The repetitiousness, the sloppiness, and the uncertainty of the earlier novel are all gone – though I miss the earlier book's assumption that not only the dehumanized astronauts but everyone in the program (and in the government) was insane. Again we have the protagonist's wife as the one human being who knows that something has gone wrong, again the false, rational, "cool," bureaucratic-analytic tone of voice is shot with errors, and undermined by little mistakes ("committed sexual acts") which carry it easily and reasonably to the point of lunacy. The novel is lyrical, even circular, in structure, although it presents a straightforward, detective-story problem: How did the Venus flight fail? There is an answer, but the answer cannot be paraphrased. Words like "seriously," like "understand," like "believe," like "insane," are used seriously, are believed in, are insane, are understood – seriously – until they become a kind of Greek chorus, a terrible, poignant insistence on something that is not quite in the story but yet comes through the story. Reason is crazy, madness is sane. As the protagonist writes in his diary:

> The Captain ... said that he had always had homosexual impulses and by God now he was going to act on them; *if you couldn't do what you wanted to do thirty million miles from earth, when were you going to get to do it?* (pp. 27–28, italics mine)

In his cell, meditating on What Went Wrong, doing cryptograms (he knows this is the only truly sane activity), Harry Evans – madman, failed astronaut – tells us over and over again How It Really Happened, a different story each time. *Apollo* is the *cri du coeur* of the Galactic Amurrican Square who read *Pandora's Planet* at fourteen and believed it would really be like that, a series of false perspectives, an exquisite tangle of self-deception. Only the protagonist's sexuality reminds him that he's human; yet sex itself has been deformed, has turned bodies into machinery, women into knives; it spills over and informs the most excessive, desperate metaphors of this astonishing book. There are veins of gold: "Her chin juts, reminding me of that other wedge of bone which rushed me in the night." Or:

> I am back in my bed, crawling out of the dream in small pieces, sweating and fussing, muttering to myself, or perhaps I am only clambering back into a dream, coming into my room in small sections, but in any event it is very complex and uncontrollable and I can make nothing of it … (p. 64)

> Doors slam up and down my wife's body; lights are extinguished. She pants; she groans. (p. 76)

Which is the real story – the almost Trafalmadorian Venusians who murdered the Captain and forced Evans to return? Or the mad Captain who kept Evans guessing the purpose of the trip to Venus, literally for weeks? Or the homosexual, murderous Captain? Or the man who simply couldn't stand it any more? The answer comes from reading the whole book, not from picking up separate clues as in a detective story. Still, the only way to read the whole book is to let oneself be taken in, to try and make sense of what doesn't make that kind of sense. As far as I can tell, there are only two straightforward moments in the novel, both occurring paradoxically when the protagonist is farthest into his madness: the remarks the two Evanses make about themselves near the end ("They made a machine of me") and the altered meaning of the first paragraph of the novel, repeated at the end:

> "I loved the Captain in my own way, although I knew that he was insane, the poor bastard … one must consider the conditions. The conditions were intolerable." (p. 3)

The Captain, of course, may be nothing more than Evans' alter ego, or an object in the madness that permeates this beautiful and heartbreaking book. There are horrid ironies, like Evans' pride in being so "highly qualified." There are gorgeous turns of phrase, bridge problems and cryptograms like "lovely small neurasthenic tentacles," "the little knifelike slant of his abused genitals ... It is all for Venus."

Mr. Malzberg has been writing good books for some time. *Beyond Apollo* is a passionate, fine, completely realized work. The Galactic Square won't like it.

("The universe", writes Harry Evans on p. 112, "was invented by man in 1976 as a cheap and easy explanation for all of his difficulties in conquering it.")

What Entropy Means To Me by George Alec Effinger is a promising first novel, a kind of camp epic in which the hero's Quest is invented – chapter by chapter – by his younger brother, while family squabbles rage as to what religious status the now-gone brother is to enjoy in the family pantheon. (The story has the air of games by which children transform their own back yards into Mars.) The family theology seems to recapitulate early Christian battles about the Trinity, with the addition here that the religion is a mythification of a family life which we actually see. Thus we have our (leucotomized) mother whose perpetual tears are the source of the River of Life, the thrones (chairs) in the back yard, which belong to different principles (children) and so on. Some of this is fine, in particular the siblings' dealings with each other (they sign notes "Yours truly" even when the notes are threats on other siblings' lives) and the younger brother's literary throes (complicated by the family Conscience Monitor and the children's doctrinal wars). The parents, however, are very bald stereotypes and the scenes of the Quest are often vulgar without being funny or far too cheaply silly, e.g. phrases like "You're really weird" intruding into a bad satire of a love scene (p. 25). Mr. Effinger's book is uneven, despite the fine quantum jump of an ending, but parts are genuinely sweet and deceptively slight. At its best the story achieves a fine suffusion of emotion. I hope Mr. Effinger will go on to better things; the imagination and individuality are already there. The novel is dedicated to (among others) "my parents, for enabling me to write unfettered by the bonds of nonexistence."

Village Voice, June 16, 1973

Mystification about (gulp) marriage

The Future of Marriage. Jessie Bernard (World, $9.95). *Marriage: For and Against.* Ed. Harold H. Hart (Hart, $7.50 and $2.45)

Glomph is bad. Glomph is good. Everybody ought to have a glomph. Glomph will kill you and make your toes fall off. Glomph is the only way to lead a normal life.

There is something quintessential, ineffable, mystical, and inexpressible about glomph – sorry, I mean "marriage" – but what in God's name *is* marriage? If you were a Martian and read these books, you couldn't tell. Like the old warnings about sex (which never told you what it was) controversy about marriage nowadays escalates instantly into the Dance of the Seven Obfuscations. Definitions of marriage are either economic-cum-role-playing or they are mystifying. Still, the fight goes on, as if "marriage" were substantive, unalterable, monolithic, and autonomous. I don't understand what they think they are talking about and I've *been* married.

Marriage as an economic contract and a promise to undertake certain role behavior has been taken to pieces and condemned by many feminists. This version of marriage is not an interesting one. What is interesting is the intense emotionality that surrounds the subject. People seem to react to "marriage" as they react to "youth" or "immorality"; these are content-free terms and the discussion of them tends to be content-free, but the sheer quantity of upset that surrounds all these topics shows that the discussants are talking about something very dear to them, even though nobody seems to know what it is.

As far as the ostensible subject goes, *Marriage For and Against* is worthless. Even Jessie Bernard's *The Future of Marriage* provides only one analytic tool – the distinction between "his" marriage and "her" marriage – and is otherwise quite baffling. Dr. Bernard cites all sorts of studies about who marries whom, when, how many times, what they say about each other, who does what domestic chores, and so on, but none of this seems to clarify or illuminate the subject. Talking about marital behavior without deciding what marriage *is* is like compiling statistics about where and when people take their vacations without ever deciding what play is.

The Future of Marriage is valuable as a mine of citations from the literature and has some interesting details. There is enough material to damn the wife's marriage several times over (Dr. Bernard's viewpoint is feminist) and there is a good short discussion of leftist sexism. But is there not also the bank's marriage, the advertiser's marriage, the state's marriage, the children's marriage – and if "marriage" is not autonomous but connected with every other institution in our society (both books treat only of Western, even American marriage), how can one talk about it without some theoretical underpinning? Dr. Bernard gets awfully mixed up about this.

As most sociologists do, she ignores institutional functions and analyzes roles, with a desultory nod toward people's motivations for entering into institutions. She seems to assume, for example, that the functions served by marriage (both to the participants and to the society) will remain the same in future, but that "marriage" will change. (Sometimes she says the functions *will* change. It's very confusing.) I cannot see how this is possible. Moreover, the personal effects of marriage and its social functions are not disentangled.

Dr. Bernard succumbs to the worst mystification at one point – she states that there is "something timeless running through the accounts of specific husbands and wives" and then quotes vignettes from the Greek and the Old Testament without inquiring whether husband–wife interaction is similar when limited to one husband and one wife, persons who know each other, persons of different sexes, of the same sex, many husbands and/or many wives, persons who like each other, persons who hate each other, persons whose relation is distant, persons for whom marriage matters little compared with other relations, and so on. That is, she is anthropologically naive.

It is just this "monolithism", this comfy timelessness that Juliet Mitchell shreds to pieces in *Woman's Estate*, the only book I can find that gives a systematic social analysis of the institutional functions of marriage, as distinct from both its ostensible institutional functions and the motives that propel people into it. Dr. Bernard's theoretical statements about marriage (and the methods of research she cites) could be applied to any relationship at all – for example, it would be perfectly easy to argue that the landlord–tenant relationship is "timeless" – because it is. The "timelessness" of marriage means only that people brought up in similar traditions (Western patriarchal, no?) and in similar institutions, playing similar roles, behave similarly.

The distinctions between institutional function, ostensible function, and personal motive are what is left out of both books (and most discussions). In the absence of such distinctions there can hardly be anything but moralizing, "umbrella-ology" (fussing around with the factual details without relating them to one another), or bafflement. (Some of the essays in *For and Against* are palpably frustrated by the request to write "something about marriage" – you can almost hear them protesting: "but what am I supposed to say?") The major trend of radical thinking in the last decade (perhaps always?) has been to disentangle ostensible from real functions and then to explode: Look! They don't match! In the case of the public schools, for example, it comes as no surprise to hear that although the public school system is supposed to educate the young (ostensible function) it really makes sure that upward mobility is confined to the "right" people (real function), and that children do not attend public school in order to be educated but because they are coerced, either directly or by economic pressure (motives).

No comparable analysis has been done on marriage. (*Woman's Estate* is again an exception.) The reasons people get married, or say they do, are not the same as the social functions marriage is supposed to serve (sex, socializing the young, affectionate companionship, and production, i.e. maintaining certain physical and emotional living conditions for the family), and the ostensible function is not the same as the real function. Literature on marriage seems to make some distinction between the first and second (it doesn't mention the third) but assumes that the first and second are harmonious. One could doubt it.

Taking the statistics in *Future of Marriage* as a starting point, it seems that people's sex lives are often terrible, that women suffer from having exclusive responsibility for socializing the young, that spouses, certainly wives, and certainly in the working class, don't get the affectionate companionship they want, and that the divorce rate in the U.S. is now 44 out of 100 marriages.

All this gets thrown around in *For and Against* but, as in the great gray *Times*, there is no real discussion of the subject. One of the gackiest assumptions in modern American "controversy" is that if there are two points of view, the truth must be exactly between them. To get an objective, "balanced" view, you measure the distance between one view and t'other and plop yourself down in the geometric center. Essential is a cop-out introduction which keeps saying on-the-one-hand, on-the-other-hand. (The book has one.) It is also very important to ask people to testify who know nothing about the subject. (Thus we have such experts on marital activity as Judith Crist and Max Lerner.) A vast array of opinions, the more superficially varied the better, guarantees truth; that it may guarantee nothing more elevated than confusion doesn't seem to occur to anybody. (That is, opinions are treated as *phenomena*, not as statements which might be true or false.)

An old and honored ploy, when discussing an institution, is that the institution is fine but the people are at fault – i.e. people aren't adapting themselves to the institution or being trained properly for it or being "motivated" enough. We exist for the Sabbath; the Sabbath does not exist for us. A book about marriage that has four women essayists and 11 men essayists is damned from the start, to my mind; but the book has been more careful in balancing experts and non-experts – 50 percent of each, roughly. People who combine boldly radical statements ("Marriage is obsolete") with cop-out remedies (rituals like engagement showers must cease) must constitute a significant number of your discussants. It is essential never to define the subject and to use the kind of single-variable thinking that good science fiction writers try so hard to avoid – i.e. if you change one variable, you must be careful to assume that everything else will remain the same. That is why the changed variable "won't work." For example, if you are Ira Reiss, say that polygamy (I suspect he means plural spouses of both sexes) cannot work because human relations are difficult enough between two people. (That is, never consider that relations among several people may be less intense than dyadic relations, and hence less difficult.) If you are Judith Crist, assume implicitly that all women are wealthy and middle-class and that alimony exists for more than a very tiny minority. If you are a woman, it is also good to denounce female "parasites" and glorify hard work and serious commitment (another name for monogamy). After all, everybody knows housewives do nothing but eat chocolates all day.

You must be absolutely sure to ignore the economic or contractual base of whatever phenomenon you are discussing. Only one person may be allowed to mention the awful truth that sexuality does not create *permanent* pair-bonds (Joseph Fletcher) and thus cannot serve as a natural basis for monogamy. You may, nowadays, have one moderate feminist (Caroline Bird) who is actually allowed some analysis and some knowledge that marriage is not an autonomous institution. When asked to define marriage, your discussants must be humane and disembodied and talk about companionship – but when they actually talk about the suitability of marriage to modern life, they must rush like lemmings to the areas of sex and exclusivity, especially if they are men; either adultery is bad and a "problem" or the exclusivity of sex is a problem and monogamy is bad.

Of course most of us are hopelessly confused about the nature of the institutional and ideological forces in our lives. Most "controversial" discussions are sheer ideology-yelling which never gets anywhere; at their best, they are descriptions of roles (this is Juliet Mitchell's complaint about sociology) which lead to what I think is an unwarranted optimism. Jessie Bernard's book is largely an inventory of roles, treated as autonomous; so the (easy) cure, of course, is education. (If there were social reasons, apart from the personal motives that led people into marriage, for keeping marriage as it is, education would not be enough to change the institution.) Even untangling an institution's real functions from its ostensible functions only clears away the rubble from the real question: What do people actually need and want?

It seems extremely strange to me (for example) that although there have been so many investigations of marital roles, nobody has investigated what people get from each other, what people need in other people, in short, friendship. There has been some of this, mostly speculative psychology. Sociology seems to have left it alone. Even the most reactionary essays in *For and Against* assume that people marry for affection; Jessie Bernard assumes the same thing; in fact, she sees affection as the one function that will give marriage a future once sex, child-rearing, and housework are dealt with in other ways. (I do not see why the need for affection must lead to marriage, unless one defines "marriage" as any relation obtaining between people who are fond of each other – a definition that would include some really surprising things.)

But what is affection? Nobody knows. Yet surely the relation least contaminated by contract and role behavior can surely tell us the most about what people seek freely and without practical motive – e.g. we all distinguish, I think, between friendships and mutual-admiration societies, which (though informal) are based on a kind of contract. But nobody bothers to investigate friendship.

I would very much like to know what people seek in each other and get from each other when their work, their reproductive obligations, and their means of getting a living are provided for in some other way. Is it necessary, for example, to work together in order to have friendships? Are "colleague" friends different from "playmate" friends? Does one need both in the same relation? Nobody seems to know.

Perhaps the heat generated by the topic of "marriage" is an index of our secret knowledge that we are in fact talking about nothing. When you have described the role behavior required by marriage and the economic contract that is its base, you have described all there is – the substantive, really-existing Essence the ideology insists on just isn't there. It's very easy to tear marriage and marital orthodoxy into little pieces if you treat them as concrete phenomena (like anything else). Ruth Dickson did just this in 1968 in a nice book called *Marriage is a Bad Habit* (Sherbourne Press, Los Angeles). Nobody listened. I found *Bad Habit* withering away on a second-hand counter – this although she includes every feminist argument ever penned.

Until we start looking at the real functions of institutions, at who profits, at how, at who really knows about the profiting and who has concealed the knowledge, and how much, and to what end, we will know nothing.

George Bernard Shaw has somewhere a statement to the effect that people keep asking him what social phenomena "mean" and he has to tell them that what they're talking about doesn't even exist, let alone have a meaning. I suspect that the real horror of our noisy, elaborate controversy about marriage is a *horror vacui;* the function of ideology is to conceal the fact that it's talking about nothing; hence the mystification, hence the secret knowledge of falsity, hence the fear of finding out the falsity, hence the extraordinarily excessive emotion.

So much for "marriage."

The Magazine of Fantasy and Science Fiction, July 1973

Eros In Orbit: A Collection of All New Science Fiction Stories About Sex. Ed. Joseph Elder (Trident Press, $6.95). *Strange Bedfellows: Sex and Science Fiction.* Ed. Thomas N. Scortia (Random House, $5.95). *The Iron Dream.* Norman Spinrad (Avon, $.95). *The Listeners.* James Gunn (Scribners, $6.95). *Dying Inside.* Robert Silverberg (Scribners, $6.95)

The topic of sex seems to bring out the worst in a lot of us: embarrassment, 1930s obviousness, and the assumption that just mentioning love-making is somehow funny. Joseph Elder's introduction to *Eros In Orbit* contains such phrases as "the pleasures of the flesh," "carnal love," "the age-old itch," and the question "Where will it all end?" which only occurs to nervous Americans when they don't know where a lot of other societies have already been. Thomas Scortia is also seized with editorial coyness; he perpetrates "hypermammiferous females" and "raunchy writers ... like naughty schoolboys." These are symptoms of embarrassment, i.e. the assimilation of novelty.

Both anthologies range from the fine to the awful. (By the way, it's good to see publishing houses like Trident, Random House, and Scribners getting into science fiction.) Anthologies "about" this or that theme are bound to be uneven, especially in science fiction where the "topic" is only ostensible – e.g. Philip Jose Farmer's "The Lovers" is really a story of alien mimicry like Avram Davidson's "Or All the Seas with Oysters," and Theodore

Sturgeon's "The World Well Lost" (which is reprinted in *Strange Bedfellows*) is not about homosexuality *per se*, but about the effects of enforced secrecy on the human soul. If the anthologies are uneven I suspect the topic is at fault; sex is both endlessly interesting and very hard to write about. Either writers succumb to social taboos and write hartyhars or they break the taboos and are so dazzled by the mere fact of having done so that they manage to express only the most obvious science fiction ideas. Most of the stories in both books don't get beyond the idea of mechanical substitutes for sex – gadgets or android partners or recordings. There is practically no group sex, no promiscuity rendered genuinely and from the inside, and (except for the Sturgeon reprint) no homosexuality. Alien–human love fares a little better, but the only new attempt at perversion, technically speaking, is a story about paedophilia[1] which studiously avoids showing any. *Bedfellows* (half reprint, half new stories) is the more thoughtful anthology, illustrating James Blish's dictum that ideas alone are worthless; what counts is ideas *about* ideas. Sex, like all primary experiences, can be named directly but not described directly; one can only describe its effect on people, its experiential dimension, so to speak. In the newness of taboo-breaking, many writers forget this, and the result is descriptions of love-making which are interchangeable from story to story. What matters is not organ grinding but the explosions sex produces in the head; some writers in the anthologies know this. Most are learning. Some are hopeless.

The best new story in *Eros* (either book, really) is Robert Silverberg's "In the Group" which deals with a splendidly pathological future of group-sex (actually they use mechanical telepathy) and the one monogamous throwback who can't fit in, the sort of thing Kingsley Amis once called conservatively progressive. The motives for the protagonist's present-day attitudes are never explained (the story's one flaw) but moment-to-moment rendering of experience is fine, especially the joyless priggishness of that wretched Group from which the obsessed hero finally flees.

Silverberg's prose very occasionally slips ("taut globes") but at its best it's very good – "her jolly slithers and slides" or the Group's "olla podrida of copulations." Good also is Ron Goulart's "Whistler" which one might call a tragedy of misfitting morals to situation, except that Goulart's style is far too cool, detached, and comic to merit such a heated definition. It's the usual blend of the homey and the freaky; in this conventional world in which businessmen leave their middle-aged wives lonely in Westport the heroine buys a mechanical hand called Wakzoff for the hero; she says, "If you love someone, you give them things." Goulart Man finally does in

---

1 Not love of feet (which you might suspect) but love of children.

slender, intense Goulart Woman, a hopeful sign that Goulart may be moving into new territory. George Zebrowski's "Starcrossed," another fine story, is too genuinely science-fictionally far-out to summarize easily; in essence it's a love affair between two parts of a cyborg brain. It's the only story in both books to realize the sense of the subjectively erotic; Zebrowski knows that the experience of sex can be approached only through its effects, and when he writes of the "awesome reliability and domination" of the sex act he's closer to the real thing than all the thighs and globes in the world. There are other stories in the book that have a touch of this, especially Gordon Eklund's "Lovemaker" with its exploration of an android consciousness (for which sex is the only real act in the world) and Barry Malzberg's "Ups and Downs," with its first-rate Malzbergian grasp of a certain kind of mental process (though I wish he'd cross into new territory, as he's done a lot of the same thing lately). Pamela Sargent's "Clone Sister" and Ed Bryant's "2.46593" are fairly good, and there are three failures: Thomas Scortia's "Flowering Narcissus" (a Hell's Angel Mama is not a Hell's Angel with estrogen added but a very different personality type – nor is the H.A. in the story anything more than a stereotype); John Stopa's "Kiddy-Lib" which is an even worse example of a middle-class outsider's idea of hippies, old men who letch after little girls, and children themselves (the schematic shifting of counters doesn't help), all with a careful evasion of the real subject; and Thomas Brand's "Don Slow," an incoherent farce-parody which not only believes that prostitutes are nymphomaniacs and homosexuals limp-wristed sissies, but (worse) does not know that parody must restrict itself to one target and farce must not invent new plot zigzags whenever it has plot problems.

The best stories in *Bedfellows* are reprints: Theodore Sturgeon's loverbird story and Philip Jose Farmer's classic, "Mother." The Sturgeon story worries the editor, who reassures you that Sturgeon is "virile," "sexual," and "devoutly heterosexual." (He also has "a fierce beard.") The relationship in the story is far more bizarre than Mr. Scortia even suspects; if mere homosexuality frightens him, what would he make of the intense, secret romanticism that is the real subject? Brian Aldiss's "Lambeth Blossom," a splendid playing with reality, seems to be a reprint, although I haven't seen it before (maybe England?) as is Reginald Bretnor's "Doctor Birdmouse," a well-done story that tries to present loneliness and sexual frustration as funny. In truth Mr. Bretnor doesn't believe it, but his real theme is too God-awfully horrifying to treat straight – though I think the idea began as a gentle whimsicality; his Miss Cowturtle sounds very like Tenniel's Mock Turtle in *Alice in Wonderland*. But Mr. Bretnor is too good a writer not to feel the grimness of his alien/human mating joke. The lyricism of Laurence Yep's "Looking Glass Sea" presents the positive side of love between species with its marvelously strange silicon/crystalline world, and George Zebrowski's "First Love, First Fear" (although a little too long) shows what can be done with "rationalized" fantasy (a major source of s.f.). The biology is flawed (what is an alien doing with mammaries when her babies eat their way out of her like insect babies?) but the story creates authentic strangeness and springs from real sexual feelings (the fear–attraction of inexperience). The formidable Silverberg is present with "Push No More," a fine, awful, comic portrait of the same fourteen-year-old seen from a very different perspective ("suave as a pig" and his pimples light up like beacons when he blushes) although the story is written from the wrong point of view – there is too much of a split between the teller and what he must describe, i.e. himself. Another good story is "False Dawn," one of Chelsea Quinn Yarbro's series about her future-disaster world, which contains (among other things) a rape told from the point of view of the victim – it's not good clean fun, kiddies. Not as accomplished but equally interesting stories are Jack Dann's "I'm With You in Rockland" and Mel Gilden's "What About Us Grils," the most science-fictionally far-out stories in the book. The first expresses alienation from one's body in a metaphor-made-literal that is pure s.f. – this is the kind of originality both anthologies could use more of – and the second captures something of the effect of what-on-earth-do-they-see-in-each-other, one of the legitimate effects of s.f. sex, especially in the very last paragraph. Failures (and some are awful) include a slight anecdote by Walt Leibscher ("Do Androids Dream of Electric Love?"); the oddly inconclusive "Genetic Faux Pas" by Harvey Bilker, which probably had more point in its original context; "Dinner at Helen's" by William Carlson, another middle-class conventional pretense at unisex and hippiedom; G. A. Alpher's "The Mechanical Sweetheart," a talented but derivative (Nabokov) and overwritten piece – grotesquerie is not as easily come by as that, although the ending picks up; and four hartyhars, the dimmest of which is Joe Gores' "The Criminal," which ought to have been left to languish pornographically in *Adam*, from which it came. Mr. Gores thinks rape is chucklesome; he ought to read Chelsea Quinn Yarbro's story. Miriam Allen de Ford's "The Daughter of the Tree" is pleasant, but it's not s.f. and doesn't belong here.

Norman Spinrad's *The Iron Dream* is really a science fiction novel by Adolf Hitler called *Lord of The Swastika* but Avon copped out. Spinrad has been trying to convict humanity of sin for some time now; here he finally does it. *Lord* is a changeling that Spinrad has plopped into our sword-and-sorcery cradle and the damned creature is so close to the real thing that we can't disown it. The narcissism, the beautifully done self-righteousness, the preoccupation with clothes and gear, the magical ease of victory, the screamingly funny phallic obsession – it's all there, so exciting that you can't help enjoying it and so God-awful that you ought to hate yourself for it. There are patches of pure fun, but by some eerie artistry "Hitler's" novel is both serious and seriously written. Moreover the book is a fascinating, genuine, alternative universe – part of this is in Hitler's novel (which is itself a garbled account of Hitler's real rise to power) and part in the blurbs, the Afterword (by Homer Whipple, New York, N.Y., 1959), the puffs on the back, and the list of Hitler's other novels, which segue slowly from *Emperor of the Asteroids* to *Tomorrow the World*. As Michael Moorcock, the famous sword-and-sorcery writer, comments on the back cover, "This exciting and tense fantasy adventure ... is bound to earn Hitler the credit he so richly deserves!" A lovely book, and a deserved crack on the knuckles of more than just sword-and-sorcery addicts.

When will science fiction learn that we love it for itself alone? James Gunn's *The Listeners* is two books, a wonderful science fiction novel (concentrated in sections called *Computer Run* and some of the scientific work on the novel's Project to communicate with extra-terrestrial civilizations) and carefully variegated impossible people who all have their faith in life revived by the Project (five of them!) and go drearily through "human interest" situations, e.g. lonely wifehood, father–son conflict, etc. Periodically we have to sit still for this "human" stuff – it's not inept or crude, just dead – to be rewarded by the following (the static of space):

> He turned the knob once more, and the sound was a babble of distant voices, some shouting, some screaming, some conversing calmly, some whispering – all of them trying beyond desperation to communicate, and everything just below the level of intelligibility. If he closed his eyes, MacDonald could almost see their faces, pressed against a distant screen, distorted with the awful effort to make themselves heard and understood. (p. 18)

This is the subject. This is the soul of the book. The rest is flubdub. If Scribners insisted on it, Scribner must learn, and if part of Mr. Gunn insisted on it, *he* must learn. The good parts are so good that the bad become insupportable – there are real scientific quotations (which give the effect of a dialogue between real scientists who have in fact never met) and catalogs of star names and other wonders, and then there are silly things you could pick up in any kind of routine fiction. Despite this, and despite the plethora of literary quotations (no writers ought to expose their own prose to that kind of comparison) the book is good enough to be worth reading. But it hurts.

Robert Silverberg's *Dying Inside* is a dry, often witty, low-keyed, realistic novel about a present-day telepath who is losing his gift (the only thing that makes his life worthwhile), as close to mainstream realism as science fiction can get without moving out of s.f. altogether. Telepathy (reception only) is presented as a kind of addiction, something like a schizoid inner life. I find the book interesting but not moving; I suspect I'm just not on its wavelength and that readers who are will react to it as heavy tragedy (which it is). Everything in it is present in fine detail: the psychoanalytic-Jewish milieu, the overly bright child, the lying parents, the dreadful closeness which is paradoxically linked to lovelessness and isolation. Unlike the quick, flashy bizarrerie of most s.f., *Dying* has the density and length of a realistic novel (which essentially it is). One might quarrel with the subject (this kind of hero is common in recent mainstream fiction) or with some of the writing (there's occasional redundancy and the book could've benefited from a final careful trim), but the solidity of it is beyond question, as is the quality. It's also the first time Mr. Silverberg has used his extraordinary wit in print, e.g.:

> In those days there was an old cast-iron kiosk at street level marking the entrance to the depths; it was positioned between two lanes of traffic, and students, their absent minds full of Kierkegaard and Sophocles and Fitzgerald, were forever stepping in front of cars and getting killed. Now the kiosk is gone and the subway entrances are placed more rationally, on the sidewalks. (p. 7)

In my February 1971 column I mentioned a book called *The Way It Spozed To Be* and (as usual) got my references wrong. The book is by James Herndon and is the record of his one year's teaching in a metropolitan ghetto school. It's a good book but it is not (as I called it) a collection of writing done by Harlem schoolchildren. I would appreciate any information about such a collection which, as I remember, did come out at about that time.

The Magazine of Fantasy and Science Fiction, **February 1974**

Bad Moon Rising. Ed. Thomas Disch (Harper & Row, $6.95). *Paradox Lost.* Frederic Brown (Random House, $5.95). *The Star Road.* Gordon Dickson (Doubleday, $5.95). *Complex Man.* Marie Farca (Doubleday, $5.95)

> Intellectuals try to cope with their anxiety by telling each other atrocity stories about America ... What is the consequence? A stiffening of spines? A clearing of the mind and will for action? I doubt it ... People who tell such stories are, unconsciously, seeking to create a climate which will justify in their own minds the concessions they are making.[1]

> Radical movements are always plagued with people who want to lose ... want in effect to be put under protective custody.[2]

In the 1950s somebody defined urban renewal as "replacing Negroes with trees," and I'm beginning to think that in the same way too many typical science fiction horror stories are not the universal dystopias they pretend to be, but rather the unhappy wails of privilege-coming-to-an-end. Take, for example, the usual Overpopulation Story, in which Americans have to live without private ranch houses, or the typical Pollution Story in which far too often the real gripe is that "we" must subsist on soybeans and vegetable starch (as if the vast majority of the human race since the Bronze Age hadn't been doing just that) or the Violence Story which deplores the fact (as someone recently pointed out) that violence is becoming democratized.

As Thomas Disch, editor of *Bad Moon Rising*, says in his Introduction, science fiction is "a partisan literature" inevitably involved with the didactic because it presents not what exists (about which one can at least pretend to be objective) but what might exist. Like a liberal late Roman Mr. Disch prefaces his collection with the statement that "almost everything is going from bad to worse," but the collection doesn't think so; it is really on the side of the early Christian radicals and so am I. Keep this in mind as I tell you that I judge *Bad Moon* to be a splendid book. It is (by the way) not

---

[1] David Reisman, *Individualism Reconsidered*, MacMillan (The Free Press), pp. 124–27.
[2] Philip Slater, *The Pursuit of Loneliness*, Beacon Press, p. 122.

labeled "science fiction," but a recent article of Samuel Delany's[3] has convinced me that we're fighting a losing battle, *not* in trying to get public recognition of s.f. (which is possible) but in trying to get *the distributors* to let us out of our ghetto. *Bad Moon* will at least be read by people not yet acquainted with science fiction, for most of the book is indeed s.f. and most of it is extraordinarily good.

Not only does *Bad Moon* have a cumulative impact, which is rare among anthologies, but Mr. Disch has managed to split almost all the themes treated into at least two stories, this odd doubleness – the Look Again technique – being the essence of propaganda. Thus we have two stories by George Effinger, one a Kafkaesque tale of Little Man vs. Big Government ("Relatives") that is frankly awful, and another ("Two Sadnesses") which will enchant all lovers of *Winnie the Pooh* and *Wind in the Willows*, though they may find themselves hiding under their beds afterwards. There is a passionate, fully detailed, well-written New York paranoia story by Harlan Ellison[4] ("The Whimper of Whipped Dogs") which puts forward the (to my mind, untenable) view that violence is caused by Satan or maybe Original Sin; there is a similar, quiet, well-written tale by Charles Naylor ("We Are Dainty Little People") which not only shows you what but also why. One might contrast Malcolm Braly's "An Outline of History," an old-fashioned *Analog* tale that not only operates on the village-atheist level but also has (Black) characters the author has gotten from bad movies, with Gene Wolfe's "Hour of Trust," which watches the next American revolution from the viewpoint of an expatriate businessman. Mr. Wolfe not only has complicated, real, human characters – although I think he romanticizes his revolutionaries – but also he knows the how and why of what's happening. He is the only writer in the book to ask the crucial question "Who profits?" right out loud, and the only one to display a tired, detached sympathy I can only call "European" (because I don't know what else to call it, really). Mr. Wolfe's astonishing qualities as a writer now extend to historical analysis; his *raisonneur* is the perfect character, historically speaking, a parasite/jester in the person of an expensive, ironic, intelligent pimp.

Dropping the pairing-up game (which is becoming unmanageable) the best piece of propaganda I have ever read is in this book: Kate Wilhelm's "The Village." It carries its own split; its subject (the war in Southeast Asia) is folded back on itself in a doubleness that *is* the subject of the story. This

3 "Popular Culture, S-F Publishing, and Poetry: A Letter To a Critic," *Science Fiction Studies*, Spring 1973, pp. 29–43.
4 In West Coast paranoia stories only the police are Bad; in New York City paranoia stories everybody is Bad. Needless to say, much paranoia is socially justified, but genre ordinarily evades the why, which is all-important.

is the first time I've seen Ms. Wilhelm use the slick-magazine origins of her people and places (not her treatment of them) so savagely and well. The tale, which was written several years ago, was good enough to frighten the slick magazines into rejecting it; only now does it see print. At the same level of effect – and even more frightening now – is Norman Rush's "Riding," a perfect commentary on the quotations at the beginning of this review. Mr. Rush calls it "riding to the trap," i.e. the gallows; it is criticism of the Left (?) made from the Left. (Mr. Rush's other story, "Fighting Fascism," is equally understated and also ironic, but I'm afraid it lost me.) Kit Reed's "On Behalf of the Product" has a somewhat smaller target in view ("Miss Wonderful Land of Ours") but covers it very thoroughly indeed, and Carol Emshwiller's "Strangers" is routine Emshwiller, which means very, very good; she has not, as usual, wasted one word. Mr. Disch's own "Everyday Life in the Later Roman Empire" is merely brilliant; it is part of a novel about a future New York City, parts of which have come out lately in various places. This piece is not quite the best, which means (if one can judge by what's already been printed) that the novel will be a stunner.[5] There are also two fine poems by Peter Schjeldahl, "Ho Chi Minh Elegy" and "For Apollo 11," the first New Left, the second hair-raisingly good science fiction. John Sladek's "The Great Wall of Mexico" attacks its subject by way of an eerie, funny, subversive, almost-surrealism quite impossible to describe; you may get some of the flavor of it if I tell you that the FBI is using retired Senior Citizens to listen to bugged conversations in public places, and that one of them, loyal as he is, vows after his first two hours' excruciating listening that he will never say anything dull in a public place again.

    Marilyn Hacker has two poems, "Elegy for Janis Joplin" and "Untoward Occurrence at Embassy Poetry Reading," that strike me as not her best; there is a charming but slight pastiche by Ron Padgett and Dick Gallup ("Cold Turkey"), and a bad West Coast paranoia story by Raylyn Moore called "Where Have All the Followers Gone," whose characters are obviously doomed to expire from sheer grubbiness long before they get gassed. Michael Moorcock's "An Apocalypse: Some Scenes from European Life" is well-intentioned but awfully clunky, i.e. one of those stories in which people speak translatorese ("Are those the bad soldiers, Mother?" "No, Karl, they are the good soldiers. They are freeing Paris of those who have brought the city to ruin.") and – as in bad propaganda movies –

---

5 *Author's Note*: It was a stunner. It was *334*, published in 1974 by Avon. Unfortunately someone messed up the order of the novel's parts. Read first "The Death of Socrates," second "Emancipation," third "Angouleme," fourth "Bodies," fifth "Everyday Life" (etc.), and sixth "334."

nothing is there for its own sake but only for the grim, grim lesson. As another critic once put it, the minute you see a flower growing in the dreary mud of the back yard, you know it's only there so a brutal Cossack can step on it. (Mr. Moorcock's recent novel, *Warlord of the Air* makes similar historical points and does so much better.)

Bad Moon ends with "Notes from the Pre-dynastic Epoch," the best story by Robert Silverberg I have ever read. To my mind his work has always suffered from the lack of really strict cutting, but here he has made every word tell. Moreover, the chilliness that hangs around even his best work is gone, and the result is a direct appeal of extraordinary poignancy.

Paradox Lost by the late Frederic Brown is a collection of stories "never before published in book form" (according to the jacket copy), four from the '40s, three from 1950/51, and the rest from the early '60s. The early tales are raw wonders-and-marvels with homey-pulp characters and large holes in the science; the execution improves in the later stories, but they remain slick mousetraps at which the reader must collude by accepting a lot of arbitrary givens for the sake of one final twist. In James Blish's terms, only "Puppet Show" (here) has an idea about its idea; it (like so many of the stories) would make a perfect TV show because actors and production can supply the characterization, the scenery, in short the denseness of texture, that Mr. Brown doesn't. At bottom these stories are padded anecdotes. (The funniest, "Aelurophobe," almost makes it as pure anecdote.) Some Brownian notions are fascinating – for example, "Double Standard" explores the world of TV characters who exist not as actors but as persons in another world – but even here the only difference the author can find between art and life is sex and profanity. The book contains the famous "Knock," as well as "Something Green," a story I found breathtaking at fourteen, but which now looks much the worse for wear. Others are "Eine Kleine Nachtmusik," "Paradox Lost," "The Last Train," "It Didn't Happen," "Obedience," "Ten-Percenter," "Nothing Sirius," and "The New One" (the kind of American myth Stephen Vincent Benet did so much better). The stories are badly over-written (you can skip every second word and still follow them perfectly well), and aside from some nice bits of humor (a baby fire elemental says, "I'm going to look out through the curtain, Papa. I'll keep my glow down to a glimmer") there's nothing here to think or feel about.

Gordon Dickson's *The Star Road* starts with a slick mousetrap of a story (entitled "Mousetrap"!) but even this one, written in 1952, has more to it than the single plot twist. Mr. Dickson never constructs an ingenious toy merely for the sake of seeing it spin. The collection, which ranges from the late '50s through the '60s, has the usual interesting and varied Dickson aliens, good if they're powerless and/or furry, usually bad if they're powerful. Each story has both an intellectual puzzle *and* something else: in "On Messenger Mountain" an exceptional man learns that he will always be lonely; "Jackal's Meal" shows us the conflict of military and diplomatic temperaments (and aims); "Mousetrap" deals with the tragedy of a brainwashed wreck who wants to respond to good (and furry) aliens but can't; "Whatever Gods There Be" illustrates the self-command of the title (Henley's *Invictus* – Mr. Dickson often quotes poems); and "Hilifter" is a future Boston Tea Party that dwells on the contrast between romantic expectations and reality. Less successful stories are "The Catch," which ought not simply name the seduction of power and authority but show it; "The Christmas Present," in which the sacrifice of alien for human seems not only sentimentally excessive but also unnecessary; and "3-Part Puzzle" which posits that humans are superior to aliens because we have moral ideals, a proposition George Bernard Shaw took a much dimmer view of in his play *Man of Destiny*. (He argues that the English are the most dangerous nation on earth because they can convince themselves that what they *want* is also *virtuous*.) Mr. Dickson is a propagandist whose propaganda passes unnoticed because it's so familiar; "Building on the Line" (the most recent story in the book) is pure Kipling, and I find it, as I do much of Kipling, morally revolting. The author carefully makes his s.f. situation parallel with the building of the railroads across America in the 19th century, from the song the men sing to the ghastly conditions under which they work. (Who profits by saving all that money and time?) As in Kipling, it's not the importance of the job that justifies the romantic heroism but vice versa; according to the author's spokesman, "fat tourists" will use the Line when it's complete. Mr. Dickson even duplicates Kipling's contempt for the remote administrator (here the Research Department, which doesn't understand front-line conditions), his disregard for the annoyed natives, whose front parlors are being dug up (so to speak), and his mystique about "team spirit" – though the animal analogies used in the story are actually species solidarity, a characteristic human beings either don't have or manage to control (at times) with great ease. There are no underpaid Chinese working on the Line or Irishmen who can't get jobs anywhere else; all are volunteers so it's O.K. to ruin their comfort, health, and even lives, and then pay them with Glory. I should add that Mr. Dickson writes magnificently of the psychology of stress and delirium, little as I like his politics, his Men's House mystique, or the appointment ceremony in which the human race is the Line and the Line is the Team and so on, all of which has eerie overtones of Fuehrer = Volk = Partei. (But the protagonist is delirious at the time so maybe he's distorting things.) The collection is half fair and half good, the line of demarcation coinciding pretty much with the age of the stories, the later ones being the better ones.

For reasons known only to itself, Doubleday has published a non-book called *Complex Man* by Marie Farca. It's very hard to read and is full of awful scientific bloopers: e.g. people no longer sleep ("Food, drugs, and purity of air compensate for this"), people whose legs have atrophied from birth onwards can learn to walk at age twenty-five, everybody uses motorized chairs hovering on "air jets" (imagine what a storm this would kick up indoors!), and there are "island" satellites of earth which have Earth-normal atmospheres and gravity. The author seems caught up in some very detailed, private, untransformed fantasy; you never get the details you need (e.g. something that will enable you to tell the characters apart during the first 100 pages), and you get vast amounts of dramatically irrelevant detail (mostly architectural, including diagrams). Almost nothing is dramatized until the last fifth of the book. Ms. Farca might eventually turn into an s.f. writer, for she has lots of utterly uncontrolled imagination, but she is not any kind of writer now.

The book I asked for in my last column is *The Me Nobody Knows*, ed. Stephen Joseph (Avon, 1969). I want to thank all those who wrote in, especially Mr. Leonard Bloomfield of Manhattan, whose address I mislaid and to whom, therefore, I can't write a personal letter.

The Magazine of Fantasy and Science Fiction, January 1975

Born With the Dead. Robert Silverberg (Random House, $5.95). *Some Dreams Are Nightmares*. James Gunn (Scribners, $6.95). *Total Eclipse*. John Brunner (Doubleday, $5.95). *Flow My Tears, The Policeman Said*. Philip. K. Dick (Doubleday $6.95). *The Texas–Israeli War: 1999*. Howard Waldrop & Jake Saunders (Ballantine, $1.25)

A reviewer's hardest task is to define standards. "Good" can mean almost anything: what the British call "a good read," "for those who like it, this is what they'll like," "it won't poison you," "good enough for minor entertainment," "mildly pleasant," "intelligent, thoughtful, and interesting," "charming!" and just plain "good" – excluding the range of better, from fine to splendid to superb to great. Reviewers also tend to adopt a paradoxical sliding scale in measuring a book's quality, i.e. the more ambitious a book, the more it's likely to fail; yet the competent, low-level "success" can be less valuable and interesting than the flawed, fascinating, incomplete "failure." For example, in July 1973 I reviewed James Gunn's *The Listeners* (which belongs emphatically in category two, above) and managed to make it sound worse than Norman Spinrad's *The Iron Dream*, a considerably lower-level (although fun and interesting) category one. Novels don't only provide different kinds of pleasures; they involve a reader more or less profoundly. *Listeners* was "bad" because parts of it were so wonderfully good. *Dream* was "good" partly because it demanded so little of the reader – some of this by the author's deliberate choice, which only adds to the complexity of the whole business.

None of this month's hardcover novels lives up to its author's own best work and in that sense they are not good books. They're certainly not in the "good-by-any-standards" class. Yet none of them is in the droopy-eyeball or loathsome class, either, and all have some excellences. The reviewer's business (as so many reviewers have said) is distinguishing between various levels of failure, keeping in mind that by "good" here I mean very high standards indeed.

Robert Silverberg is a sossidge-factory trying to become an artist.[1] To my mind he's done so only twice, in "Notes from the Pre-Dynastic Epoch" (Tom Disch's *Bad Moon Rising*) and "Schwartz Between the Galaxies" (Judy-Lynn del Rey's *Stellar 1*, reviewed next month). *Born* consists of three related novellas written from 1971 on, two of them ("Born With the Dead" and "Thomas the Proclaimer") interesting but eventually unsatisfying, and one ("Going") just as unsatisfying and considerably less interesting. Mr. Silverberg has hit on a fine idea for making quasi-novels; there are some unnecessary chronological connections (the tales are supposed to happen in the same future world but quite obviously needn't); yet the similarity of theme does enhance all three. They are good – and bad – in exactly the same way: in each some final enlightenment is promised but in none does it occur. Silverberg gets close, especially in the first, "Born With the Dead."

1 *Author's Note*: Seeing this statement in print today makes me cringe as I did then (1975), as it had no relation to what I had intended to say and what I thought I *had* said. Please ignore it.

The details here are almost perfect: the "Deads" (who have been "rekindled") living in their "Cold Towns," segregated from the "warms," attracted to tombs, shooting living re-creations of extinct animals, eating but not caring what they eat, hating the vibrations of life, oddly waxy-looking, very slowly-aging, almost telepathic among themselves, people to whom "nothing matters ... it's all only a joke" and who have lost every aesthetic sense in the present (to judge from the monumental bleakness of their Cold Towns) and who live, in some elaborate, soulless fashion, behind the psychic equivalent of a sheet of glass. They are modern cousins of our old friends, the Undead; yet when the hero's obsession with tracking down his Dead wife (an inexplicable mania unless he is really trying to become a Dead himself, which doesn't seem to be the case) brings him into the world of the Deads in earnest – he's such a nuisance that his wife and her companions have him killed and rekindled – we find out no more about the Deads than we knew before. Up to a point the story is immensely suggestive, but when it comes to the crunch, Silverberg knows more about it than we do, despite the obvious tremendousness of the theme (life and letting go vs. static soullessness) and some extraordinarily fine touches, e.g. the wife's archaeological "find," which she has invented, is not only an elaborate joke but an elliptical description of the interaction between her live husband and herself. The story simply does not deliver. And it's the best of the three.

The second novella, "Thomas the Proclaimer" (under its highly polished surface) is another of James Blish's "one-lung catastrophes." Again there is so much detail to admire that the fundamental staleness at the center is almost lost – until the very end, when one realizes that the "miracle" which begins the story (the Earth's standing still for twenty-four hours without any of the physical effects that ought to occur therefrom) will never be explained, that the author (again) knows no more than you or I, and that the story, for all its echoes of the story of Christ and its discussions of religion, is basically that old-time world-catastrophe, to which (as Blish pointed out) the range of characters' reactions must necessarily be pretty narrow. The periphery of the tale is as interesting as it can be made: prophet Thomas has a manager/inspirer called "Saul Kraft" who does to Thomas's religion something like what St. Paul (formerly "Saul"!) did to Christ's; the chapter entitled "The Sleep of Reason Produces Monsters" (about the conversion of an atheist physicist) is extremely funny – "And the laws of momentum were confounded, as was I" – but the main event still seems to me merely Silverberg in love with gloom and doom. The inner life of Thomas (which might be the story) is never made concrete, and Thomas's death is neither moving nor interesting but merely annoying.

"Going", the third novella, is about voluntary dying in a long-lived Utopia of 2095. One would swear the author had been reading Max Beerbohm's diabolical parody of Wells ("Sitting Up For the Dawn" in *A Christmas Garland*) with its ceremony of "Making Way," its visit of the doomed man's entire family, and the sickly-sweet, sentimental "healthiness" of the whole business. There are interesting details here too, but the real problem – when (and why) will the hero choose to die? – is answered with pure argle-bargle ("in my unreadiness lies my readiness") while the realistic psychological progression that leads to the end doesn't allow you to deduce what in God's name *is* going on. Perhaps death is not a possible subject (as Wittgenstein said, "it is not lived through"); perhaps private, untransformed material intrudes in the stories without being fully expressed.

James Gunn's *Nightmares* (another collection of quasi-related pieces) has an excellent, even brilliant, introduction in which he points out that the novella is the ideal length for s.f. (I agree) and then refutes himself by providing two novellas, a long short story, and a short story, of which the short story is by far the best. The introduction is so good that is ought to be printed in a more portable place (*S.-F. Studies? Extrapolation?*) Mr. Gunn not only indicates the peculiar problems of the novel length but also carefully lists the false solutions to them, all of which are, unfortunately, familiar to s.f. readers. The fiction (which would be entertaining enough in another context) is here put to considerable shame by the excellence of the introduction – actually the two come not only from different worlds, but also from different decades, "The Cave of Night" (a very good read) having been first published in 1955, "The Hedonist" in 1954, "New Blood" in 1962, and "The Medic" in 1957. All are pleasantly old-fashioned, sometimes a little foolishly so, but in general they are obvious, noble, colorful, satisfying stories of good behavior on the part of people who find out that they're living in tyrannies (the two novellas) or (in the long short story) represent evolution and life as against power and its rigidity. There are discussions about happiness ("The Hedonist"), the tyranny of medicine and the fear of death ("The Medic"), power &c. (see above, "New Blood") which are solved by personal virtue and conversion to the too-simple, old fashioned s.f. answers, i.e. fear of death must not become "excessive" (?), freedom is better than happiness, and so on, which are fun but which promptly lower to almost nothing the reasonably sophisticated level on which the discussions were conducted in the first place. The only piece that really explores its theme is "The Cave of Night," with a triply-ironic ending that transforms the obvious (apparent) heroics of the story into something very different. The author's only real errors are in "New Blood," in which a man sheds thirty years in a week, which means that his hair is growing at a rate 52 times faster than normal and his teeth 365 times faster.

He doesn't even eat more than usual; where does the energy for this come from? Nor did Mr. Gunn realize in 1962 that hair cannot change color except by growth from the roots, that teeth can't grow without tooth-buds (and how long do they take to form?), and that brain cells do not divide after birth. Gunn has the odd quirk of highlighting his worst bits by placing them next to his best; here the errors are in a story which is otherwise almost pedantically accurate about medical details.

John Brunner's *Total Eclipse* and Philip Dick's *Flow My Tears, the Policeman Said*. (sic) are hard to assess, since Mr. Brunner can no more be unintelligent than Mr. Dick can lose his feeling for the gritty, chancy irrelevancies of real life. But neither book coheres. *Eclipse* reads like the first draft of a fine novel John Brunner ought to write some day and *Tears* like a beginning that could not find an end – the book literally ends with the equivalent of "He woke up and found it was all a dream."

Eclipse deals with several things: a fine scientific puzzle about the sudden, planet-wide demise of genuinely alien aliens (almost the whole book), the death of a human colony on the same planet (the last forty pages of 187), a man's "becoming" one of the aliens in a prosthetic simulacrum (twenty-odd pages, some of them brilliant), parallels between the aliens' fatal flaw (the solution to this one is smashingly good) and the humans' (conventional stuff about war, &c., which gets natural and unforced only long after the human research team becomes isolated from Earth), and the conversion of a tyrannical Blue Meanie by plain-speaking, which is damn-fool nonsense and occupies fifty pages of padding.

It's easy to see how these fit together intellectually (the paranoid tyrant, the possible death of Earth, the parallel flaws, and the two races lying dead on one planet, done in by the same preference for individual gain over species gain) but they have not been made to cohere dramatically. *Eclipse* is worth reading for the scientific puzzle alone and the way the author sets up a logical, rigorous process of reasoning which only appears to lead deeper and deeper into mystery: here all the details cohere, and in one moment. Knowing what Doubleday usually pays for science fiction (I will be glad to be refuted, but $2000 is the highest figure I've ever heard of) I can only conclude that if Brunner had had the time, we'd have a better book.

Tears (also Doubleday's) is non-coherent in the opposite way; Dick apparently starts with the overtones and lets them (when he is at his best, as in *Counter-Clock World*) produce their own organically whole plot.[2] *Tears*

---

[2] *Counter-Clock World* is built on the dichotomy of the Hobart Effect, i.e. the physical resurrection of the dead, and the deaths of almost everyone you care about in the book – as a line of poetry (which is quoted more than once) says, "It is the lives, the lives, the lives, that die."

is best in its digressions and at its periphery and weakest at the center; the genetically special hero is a very unconvincing superman who in fact has only his charm (and perpetually bad judgment). The theme of finding out what life is like among the proles (i.e. losing your money and power) is God-awfully stale, nor does the author really care about it, and his attempt at the end – I mean I *think* so – to replace the hero's second reality by a third only piles up inconsistencies and unanswered questions instead of attacking our very perceptions of reality. Some of the digressions are fine by any standards; for example the telepathic clerk in a cheap hotel who says cheerfully, "I know this hotel isn't much, but we have no bugs. Once we had Martian sand fleas, but no more"; Monica Buff who is a compulsive shoplifter, with a big wicker bag she got in Baja California once, and who never wears shoes or washes her hair (she's only talked about!); Ruth Rae (something of a character herself) who tells a marvelous story about the pet rabbit ("lipperty-lipperty") who wanted to be a cat; the agreeable Jesus-Freak cop who answers Ruth Rae's frightened, "I *hate* L. A." (she's being arrested) with an earnest, "So do I. But we must learn to live with it; it's there." The most brilliant character in the book is a waif called Kathy, all innocence and psychotic emotional blackmail, who has violent temper tantrums in which she goes rigid and screams (she calls them "mystical trances") and who allows the author to render with frightening verisimilitude what happens when you try to tightrope-walk a conversation with a skillful, vicious, grown-up eight-month-old. Unfortunately the book also has failures like Alys Buckman, who is a lesbian *and* married to her brother *and* a drug freak *and* an undefined "fetishist" (she wears tight pants, a leather shirt, hoop earrings, and a chain-link belt), *and* a sadist (her stiletto-heeled boots are hardly lesbian), *and* an electronic-sex addict *and* lobotomized in some way never clearly described, *and* a collector of "bondage" photos (another male specialty). In short, she is pure *diabola ex machina*, a male fantasy of a macho, homosexual, leather, S & M freak projected on to a woman.[3] The Epilog is unfortunately like a cartoon *Punch* once printed: author-at-typewriter with the caption "The hell with it. Several shots rang out and they all fell dead. The End." In any other profession *Tears* would be called a good, sometimes fascinating, example of overwork and the prolific author would be pensioned generously for several years in order to mellow and recuperate.

---

3 John Rechy, a homosexual author, has a character very like this in one of his recent books and C. S. Lewis's Fairy Hardcastle in *That Hideous Strength* is another. If a woman can't be a lady, she automatically becomes Marlon Brando in *The Wild Ones*. Pfeh. See other recent stories about hairy, muscled Women's Libbers (yech) who smoke cigars (chomp) and cut up men (help!)

The Texas–Israeli War: 1999 is a pacifist's dream. It is literally a bloody bore. A war story with (few) futuristic frills, it is about nothing else and appeals to nothing else. What is being celebrated or exorcised here I do not know, although I can tell (for example) what makes *Patron of the Arts*, William Rotsler's giant, marshmallow-filled waterbed of a fuzzy non-novel, so appealing to horny, fourteen-year-old male virgins who are dying of loneliness and so unbearably numbing to anybody else. The minutiae of war (in *War*) are vivid and accurate, the people non-existent, and the whole novel somehow accidental, as if it had been founded on the Bright Idea of a one-line joke (the title). There are lots of better war stories around by strange authors like "Norman Mailer," "James Jones," "Bill Mauldin," and a promising newcomer called "Ernest Hemingway." Look them up. You'll be pleasantly surprised.

The Magazine of Fantasy and Science Fiction, March 1975

Frankenstein Unbound. Brian Aldiss (Random House, $5.95). *The Dispossessed*. Ursula K. Le Guin (Harper & Row, $7.95). *Joy in Our Cause*. Carol Emshwiller (Harper & Row, $6.95). *Stellar 1*. Ed. Judy Lynn del Rey (Ballantine, $1.25)

In the words of Noel Coward, Aldiss Is At It Again, frolicking with Time, merrily imitating other people's writing styles, and naturally bewildering the poor critic of *Locus* who cannot peg a late 18th-century novel written in modern English (and impossible American), a hero who's supposed to be Everyman but is really Nobody, and the out-and-out treachery of any novel (except *Dracula*) which begins with a letter to "My dearest Mina"! Aldiss's description of Mary Shelley's book in his critical work, *Billion Year Spree*, fits his own novel perfectly:

> a quilt of varied colour ... and occasional strong scenes. Contrast is what she is after ... the preoccupation with plot had not yet arrived. (p. 22)

While Percy Shelley was writing *Prometheus Unbound*, Mary Shelley (at eighteen) was writing *Frankenstein: A Modern Prometheus* – two opposing views of the consequences of modern industrialization. Hence Aldiss's title and his fascination with "this first great myth of the industrial age."[1] The structure of *Unbound* is not the usual cause-and-effect dramatic narrative, but a hyperbolic curve: from a deliberately flattened, neutral, conventional, s.f. twenty-first-century to the clumsy world of Mary Shelley's clumsy novel, to the historical milieu of its author (the portrayal of the literary circle of Percy, Lord Byron, and Mary at the Villa Diodati is particularly good) back to a sophisticated, "opened-up" version of Mary Shelley's novel, and from there to a splendid far-future world (with odd echoes of Hodgson's *The Night Land*). The aesthetic spiral from the flat, twenty-first century of the beginning to the marvelous far-future world of the end are part of what the novel is about; so is the "unfolding" of Mary Shelley's book *in* Brian Aldiss's book – *Spree* calls the original *Frankenstein* "an exhausting journey without maps."[2] So is *Unbound*.

There is no question, I think, about the last quarter of the novel, where Aldiss breaks free of history, as it were, and writes his own version of the myth, but Joe Bodenland (New-Texan and former Presidential advisor) is such a clunkhead that it may not be possible to use him as a first-person narrator. Sometimes the results are extremely funny, as in his letter to Mary Shelley complaining that two of her characters, Clerval and Elizabeth, have been treating him very badly, and that she doesn't really understand Elizabeth's personality at all. But parts sag – for example, Joe's trudging ruminations on the book's theme, handled so much better by Percy and Byron at the Villa Diodati; there Aldiss knows exactly when to interrupt a didactic passage, but Joe (alas) is unstoppable and far too dense to realize (another example) that his "timeslips" are merely novelistic time. When it occurs to him at the end of the book that he may be a character in a novel by Brian Aldiss, he comes out with it in a painfully flat-footed way.

Somewhere James Blish says, apropos of the anti-novel, *Report on Probability A*, that even Aldiss's failures are definitive. This is waffling, but it does describe the effect of *Unbound*. The book is complex, cool, unemotional (except at the end), and very distanced. It is sometimes boring and large parts of it require Brian Aldiss to pretend to be a bad writer. Yet the novel sticks in my mind with extraordinary force. Even the fact that Part One is epistolary (a technique not used seriously in literature for more than a century) evokes a kind of senseless pleasure. *Unbound*, a book very much about time, flowers in one's memory just as its impressive ending grows

1 Brian Aldiss, *Billion Year Spree*, Doubleday, N.Y., 1973, p. 23.
2 *Ibid.*, p. 23.

out of its superficially bad beginning, just as Bodenland[3] is the necessary cipher in the story, like the zero: a living place-mark. A definitive failure? A definition of failure? Something like that. And at times very beautiful. (But read *Frankenstein* first.)

Robert Edmond Jones, the Great American stage designer, once said that a theatrical *mise-en-scène* is not a picture, but an image. Similarly, no Utopia can provide a genuine blueprint for social change, only a poetic image of what we need or want, and can thus (like a good Dystopia) illuminate the questions we need to ask. For all its beauty, *The Dispossessed* wrecks itself on just this issue, and since Ursula Le Guin is neither hack nor craftswoman, but an artist, the inauthenticities show.

The rift between authentic and unauthentic runs through the whole book. Anarres, the novel's Utopia, is bleak, beautiful, and brilliantly realized, but Urras is a stand-in for Earth, and once you spot the models (Ben-bili is the Third World, Thu the Soviet Union, A-Io the Western Democracies) Urras becomes redundant; why should we be interested in a fancy way of disguising what we already know? *Dispossessed* is not satire, which would thrive on such one-to-one correspondence. In fact, A-Io is not even American; it's literary-European (a copy of a copy) which leads the author to some awful inconsistencies: a capitalism that neither expands uncontrollably nor experiences drastic depressions, women with the social position of the 1840s but with contraception and a stable population (hence few children), ultra-modern technology plus an Edwardian (at the latest) social structure. Even the scenery evaporates – it's all *kleggitch* (the Annaresti word for drudgery as opposed to meaningful play-work) technically polished but unreal. One has only to compare the mass protest in A-Io with a similar scene in *When the Sleeper Wakes* to see that Le Guin does not know slums, the poor, mass strikes, police riots, politics, economics, revolutionary undergrounds, society ladies, or aristocrats. Few writers do. The oddity is that she conscientiously insists on writing about them anyway. (One extraordinary goof is that women's fashions haven't changed in a century and a half – haven't the Ioti capitalists invented planned obsolescence?)

There are rifts even in Anarres, generally between what we are shown and what we are told. The anarchism/syndicalism of the society is all there, right down to its roots, like the climate, but (for example) we are *told* that Anarresti children copulate with each other bisexually, breaking no taboos, yet we *see* adolescent boys clubbing together to avoid girls and the disturbing advent of sex. We are *told* that much of the adult population remains promiscuous throughout life, but the only such person we *see* is prying,

---

3 The name obviously bodes something, but I can't catch the reference.

nasty, meddling and comical. We are *told* that one (male) character is homosexual, yet he acts asexual[4] and has no love affairs (except once, with the hero, but the hero only does it out of friendship because the hero is heterosexual). We *see* no other homosexual men, and never even hear of homosexual women (this is not explained). We are *told*, near the *end* of the book, that it is common for a child's father to be the nurturing parent; yet Shevek, the hero, suffers from his mother's absence (*early* in the book), and she herself seems to feel guilty about it. In all the partnerships we *see*, it is assumed that children stay with the mother. Furthermore, although we are *told* that children are raised communally after the age of about three, the only children besides Shevek that we *see* at close range have (by some fluke) been raised privately. (We never find out what happens to the children of unpartnered people.) Even the theatre, which we are *told* is the most important Anarresti art form, and which causes the downfall of the one artist in the book (he is a playwright), is invisible. Instead we have many fine descriptions of – music! Anarres is without artificial gender-roles (a point Shevek makes explicitly in conversation on Urras) but except for female administrators (for whom Le Guin seems to have a penchant: diplomats, work bosses, and such) what we see does not quite match what we are told. For example, women are physicists et cetera, but most conversations on Urras are between men, and the one female physicist in the book is senile; we are *told* that she *has done* fine work, but she never does it on stage, while Shevek's intellectual life is absolutely and authentically concrete. (I might add that the constant use of "brother" as a form of address is enough to make your head spin, especially when used for women – and yet the Anarresti have an invented word, *ammar*, which could easily be made genderless, if Le Guin wanted it to be.) The author's artistic and intellectual impulses seem to be traveling subtly, but persistently, in different directions, and the (unintentional) result is a romantic radicalism, a radicalism without teeth.

Something has gone wrong; what, I can only guess at. I suspect that Le Guin, who is relatively young as an artist, is still in the process of finding her own voice, a process partly hidden (as in Virginia Woolf's early work) by her extraordinary talent. *Dispossessed* makes uncomfortable forays (mostly on Urras) into Big, Public Subjects when the author's real talent lies elsewhere; Big Subjects begin to glow in her books only when they are exotic or magical (as in *The Left Hand of Darkness* or the children's books) or have happened long ago or will happen in some indefinite future. In fact, Le Guin's talent is not (strictly speaking) dramatic at all, but lyrical, and such talent can't deal conventionally with conventional Big

4 A mistake made in *And Chaos Died* by Ross – um – Roos? Rouse? Somehow I forget.

Happenings, nor should it. What works (and magnificently) in *Dispossessed* is indeed what the hero, at one point, calls, "a time outside time ... unreal, enduring, enchanted." The novel's Utopia rejects the categories of higher/lower in favor of central/peripheral (the material on this is fascinating) but the author seems caught in a conventional hierarchy of what makes subject-matter important. One thing she might try is abandoning male protagonists, with the burden of tour-de-force characterization they inevitably impose on a female writer. (And the third-person point of view, which often produces the same kind of strain – in fact, *Dispossessed* is author-omniscient!) Another is to develop the artistic "irresponsibility" (actually the highest form of responsibility) simply to *leave out* what doesn't interest her; when intellect and emotion part company, it's intellect that ought to be abandoned (after a struggle, true, but abandoned).

Needless to say, I carp because the book has earned the right to be judged by the very highest standards. That it fails as an organic whole by these standards is both a criticism and a tribute. (The author is, in addition, exploring new territory; Aldiss's *Unbound*, both a more successful and a lesser book, employs territory Aldiss mapped out long ago.) Anyone who can write that description of the rocket port on Anarres (the first few paragraphs of the book) with its thrilling and intensely meaningful figure-ground reversal is potentially a writer of masterpieces. There are parts of a masterpiece in *Dispossessed* (though the title's echo of Dostoevsky is too easy) and while carping, I will also wait. As George Bernard Shaw (also a late starter) once said, the strength of a work of art lies in its strongest, not its weakest link, and where *The Dispossessed* is strong, it's strong indeed.

Nothing can justly describe Carol Emshwiller's collection of short stories, *Joy in Our Cause*. It is a terrifying, inexplicable, totally authentic world in which even the commas are eloquent. People either drop from the sky, are brought in forcibly from the woods, walk in from the desert or otherwise appear inexplicably out of place (What am I doing *here?*) or "I" is squashed under desks, into kitchen corners, or into the eaves of attics (What am I *doing* here?) The publisher has packaged the book as feminist, but it isn't; it's only absolutely faithful to the center, "little bits of fun or little bits of reality" as the author says ("Stories! I don't believe in them any more than I believe in pictures on the walls"), sometimes excruciatingly funny, sometimes just excruciating, the unsupportable taken cheerily for granted, Hell loyally lived in ("As a mother I have served longer than I expected"), Heaven profoundly melancholy with intimations of death (as in "The Childhood of the Human Hero," a painfully loving portrait of a son).[5] There

---

5 Heaven and Hell exist simultaneously in the same activities, of course.

are sentences that follow the wrinkles of thought in one, secure, impeccable line, gallows humor so fresh and innocent that you swallow it sentimentally before you realize what it is, trivia that can kill – remember the fencer who didn't know he'd been cut in half until he tried to walk? – in short, feathers made of neutronium because there are no big subjects or little subjects, only life.

A sample beginning (from "I Love You"):

> The person you care about the most has just told you you're no good.
> It rings true, but there's an element of surprise in it.
> He has wonderful hands and always gives free advice even if he is, basically, a nonverbal person.
> (These tears are just from yawning.)

Or (in a story indescribably mixed up with Johann Sebastian Bach):

> BACH'S SEX LIFE
> Orthodox Lutheran.

(This is followed by a list of his twenty children, only nine of whom lived to adulthood, one of them feeble-minded and the words, both funny and horrible): "Is this any way to write a Saint Matthew passion!" Or:

> I have one more thing to tell them before the trap door is opened or the sergeant of the firing squad says, "Fire." In fact, I'm sure of it. "Wait," I'll say.

The last story in the book should not be "Maybe Another Long March Across China 80,000 Strong," a very funny story about the women's movement (she's game but has her doubts; the baby girl she carries turns out to be a boy; her best friends are two transvestites in miniskirts; and after clonking one man on the head with a rubber dildo she jumps into the arms of another whom – she brags – is "noted for his leadership qualities"). It should be "Peninsula" (John Donne?) in which "I," driven into the attic by obscene telephone calls, imagines beautiful acrobats on the telephone wires ("the boys wear tights and colored vests and the girls have short skirts and flowery hats") who go South for "Carnival" like migratory birds. The story ends as "I" (who used to be ornamental but is now alone) steps out – to freedom or death? – on the wire:

> "Oh, those untold stories! ... If mine could only ring in your ears like that!"

And they do. They do.

As Baird Searles once said, the golden age of s.f. is twelve, and *Stellar 1*'s efforts to pursue the bubble Entertainment ev'n in the plethora's mouth (the introduction is full of vague, sinister assertions about "second-rate academics" who are taking the fun out of s.f. and grumblements about significance and other dangers, as if science fiction hadn't been born didactic) only lead to a host of newly made antiques, a good Lafferty ("Mr. Hamadryad"), a pleasant Clement ("The Logical Life") and Robert Silverberg's "Schwartz Between the Galaxies," which story is worth the rest of the book put together. I will delicately omit the other participants except for Milt Rothman's "Fusion," a 30-page essay on hydrogen fusion interrupted by names who drink coffee – this is the editor's mistake; Rothman is a fusion technologist himself and only wants to burble. Actually, *Stellar 1* may not be the editor's fault alone; a well-meaning steam dynamo named Roger Elwood has been diluting the anthology market to death lately, innocently unaware that an increase in titles published may not mean reaching a new audience, but only overloading the existing one, and that good fiction can't be cranked out like haggis; there aren't enough good stories written in one year to fill fifty extra anthologies. Let us tiptoe past *Stellar 1* and wish *Stellar 2* a wider selection to choose from.

The Magazine of Fantasy and Science Fiction, April 1975

Cliffs Notes: Science Fiction, An Introduction. L. David Allen (Cliffs Notes Inc., Lincoln, Nebraska, $1.95). *Political Science Fiction: An Introductory Reader.* Eds. Martin Harry Greenberg, Patricia S. Warrick (Prentice-Hall, Inc., $5.95, cloth $9.95). *As Tomorrow Becomes Today.* Ed. Charles Wm. Sullivan, III (Prentice-Hall, Inc., $4.95, cloth $7.95). *Speculations: An Introduction to Literature Through Fantasy and Science Fiction.* Ed. Thomas E. Sanders (Glencoe Press, Beverly Hills, California, $6.95). *Modern Science Fiction.* Ed. Norman Spinrad (Anchor Press, New York, $3.50). *Science Fiction: The Classroom in Orbit.* Beverly Friend (Educational Impact, Inc., Glassboro, N.J., 1974, $3.75; $3.00 for 20 or more). *The English Assassin.* Michael Moorcock (Harper & Row, $6.95)

It's important to kill mosquitoes, especially malaria-carrying ones. *Cliffs Notes* may be refreshing to masochists in search of a new intellectual thrill, but every teacher of Frosh Comp will find this volume wearisomely familiar; it is the ultimate bad paper that drives us all stark, staring bonkers: the compulsive (usually polysyllabic) hedging, the endless plot summaries (redundant if you've read the book, baffling if you haven't), the blank ignorance of anything more than two years old (the "tremendous effect" of *Dune* on the young is mentioned as being without parallel; *sic transit gloria Stranger*), the cumulatively unsettling inaccuracies, the eerie sloppiness (based on an intense, unspoken belief that words don't really mean anything), and worst of all – because ignorant, desperate, or hurried students are particularly vulnerable – the assumption that fiction is put together assembly-line fashion, out of detachable pieces (except for titles, all italics in the following quotes are mine):

> [A] rite of passage ... the sociology of a closed society ... the politics of power ... *are brought together smoothly* and successfully. (p. 93)

> There are six factors which *compose* a literary work ... which can be separated *rather easily* for analysis: character, story, plot, narrative point of view, setting, and language. (p. 133) ("language" is given short shrift here and elsewhere, as you may infer from the misuse of "compose")

> [*Left Hand of Darkness* provides] the first "contact" [sic] theme handled differently and well ... an excellent adventure ... the world and its people. Accomplishing *any one of these well* would deserve praise; to do *three of them well* should insure the author of a permanent place ... (pp. 101–02)

A good example of hedging:

> [Verne's *20,000 Leagues Under the Sea*] *seems* to have introduced *many* readers to a new *kind of* world, one which *most of them* would have had *little* opportunity to have known *very much* about *at all*. (p. 15)

Here is *Conjure Wife* gutted (witchcraft only might be real and women only "tend" to be witches), *Canticle for Leibowitz* without its Roman Catholic theology, *Left Hand of Darkness* bereft both of love-affair and *leibestod*, *The Time Machine* without either Marxism or the second law of entropy (!), and plot summaries of *Dune, The Demolished Man,* and *Ringworld* which would make the authors' heads spin. Most unnerving is the cumulative inaccuracy; in Wells' book the Time Traveller resembles the Morlocks more than he does the Eloi, Stephen Byerly (*I, Robot*) might really be human (which destroys the story's point about ethics), Jan (in *Childhood's End*) "it is interesting to note" bases the calculations for his trip "on Einstein's relativity theory" (heck, I thought he used Newton's Fluxions), "wisely" Panshin does not describe faster-than-light travel in *Rite of Passage* because it "might be impossible to do convincingly," Mia "is initiated sexually by Jimmy" (he's a virgin too), *kemmer* (in *Left Hand*) has "little legal status" (it has none), Gethenians are "humanoid" (they're human), the Ekumen is "somewhat of a failure" and yet "extremely successful" (no, I'm not making this up), the engineering of *Ringworld* is theoretically sound (never mind that plane-of-rotation thing, Larry), and the sex of the "hero" in *Babel-17* is a "twist" (Delany, known for his flashy commercial novelties). This is not merely a useless book; it is obscene, exploitative, and part of the obscure reasons why Americans cannot read. No student, exposed to this ghastliness, would ever want to; and she or he would be right.

Almost (but not quite) as ravaged is *Political Science Fiction*, a big, bland, Platonic Idea of a high-school textbook, which delivers such gems of profundity as "In the United States, political leadership at the national level is determined by voting" (p. 74) and such droning non-questions as "Who is to be the political and literal master – man or his technology?" (p. 5). Students faced with this kind of numbing gorp will instantly flee into pornography, violence, megalomaniac power-tripping, and (just possibly) science fiction, i.e. anything septic. The use of the masculine-preferred[1] is more offensive here than elsewhere (all the teaching anthologies commit it) simply because there is so little else in the book; to write an "inoffensive" high-school civics text (which is what the editors seem to want to attempt) means omitting race, sex, economics, drugs, culture, perception, biology, i.e. the entire human context of political behavior. One author is a male man and the other a female man but neither gets much beyond Matthew Arnold; here is *Political S.F.* at its most fiery and intransigent (italics mine):

> The anger and frustration felt by many American blacks, *for example, may* derive *in part* from the *feeling* that statements about equality and

---

1 Not only do the authors talk endlessly about "Man" and "men"; they also complain about the abstraction of other textbooks! The vast, monolithic figure of Man the Empire Builder, Man the Toolmaker, and Man the Problem-Solver is a standing invitation to falsification and enlarging rhetoric, and an irresistible temptation to invent Man the Blatherer, Man the Dandruff-Shedder, and Man the Lettuce-Slicer. Woody Allen, thou shouldst be with us at this hour.

justice contained in documents *like* the Declaration of Independence and the Bill of Rights do not *have meaning* for them. (p. 10)

The stories – mostly powerfully dull – peak in the mid-'50s and mid-'60s, median date 1959. The few good ones can be found elsewhere; "Remember the Alamo" by R. R. Fehrenbach and Herbert Gold's "The Day They Got Boston" are the only interesting rarities.

Neither Prentice-Hall book shows any definite personality, although *As Tomorrow Becomes Today* has a better selection of stories (possibly due to the aid of the four s.f. authors whom the editor thanks on p. xv). The introductions rehearse the obvious very lumpily ("One danger for the man who travels into the near past is that he may get caught in a time loop" p. 7), tub-thump for s.f. as the handmaid of futurology, which was one thing in the 1930s (a voice crying in the wilderness will use all the arguments it can get, even bad ones) and is quite another in 1974, especially when the crier-in-the-wilderness gets the plot of *The Einstein Intersection* as staggeringly wrong as this one does (pp. 93–94). A good teacher could avoid (or argue with) the intermatter and concentrate on the stories (Sullivan, like Allen, thinks fiction is made of detachable parts like a watch – "a work of art was *broken down* into its various *components, examined,* and then *reassembled*" p. 3); so the final criticism of the book could be simply its contents page. One of the (doubtful) pleasures of such a volume is discovering how good writers like Heinlein and Clarke can be when they're good (as they are here). Best in the book: Heinlein's "All You Zombies" and "And He Built a Crooked House," Bester's "The Man Who Murdered Mohammad," Lafferty's "Primary Education of the Camiroi" and "Thus We Frustrate Charlemagne," Ellison's "A Boy and His Dog"[2] and "Repent, Harlequin," Asimov's "Runaround," Knight's sinister "Masks" with its smashing last five words, Sheckley's "Specialist," Clarke's "Sentinel," Cordwainer Smith's "Game of Rat and Dragon" (I'm reminded of Christina Rossetti, who preferred moles and wombats to men), Worthington's "Plenitude," Pohl's "Wizard of Pung's Corners," and Le Guin's "Nine Lives." Less well known but very good is Burt Filer's "Back-tracked" and a brief stunneroo by Tuli Kupferberg called "Personal."

Speculations has less intermatter, more real personality (sometimes offensively snobbish as in a belligerently silly attack on lit. crit. written by some anti-Asimov who must inhabit the ghostly interstices of the Good Doctor's

---

2 Oddly affectionate-cum-horrific as it is: its last line is literally true.

cranium like the Dr. Edward anti-Teller of the *New Yorker* poem), and a much more mixed bag of science fiction, including fine nineteenth-century material and poetry, plus an essay on overpopulation by Arthur Koestler ("Age of Climax"). The "voice" of the anthology, overall, is sentimentally liberal and artistically conservative (the editor believes "the human condition" – there's only one – to be "unchanged and unchanging" on p. 45, cheerily disregarding Asimov's wrath at the back of the book on just this point) and somewhat lacking in the middle types of fiction – you have Lafferty and Lovecraft on one side, Sheckley and Pohl on the other. Most of the fiction filling this gap in tone is older material like Kipling's "Easy As A.B.C." or Benet's "Nightmare Number Three." The editor is a curious, goshwowing fellow who thinks that speculative fiction is about controlling inanimate matter because you can't control yourself (and that's jimdandy – p. 11), that fantasy (which is identical with science fiction) is good because it creates "metaphorical reality wherein evil is truly evil without the necessity of rational study of extenuating circumstances" (p. 5), i.e. he is ahistorical, apolitical, and an academickal tragedy-addict. He is also a burbling neofan. Consider (italics mine):

> "Have superior beings visited Earth, programmed primitive Earthlings to become intelligent beings or destroy themselves ...? Such questions are as unanswerable *as they are undismissable*." (p. 8)

He is also vividly human, in a Preface worth the rest of the intermatter put together: a youngster in Picher, Oklahoma, lusting after Dale Arden ("a dress like no one in my town would ever wear"), intensely admiring Flash Gordon, "that clean, blond-haired god" with his "yellow ringlets," and finally throwing up (at the horrible rats in the story) while being driven home by ... his Cherokee father (pp. xvi–xvii).

The poems include goodies by Ammons, Auden, Ginsberg, Poulin, Swenson, William Carlos Williams, and a gorgeous but obscure writer called Walt Whitman ("When I Heard the Learned Astronomer" is *good*). There is a blather of bad, fancy poems about the Apollo landing. Best of the fiction: Benet's "By the Waters of Babylon" and "Repent, Harlequin," Graham Greene's "Discovery in the Woods," Nathaniel Hawthorne's "Earth's Holocaust" (yum), Lafferty's "Continued on the Next Rock," Leiber's "A Pail of Air," Lovecraft's "The Outsider," Katherine MacLean's "Pictures Don't Lie," Melville's astonishing "The Tartarus of Maids" (about which the editor is awfully obtuse, but maybe he's just being sneaky), Niven's "Neutron Star", Poe's "Mellonta Tauta" (nice to see it around), Saki's "Sredni Vashtar," Silverberg's "Sundance," and two curiosa: a very chopped-up condensation of Mary Shelley's *The Last Man* (somebody ought to try publishing it all the way through, despite the apparent hazards) and H. G. Wells's *Chronic Argonauts*, the novella which became *The Time Machine*.

Subtle, sophisticated, intelligent, accurate (and inexpensive), *Modern Science Fiction* is the gem of the bunch. He burbleth not; neither doth he drone. He knows the subject. He even talks about the economics of s.f. and the effects of packaging (though he doesn't mention that paperback distributors and retail outlets don't share the publisher's financial risk). In plain English he says fine, illuminating things: "People weren't so sure that they knew what was real and what was not until the eighteenth century" (p. 4) or science fiction is "living metaphor" (p. 10 – exactly what Samuel Delany says about s.f.'s effect on language). The book's intermatter is too compressed, if anything; on p. 402 Judith Merril appears unidentified and shorn of her first name; likewise, much more that the editor says is worth further explanation and illustration. The selections (chronologically arranged, beautifully illustrating the history of the field) are excellent, and – unlike neofan professors – Spinrad is not taken in by naive power-tripping; in fact he loathes it (as one would expect from the author of *The Iron Dream*).[3] I would quibble with some of his choices (e.g. Farmer's "Don't Wash the Carats," far from being the only dangerous story in *Dangerous Visions*, is plain silly – Spinrad's interest in the human sensorium is leading him astray here) but the best praise is simply to list the contents: Campbell's "Twilight," Van Vogt's "Enchanted Village," Del Rey's "Helen O'Loy," Asimov's "Nightfall," Clarke's "The Star," Sturgeon's "Affair with a Green Monkey," Knight's "Stranger Station," "Godwin's "The Cold Equations" (rather Eichmannesque, this one), Kornbluth's "The Marching Morons," Bester's "5,271,009" (jeez parbloo cheers!), Ballard's "The Voices of Time," Moorcock's "Pleasure Garden of Felipe Sagittarius," Spinrad's "No Direction Home" (the most genuine and sophisticated s.f. drug story I've ever read, miles from the usual Unspeakable Temptation or It Isn't Real – it's about epistemology), Disch's "Descending" (really a fantasy), Zelazny's "For a Breath I Tarry," the aforesaid story by Farmer, Dick's "Faith of Our Fathers," Delany's "Aye, and Gomorrah ...," Ellison's "At the Mouse

3 A man (not woman) who writes of "pseudo-Wagnerian superpowered hugger-mugger" (p. 13), "murky, adolescent longings for power, strength, peer-group solidarity, and mystic transcendence" (p. 110), and "a machismo of production" (p. 191) may find himself in the same position as Damon Knight and Theodore Sturgeon, who challenged a lot of he-man nonsense but never really overturned it (fictionally that is) because they were working with only one-half of the social equation. Worried – and sincere – discussions in the Men's House which do not also consider what is happening in the Women's Lodge (are those smoke signals? machine guns? what are they really thinking?) are self-defeating. This is not a criticism of the book.

Circus," Silverberg's "In Entropy's Jaws," and Le Guin's "Nine Lives." There is a bibliography of additional works (including novels). A fine book for both students and teachers, as well as plain old readers.

A jazzy, goshwow, speed-of-light, quirky "mini-course" packed with information, with a natural grouping of themes and subjects, considerable history, and a wealth of games and questions (called "probes") which ought to keep everyone higher than a kite for months (they're sometimes booby-trapped; one is "Try to say ISHFE" p. 83), *Classroom in Orbit* is a fine resource book – not an anthology but an old trunk which you open in the attic and find full of treasures: quotations, questions, hints, games, flat statements (most of them accurate), bibliographies, horrors, provocations, poignancies, everything fast and pointed and designed for take-off. It is more complex and subtle than it seems (although Friend fumbles some things, e.g. the *auteur* theory of film, p. 67) and by approaching the subject the way a fan or writer would, manages to be suitable for any level from (possibly) junior high on up. The book is infinitely sophisticatable. What it needs is a teacher or class that can *fill in* – this is designed to get classes started. The art is scribbly-funny (although the illustration for *Slaughterhouse Five* utterly spoils one of the saddest parts of the novel) and if Heinlein says don't rewrite, don't believe him. (Man the Black Monolith appears again,[4] despite a chapter on women in s.f., but who's perfect? Anyhow the book invites quarreling.) There is a Supplement which the author wishes to have bound with her text; it is full of lists of anthologies, textbooks, thematic works, critical articles, articles on teaching, films available for classroom use, Hugo winners, &c. and can be ordered separately and inexpensively from the same publisher. The book itself includes material on s.f. films, TV, *Star Trek*, and fandom.

The English Assassin got squeezed out of my last review by problems of space, not quality. It is Michael Moorcock's third Jerry Cornelius novel, and – less vividly raw than the first, *The Final Programme* (I haven't read *A Cure for Cancer*) – it is sadder, stranger, more crafted, sometimes more beautiful, and far more complex. It is also much more concretely English in its references than the first book and hence somewhat baffling to an American: a kind of subjective world in which everything opens on to Ladbroke Grove (which I take to be something like the Greenwich Village of the '20s), in which disasters happen over and over again and yet people come back after death (to die again), with everything always on the verge of ending,

---

4 Yes, I know there's someone out there turning purple with rage at this point. But I'll leave the subject alone when it leaves me alone.

beautiful, odd, funny-melancholy, flatly horrible, take your pick (tanks at Dove Cottage). The book is full of decay, death, war, what Moorcock calls "the poverty trance," the mixing of alternate histories, alternate technologies – well, it calls itself "A Romance of Entropy" and it *is* a romance – people appear, die, reappear – and die – vitality passes from one character to another (Jerry has to steal his brother's life-force in order to become human at the very end; sister Cathy comments "What a wonderful surprise!" and then "It's time Frank had a turn"); they sail out to sea ("goodbye, England") with Woman-Mountain-Mum-Mrs. Cornelius asleep at the seaside and about to be shelled by a destroyer (she may not be indestructible, after all); and one recalls with mixed feelings Bishop Beezley's munching a young, chocolate-covered ex-nun (he loves candy bars). There are also newspaper clippings about violence and death, often children's – Moorcock doesn't like death, or violence. The author's first Jerry Cornelius book was printed by Avon in paperback; I'm glad he's finally gotten a good publisher and hope S & S readers of Moorcock's other (and vastly inferior) books will all run out and buy *The English Assassin* under the mistaken belief it's all about Prince Elric of Whatchamacallit. They will have exchanged fake-exoticism for real strangeness and (despite the difficulty of pegging English locales and Erté tea gowns) may find they like it. I do. Goodbye, England, Goodbye. Goodbye (Good luck.)

NOTE: Two new fanzines have appeared recently: a feminist one, *The Witch and the Chameleon,* Amanda Bankier, 2 Paisley Avenue South, Hamilton, Ontario, Canada ($3.25/yr and *Red Planet Earth*, Craig Strete, R.R. #1, Box 208, Celina, Ohio 45822 ($.50 each), "an inter-tribal effort to help Indian writers." There are aliens among us. (*Us?*)

REPENTANT – SILVERBERG NOTE:
In my January 1975 review I committed the kind of blooper about *Born With the Dead* that has made me wish *I* were dead. I didn't say what I meant. I called the book's extremely talented writer "a sossidge-factory trying to become an artist," assuming that everybody knew Mr. Silverberg's factory days ended fifteen years ago and that by "artist" I meant work so faultless and fully realized that one would not wish a word of it changed. Then I went and did it again, reviewing *Stellar 1*. I wish to apologize publicly for my ghastly fumble. Silverberg is a *very*-ex-sossidge-factory *still in the process of developing as an artist*; "Schwartz Between the Galaxies" and "Notes for the Pre-Dynastic Epoch" are true quantum-jumps in this process; to my mind they are absolutely satisfying works, without reservations, the kind of fully fused writing that's rare in any writer's career. And *that* is what I meant.

The Magazine of Fantasy and Science Fiction, **November 1976**

The Clewiston Test. Kate Wilhelm (Farrar Straus Giroux, $8.95). *Millennium.* Ben Bova (Random House, $7.95). *Star Mother.* Sydney J. Van Scyoc (Berkley Putnam, $6.95). *Comet.* Jane White (Harper, $7.95). *Cloned Lives.* Pamela Sargent (Fawcett Gold Medal, $1.50). *Star Trek: The New Voyages.* Eds. Sondra Marshak and Myrna Culbreath (Bantam, $1.75)

In the course of her writing career Kate Wilhelm has progressed from being a "story *teller*" (her own phrase at a writer's conference once attended) to a "manager of words" – T. S. Eliot's phrase – through sheer intelligence and dogged hard work. Verbal lyricism remains either outside her repertoire or not to her taste; what she has done in *The Clewiston Test* as part of her continuing progress is to develop her "telling" into dramatic crosslighting. There are no less than sixty-four changes of point-of-view in the book (I may have missed some) and the crucial questions on which the book turns are questions organic to the crosslighting method: who is sane, who is honest, and whose perceptions are to be trusted. *Test* is a bare book, puzzling perhaps at first reading (it puzzled me) because of the solidity, simplicity and unusualness of the method, but eventually clear and often very powerful.

There is an eerie idea current in much popular criticism that a critic ought to judge only the "technique" of a novel and not its "content;" yet beyond the point of minimal competence technique *is* content. To judge science fiction by "technique" only is like judging buildings only by whether they remain standing or not; in these terms, I. M. Pei's NCAR building at Boulder and McDonald's golden arches are equally valuable. Literature is not only beautiful, like music and architecture; it is also referential, which means that literary criticism inevitably becomes referential also, and hence moral. As George Bernard Shaw once said of plays, mechanical rabbits are fun because they are ingenious, cheap, or resemble real rabbits; but real rabbits appeal to entirely different concerns and provoke entirely different questions. You don't, for example, praise a live rabbit for ingeniously looking like a live rabbit; you expect it to; after all, it *is* a live rabbit. In Shaw's metaphor the artificially constructed commercial work is the wind-up toy, the organic work of art the live animal. Science fiction, like all literature, is overrun by artificial rabbits; *Test* is one of our very few live rabbits (Kate Wilhelm has in the past written mechanical – though sometimes deeply felt – wind-up rabbits) so criticism from now on will be, among other things, moral.

I have two objections to the book, one minor and technical, one major and non-technical. The technical objection is to the point-of-view changes, which proliferate a little too much, even once (for a single sentence) into the mind of a passing waitress. Wilhelm's dramatic crosslighting demands a lot of athleticism in the reader, and these jumping points of view add to the demands; there are also too many spear-carriers unnecessarily identified by name, although these painstaking details, among others, do make Prather Pharmaceuticals extraordinarily solid. Scenes also often start with the objective camera-eye and then slide into a particular mind; and sometimes shifts occur within paragraphs.

My major objection inevitably takes us outside the book. At first what bothered me was the constriction of the characters' lives; although they are scientists and one of them is a genius, there is no intellectual playfulness here, no culture, no politics, no international affairs, no sports, and hardly any gossip. (This odd deprivation has one effect at least that is fine: The heroine's few escapes into fantasy stand out brilliantly.) Perhaps Wilhelm means to demonstrate the provinciality and deprivation of her scientists' lives; yet narrow-minded people don't really banish all the above from their conversation; they have their own versions of them. The book seems to oversimplify reality for dramatic effect. In another area this is just what the book does, thus turning a qualified social situation into a simpler kind of tragedy and a simpler kind of triumph than it might be. I mean the heroine's isolation from other women.

Women in the sciences are certainly more isolated from other women than their humanist cousins, but *Test* does not offer this (or any other) explanation for Anne Clewiston's being alone; not only that, the author seems to have deliberately loaded the dice so that her heroine's isolation will be total. A book about a strong, independent, gifted woman who challenges the establishment and her own husband is clearly a feminist book. Yet Wilhelm, writing page after page about her own version of one-half of the feminist equation – that much misunderstood phrase, "The personal is political" – completely neglects the other half, i.e. solidarity between women. It is no more possible to be a feminist single-handed (or make what is essentially a feminist protest) than it's possible to have a one-woman trade union. Our cultural tradition be-mystifies the question of support and solidarity for everybody but especially so for women; not only can no woman (or man) today succeed in any social protest (including feminism) without support from others, nobody ever could. The official portraits of women artists, for example, as operating in a supportive setting of husbands and male colleagues, tend to censor the importance of female colleagues and female friends, such unlikely-appearing pairs as Elizabeth Barrett Browning and George Sand, for example, or the very isolated – *but not that isolated* – Emily Dickinson. It was with this quite verifiable historical fact in mind that I read about Anne Clewiston, who is neither a feminist, misinformed about feminism, nor even afraid of it; she seems to live in a world in which it simply does not exist. Now no woman or man in this country can have escaped hearing something, however sketchy, about the women's movement in the last few years, and any white, middle-class woman (I would be presumptuous if I spoke outside my own experience, but this much I know) who is not too far from a big city or a large university can find some kind of support from other women if she chooses to look for it. In *Test* Anne Clewiston hasn't made any such choice, nor do we see for what reasons she might have made it or the information or misinformation she had to base a choice on. In real life it takes time to find the "right" group and feminists are always complaining that the groups they do find are "wrong" – too conservative, too radical, too young, too old, too lesbian, too non-lesbian, too political, too subjective – but Wilhelm's heroine hasn't had this experience, either. If anything, *Test* proposes that an independent woman can expect support *least* from other women; when it comes to the crunch there are three good men who stand up for Anne (her boss, her uncle, and her lawyer) but the women Anne might possibly turn to are as repellent a pair as you will find: a mother so totally destructive that she has openly parted company with reality, and a feminist colleague (ditto) who is an unstable, treacherous lesbian and whose thwarted passion for the heroine heads directly to the heroine's being presumed mad. The one good woman in the book is Anne's nurse-companion, but the social distance between them is so great (and so unbreached by either) that only on p. 232 does the loyal Ronnie finally ask her employer if anything's wrong. This is not to say that Wilhelm is obliged to show her heroine being supported by other women, but the sheer possibility doesn't seem to enter the book's social calculus at all.

In a novel that depends heavily on social analysis, conventional or ambiguous material is fatal. There is some of this in *Test*. The novel indicates at one point that Deena, the lesbian, is not typical of feminists but gets the dynamics of her c.r. group wrong; any leader who was "sharp" with a member would face at the very least the flat rebellion of the other members, probably enriched by three hours' kvetching about elitism. Moreover it's not clear whether Deena is a lesbian because she's crazy or crazy because she's a lesbian. The humane view, of course, would be that it's the repression of her lesbianism that's driven her crazy, just as the humane view of the heroine's mother – explicitly put forward by good Uncle Harry – is that it's the suppression of her intelligence that's made her bitchy. Since we never see the dynamics either of Deena's madness or the mother's frustration (how? why? who did it to them? in what ways?) we are left with unpleasant people who can be interpreted in the conventional way, i.e. it's their own fault. I think Anne's alcoholic boss fails in the same way; the book tells us his life was ruined by being kicked upstairs into an uncongenial job, but what we see dramatically is a spineless, whining hypochondriac. One can only conclude that his alcoholism, his hypochondria, and his acceptance of the uncongenial job are all caused by his weak character.

It is, I think, in the details of the business at Prather, and especially in Anne's relation to her husband, that the novel is most solid, though even here the reasons why the Symons marriage breaks up shift bewilderingly. Wilhelm seems to be saying in one place that sexual dissatisfaction causes feminism, in another that Anne's confinement at home after her accident gives her a taste of the life most wives lead all the time, and still elsewhere that she blames her husband for the car accident. After the rape the question is no longer up for grabs, of course, and I especially liked Anne's "sly" look at her boss (she asks him if a man can rape his own wife and Goodguy answers no) and the theatrical, self-aggrandizing nature of her husband's grief, a masculine phenomenon insisted upon by such diverse works as Samuel Delany's *Triton* and "Mary Hartman, Mary Hartman." Much in the novel is sheer tour-de-force, especially the domestic detail of Anne's surroundings. Emphasizing the contradictions in the book only points up that contradictions are inevitable when you deal with real, difficult subject-matter. Ms. Wilhelm is blasting out living space in the middle of solid rock, something not one book in ten thousand has the nerve to do. Confusion is inevitable; what's exhilarating is that the process is nonetheless alive and continuing.

Ben Bova's *Millennium* is an artificial rabbit. My copy tried to eat real grass in the back yard and died. It's a slick, optimistic replay of 1776 in which a predictably humane-and-decent society on the moon revolts against a predictable dystopia on earth. The moon society is half American and half Russian, which gives the author a chance for a lot of International Understanding (there are, luckily, no Maoist Chinese practicing self-criticism in the corridors) with a lot of sloppiness in the beginning, great wedges of exposition, and some Sears Roebuck eroticism that annoyed me until I realized the author was simply trying to trot out his characters as fast as possible (this is done by listing the features that make the women sexy and grading the men on degrees of being "in condition"). The story that unrolls after this, however, is slick enough to be fun, and even moving if you can forget that its assumptions are more-than-twice-told tales. I'm tempted to call the novel "Executive to the Stars" but that only pegs the school to which it belongs, and however stodgy the school (and the ideas thereof) the book is an O.K., intelligent workout for an idle hour or for people who are terrified of live books.

In *Star Mother* Sydney Van Scyoc has invented the first hybrid gothic-cum-science fiction, a combination quite as horrid as it sounds. The heroine, a Peace Corps type, is your routine sheltered, spunky and incompetent miss; there is a dark, arrogant, brusque, mysterious hero who lives in a castle, hauls the heroine about, and refuses to answer her questions; heck, there's even a loyal housekeeper.[1] The hero and heroine do not get married and there is no glamorous and wicked other woman for the heroine to be jealous of, but there is your usual heroine's alter ego, who is carefully developed through chapter after chapter only to get killed as a stand-in for the heroine (who blunders badly the only time she actually does something on her own). In fact there are two alter egos, one of which kills the other – a worn-out drudge from a Fundamentalist community that kills its mutants (brilliantly novel, eh?) and a rebellious girl from a savage tribe who has a bad case of pelt-envy (males are very hairy on this world) and wants to be a man. By contrast Jahna, the heroine, is presented as a free, independent, but not aggressive or hostile, representative of liberated womanhood, who is going to raise the status of the native savage women because she is beautiful (!), intelligent (an assumption not borne out by her actions), and will provide a figurehead around which they can rally. The book's idea of how to make men value you is to be very pretty and have lots of babies (though not, on this world, in the usual way), an idea you'd think the last eight thousand years of human history would have thrown a teeny bit into doubt, but *Star Mother* is a rabbit so absurdly artificial (purple and with pom-poms) that only those who try to eat it or breed it will be disappointed. It's a lively, silly, colorful, wholly derivative book, with some promising biological inventions the author never really develops. I don't actually mind the book itself, but I do have unsettling visions of inspired adolescents among the readership typing out mss like "Governess to the Stars" and "Interstellar Nurse." Star-executives have to know a considerable amount about the real world, even if such knowledge doesn't include anything about people. Star-governesses need to know (and do) nothing.

A wind-up rabbit that doesn't even go is Jane White's *Comet*, a dreadfully pretentious re-play of the birth of Christ and early Christianity in which everybody speaks Basic Peasant ("A baby. There has never been a baby here. Not even in the village, not now. It is forbidden") and they are all so simple and elemental that they've forgotten the word for fucking, a proposition I absolutely refuse to believe. *Comet* is a post-holocaust world, the

---

1 Joanna Russ, "Someone's Trying To Kill Me and I Think It's My Husband: The Modern Gothic," *Journal of Popular Culture*, Spring 1973, q.v.

holocaust in this case having been the dearth of raw materials needed for a machine civilization. Thus the populace lives in squalor and the rulers run tanks and planes (on what, for Heaven's sake?) and wear plastic clothes, apparently having located their hideout over a petroleum mine. The book has a terminal case of Archibald MacLeish-itis, i.e. the idea that you can arbitrarily substitute any patch of history for any other because the Eternal Verities make them identical. One would expect this book to come from Doubleday in one of its barrel-scraping moments, but even books like *Pig World* and *Complex Man* hop erratically and luridly about the room; *Comet* (from *Harper and Row*, of all people!) just lies there with its gears grinding. It is a portentously dull, thoroughly bad book.

To drop the rabbit metaphor, Pamela Sargent's *Cloned Lives* is an interesting and promising first novel, sketchily and badly put together from episodes that first appeared elsewhere. The first 120 pages are jumpily expository and dull, with no indication of how the violent millennial riots of the beginning ever lead to the rational, affluent, decent world of the middle and end. Once we get into the adult lives of the six clones, however, the author reveals a talent for tracing the psychology and human relations of her characters, projecting a kind of ideal decency that is pleasant and refreshing. Much in the book is clumsy (like the technology, which seems an afterthought) but there is a kind of innocence which carries much before it. The clones, I am glad to say, turn out to be different people, realistically bothered by their notoriety and the peculiarity of their birth; despite the excitingly revolutionary and inflammatory claims made by the various epigraphs, the book shows not big changes but little ones; its world is quiet, low-keyed, and not flamboyant, but often authentically different.

The Kindly Editor sent me *Star Trek: The New Voyages* with the comment that *Fantasy and Science Fiction* has an obligation to cover "one of these" books. But *New Voyages* isn't one of these books; it's neither about the program (like *The Making of Star Trek*) or a novelization by a professional writer of produced or unproduced scripts. *Voyages* is a collection of fan fiction, i.e. a ten-year-old's toy rabbit made very carefully with love and effort but a lot of the little wheels and things got left on the kitchen table and when you try to make it stand up it collapses. Most of the authors are ignorant of such fictional niceties as point of view, to mention only one mess-up, and the strain of reading stories that can't or won't distinguish between the television medium and written prose narrative finally did me in. I survived part-way into each story (considering this better than not reading any of them) and if you think this impairs my credentials as a critic, remember the story of the playwright who fell asleep during a neophyte's play, and afterwards, to the young person's pained protest, replied, "Young man, sleep *is* an opinion." What seems to be wrong with the stories (besides their technical faults, which I would deal with in a writing class – where some of the authors might get A's, by the way – but not here) is that they mechanically re-create the stalest trivia of the show – its names, its star dates, its log, its mannerisms – without in the least trying to replicate the essence of its appeal. The best story I've ever seen about *Star Trek* (which carefully avoids trying to ritualistically re-create the superficialities) is James Tiptree's "Beam Us Home," which can be found in his *Ten Thousand Light Years From Home* (Ace, 95¢). I recommend it to the Little League writers in *New Voyages*, as a way of learning how to play with the big folks.[2]

NOTE: Fan fiction is extremely interesting as a sociological phenomenon, sociological value being – of course – separate from literary value. Analyses along many dimensions are needed, e.g. the perennial interest in Spock, the s.f. themes that crop up, the kinds of alien worlds created, the imaginary–real interface, and so on. Some comments on the sexism of *New Voyages*, especially interesting because the editors and most of the writers are women, appear in a pamphlet sent to me, which was written and distributed by Joyce Rosenfield at the Science Fiction Fair held May 22, 1976 for the Children's Brain Diseases Foundation in California. This is only one possibility and perhaps the most obvious. *New Voyages* represents the taste of its editors, and is not (I would assume) representative of the range or typicality of fan fiction. Some popular culture scholar might go through the fanzines in search of all this material. As an old *Trek* watcher I would be interested in the results of such a search ... as long as somebody else did the large quantities of reading required.

---

2 *Author's Note*: Years after the publication of this review, I was told that the stories suffered, not from the authors' limitations, but from having been altered by someone during the production process. Unfortunately I don't know who or how.

The High Cost of Living. Marge Piercy (New York, Harper and Row, 1978, 268pp., $10.00)

I find Marge Piercy's new book, *The High Cost of Living,* not quite as good as her other works, which probably means it's better. I felt the same way about *Woman on the Edge of Time* until I lived with it a little. Books that are truly alive and individual don't fit easily into preconceptions about what "the novel" should be doing. In addition, Piercy tackles subjects in such an uncompromising, straightforward way that her novels carry an odd air of obviousness about them; surely (one says, reading) something this clear can't be good. Why, everybody knows what this book tells me. But, ah, look around you! They don't.

"All the things you don't know about me would make a new world," wrote Ida Mae Tassin from Bedford Hills Penitentiary.[1] Not that I know these things, either, mind you; I'm quoting Elizabeth Janeway quoting Kathryn Watterson Burckhardt quoting Ida Mae Tassin – thus (third-hand) do the statements of the poor and powerless enter even that marginal part of academia devoted to feminist scholarship. *The High Cost of Living* is a truth of this sort: the price exacted from those who are both poor and homosexual. This subject is grim, gritty, and gray, and Piercy makes it neither elegant, stylistically ingenious, nor luridly false. Thus the most astonishing thing about *Living* is not that it was written (if you know Piercy's other work, that won't surprise you) but that Piercy, in some working-class survival dodge unknown to middle-class academics like myself, *got it published.*

The jacket blurb is a study in confusion, from the assertion that the heroine's boss is a "spoiled parasitic academic" (in his milder forms he is a very common type in the circles I travel in) to the zany notion that the heroine's isolation is caused by "relentless ideology" (she is poor and lesbian; if she moved into the lesbian, feminist community, as the book makes clear, she could stop being lonely), or that her homosexual friend, Bernard, is converted to heterosexuality (he finds that with the help of a good deal of fantasy, he can *once* fuck a particular woman, which is not at all the same thing), or that the heroine, Leslie, is "a moralist whose high

---

1 Elizabeth Janeway, *Between Myth and Morning,* William Morrow & Co., New York, 1974, p. 259.

standards inevitably blind her to those crucial moments when reality refuses to dissolve itself into clear categories of right and wrong." Alas, there are no such moments in *Living*, which is concerned rather with the slow grinding down of those who are deviant in too many ways at once, class being the main killer here. Piercy is honest about the alertness to self-defense required of homosexual people, the vulnerability, and the emotional fatigue of living in a constantly, unpredictably hostile world (there are queer jokes in here you don't even notice on a first reading) and yet what could Leslie do if she were heterosexual? Perhaps what silly, pretty, charming, seventeen-year-old Honor does, i.e. get screwed. The characters in this novel, initially so different and unrelated, begin to form (as one watches) an eerie pyramid of oppression: Honor, naive and ambitious, trying to be Somebody via the traditional feminine methods and hence caught by what she ought to know better than; Honor's mother (originally seen by Leslie as a villain), herself deprived and rightly ferocious about her daughter's future; Bernard and Leslie, thinking it makes sense to fight over the very limited stock of pretties available to them; Leslie's ex-lover, as stupidified and paid for as the most unhappy suburban housewife; the woman keeping her, one of the rich lesbians Leslie used to know, with their silk shirts and edged jokes but still closeted, still only playing at achievement; the faculty wife, Sue, profiting a little from her position (largely because she herself is rich) but still unhappy and insecure (her husband's idea of an open marriage doesn't really include her freedom, too). At the top of this small heap is the white professional man, George, but George is only a little fish whose own fears point straight up the pyramid, to the moneyed interests in Detroit he dare not offend. None of these people is weak or pathetic; they are all strong, whether pleasant or unpleasant; Piercy knows that the measure of a society is how much passion, courage, and sheer love of living it can crush. This is not a novel about The Oppressed written from above (Robin Morgan once called that sort of thing, "Lenin Leading the Schlemiels"), nor does the book stand outside its characters, thus allowing us to do so. Nor does Piercy claim that proper ideology is the answer – one of the best things here is the implicit portrait of the limitations of the lesbian feminist counterculture: its surface sweetness, its closed-in-ness, the dreadful demands it makes (must make) on everyone's time, and the ghetto acceptance that lasts only as long as one obeys tribal custom. For the main characters in the book, the wrenchingly high cost of living is that they *do know* their situation ... and that understanding doesn't help. They are tough, informed, determined, even desperate people, and by all the rules of fiction, *they ought to succeed*. But they don't, and Piercy shows you why, which is much harder than telling you why. Not are there villains, except off-stage; even George, creep that he is, exists in response to temptations and privileges that are not at all uncommon.

It might be objected here that the very act of writing about dead-end desperation is itself a kind of escape; and yet, if it is, it is surely one unavailable to most people. The characters in *Living*, for example, for all their intelligence, do not possess any special talent for writing novels, nor do they enjoy intimate chats with God. Neither visionaries nor artists, they possess no special escape routes and hence don't escape; they merely draw together, are tempted by the possibility of real community (which doesn't pan out: Piercy is much more pessimistic about sudden conversions of any kind than the blurb writer is), but cannot overcome the social forces which act against that community, and so drift apart. Leslie may make it – or rather, she may find life somewhat easier than before, since the pupils in her new, all-woman karate class may fall in love with her. But the separatist solution is, at best, partial, like everything else. It is also (like everything else) *too costly*. The last sentence of the book has Leslie heading back to academia and George.

Marge Piercy is a realist born out of her time, which is one of the reasons she could write so (technically speaking) nineteenth-century a Utopian novel as *Woman on the Edge of Time*. Nor is there anything strange or idiosyncratic about this. One could say the same thing of Lorraine Hansbery's *Raisin in the Sun*, for example. Material finds it own form, and when creative work first begins to be written, authors tend to take two approaches: the subjective and lyrical sort of work where the material exists as the unnamed and possibly unnameable thematic center of the work, and then (once the material can be named, i.e. pinned down) as those pioneering forms which long ago dealt with similar matters. If the brothers Goncourt had written about class and sexism from the viewpoint of an upwardly mobile, poor lesbian, Marge Piercy would be doing something else today. But they didn't and so she must. Indeed, so pronounced is this nineteenth-century ghost hovering behind Piercy's book that the jacket blurb (for once fairly accurate) calls the novel "Victorian." I was taken in by the apparent anachronism of *Living* to the point that I wanted to describe Piercy's style as that "duffle gray blanket which wears well and suits everything" – a phrase Woolf invents to express her sense of Scott and Trollope.[2] But such a description would be unfair to Piercy. Her style is plain and unspectacular (the intellectual beauty of the book may pass unnoticed) but *Living* is realism lightened and much speeded-up. Piercy is no Trollope. And when fine shading is needed, Piercy gives it, especially in the realm of charac-

---

2 Virginia Woolf, *Granite & Rainbow*, Harcourt Brace, New York, 1975, p. 133.

terization. For example, note the many quirks of Honor, that splendid character (every woman has known or been an Honor in her teens) who is capable of saying, "that incident is hazy in my mind, which proves I feel dissatisfied with my role" (p. 206), and who is cynical about romantic love – she says it means only Quaaludes and crying – but who ends up crying for "an hour straight" and exclaiming, "He said he loved me, he said it twenty times, I swear it" (p. 265).

There's something abrasive about the reality of Piercy's books; they're too authentic to be comfortable. I don't mean that the truths they tell are in themselves unpleasant (although here they are) but that there's something about authenticity in fiction which need not be immediately pleasing or charming, though it may be impressive. This has little to do with one's politics and much to do with the nature of literary cues and expectations; as Wilhelm Reich says in *The Sexual Revolution*, turning "an ordinary detective story" into "a White spy pursued by an O.G.P.U. man" does not really change the story.[3] Piercy has chosen the dangerous method of really changing the story, and as if to burden herself further, uses a method which looks (at least superficially) old-fashioned. This is what makes reviewers angry and publishers uninterested and readers (except for those who need the new truth so desperately that they'll take it in any form) puzzled at best. *Rubyfruit Jungle* is a much cuter book than *The High Cost of Living*, an infinitely more winsome and boring book. It's not surprising that it's *Rubyfruit Jungle* that's going to be made into a movie; it's Hollywood's idea of what the well-behaved lesbian should be. I don't want to downgrade Rita Mae Brown's book (it's fun and its *chutzpah* is a virtue) but Piercy's is a much more humane, complex, and truthful work. In fact I could find it in my heart to wish *Living* on every women's studies class in the country; it accomplishes some very difficult tasks and does so without romanticism or prettification, or, out of sheer desperation, leaving half the topic out. For example, one of the most difficult things a novelist can do is to present affectionate, good feeling (and the eroticism that goes with it) outside the conventional categories of how and where one ought to feel it. Piercy's lesbian love scene is detailed and authentic, but her re-creation of the simple joy people can feel in each other's company (the joy that suffuses the utopian society of *Woman on the Edge of Time* but here occurs only briefly) is an even better accomplishment.

Literature (that means people like me) has for too long used the poor of this world as spear-carriers or ignored them completely. As Elizabeth Janeway comments, "To the powerful, the experience of the poor isn't

---

3 Wilhelm Reich, *The Sexual Revolution*, Farrar, Straus and Giroux, Inc., New York, 1974, p. 215.

interesting; their deviance raises no questions that seem to warrant exploring, and the trouble they make is dealt with by labeling it criminal."[4] In this sense the poor, like women, like homosexuals, like nonwhite people, have been with us in white Western literature for a long, long time. That is, they have been used (if at all) as projection screens for other people's desires and fears, typically those of the upper class, of men, of heterosexuals, of whites. Consider, for example, The Homosexual as tragic grotesque in movies and books. Piercy neither ignores, condescends, nor (as far as my class bias allows me to see) distorts. Nor does she sing us siren songs of daydreams fulfilled, or ornament the whole mess, verbally or otherwise. As Woolf, herself a very charming writer, once remarked, lack of charm counts in a woman (even among women, I would add). *Living* is not charming. But it has more formidable virtues: an intense sense of character, a direct dignity, and genuine weight. It neither snoozles up to you, gushes, nor complains, and that's rare.

By all means, read it. It's an impressive achievement.

The Magazine of Fantasy and Science Fiction, February 1979

What Happened to Emily Goode After the Great Exhibition. Raylyn Moore (Donning [Scarblaze] (Norfolk, Va., 1978, $4.95). *Rime Isle*. Fritz Leiber (Whispers Press, Chapel Hill, N.C., 1977, $10.00). *The Year's Finest Fantasy*. Ed. Terry Carr (Berkley Putnam, New York, 1978). *Lord Foul's Bane*. Stephen Donaldson (Holt, Rinehart and Winston, New York, 1977, Ballantine, 1978, paper, $2.50). *The Grey Mane of Morning*. Joy Chant (George Allen & Unwin, London, 1977)

Emily Goode is an archetypal female fantasy – Victorian lady in twentieth-century America – whose appeal (I suspect) is the chance it offers for moral cheating; one can have the thrill of being daringly improper (in nineteenth-

---

4 Janeway, *Between Myth and Morning*, p. 259.

century terms) while remaining extremely ladylike and staid (in twentieth-century ones). To send her heroine across the modern United States, Moore resorts to what Damon Knight once called an idiot plot (i.e. one that works only because everyone involved in it is an idiot). Emily, supposedly so respectable that she can't mention sex to a suitor, even by euphemism (and she's a widow of thirty, not a maiden of twenty), nonetheless runs *from* authority, not *to* it, the moment she finds herself in trouble, a piece of plotting that not only detracts from her reality as a character but also insures that the novel will be an adventure story, and (therefore) that there will be no real confrontation between the values of the two eras – the only possible point in a story with a time-displaced protagonist.[1] Either the nineteenth century can win and the heroine reject our time, or we can win and she can accept the modern world, or (the most interesting possibility, dramatically) she can outdo the twentieth century. Moore chooses the first and dullest alternative; near the end of the book the heroine denounces modern life, and the psychiatrist she's seeing is impressed and agrees with her. That is, the era of child labor, Jim Crow, robber barons, rampant prostitution, and virtual female slavery in marriage feebly condemns the nineteen-seventies for smog, inflation, tasteless food,[2] television pictures of the moon, unisex clothing, and "wars fought without reason and without honor." The list is an odd one: inflation has been going on for eight centuries, smog is surely preferable to tetanus, and if Moore wants reasonable and honorable wars, one can only send her (with an ironic grin) to a history of the entire world, which she may open at any page she chooses. (The Civil War, for example, was not fought over slavery, though Moore seems to think it was; emancipation was something of an improvisation by Lincoln – who believed, by the way, in black inferiority.)

The trouble is that *Emily Goode* doesn't see the nineteenth century as a real era in which real people lived, suffered, enjoyed, and died. (Neither does Bradbury, but he connects his idyll with childhood, which is everybody's Golden Age.) This might not matter if its twentieth century were real, but the characters that impossible-stereotype-Emily meets on her travels are even worse clichés than she: the philosophical cabbie and his whiny, vulgar, insensitive wife (both with fake Brooklyn accents); the swinging, divorced, wealthy ad-man who talks about male prerogatives in intercourse (to a woman he's trying to seduce!); the mannish, criminal lesbian (who is both an orphan and an ex-WAC sergeant); and the colorful,

---

[1] Unless you want to show cosmic catastrophe, as in the end of Wells's *The Time Machine*.
[2] Food also without the germs of tuberculosis, undulant fever, typhoid and botulism.

liberal lawyer who talks feminism on one page and praises gallantry on another. In short, the book is riddled with class snobbery, sexism, and homophobia, even though Moore tries to "redeem" her characters by telling us that the vulgar, insensitive wife is *really* sorry for her husband's death, that the exploitative swinger isn't *really* a cold-blooded rapist, and that the lesbian is *really* pitiable, all of which, alas, only adds condescension to the bigotry. Moore judges her women much more harshly than her men, without, I think, being aware that she's doing so; the book shows one incompetent woman professional (a lawyer) who is squashed by a *black Federal judge* – brought out triumphantly on p. 124 to validate the book's liberal credentials. Moore dedicates the book to her two daughters, who will, I hope, spurn it for the cultural prussic acid that it is and instead instantly read Juliet Mitchell's *Woman's Estate*, which will tell them why the initial fantasy of *Emily Goode* is so compelling (the female role, argues Mitchell, is in fact anachronistic). I would be less cross if the book were better written, but Moore shows her heroine's nineteenth-century propriety by a stiff, abstruse, polysyllabic style which leads to howlers like "a sensible mood of calm," "Emily lost the quality of immediacy in her resolve," "a vendor peered boredly from a booth," and the awkwardness of the one sentence that does convey a sense of wonder (a plane trip): "Joshua had stopped the sun; who had ripped loose the seam which joined the land to the sky?"

Nehwon addicts will probably like *Rime Isle*, though I suspect Fritz Leiber didn't. Everything's here: strange scenery, properly lurid monsters and gods, lots of (sometimes aimless) action, two beautiful women (indistinguishable from Leiber's other pairs in other books), but the whole business is tired; it starts with a typical mid-life crisis and ends with both heroes in debt and (almost) married. In between, two gods intimately connected with Fafhrd and the Mouser are dismissed to non-existence, loose ends from other Nehwon stories are carefully tied up, the heroes learn that adventures are for idiots, and a major war is not fought, but averted. There is a fascinating wizard with a fine name who does almost nothing and more imitation late Jacobean than usual, used here as a form of telegraphy:

> Would Mingol mariners fight fiercely 'gainst their own in a pinch? Mingols were ever deemed treacherous. Yet 'twas always good to have some of the enemy on your side, the better to understand 'em. And from them he might even get wider insight into the motives behind the Mingol excursions naval. (p. 14)

In books as well as on TV, series tend to decay after their templates satisfactorily establish who's who and what's what. I wonder if the very early

"Adept's Gambit" was not the last of the Fafhrd–Mouser stories in which something really happened humanly, that is, in which somebody actually changed. *Rime Isle* has one good joke, the Mingol shamans' Talmudic debate as to whether it "is sufficient to burn a city to the ground or must it also be trampled to rubble?" and one genuinely sinister and poetic incident – Odin's noose – but everything happens much too fast and, except for some sparkling scenery, Leiber (I suspect) is trying hard to get rid of both heroes. *Rime Isle* may be his way of doing it. The novel has very much the air of an intelligent grownup (much more at home in a civilized fantasy like *Our Lady of Darkness*) trying, for the last time, to please the kids. The kids may have noticed; *Rime Isle* is put out not by a major publisher, but in a special edition by Whispers Press, with pictures by Tim Kirk.[3]

The Year's Finest Fantasy is a good collection with only one outright failure, a clumsy piece of grue by Stephen King called "The Cat from Hell" which doesn't belong here, though King's name (he's the author of *Carrie*) makes for good jacket copy. "Probability Storm" by Julian Reis is pleasant enough but very derivative; "Getting Back to Where It All Began" by Raylyn Moore is the essence of F&SF idyllic pastoral with nice names; and T. Coraghessan Boyle's "Descent of Man" is the kind of male competition-inferiority fantasy modern high culture deals in a lot ("his is bigger than mine"), verbally polished but full of unearned clichés – it appeared in *The Paris Review* and not one of ours, you will be glad to hear. Another pastiche, youthfully energetic and rather appealing, is Steven Utley and Howard Waldrop's "Black as the Pit from Pole to Pole," which gives Frankenstein's creature further adventures and a beautiful, blind lady to fall in love with. Without the charm of the borrowings, however (Lovecraft, Henley, Poe, Melville, Symmes, [Mary] Shelley, Edgar Rice Burroughs and doubtless others I missed), the story would not make it, and although it's genuinely enjoyable to watch the Malaprop Kids excitedly rummaging through The Classics, somebody should've warned them against putting "erstwhile" and "displacement activity" in the same sentence (except in straight parody) and that "arcing" and "stomped" are not words. There are other screamers, my favorite being "willing to cope with the basin's large predators on a moment-to-moment basis." There is also an Expository Lump on p. 91 that should've been given to the brontosaur (on p. 82) to eat.

In the top half of the anthology is "The Bagful of Dreams," a Cugel the Clever story by Jack Vance, as cynical, elegant, and sour as the best of them (Vance appears not at all bored or stale). Avram Davidson's "Manatee Gal,

---

3 *Author's Note*: I was wrong. Whispers Press had published *Rime Isle* as a *reprint*, surely a sign of the book's success with its audience.

Ain't You Comin' Out Tonight?" is ostensibly a horror story but really a beautifully detailed creation of a tiny Central American country he calls British Hidalgo, including a fine ear for accents. Woody Allen's wispy, very funny "The Kugelmass Episode" is perfect Woody Allen ("'My God, I'm doing it with Madame Bovary!' Kugelmass whispered to himself, 'Me, who failed freshman English!'"), and "Growing Boys" by Robert Aickman is a strange, very British story whose exoticism may be due simply to its appearance on this side of the ocean. I can't shake off the impression that "Robert Aickman" is a pseudonym and the author is a woman, since the tale's subject is the cannibalistic horror of family life, from which the Everywoman heroine is offered two escapes: decamping with another, friendly woman (the heroine dreams at one point that they're happily climbing the Himalayas together) and an ideal, protective substitute father. The ending is the kind mothers – but not fathers – dream of.

Harlan Ellison is a born dramatist. His gift of creating extreme situations and of communicating the intense emotion evoked by them is quintessentially a dramatist's gift – *all* situations in drama are extreme (including Chekhov's, although the seemingly discursive texture of Chekhov's plays tends to hide this), and in drama character is an attribute of action and not vice-versa.[4] One of the problems I think Ellison has had as a short-story writer is that there is no narrative scrape his dramatic gifts can't get him out of, which means in practice that until fairly recently he's stayed with the kind of subject that can be dealt with dramatically. (I have seen analyses of "Pretty Maggie Moneyeyes" and "The Ticktockman" which thoroughly – and mistakenly – demolished them from the point of view of novelistic social realism. Then that ultra-novelistic novel, *Dahlgren,* appeared and fandom thoroughly demolished it – just as mistakenly – from the opposite point of view.) But without anybody's noticing particularly, Ellison has begun to move into areas drama can't cover; "Jeffty is Five" is just such a story. It is, I think, Ellison in transition. On one page there is a phrase as precise as "gentle dread and dulled loathing," on another, "I realized I was looking at it without comprehending what it was for a long time," which fails because it's sloppy – though I admit that surprise (the easiest emotion to induce in drama) is the toughest to evoke in prose narrative.[5]

---

4 Ellison wrote the best script *Star Trek* ever did, "City on the Edge of Forever" (even better in his original version), and the best I've seen on *The Outer Limits* – the one about the soldier from the future; "Demon with a Glass Hand" tries for much more and therefore doesn't cover its subject with such absolute thoroughness. (I would almost swear he had a hand in "The Inheritors"; does anyone know?)

5 *Author's Note*: I would not agree with this judgment now as the second sentence quoted strikes me now as just as precise as the first.

In short, Ellison was too impatient or busy or involved with his material to sit down and pick the verbal fluff out of "Jeffty" – though again and again he's demonstrated that if he wants to, he can. There are times I could wish a talent-sabbatical on him, if only to force him to handle the printed word as print, not spoken voice ("Jeffty" is full of the italics and repetitions that are the devices of the story-teller, not the word-writer). Bradbury, also a dramatist at heart (and with less to say than Ellison) is one of the most economical writers alive and therefore one of the most effective. A singing teacher once told me that voices are not made but carefully (layer by layer) unwrapped. "Jeffty" is still half-smothered in wrappings (largely because the material isn't the kind that can be treated dramatically), and the problem now is to unwrap him, that is, to make every sentence as clean as the first. Nobody knows popular culture better than Ellison and nobody loves it and hates it as he does. I couldn't imagine Jeffty any more than I can fly, but I do know that the last sentence of the story should be "They die from new ones." And I suspect, hopefully, that the story refuses to smooth itself out precisely because the material is so alive and charged with emotion, which means it may have to be wrestled with but the wrestling will be worth it. Ellison ought not to be writing "the best of the year" but something much better, and although he may not like the idea of his works being taught in Lit. 101 a hundred years from now, I do. Only the preservative of style can make things not only enter people's heads and hearts, but also stay there. I hope he does it.

Fantasies like Ellison's, Moore's, or Davidson's have nothing to do with "heroic fantasy," that form of twentieth-century escapism pillaged from genuine medieval culture. Samuel Delany is, I believe, writing something he calls sword and sorcery at this very moment and may revolutionize the genre for all we know, but until then rocky caverns full of rank stench inhabited by evil entities with red eyes, sentences like "Peace lay over the realm of the Wide Land," and other signs of secondary universes in the brewage only send me into fits of giggling followed by stupefying boredom. (I was not so sensitive before the eighth – or was it tenth? – laser battle in *Star Wars*, from which I had to be awakened several times, or so my friends tell me; I have only a confused and whimpering recollection of the last hour of the film.) George Bernard Shaw once said that those who have grappled face to face with reality have little patience with fools' paradises, and another political radical, Virginia Woolf, stated flatly that "books of sensation and adventure" quickly grow dull because they can only present the same kind of thrill over and over:

> It is unlikely that a lady confronted by a male body stark naked, wreathed in worms where she had looked, maybe, for a pleasant

landscape in oils, should do more than give a loud cry and drop senseless. And women who give loud cries and drop senseless do it in much the same way.[6]

Woolf was talking about Mrs. Radcliffe, but when the sensation is heroic virtue instead of brooding terror, things get no better; as Suzy Charnas once wrote to me about the fixity of Lewis's and Tolkien's characters: "Arrowshirt, son of Arrowroot, son of Stuffed Shirt, THIS IS YOUR VIRTUE!" In short, fiction's only real subject is the changes that occur in human beings, and since real change is the one thing that "heroic fantasy" (with its aim of wish-fulfillment) must avoid at all costs, such fantasies often begin with a delicious sense of freedom and possibility, only to turn dismayingly familiar and stale unless well salted with comedy (Leiber's technique)[7] or adorned with rapidly changing, interesting, and colorful scenery. C. S. Lewis, who is very good at scenery, manages in this way partly to disguise the dreadful predictability of his Narnia books – i.e. aristocrats stay noble, dwarves cunning, animals loyal, and peasants stupid unless pushed by God or the Devil. After the marvelous opening of *The Lion, the Witch, and the Wardrobe*, Lewis can find no story for his world but Christian myth imposed like a straitjacket over the plot and no antagonist but that old sexist stereotype, the proud, independent, and therefore wicked, woman. Nor does George MacDonald fare much better. What to do in these wonderful Other worlds is always the problem,[8] for although reality can't be escaped (it being all there is), it can be impoverished and sooner or later the mechanical predictability of the whole awful business sends you back to such comparatively heartening works as "The Penal Colony" or "The

---

6 Virginia Woolf, "Gothic Romance," *Granite and Rainbows: Essays*, Harcourt Jovanovich (Harvest), N.Y., 1975, pp. 58–59.
7 Moorcock substitutes the purple perversities of a very-late-in-the-day Byronism with much less success.
8 It is in *Star Wars*, whose plot events are (to put it mildly) derivative. In Le Guin's *Earthsea* trilogy there is no problem because Le Guin is concerned precisely with the reality – i.e. the non-Otherness – of what at first appears to be Other. (This is the subject of *The Left Hand of Darkness*.) The first book of the trilogy ends with an explicit statement of this position: the young wizard, Ged, having called up an evil shadow and pursued it across the world, finally confronts it and is able to call it by its true name, which is "Ged." It's part of himself and must be incorporated, not destroyed. Le Guin's position on "evil" is absolutely opposite to Lewis's, Tolkien's or any other heroic fantasist's I know; it's close to existentialism or psychoanalysis. Le Guin is interested in illuminating and confronting reality *via* an invented world, not escaping from the real into an invented world. Thus she welcomes tragedy, which "heroic fantasy" avoids like the plague except in the ersatz form of Moorcockian Byronism.

Death of Ivan Ilyitch" where there is humanity, contingency, and reality.

The desire for escape is understandable. It's the supply that's spurious. Unfortunately, after Tolkien had wrung the last drop of meaning-freighted landscape out of an extremely tiny genre, the cry went up, "Now we know how to do it!" and another, "There's money in it!" and the flood began.

With orthodox heroic fantasy, one judges the quality not of books but of guided daydreams: *Lord Foul* is a daydream of Byronic suffering and self-importance in which weakness is strength and vice versa and the hero's terrible secret is leprosy (if only he'd explained it patiently in Chapter Five, three-quarters of the plot would be rendered useless and much lurid suffering avoided, but I daresay Donaldson's attitude toward probability isn't mine). It's an energetic, crude, lurid work with Tolkienesque echoes, evil entities with names like "Drool Rockworm," and a brow-smiting playing with disease only possible to the young and healthy. *Grey Mane* is a daydream of primitive, idyllic, nomad life which celebrates the beauty, prowess, wonder, glory and general worthiness of male persons in the way that only a woman can do (men know better). I hope that some day its British author will try to claim some of this admirableness for herself, but remembering Henry James' remarks about Englishwomen and their brothers (in *Portrait of a Lady*), I doubt it. This daydream is much more smoothly crafted and self-consistent than the other, but both are impenetrably formulaic, ahistorical, full of magic (*Foul*) or religious ritual (*Mane*) and almost totally devoid of economics and work, though *Mane* makes a couple of shies at trade (the only kind of work middle-class people are familiar with). Both make vague gestures in the direction of ecology, and Donaldson tries to be liberal about women but clearly doesn't know how. Chant (ever the one for self-immolation) includes in her daydream an independent, bitchy girl who dislikes male control and doesn't want to spend her life pregnant; she is "afraid of the life of a woman" and ends up dead, while the self-effacing, suffering heroine gets the man.

Lord Foul is ersatz tragedy, *Grey Mane* is ersatz history, and both are stone dead. Both are parts of a series, not surprising since life ends (its final change) and art ends (its final satisfaction) while escape – never quite satisfying enough – is condemned to tread over and over the same barren ground.

"Book World," *The Washington Post*, April 1, 1979

In Memory Yet Green: The Autobiography of Isaac Asimov, 1920–1954 (Doubleday, 732pp., $15.95). *Opus 200.* Isaac Asimov (Houghton Mifflin, 329pp., $10.95)

Science fiction readers devoted to the work of Isaac Asimov, that elder statesman of the field, will enjoy this account of his childhood, his growing up in Brooklyn, and the years in which he wrote the earliest (and most famous) of his works. Those familiar only with his popularization of science or those who don't know his work at all will probably not like the book and may even wonder what moved him to write it.

Biography is as close to impossible as art can be and two sorts of falsification are common: the bare recital of facts, in which the shape of a life gets lost, and the imposition of a novelistic "theme" from the outside. Both under- and over-interpretation are available to the third-person biographer – but what if the biographer happens also to be the subject?

Asimov has chosen the bare-facts route; after his childhood memories (which are charming) the book becomes a fairly dry list of professional facts and a considerable number of personal ones which ought to be more interesting than they are (Asimov is surprisingly candid about a good many things) but which remain uninterpreted and hence unconnected. Either the author does not want to make the effort to treat this vast mass of material as something that demands interpreting or else he modestly regards this work as merely a mine of information for some future second-stage biographer.

Where time has provided the interpretation, Asimov accepts it, and, in his account of his childhood, the young Isaac emerges as a distinct and delightful personality – as sunny, playful, and sensible as Asimov's own persona as a writer of nonfiction. His family's remembered eccentricities are lovingly presented, like his father's theories about germs and his mother's cooking. (Regarding the latter, the adult Asimov notes happily that anyone attempting to eat Eastern European Jewish cuisine without slow acclimatization is risking death by "pernicious dyspepsia," but he loves it.) There is much fascinating material here about the lives of Eastern European Jewish immigrants in the New York of the '20s and '30s, about the small businesses which drained the time and energy of whole families (the Asimovs were slaves to their seven-day-a-week candy store: a combination of newspaper stand, ice cream parlor, and miniature Woolworth's).

He talks about the asceticism of outright poverty (dental work was an impossible luxury), and the intellectual striving, describing it without explicitly pointing to it as a source for his own career.

A third-person biographer might dig much out of this book: Asimov's sheltered childhood and adolescence, his isolation (the candy store was a severe controller of his free time and thus of his social life), his situation as a favored child, his unselfconscious precocity, and his matter-of-fact training in work and the enjoyment of work. What is not here – possibly because Asimov is not conscious of how much he differs from other people in this respect – is an explanation of the extraordinary imaginativeness that produced his fiction, or the corresponding quality in that peculiar group of eccentric and poverty-stricken youngsters who created science fiction's Golden Age in the 1940s. The hard-working, precocious, naive young man described here could well have written Asimov's nonfiction. But the writer of such works as "Nightfall" or the *Foundation* series (two of the classics for which Asimov is famous) is not in this book.

Nor is he represented by much in *Opus 200*, a sampler of Asimovian fiction and nonfiction culled from the author's second 100 books. (Yes, he works hard!) *Opus 200* emphasizes nonfiction – somewhat grayly – and of the fiction the best is an excerpt from his recent novel, *The Gods Themselves*, a charming, recent story called "Good Taste," and two good science-fiction mystery stories ("Light Verse" and "Earthset and the Evening Star"). Polemical intention gives vitality to one nonfiction piece, "Lost in Mistranslation," but the rest is fairly routine science fact with a bow at history and the historical (not literary, as Asimov points out) annotation of literature. (Also a very early, entertainingly bad story, "The Weapon," is reprinted in *In Memory Yet Green*. First published under a pseudonym in *Super Science* in 1942, it was for years thought lost.)

Both of these books are useful and interesting, although the material reprinted in *Opus 200* may be found elsewhere. But neither is nearly as good throughout as the episode of *In Memory Yet Green* when Isaac, promoted to 1B2, hides at the back of his old classroom (because he likes the teacher), "hoping no one would notice me," until he is led, sobbing, into his new one. The same little Asimov cried lustily at having to walk home alone from elementary school. He was not, it seems, "frightened or unhappy. It was just the appropriate response to being alone ... a man, his heart touched at the sight of a five-year-old boy walking down the street, crying, stopped and said, 'Are you lost little boy? Where do you live?' ... I stopped crying at once, looked up at him in indignation, and said, 'Of course I'm not lost, I know where I live' ... Having put him in his place, I resumed my wailing and continued to walk down the street."

Asimov still knows where he's going, but the subjective alchemy that enables him to know (and to get there) is never revealed in *In Memory Yet Green*. It remains a useful, limited, special-audience volume rather than the fascinating human exploration it might have been.

"Book World," *The Washington Post*, May 9, 1979

On Lies, Secrets, and Silence: Selected Prose, 1966–1978. Adrienne Rich (Norton, 310pp., $13.95)

Adrienne Rich notes dryly that "the first verbal attack, slung at the woman who demonstrates a primary loyalty to herself and other women is *man-hater*." After the bad reviews of her previous prose work, *Of Woman Born*, Rich might well have extended "the invitation to men" (in Mary Daly's phrase), whether sincerely or not, out of simple self-preservation. Instead *On Lies, Secrets, and Silence* continues to offer its primary loyalties to women. The author also refuses to allow her very real compassion for men (which an astute reader will not miss) to defuse her conclusions, nor does she parade evidence of her "humanism" (a word Rich has elsewhere said she finds false and will no longer use).

On Lies, Secrets, and Silence can be seen as one woman's journey past obligatory "humanism" (early in the book Rich quotes Virginia Woolf's constant sense that male critics are her audience; "I hear them even as I write," Woolf says), to the position of a woman who does not give a damn about such voices because she is talking to women. (Robin Morgan's feminist essays in the recent *Going Too Far* chronicle the same change and comment explicitly on it.) The shift occurs halfway through the book, in 1974. The earlier Rich is capable of assuming (in "The Antifeminist Woman") that equal pay is "serious" and housework trivial; the later Rich, freed from attending to the voices that so tormented Woolf, can state, "it is the realities civilization has told (women) are unimportant, regressive, or unspeakable which prove our most essential resources."

Not a popular stand. But its uncompromising honesty frees her for some fine things, from the bitter accuracy of "Toward a Woman-centered University" to the splendid "Vesuvius at Home: The Power of Emily Dickinson" (a title taken from one of Dickinson's poems). At her best Rich is inimitable: driving through the sentimental legend of Dickinson (Rich points to examples like Ransom and MacLeish's comments on her, and the recent play, *The Belle of Amherst*) to the truth: Dickinson's three words to her niece (locking the door of her bedroom with an imaginary key), "Matty: here's freedom." Or "Husband-right and Father-right" in which Rich (as usual) says terrifying things about "the contemporary, middle-class facade of free choice, love, and partnership" and then, Heaven help us, backs her judgments up (as usual).

Inevitably the book is uneven. Among the best of the literary essays are those on Dickinson, *Jane Eyre* (although Rich scants the difficulties of the novel's ending), and the contemporary poet, Judy Grahn. The others include "Toward a Woman-centered University", "Husband-right and Father-right", and "Conditions for Work." Rich's essays on lesbianism, like the last essay in the book (a meditation on racism and women), are more promising and less complete than the others, the other subjects being matters she understands more thoroughly because they are more limited. Her history of her own development as a poet is also here ("When We Dead Awaken: Writing As Re-Vision").

As Woolf has noted, charm is considered important in a woman writer and Rich is not charming; moreover, her uncomfortable honesty takes place in an atmosphere of passionately felt tragedy. The integrity and clarity of this book are very old-fashioned virtues, as evident in her condemnation of Pablo Neruda's dishonesty (a strikingly good piece of political insight in "Caryatid: Two Columns") as in her silly attack on television (she attributes to the medium itself all the vices intellectuals used to see in the movies), or as in the too-gnomic epigrams of "Women and Honor."

It will be no surprise if this book receives the same treatment as *Of Woman Born*; those who assume that female forgiveness must inevitably be the consequence of female compassion will be especially enraged. The attack of "man-hater" will most likely be made. Rich, mentioning wife-battering, father–daughter incest, the sadism of pornography, and the forced sterilization of poor and Third World women, asks simply, "who ... hates whom."

This is a fine book to read if you want to find out.

The Magazine of Fantasy and Science Fiction, June 1979

Immortal: Short Novels of the Transhuman Future. Ed. Jack Dann (Harper & Row, New York, $9.95). *Anticipations: Eight New Stories.* Ed. Christopher Priest (Scribner's, New York, $8.95). *Ursula K. Le Guin's Science Fiction Writing Workshop: The Altered I.* Ed. Lee Harding (Berkley, New York, $3.95). *A Place Beyond Man.* Cary Neeper (Dell, New York, $1.50)

Immortality – like death – is one of the great unrealizables, powerful in artists' hands not because they are capable of saying anything about it, but because they can use it to say so much about everything else. Probably the only interesting use of the subject can be made by the religious mystics, since they use immortality as a metaphor for transcendence; thus in science fiction we have Shaw's "Ancients" (experienced, serious, memory-reliant, detached from the body) and Stapledon's "Last Men" (playful, wild, physical, paradoxical, immediate, sensuous). Without the mysticism and hence the belief in progress-as-transcendence, extrapolating from old age results not in Shaw's wonderful Ancients but in Swift's horrible Struldbrugs, while the neoteny of the Last Men decays to silly hedonism: the immortal as game-player.

In *Immortal* editor Dann has assembled four novellas in which immortality (conceived differently by each author) is neither transcendent nor particularly appealing – therefore making R. C. W. Ettinger's technophile introduction look even odder than it is. Ettinger says that human nature is radically imperfect and should be improved, but if so, are not the improvements suggested to us by the radically imperfect judgment of our radically imperfect natures also radically imperfect? Ettinger thinks not, nor does he answer the question of *who* the "we" is who will judge what constitutes improvement (Gene Wolfe does in "The Doctor of Death Island" and the answer is a chilling one). Ettinger does agree with one of the stories; both he and George Zebrowski ("Transfigured Night") disapprove of an immortality devoted to immediate sensation in the interests of wish-fulfillment. Zebrowski tries hard to avoid the fallacy of imitative form (as one of his characters comments, without the refractoriness of reality, wish-fulfillment can get pretty dull) but he can only up the ante by luridness and violence, since the story is without real conflict. The best line in it is a visiting alien's dry comment, "I am glad that you are not mobile." There are signs also that attempting to make meaningless events matter has pushed the author into forcing the tone; there are lines like "inertia imprisoned him in the chair as a desire to visit Evelyn seized him" and "He slowed suddenly." The quotes from Toffler, Ettinger, Blake, Dali, Feinberg, Plato, "Song," and Anonymous don't help; the material by Haldane does.

If Zebrowski's immortality is meaningless hedonism (based on a false dichotomy of "sensation" vs. "knowledge"), Wolfe's is grimly opposite – immortal, we are merely our old selves with all our old (and fatal) sins upon our heads. The world of "Doctor of Death Island" is the world of Wells' giant corporations, a story of drab and shining detail (the understatement and the texture work even better the second time round) in which long life – precarious as any, as the author makes clear – is simply another commodity to be controlled by ambition and corporate greed. As usual in Wolfe's stories, people do appalling things in the quietest way and technically the story's lovely, with simple (and terrifying) lines like "The book was near his head now." And as in much Wolfe, there is a delayed-action bang long after the last page, in this case the incidental destruction of an entire society. Yet the story is flawed by the moralism (not morality) that hangs over it like the shadow of Wolfe's giant spacecraft over the prison. The "poetic justice" of female jealousy is there (I suspect) merely because the author can't bear to let his protagonist go unpunished for a murder which is, also, not quite plausible.

Pamela Sargent, with less showiness than any of the others, gets more done; her version of immortality (the dullest: simple continuance) is incidental to a generation gap between the long-lived humans and their genetically changed, "rational" children, the children a fine mixture of the admirable and the unappealing, a balance Sargent attains by careful, realistic detail. "The Renewal" is a world in which the refractoriness of outside reality (and other people) looms large; it is, for just this reason, the most interesting tale of the lot. (The intractability of reality in "Death Island" is largely author-fabricated.) Sargent presents evasiveness, ordinariness, fear, and keeping a low profile as high-survival traits, though tragic ones. The (hermaphroditic) children are very good in their awful way, and it took me a while to notice the splendid things Sargent was doing with pronouns (they're not there and you don't miss them).

"Chanson Perpetuelle" by Thomas Disch, along with "Mutability" in *Anticipations* (and several other pieces in various science fiction magazines) is part of a forthcoming novel, *The Pressure of Time*. As an admirer even to idolatry of Disch's *334*, which I consider as brilliant as early H. G. Wells, I must nonetheless report that the so-far-published sections of *Time* appear to me not to be science fiction at all, but a mundane novel (in Delany's phrase, "mundus" meaning "the world") of an in-group of aging, jaded, experienced, sophisticated initiates interacting with an out-group of inexperienced, uninitiated, passionate young, the medium of action being sexual intrigue. Despite Disch's attempts to set the novel in the future, the science-fictional details (of the fragments published, at least) don't add up, and I include the section on a spaceship. Phrase by phrase Disch is a splendid writer, but his attempt to move a contemporary story into a (nebulous) future results, for me, in the kind of emptiness in which a writer's mannerisms become annoying, in this case the foreignisms and a Mauve Decade preciosity which were quite invisible in, say, *Camp Concentration*. I suspect that Disch's change of locale, from the United States to England and Europe, has disturbed that unfamiliarity-in-familiarity that is at the heart of science fiction. While even the most obvious details in *334*[1] like the dream-slow passage of those great ships, the *U.S.S. Melville* and the *U.S.S. Dana*, past the Battery evoked complex social overtones, similar details in "Chanson" like the Brighton Wall or the pudding clubs are merely embellishments on a landscape Disch already sees as strange, and hence already science-fictional. (For the transformation of modern London into the strangeness of science fiction, one must look to Michael Moorcock's Jerry Cornelius books – he doesn't do it as well as Disch does New York in *334* but he does it.) One of the difficulties of the science fiction ghetto is that of getting out of it conceptually. I would like to see the mundane novel hidden under the science fiction embellishments of *The Pressure of Time*; I suspect it would be chilly, disagreeable and impressive.

Christopher Priest's introduction to *Anticipations* falls into the same error as Disch's novel; i.e. (as Priest says) "all good science fiction hovers on the edge of being something other than science fiction." I can understand Priest's annoyance at critics' calling science fiction trash, but is it necessary to erase the mode entirely in order to be respectable? Time and again somebody in the field tries this only to come up with an indigestible cold hash of science-fiction-plus-soap-opera or the late James Blish's smeerps (call it a "smeerp" instead of a rabbit). If trendy academics say that *1984* is too good to be science fiction (as Priest reports), it doesn't help matters to agree with them by saying that anything good isn't science fiction (as Priest does). Perhaps it's the idea that science fiction ought to resemble received ideas about what "literature" is that led the editor to the first four stories in the anthology, none of which is first-rate and all of which are familiar ideas worked out in thorough, but oddly muted, detail. Robert Scheckley's

---

1 If the sections are read in the original order of publication. The "chronological" order of novel publication is aesthetically destructive. Delany recommends: "The Death of Socrates," "Emancipation," "Angoulême," "Bodies," "Everyday Life in the Later Roman Empire," and "334."

"Is *That* What People Do?" is a slight fantasy; Bob Shaw's "The Amphitheatre" is a realistically detailed (but twice-told) alien monster which ought to count for much more in the story than it does, as should the alien rescuer. Priest's own "The Negation" is pure smeerp, a fake-European allegory that could easily happen in a real country and ought to. Ian Watson's "The Very Slow Time Machine" has some nice intellectual athletics, but it sets up one of those tremendously mysterious events for which it is hard to find a plausibly tremendous explanation. Watson rings in a Messiah, which will disappoint those who remember the last line of Van Vogt's *The Weapon Shops of Isher*. Whatever blight hit the first four tales (the fear of being too vivid or lurid?) also clouds J. G. Ballard's "One Afternoon at Utah Beach," a surprisingly flat story which promises much more dislocation of reality than it finally delivers. Of Disch's "Mutability" I've already spoken.

There remain the slight, pleasant "The Greening of the Green" by Harry Harrison and the good "A Chinese Perspective" by Brian Aldiss, which backs a bit woozily into Phil Dick country – in some of its details, not in its tone, which is sprightly and optimistic.

From the other side of the world comes *Ursula K. Le Guin's Science Fiction Workshop: The Altered I*. Lee Harding, a student at the First Australian Science Fiction Writers' Workshop of 1975, has put together a potpourri of stories by students and teacher, introductions, comments, postludes, writing exercises, and general impressions of workshopping that together convey very well the whole process of the intensive science-fiction workshop for new writers. (There were even the grongs. As Le Guin exclaims, "That dolphin-torn, that grong-tormented sea!" There's always something. I remember one workshop in which it was breakfast cereals like Cream of Flax.) The nonfiction is excellent although most of the fiction suffers unavoidably from its shortness and the hurried nature of its composition. There is a first- and second-draft Le Guin story plus comments in between (interesting but minor for Le Guin). Of the others, Annis Shepherd's "Duplicates" is a vignette which needs more social background and explanation than it has (its complaint about the female predicament hasn't been fully converted into an objective, science-fictional situation); John Edward Clark's "Lonely Are the Only Ones" is another vignette, one of those frustrating, exciting situations for which you can't find a proper ending (he doesn't); and David Grigg's "Islands" and "Crippled Spinner," despite their nicely atmospheric treatment of the loneliness and beauty of space, are vignettes, not stories. Predictably, as with most young writers, the love stories are the worst in the book – in general, they point to a situation and shout "Look! Look!" – from John Edward Clark's inflatable doll in "Emily,

My Emily" to Rob Gerrand's tragic "Song and Dance" to Bruce Gillespie's sex joke, "Vegetable Love," to Stefan Vucak's feverish "Fulfillment." Randal Flyn's "Downward to the Sun" has more substance (a solid psychological speculation) but needs much more detail to bring out its feeling. (Most of the "love stories" are despairing, bitter, hopeless, or disgusted.) Of the dialogues, Andrew Whittemore's "Process" is stylized and good, but the others strike me as the too-bald ones novelists *would* write. (We playwrights know better.)

Of the other works Rob Gerrand's "The Healing Orgy" is an interesting initial situation and a good try at an imposed subject, although again a vignette and not a story, and Barbara J. Coleman's single-change tale is a clever idea restricted to one or two consequences and not the thoroughgoing revision of society that is science fiction's *sine qua non*. The only writer in the book I would actively warn is Edward Mundie whose "The Gift" commits two classic mistakes: an enormously too-long time-span and the substitution of over-abstract feeling for specific action. There remain two superior single-change stories, David Grigg's and Pip Maddern's, both of which have the authentic strangeness of science fiction. Pip Maddern is indeed a very promising writer with her atmospheric (and oddly Le Guinian) "The Ins and Outs of the Hadhya City-State" (though I never believed that the communications taboos were severe enough to keep two sane beings from communicating a secret *quite* that simple) and "The Broken Pit" which is a first-rate story by any standards: funny, appealing, and economical (I especially liked the "bang-crash stuff").

And now I'm going to step right out of that story and kick it – and something else – to pieces.

For there is this alien dwarf Filek, see, and there's the alien dwarf Garn, and he's "he" and *he's* a "he" and the Gethenians are "he" and Pip Maddern's single-change story character is "he" and I'll *bet* you that Maddern's explorer of the Hadhya city-state is a "he" (the Hadhyan is) and yet both Le Guin and Maddern are *shes*, dammit, *shes*.

So what's up?

What's up is the nominally male, normatively masculine usage that ensures that males will be the normal, the ordinary, and the neutral, and females the abnormal, special, and extraordinary all over the Galaxy – even when a female author is talking about child-like, dwarf extra-terrestrials who are (apparently) as sexless as turnips. This is not Pip Maddern's fault (or Ursula K. Le Guin's either) but surely science fiction writers, of all people, ought not to submit tamely to this wholesale theft of pronomial normativeness. Bite your tongue and write "she"; if you look at it long enough, it will actually start looking human. And for extra-terrestrials, invent. What the normative-male usage does is to insist, usually below the level of conscious awareness, that all us shes are *special* people, confined to *special* (not broadly human) functions – or that we, like Gethenians, are (sort-of) male ninety percent of the time except when we revert to being (truly) female for the purposes of that special chapter of the human story called Sex and Reproduction. (It's enough to drive one piebald.) In a world that can naively produce Jacob Bronowski's "The Ascent of Man" (two of my writer friends call it "The Ascent of Guess Who" and "The Ascent of You Know Who") how does "she" enter the verbal world of science fiction when not pitchforked there by feminists or kept on the sidelines as an accessory for the special-topics business?

Simple: The Special Topic is expanded to overshadow all human activity.

This is what Cary Neeper does in *A Place Beyond Man* (a Bronowskiesque title, surely). "Tandra Grey," Neeper's heroine (and a Harlequin-romance name if I ever heard one), although ostensibly a biologist recruited by aliens to save Earth, really spends more than two hundred pages teasing the bejezus out of two yummy alien males: one humanoid, rational, mild, and ultra-controlled (but vulnerable) and one amphibian, explosive, sensual, and all over delectable green feathers (but also vulnerable). Neeper's biology backgrounds are detailed and she has imaginative energy, but she also brings in a Hollywood tot who talks baby-ese, indulges in a point-of-view that wanders all over the place, and goes on a lot about a vaguely conceived "ecology" (anti-greed and anti-shortsightedness) which is Neeper's substitute for politics. *Place* is, in fact, stupefyingly apolitical, since Neeper is not really interested in saving Earth from ecological disaster but in female erotic fantasy. She's fairly good at it, it's fun, and it's certainly a relief from the plethora of male erotic fantasy in literature (I also enjoy it much more, naturally, although neither kind is better or worse *per se* than the other).

But *what* a fantasy!

For the erotics of *Place* is the classical anti-genital, feminine "romance" – libido as frustration. Time after time the characters indulge in super-heated hanky-panky only to roll over and go to sleep, frustrating the reader beyond endurance (if this is the direction you frustrate in). Twice the heroine and an alien male strip and feel each other all over (no, I am not making this up) after which one of them remarks, ah yes, our species are very different, and they go placidly away. In a modern comedy like *MASH*, such goings-on would lead to heavy breathing in the supply room, and although writers aren't obliged to put erotics into science fiction at all (though I don't mind if they give me fantasies *I* like; I'm as placable as the next critic) it does seem reasonable to ask that horniness shall appear *as such*, not distorted into the super-subtle analysis of non-existent emotion (this sort of thing occupies a lot of room in *Place*) or endless physical teasing.

The heroine never gets together with one alien; she does with the other only after a marriage so monogamous it makes early Heinlein look like Hugh Hefner[2] and then after 221 pages of torrid build-up:

> ... the joy of conscious passion swept him ... into full, welcome release as their bodies sought and found each other in easy acceptance. (p. 222)

Pfaw.

Neeper didn't invent this kind of "romantic" fantasy any more than Poul Anderson (for example) is personally responsible for the eerily homosexual overtones of *The Star Fox* – both writers could hardly avoid them, since they are floating about in the cultural atmosphere – and Anderson, in addition, is certainly capable (like Michael Moorcock in his heroic romances) of putting his readers on. But writers ought to question the Blue Meanies that turn up in their typewriters, not just accept them gratefully. The anti-genital sexual romance is a natural female response to sexism, but it's self-destructive (it also muddles everything up). If Tandra and her alien, Conn, could only get it on by page 20, not only could we have the erotic fun, we (and they) could also go on to other things and Cary Neeper might get to a place "beyond man" in truth where the Love and Sex specialty isn't the only thing the shes can do, and everyone can appear in all *their* variety, *person* doing what *per* wishes with *per* life, *na* proud of *nan, naself,* and *na* life.[3]

---

2 He will be monogamous but she won't, a piece of *chutzpah* of which the author seems placidly unaware.

3 The pronouns are from Marge Piercy's science fiction novel, *Woman on the Edge of Time* and June Arnold's *The Cook and the Carpenter*. The usages become natural in the long works in question, although they would have the effect of exoticism in a short one, an effect a science fiction writer might well want in certain circumstances. The feminine-preferred is another possibility, one which would say a good deal about the society that used it. The masculine-preferred says much about our society but nothing (for example) about Maddern's aliens. When it becomes visible as our usage, it's distracting. Of course pronouns are by no means the major part of sexism, even linguistic sexism (which is not the major part of sexism), but words are a writer's business. (Marge Piercy once fought with magazine editors for weeks over an article in which she had things like "What will Man be like in the twenty-first century? She will be compassionate ..." and so on.)

When we were everybody: a lost feminist utopia

Herland: A Lost Feminist Utopian Novel. Charlotte Perkins Gilman (Pantheon, New York, 1979, 147pp., $8.95; paper, $2.95)

The year is 1917. A "big steam yacht" with a "specially-made motor-boat" and a "'disassembled' biplane" starts on a secret expedition to discover a mysterious, mountain-enclosed country hidden in a remote and savage corner of the globe. On board are three young Americans: an athletic millionaire who says "Gosh!" a lot, quotes Kipling, and whose ideas about women are "the limit," and his two college chums, a sentimental Southerner who believes in gallantry and is a "good boy," and the narrator, a cocky sociologist, who is full of dogmatism about his ultra-modern profession. But what they find is neither King Kong nor a plesiosaur doing Heaven knows what to a beautiful girl in a chromium bathing suit; it is Herland, Charlotte Perkins Gilman's paradise of free women.

Gilman's feminist Utopia, written sixty-four years ago and never before available in book form (it was serialized in her monthly magazine *The Forerunner*, which Gilman wrote entirely by herself from November 1909 through December 1916), bears a striking resemblance to the feminist Utopias written in the United States during the last ten years. Like them it is classless, cooperative, peaceful, and in harmony with the natural world. Like them it diffuses the maternal role. Like them it is passionately concerned with reclaiming the public world for women (an enterprise to which Gilman dedicated her life). Her Utopia has an ancient Greek flavour, which gives the delicious freedom of Herland (a world in which women go everywhere, do everything, are everyone) a cleanliness and orderliness both pleasant and odd to modern eyes (our landscapes are wilder, our characterizations more complex, our ideas of the possible more bitter and more limited). There is the primitive delight of wish-fulfilment, i.e. escorting American men all over Herland (the book follows the classic Utopian pattern of lots of tours and discussions) and hearing them say, "Yes, you're right. You're absolutely right. Feminism is the hope of the world." (Several times, indeed, the narrator calls his Herland love, Ellador, a "wonder-woman" – did Charles Moulton, creator of *Wonder Woman* comics, read this book?) There is also immense, sly humor (those tours and discussions are booby-trapped) from Ellador's comment that Herlanders aren't accustomed to horrible ideas ("We haven't any," she says simply) to her enthusiastic praise of romantic, heterosexual marriage:

> "There is something very beautiful in the idea," she admitted ... as if she were discussing life on Mars. "This climactic expression, which, in all the other life-forms, has but the one purpose, has with you become specialized to higher, purer, nobler uses. It has – I judge from what you tell me – the most ennobling effect on character ... you have a world full of continuous lovers ... always living on that high tide of supreme emotion which we had supposed to belong only to one season and one use. And you say it has other results, stimulating all high creative work. That must mean floods, oceans of such work, blossoming from this intense happiness of every married pair! It is a beautiful idea!"
>
> She was silent, thinking. So was I.

Yet Herland is far from perfect. For one thing, unlike modern feminists working in this vein, Gilman is an open racist. More obvious in her other work, her racism is here present mainly as the white solipsism which makes Herland "Aryan" – though this decision does have the amusing effect of presenting the explorers with transformed versions of the Gibson Girls they would have been likely to meet back home.

Herland, unlike its modern cousins, is also a world without eroticism.

In her otherwise thoughtful introduction, Ann J. Lane is evasive about this issue, trying to turn into feminist theory what I believe to be the ancient female attempt to escape from the heterosexual institution by insisting that sensuality is not really important, and that it is (or ought to be) "contained" by love. In *Of Women and Economics* Gilman speaks of "excessive sex-attraction" and "excessive indulgence" and maintains that humanity's "health and happiness" are being ruined by this "morbid" and "unnatural" excess.[1] The cause? An excessive degree of sex-distinction. Her biological reasoning is false (she seems to expect only one sexual season in human life and that much later than puberty) but her tactics are clear. If excessive sex-indulgence can be linked to excessive sex-distinction, then Gilman will have secured women's freedom both from gender roles and the use of sexuality to harass and hurt and this without selfishness, separatism, lesbianism, or a real critique of heterosexuality as an institution.

The worst harm is done when the conditions change but the trade-off

---

1 Charlotte Perkins Gilman, *Women and Economics*, Harper Torchbooks, New York, 1966.

(sensuality for freedom) continues. A recent lesbian review of *The Joy of Lesbian Sex* (admittedly a somewhat nutty and confused book) ended with the narrator's stiff and self-righteous declaration that few of us "have such a cold attitude towards our bodies." We have, in the past, met so much coercion masquerading as permission that even real permission still looks like coercion. (If the book has one virtue, it's the abundant permission it gives women simply *to be sexual*, not loving, not affectionate, not "in love," but simply lustful.)

Gilman, stuck with the trade-off of sensuality for freedom, creates a Utopia with a gap in its passions. She tries to fill the gap, dramatically speaking, by emphasizing the passion of motherhood to the point where I (along with the American *macho* millionaire) wished the Herlanders would shut up about the subject. This emphasis may have been a reaction to her own situation – she had been violently attacked in the press, at the time of her divorce, for having agreed that Gilman's small daughter should live with her father and his new wife (a close friend of both Gilman and the little girl). It's certainly a clever way of answering anti-feminists who insist that motherhood is incompatible with public life (in Herland public life *is* broadened motherhood). And it is an inexpressible relief for a reader to at last enter an imaginary world in which babies exist – everywhere! – and such lovely ones. Gilman knows what babies enjoy as she knows – mostly – what grown women need, especially life's most crucial necessity – pockets.

Letter

Dear Editors,

In *Feminist Review* number five, in my review of Charlotte Perkins Gilman's *Herland*, I mentioned *Herland's* white solipsism but quickly passed on to a subject that interested me more, thus demonstrating some pretty obvious white solipsism of my own. The matter is all the worse because Gilman wasn't merely a thoughtless racist, but a genuine, explicit bigot, complete with nineteenth-century eugenics theories. In fact, Gilman's whole biological package – which she didn't create singlehandedly, of course – is the standard nineteenth-century line, from her views on the hierarchy of races to her idea that excessive sex is harmful, to the notion that females "select from competing males" (untrue for our chimp and monkey cousins, by the way).

It's not only painful to see one of our (*our*?) heroines, so sensitive to oppression-by-sex, turning around and pulling the same act on someone else; it's also extremely frustrating *not* to be able to accept *Herland* unreservedly that one (*who?*) tends to pretend that Gilman's racism is minor or doesn't matter or doesn't need talking about. The historical trade-off made by parts of the women's movement in the nineteenth/early twentieth century (we're female, but the "right" color/class) never really works in the long run. And the subject of how white women don't "see" racism when it gets in the way of something they want to enjoy is surely as important (at least) as Gilman's understandable evasion about sex.

When we were everybody. Well, not *exactly* everybody ...

Frontiers, **IV:1, 1979**

Gyn/Ecology: The Metaethics of Radical Feminism. Mary Daly (Boston: Beacon Press, 1979, 485pp., $14.95)

That's not an issue.
That's not an issue *any more*.
Then why do you keep on bringing it up?
You keep on bringing it up because you are crazy.
You keep on bringing it up because you are hostile.
You keep on bringing it up because you are intellectually irresponsible.
You keep on bringing it up because you are shrill, strident, and self-indulgent.
How can I possibly listen to anyone as crazy, hostile, intellectually irresponsible, shrill, strident, and self-indulgent as you are?
Especially since what you're talking about is simply not an issue.
(Any more.)
Mary Daly has written a wild, whirling, terrifying, ecstatic, haggard[1] book. In *Beyond God the Father* Daly was reasonable, temperate, civilized,

---

1 Merriam-Webster: "haggard: intractable, willful, wanton, unchaste, especially a woman reluctant to yield to wooing."

and continually emphasized in the most charmingly responsible way that she was speaking to men as well as women; between that and *Gyn/Ecology* a great deal of life and consciousness (and undoubtedly the book reviews of *Of Women Born* et al.) has happened; the result is a quantum leap that will be seen, beyond the shadow of a doubt, as "anti-male." Daly says so herself and adds dryly: "Even the most cautious and circumspect feminist writings are described that way" (p. 29). So what the hell. *Gyn/Ecology* does not bother to make the usual ritual gestures of deference, liberalism, compassion, humanism, and whatnot ("I'm not angry! I'm not threatening! Don't kill me!") As Daly says, the "primary intent of women who choose to be present to each other ... is not an invitation to men" (p. x). The way in which the glossy surface of patriarchy has closed over the feminism of only a few years ago is amazing: "Of course all that was true six or seven years ago, but we've taken care of those questions and it's *very rude* to mention them now. Besides, the women's movement is dead." *Gyn/Ecology* is a terrifying book because of its bad manners, because of its poetry, because it rips through the thin veils of the accommodations under which we all shelter, and because it threatens us with a return to the basics – and the anger and terror they rouse.

Gyn/Ecology has two faces, one a description and celebration of the feminist journey into authenticity, into "new space" (not colonized or conquered space but newly created space), and the other an investigation into patriarchal myth, which Daly finds always the same, whatever the culture. "Wrenching back some wordpower" (p. 11) is one method for doing both, a method both poetic and indescribable, since it depends so heavily on the whole context of the book. The simplest example of such techniques is denunciatory punning like "The Godfather" or the trinity as "the consummate conglomerate" (p. 75); the most rich and complex is Daly's use of the word "spinning" which assimilates the spinning of the Fates, galaxies, spiders, argonautic shells, whirlpools, the whirling of prophecy, and spiralling organic motion of all kinds into an image of free-being-traveling so profound that one must read the whole book to appreciate it. As Daly says of Scylla and Charybdis, "Spinsters are at home in whirlpools" (p. 377). And after two careful readings I'm still not sure what she means by the female "deep Background" which has been masked by the monodimensional male Foreground (though the usage feels right) or why her search for the archaic/obsolete meanings of words – a search she knows perfectly well does not "prove" anything – *works*. The book is one long crime of Methodicide (one Daly highly recommends, since one of the sins of patriarchy is Methodolatry).

The mythic reclaiming of the cosmos for women, the ecstatic journey and its dangers, culminates in a exorcism of the Deadly Sins of the Father, a marvelously funny piece and one it would be highly educational to see enacted at, say, the Modern Language Association annual conference, the American Psychiatric Association, and other patriarchally sacred occasions. But *Gyn/Ecology* is also about material extremely painful to read: Indian widow-murder, the crippling of female feet in China, and (contemporary) female genital mutilation in Africa. Daly's chapters on the European witch murders and American gynecology/psychotherapy aren't exactly cheery, either, but the material here is at least more familiar and hence less freshly horrifying.

But surely I mean *suttee*, foot *binding*, and *female circumcision*, not these loaded words "murder", "crippling," and "mutilation"?

No. I don't and she doesn't. It's a tribute to patriarchal conditioning that calling these horrors by their right names is frightening. Like the women in women's studies classes who insist that "the women who died in *suttee* had 'free choice'" (p. 123), the accurate naming of atrocities against women makes women very uneasy. Surely it can't be that bad! What sort of a world are we living in? *Is Daly trying to start a war*? But the war is already going on: suttee *is* murder, foot binding *is* crippling – it breaks bones and the rotting flesh continues lifelong, while genital mutilation is torture for which there is really no adequate name. According to Freud, in patriarchy it is men who suffer from the fear of having their penises cut off. Oddly enough, in patriarchy it is women who (still, in parts of the world) suffer from the fact of having their clitorises cut or burned off or their inner vaginal lips sewn together until healed shut, then cut open (with a knife) for intercourse at marriage, sewn together again, cut open again for delivery after pregnancy, sewn shut again, and so on lifelong.

Worse than the descriptions of the phenomena themselves (to readers of *Gyn/Ecology* who are presumably physically secure from them) is the obliteration, the glossing-over, of both native and imported horrors in Western scholarship or their transformation into something harmless, quaint, or (Heaven help us) erotic. Daly documents this patriarchal doublethink. If any section of her work betrays personal heat beyond the usual accusatory punning, it's her talk of witch burnings and the church[2] and a few parts of the section on gynecology/therapy. Daly is (was) a Catholic theologian who's had her face rubbed in the church's particular brand of sandpaper; what can one say, after all, about "archbishop Roberts (one of the 'radicals' at the Second Vatican Council)" who had lived for years in India and told the author, in the mid-sixties, that "*suttee* is the 'logical

---

2 Not the documentation of torture or the anger against modern authorities like Zilboorg but, for example, the use of Montague Summers, who is too easy a target.

conclusion' of female nature" (p. 120)? Daly calls modern medicine awful names, and she also documents a widespread belief in American medicine's complicity in the reconstruction of real women into The Totalled Woman or fembot (both phrases hers): breasts and uterus automatically removed as "breeding grounds" for cancer, menopause prevented by estrogen (which increases the chances of cancer), and so on. This section would be more telling if Daly remembered to remind us that J. Marion Sims, the revered "architect of the vagina," who performed dozens of operations on black slave women in the 1840s and thirty on an indigent Irishwoman in the 1850s (to develop and perfect his surgical discoveries), did so *without anesthesia*. Nor would it be amiss to see Freud's theory of the double orgasm (without anatomical evidence, but eagerly adopted) as a psychological attempt at African infibulation (the bride's vulva sewn-to-order for the size of her fiancé's penis), both being a reconstruction of female sexuality into male-designed artifact.

Why this "Sado-Ritual Syndrome"? (Daly's words.)

She contends (and I think she is right) that the fundamental myth of patriarchy is Goddess-murder – her earliest example is the story of the killing of Tiamat by Marduk – and that this murder is daily re-enacted in patriarchy on the bodies and minds of living women. Daly traces cross-cultural similarities, including the obsession with "purity" and the use of women as "token torturers." Thus it is *women* who broke the bones of little Chinese girls' feet (otherwise no *man* would marry them), *women* who mutilated African girls' genitals (otherwise no *man* would marry or sleep with them), *women* who advertise cosmetics on television or write books on how to be properly totalled, and so on.

I could not at first understand Daly's insistence that femininity has nothing to do with women, that femininity – what a bizarre assertion! – is a male trait, and yet she is right. We're still all too prone to talk as if "femininity" were produced by the selective obliteration of some natural female traits and preservation of others or the exaggeration of some traits at the expense of others. But Daly is more perceptive: *Femininity is a male projection of a solution to problems in the male situation, which is then imposed on women*. That is why Daly states that she will no longer use the word "androgyny." Femininity is not an incomplete part of anyone's character but a man-made mess from the word go. Daly is not extending an invitation to men and so does not explore the male psychology involved but Jean Baker Miller's *Towards a Psychology of Women*[3] does. Miller says the problems are vulnerability, sexuality, and dependence. I would add the terror of

---

3 Jean Baker Miller, *Towards a Psychology of Women*, Beacon Press, Boston, 1976, pp. 21–26.

freedom and the problem of evil – both of which are operative in any situation where oppressor–oppressed live as close together as men and women often do; under such conditions, the distortions that are required exact immense psychological and social energy.

In short, *the primary project of patriarchy is to get rid of women*, and failing that somewhat impractical aim – besides, if you get rid of your scapegoat once and for all, you'll only have to find a new one – to transform real, living women into the nonhuman, the subhuman, the merely-convenient, the all-but-nonexistent. Certainly this is what the myths and legends say, from the killing of Tiamat to the clear-eyed serene, sexless, maternally vigilant madonnas used to sell cold medicine on TV.

Daly also documents the male institutions' stealing of female functions, from churchly maternity (she is very funny on this) to an equally witty comparison of astronauts-who-are-fetuses (the famous Russian–American handshake in space) with fetuses-who-are-astronauts[4] (Robert Byrn's attempt to prevent abortions in New York by legally representing all fetuses due for abortion in the city).

Gyn/Ecology is not just a horror show. It is also a stunning description of a feminist journey into new space, sometimes rhapsodic, sometimes a warning. For one thing, Daly is magnificently dead-set against self-sacrifice. She also warns in the strongest terms against anti-intellectualism while cheerfully tossing academicism out the window. In her introduction she admonishes us gravely: "This book contains Big Words, even Bigger than *Beyond God the Father*, for it is written for big strong women, out of respect for strength. Moreover, I've made some of them up ..." (p. xi).

Perhaps the best things here are not even the ideas that can be detached and pointed to, but the texture of thought that *is* feminism, female in its imagery, feminist-in-its-sharing. In her introduction Daly talks about women's oral tradition, quoting Deena Metzger: "And why do you persist in thinking only one of us can use it. Shall we footnote every thought and breath ... The first man on the moon ... That isn't our game, is it? That only the first counts. Each idea they devise gets used up so quickly ... No wonder..." (p. xiv).

This is a long, hard, complicated, repetitive book whose use of language may well annoy readers the first time around. It may also frighten the dickens out of them. It is nonetheless a tremendously important work. Near the end of the book Mary Daly almost succeeds in breaking/freeing language (poets must read this book: they'll be dissatisfied with it but it will start them in the right direction). It's almost impossible to convey the

---

4 As Daly points out, both metaphors see the fetus as controlling the mother, who is envisioned as unconscious and inanimate.

effect of anything in *Gyn/Ecology* out of context – oh, how you're going to *hate* this book the first time around![5] – but here is a statement near the end, advice to the book's readers and to us all:

> "In the beginning was not the word. In the beginning is the hearing." (p. 408)

Listen.

Frontiers, IV: 2, 1979

The Mermaid and the Minotaur: Sexual Arrangements and Human Malaise. Dorothy Dinnerstein (Harper & Row, New York, 1976, 288pp., $3.95)

Dorothy Dinnerstein's *The Mermaid and the Minotaur* is not a popular book. It has crept into public notice relatively without ballyhoo. This statement is partly an excuse for writing a review, in 1979, of a book originally published in 1976 and out in paperback a year later, partly a criticism of reviewers (why didn't they sing under my pillow, flag my car down on the highway?), and partly praise for the Old Girls' network that stubbornly insisted on plugging it anyway ("Haven't you read ...?," "Maude says ...," "I found this book ..."). The vocabulary of critical praise has become so inflated nowadays that when I read Sara Blackburn's comment on the back cover of *MM* that the intellectual excitement of reading Dinnerstein is comparable to that of reading early Freud, I merely "humphed," and yet Sara Blackburn is telling the truth. Dorothy Dinnerstein's argument is so brilliant, so ingenious, so wide, so novel, *and so obvious* that I can't trust myself to do it justice, especially in a few paragraphs. What she has done

---

5 Two careful readings did not convince me: then I suddenly woke up a week later, dazzled, shouting, "It's true, It's all true!"

is to unify biology, history, and psychology in the interest of explaining not "the cause" of sexism but its profoundest motivations in both men and women. In this union of Darwin, Marx, and Freud (so to speak) none is reduced to the status of epiphenomenon or made a "reflection" of any of the others. Dinnerstein has taken one very obvious fact and much of the not-so-obvious thought of the past century-and-a-half and fused the lot in a rare intellectual triumph. To recognize that sexism is not all force and fraud seems to leave as an alternative only the craven surrender to "biology" – or rather, the kind of quasi-biology that asserts that either women are genetically inferior or men genetically horrid. Dinnerstein goes beyond such silly-simple notions to a conclusion which produced in me all the embarrassing hilarity of finally discovering the haystack after you've spent decades looking for the needle in it. The things this book explains! For example, the uneasy, unstable co-existence of feminism with protest against class privilege – and why the latter has always been so much more visible (when visible at all) than the former; why, when force and fraud are subtracted from sexism, sexism still somehow remains (while when force and fraud are subtracted from the hierarchy of class, nothing remains); why (although Dinnerstein only implies this) the modern male Left so often appeals from the unnaturalness of class domination to the supposed naturalness of the family or of the relations between the sexes; and above all why the astounding obviousness of Dinnerstein's explanation has been so long ignored by so many supposedly acute thinkers (she doesn't say this but the corollary is there).

The power of this book to illuminate more than its own data is extraordinary: Dinnerstein can explain not only much of the course of human history (which she chooses for its power to exemplify her thesis) but also random events, like best-sellers, which she did not choose and knows nothing about. Contemporary with my copy of *MM* (same week, same store, many more recommendations, though not by the same people) was a wretchedly self-contradictory best-seller called *My Mother/My Self* by Nancy Friday, as good an illustration of Dinnerstein's thesis as could be found anywhere. *My Mother/My Self* first denies and then makes the very assumptions Dinnerstein pinpoints: everything is Mommy's fault; women are women's worst enemies; men are ineffectual, glamorous presences who initiate nothing and take all their cues from women (i.e. Mother is all-powerful); and that the cure for all this is maternal self-sacrifice of the usual, impossibly angelic sort, as well as an awful lot of (heterosexual, naturally) sex.

Popular culture tends to produce these caricatures from time to time, and yet the striking thing about Friday's book is not its abundant foolishness (she calls Jane Fonda's life "sexless" and gets her psychoanalytic theory from an informant she calls "Dr. Robertiello" while he addresses her as "Nancy"), but its blatant summing up of a certain kind of female American thought. Every women's studies teacher, for example, knows the female student who comes into her office and announces defiantly *that she's going to get married* – the world is still full of girls who think that heterosexual alliances with men represent a form of rebellion against sexless Mommy. How do these young women imagine their mothers ended up where *they* were? Yet the hope persists that heterosexual activity (a little wilder than stuffy Mom's) will provide access to the men's freer, wider world. Mother's function as the forewoman who polices Daughter's sexuality, in many American families, gives some color to this notion – that an alliance with men is an alliance against Mother – and yet these girls must have at least the suspicion that Mom made the same bargain. And surely they know that heterosexual alliance can't confer membership in the men's world but only a place (Mother's place, in fact) on its sidelines. But they don't. And so they end up married, leading the same life as Mother, or – if unlucky – a worse one with less bargaining power. And *their* daughters repeat the process. Sexuality, asked to bear too much social and emotional freight, is often one of the casualties.[1]

Dorothy Dinnerstein explains why. Crucially, she takes the dictum that it's all Mommy's fault and goes one step beyond – to locating the "fault" in the inescapable conditions of human infancy and early childhood (no matter whose hand is rocking the cradle) and comes up with an analysis a review ought not to spoil by possible misrepresentation. As Dinnerstein notes, without female collusion patriarchy would collapse, and although feminist theorists have traced much of the male emotional investment in the scapegoating of women, no one has illuminated so powerfully why

---

1 It's tempting to call this the "Zelda Bargain." Surely the notion that heterosexual alliance with men will free one from the stuffy, ordinary life Mother had to live was one of the illusory promises acted upon by Zelda Sayre, the prettiest girl in Montgomery, Alabama, whose rebellion took the form of popularity with men and sexual "wildness" (of a sort daring enough in her own day) and who later, as Mrs. Scott Fitzgerald, spent much of her adult life locked in a mental asylum against her will, dying finally in an asylum fire. Her most earnest wish, near the end of her life, was the very unromantic one of being able to earn her own living. The Fitzgeralds, mutually destructive, lived out Dinnerstein's thesis: possession of the magic, feminine figure (of whom he has many fictional portraits in his work) did not make Scott happy and the heterosexual alliance did not set Zelda free. Dinnerstein actually argues that what a woman acts out in this bargain is both a wish to enter the male domain of freedom (literally so because it is out in the public world and magically so because it is seen as free of Mother's early authority) and the project of lending her person to "getting back at mama." But as Anne Sexton remarked, she *is* mama. The bargain is unworkable because it is self-contradictory, for both men and women.

and how women lend themselves to the same activity. One of the things Dinnerstein thoroughly understands is how pervasive the sexist double standard is and how a particular act, done by Joan, carries a very different meaning from the same act done by John – in short how power, selfishness, and insensitivity, seen as merely unethical or wrong when present in men, become monstrous, overwhelmingly, wickedly *unnatural* when displayed by women – and that both men and women see things this way. It's possible now (and has been at times in the past) to admire female strength if such strength is seen as nurturing (that is, something that exists for others) but female wealth, power, domination, and glory are unqualifiedly evil if nonnurturant (that is, practiced for the gratification of the woman herself) even if we immediately add honesty and competence to the list. Dinnerstein's explanations and arguments are cross-cultural here and very convincing.

I should not keep the central arguments of books a mystery, but any brief statement of the theme of *MM* is misleading. This book is a linchpin of feminist analysis and one of the most exciting (and simply useful) intellectual triumphs of the feminist movement. Dinnerstein is pessimistic in a tough-minded way that inspires a paradoxical hope in the reader – things may be unfixable (as she suspects), but surely such brilliant understanding augurs something better than despair.

MM is not a long, footnote-freighted, scholarly work but rather a distillation of years of thought. Characteristic of sexist discourse is a contention both that feminism is a protest against the human condition (that is, sexism is natural and immutable) and that it is irrelevant to the human condition (that is, trivial). Dinnerstein derives sexism right from the human condition, said human condition not imagined as a mystical unity involving the entire status quo but as an interlocking set of carefully defined, specific phenomena, in particular the uniquely human combination of self-reflective intelligence and the dependency of a prolonged infancy. She also indicates how the project of ending sexism not only joins with, but also subsumes the project of the destruction of tyranny and the dissolution of the neurotic knot formed by the human hatred of carnality, the human fear of death, and the human overloading of the unique human capacity for enterprise or labor. Her prescription is a grim one: human beings will grow up when the possibility of scapegoating is not available. (There is a specific means for doing this, by the way, although Dinnerstein can't provide a foolproof way of enforcing the means, but it would be foolish to take the book to task for not providing everything.) Dinnerstein believes that it may be too late to keep the human species from the "massive, immediate threat" of extinction (a threat she links carefully and very persuasively with sexism) and yet:

> Whether understanding makes a difference or not, we must try to understand ... To fight intelligently, armed with your central resource, which is passionate curiosity ... is for me the human way to live until you die. (p. viii)

Let us, rather, hope for a rosier future for a species of which one member could produce this brilliant, heartening, necessary, Galilean book.

Author's Note
Although I no longer think that Dinnerstein's theory explains "women's" lives – it's neither cross-class nor cross-cultural, nor does it apply to any but the white professional middle class of her generation and mine – still as a description of a particular class at a particular time in the United States it will do well enough. I can't regard it now with the enthusiasm I displayed in this review, though.

The Magazine of Fantasy and Science Fiction, November 1979

In the February 1979 issue, Joanna Russ wrote a column raking over the "barren ground" of current fantasy (and, especially, heroic fantasy). Her comments generated dozens of letters of vehement disagreement (some were published in the July issue), and the column below was written in response to those letters.

Critics seem to find it necessary, at least once in a career, to write a statement defending criticism *per se*. Shaw, Pauline Kael, Eric Bentley, and James Blish have all done it. That I'm doing it too doesn't prove I'm in the same league, but it does indicate the persistence of the issues involved and that they occur outside, as well as inside, science fiction.

I have tried to speak to general issues rather than "defend" my own criticism. Issues are, in any case, more important than personalities, although there is a (small) section of fandom which sees in aesthetic or political disagreement nothing but personal squabbling motivated by envy. It's not for me to judge how good my criticism is; if enough readers think it's bad, and the editor thinks so too, presumably he'll stop printing it, although writing book reviews (except for places like *The New York Times*) is underpaid, overworked, and a labor of love. The problem is usually to recruit reviewers, not discourage them.

Here are some of the complaints that keep coming up:

1. *Don't shove your politics into your reviews. Just review the books.*

I will – when the authors keep politics out of their stories. But they never do; in fact, it seems absolutely impossible to write anything without immediately making all sorts of assumptions about what human nature is, what good and bad behavior consists of, what men ought to be, what women ought to be, which states of mind and character are valuable, which are the opposite, and so on. Once fiction gets beyond the level of minimal technical competence, a reviewer must address these judgments of value. Generally readers don't notice the presence of familiar value judgments in stories, but do notice (and object to) unfamiliar ones as "political". Hence arises the insistence (in itself a very vehement, political judgment) that art and politics have nothing to do with one another, that artists ought to be "above" politics, and that a critic making political comments about fiction is importing something foreign into an essentially neutral area. But if "politics" means the relations of power that obtain between groups of people, and the way these are concretely embodied in personal relations, social institutions, and received ideas (among which is the idea that art ought not to be political), then such neutrality simply doesn't exist. Fiction which isn't openly polemical or didactic is nonetheless chock-full of politics. If beauty in fiction bears any relation to truth (as Matthew Arnold thought) then the human (including social and political) truth of a piece of fiction matters for aesthetic reasons. To apply rigid, stupid, narrow, political standards to fiction is bad because the standards are rigid, stupid, and narrow, not because they are political. For an example of (to my mind) profound, searching, brilliant, political criticism, see Jean-Paul Sartre's *Saint Genet*.

2. *You don't prove what you say; you just assert it.*

This statement is, I think, based on a cognitive error inculcated (probably) by American high school education. The error is that all proofs must be of the "hard" kind, i.e. cut-and-dried and susceptible of presentation in syllogistic form. An acquaintance with the modern philosophy of science would disabuse people of this notion; even a surprising amount of scientific proof is not of this kind. As philosophers since Plato have been pointing out, aesthetic and moral matters are usually not susceptible of such "hard" proof.

3. *Then your opinion is purely subjective.*

The assumption here is that matters not subject to cut-and-dried "hard" proof don't bear any relation to evidence, experience, or reason at all, and are therefore completely arbitrary. There is considerable indirect evidence one can bring against this view. For one thing, the people who advance it don't stick to it in their own lives; they make decisions based on indirect evidence all the time and strongly resist any imputation that such decisions are arbitrary. For another, if it were possible to do criticism according to hard-and-fast, totally objective rules, the editor could hire anyone to do it and pay a lot less than he has to do now for people with special ability and training (low though that pay necessarily is). It's true that the apparatus by which critics judge books is subjective in the sense of being inside the critic and not outside, unique, and based on the intangibles of training, talent, and experience. But that doesn't *per se* make it arbitrary. What can make it seem arbitrary is that the whole preliminary process of judgment, if you trace it through all its stages, is co-extensive with the critic's entire education. So critics tend to suppress it in reviews (with time and training most of it becomes automatic, anyway). Besides, much critical thinking consists of *gestalt* thinking, or the recognition of patterns, which does occur instantaneously in the critic's head, although without memory, experience, and the constant checking of novel objects against templates-in-the-head (which are constantly being revised in the light of new experience) it could not occur at all.[1] Hence angry readers can make the objections above, or add:

4. *Everyone's entitled to his own opinion.*

Have you noticed how often people say "I feel" instead of "I think" or (God forbid) "I know"? Kids who discover "It's a free country!" at seven graduate to "Everyone's entitled to his own opinion" by fourteen. The process of intimidation by which young people are made to feel humanly worthless if they don't appreciate "great literature" (literature the teacher often doesn't understand or can't explain)[2] is one of the ghastly facts of American education. Some defenses against this experience take the form of asserting there's no such thing as great art, some that whatever moves one intensely *is* great art. Both are ways of asserting the primacy and

---

1 I used to inform people of the endings of television plays (before the endings happened) until my acquaintances gently but firmly informed me they would rather the endings came as a surprise. When asked how I knew what was coming by friends who enjoyed such an odd talent (and some do) I could explain only part of the time. The cues people respond to in fiction or drama are complex and people are not always fully conscious of them.

2 Or oddities that entered the curriculum decades before and refuse to be dislodged, like "To a Waterfowl." For some reason students often end up with the most sophisticated, flawed, or least accessible works of great writers: twelve-year-olds reading *Romeo and Juliet*, for example, or *Silas Marner*.

authenticity of one's own experience, and that's fine. But whatever you (or I) like intensely isn't, just because of that, great anything, and the literary canon, although incomplete and biased, is not merely an insiders' snobbish conspiracy to make outsiders feel rotten. (Although it is certainly used that way far too often.)

The problem with literature and literary criticism is that there is no obvious craft involved, so people who wouldn't dream of challenging a dance critic's comments on an *assoluta's* line or a music critic's estimate of a *prima donna's* musicianship are conscious of no reason not to dismiss mine on J. R. R. Tolkien. We're all dealing with language, after all, aren't we? But there is a very substantial craft involved here, although its material isn't toes or larynxes. And some opinions are worth a good deal more than others.

5. *I knew it. You're a snob.*

Science fiction is a small country which for years has maintained a protective standards-tariff to encourage native manufactures. Many readers are, in fact, unacquainted with the general canon of English literature or the standards of criticism outside our own small field. Add to this the defensiveness so many people feel about high culture and you get the wholesale inflation of reputations James Blish lambastes in *The Issue At Hand*. Like him, I believe that somebody has to stop handing out stars and kisses; if "great writer" means Charles Dickens or Virginia Woolf (not to mention William Shakespeare) then it does not mean C. S. Lewis or J. R. R. Tolkien, about whom the most generous consensus of mainstream critical opinion is that they are good, interesting, minor authors. And so on.

6. *You're vitriolic too.*

It's true. Critics tend to be an irritable lot. Here are some examples:

> "That light-hearted body, the Bach Choir, has had what I may befittingly call another shy at the Mass in B minor." (George Bernard Shaw, *Music in London*, v.ii, Constable & Co., Ltd., London, 1956, p. 55)

> 'This eloquent novel', says the jacket of Taylor Caldwell's *The Devil's Advocate*, making two errors in three words ..." (Damon Knight, *In Search of Wonder*, Advent, Chicago, 1967, p. 29)

> "... Mr. Zirul has committed so many other failures of technique that a whole course in fiction writing could be erected above his hapless corpse." (William Atheling, Jr. [James Blish], *The Issue At Hand*, Advent, Chicago, 1964, p. 83)

Why do we do it?

First, there is the reactive pain. Only those who have reviewed, year in and year out, know how truly abominable most fiction is. And we can't remove ourselves from the pain. Ordinary readers can skip, or read every third word, or quit in the middle. We can't. We must read carefully, with our sensitivities at full operation and our critical-historical apparatus always in high gear – or we may miss that subtle satire which disguises itself as cliché, that first novel whose beginning, alas, was never revised, that gem of a quiet story obscured in a loud, flashy collection, that experiment in form which could be mistaken for sloppiness, that appealing tale partly marred by (but also made possible by) naiveté, that complicated situation that only pays off near the end of the book. Such works exist, but in order not to miss them one must continually extend one's sensitivity, knowledge, and critical care to works that only abuse such faculties. The mental sensation is that of eating garbage, I assure you, and if critics' accumulated suffering did not find an outlet in the vigor of our language, I don't know what we would do. And it's the critics who care the most who suffer the most; irritation is a sign of betrayed love. As Shaw puts it:

> "Criticism written without personal feeling is not worth reading. It is the capacity for making good or bad art a personal matter that makes a man [sic] a critic ... when people do less than their best, and do that less at once badly and self-complacently, I hate them, loathe them, detest them, long to tear them limb from limb and strew them in gobbets about the stage or platform ... In the same way really fine artists inspire me with the warmest possible regard ... When my critical mood is at its height, personal feeling is not the word; it is passion." (*Music in London*, v.i. Constable & Co., London, 1956, pp. 51–52)

But there are other reasons. Critical judgments are so complex (and take place in such a complicated context), the vocabulary of praise and blame available in English is so vague, so fluid, and so constantly shifting, and the physical space allowed is so small, that critics welcome any way of expressing judgments that will be both *precise* and *compact*. If *vivid* be added thereunto, fine – what else is good style? Hence critics, whenever possible, express their judgments in figurative language. Wit is a form of condensation (see Freud if you think this is my arbitrary fiat) just as parody is a form of criticism (see Dwight McDonald's Modern Library collection thereof).

Dramatization is another. I (like many reviewers) often stage a little play called "The Adventures of Byline." Byline (or "I") is the same species of creature as the Kindly Editor or The Good Doctor, who appear from time to time in these pages. That is, she is a form of shorthand. When Byline rewrites story X, that doesn't mean that I – the real, historical personage – actually did or will or wish to rewrite story X, or that I expect its real, historical author to rewrite it to Byline's prescription, any more than my saying that "my" copy of *Bug Jack Barron* tried to punch "me" in the nose means that such an event really happened. Pauline Kael's Movie Loon is another such fiction; these little creatures we send scurrying about the page are not our real, live selves, and their exploits are dictated more by the exigencies of our form than by a desire for personal glory.

7. *Never mind all that stuff. Just tell me what I'd enjoy reading.*

Bless you, what makes you think I know? (See, there goes Byline.) Actually critics can make educated guesses from time to time about the tastes of some groups of readers. Editors must, such judgments being their bread and butter – and look how often *they* fail. If judgments of beauty and truth are difficult, imagine what happens when the issue is escape reading, i.e. something as idosyncratic as guided daydreams. Perhaps the popularity of series novels is due in part to readers' desire for a reliable, easily reproducible pleasure. But the simplest good–bad scales (like *The Daily News* system of stars) is always colliding with readers' tastes. Some writers and publishers, in order to be sure of appealing to at least a stable fraction of the market, standardize their product. This can be done, but it tends to eliminate from fiction these idiosyncratic qualities other readers find valuable, art being of an order of complexity nearer to that of human beings (high) than that of facial tissues (low).

Now back to the topic of heroic fantasy, which occasioned the foregoing.

I know it's painful to be told that something in which one has invested intense emotion is not only bad art but bad for you, not only bad for you but ridiculous. I didn't do it to be mean, honest. Nor did I do it because the promise held out by heroic fantasy, the promise of escape into a wonderful Other world, is one I find temperamentally unappealing. On the contrary, it's because I understand the intensity of the demand so well (having spent my twenties reading Eddison and Tolkien; I even adapted *The Hobbit* for the stage) that I also understand the absolute impossibility of ever fullfilling that demand. The current popularity of heroic fantasy scares me; I believe it to be a symptom of political and cultural reaction due to economic depression. So does Robin Scott Wilson (who once electrified a Modern Language Association seminar by calling *Dune* a fascist book) and Michael Moorcock (see his jacket copy for Norman Spinrad's *The Iron Dream*, a novel which vehemently denounces the genre in the same terms as Wilson does),[3] and the writers of *Bored of the Rings*, the Lampoon parody from which came "Arrowroot, son of Arrowshirt."

---

3 Though *Dune* is, strictly speaking, science fiction. Wilson was talking about the great leader syndrome, and the heroic atmosphere *Dune* shares with heroic fantasy.

Briefly, to answer other statements in the letters, I apologize for implying that Tolkien's hobbits and Ents (or his other bucolic-comic creations) are as empty-sublime as the Big People's heroics. But I agree (see question 5) that Tolkien is a good, interesting, minor writer whose strong point is his *paysages moralisés*. Ditto C.S. Lewis, in his Narnia books. As for other writers mentioned, only strong, selective ignoring could miss the Vancian cynicism or the massive Dunsanian irony (sometimes spilling over into despair) which make their heroism far from simple or unquestioned by the authors themselves. As for the others, I find them gharstly when uncorrected by comedy, or satire (Morris, sometimes), or (in Beagle's case) the nostalgic wistfulness which belongs to fantasy *per se* rather than the publisher's category (that, historically, is what it is) of heroic fantasy. I don't need to badmouth Poul Anderson, James Blish having already done so, calling him (in his heroic phase) "the Thane of Minneapolis... Anderson can write well, but this is seldom evident while he is in his Scand avatar, when he seems invariably to be writing in his sleep" (*The Issue At Hand*, p. 72). That our literary heritage began with feudal epics and *märchen* is no reason to keep on writing them forever. And daydreams about being tall, handsome (or beautiful), noble, admired, and involved in thrilling deeds are not the same as the theoretical speculation which produces medical and technological advances.

It isn't the realists who find life dreadful. It's the romancers. After all, which group is trying to escape from life? Reality is horrible *and* wonderful, disappointing *and* ecstatic, beautiful *and* ugly. Reality is everything. Reality is what there is. Only the hopelessly insensitive find reality so pleasant as to never want to get away from it, but painkillers can be bad for the health, and even if they were not, I am damned if anyone will make me say that the newest fad in analgesics is equivalent to the illumination which is the other thing (besides pleasure) art ought to provide. Bravery, nobility, sublimity, and beauty that have no connection with the real world are simply fake, and once readers realize that escape *does not work*, the glamor fades, the sublime aristocrats turn silly, the profundities become simplifications, and one enters (if one is lucky) into the dreadful discipline of reality and art, like "The Penal Colony." But George Bernard Shaw said all this almost a century ago; interested readers may look up his preface to *Arms and the Man* or that wonderful little book, *The Quintessence of Ibsenism*.

It's disheartening to see how little has changed. On the other hand, there is no pleasure like finding out the realities of human life, in which joy and misery, effort and release, dread and happiness, walk hand-in-hand.

We had better enjoy it. It's what there is.

"Book World," *The Washington Post*, January 24, 1980

The Beginning Place. Ursula K. Le Guin (Harper & Row, $8.95). *Fireflood and Other Stories*. Vonda N. McIntyre (Houghton Mifflin, $10.75). *Yesterday's Children*. David Gerrold (Fawcett Popular Library, $1.95). *The Demon of Scattery*. Poul Anderson and Mildred Downey Broxon (Ace, $4.95)

In *The Beginning Place* Ursula K. Le Guin has returned to the intrapsychic landscape of her earlier fantasies (such as the *Earthsea* trilogy) and has had her characters reject it as a permanent habitation. Two modern young people, Hugh and Irena, discover a strange, fantastic realm, which Irena calls "the ain countree," and which they enter, are changed by and finally leave behind as they return to the real world.

In the essay "From Elfland to Poughkeepsie" (Pendragon Press, 1973; also included in *The Language of the Night*) Le Guin distinguished the genuine, risky Inner Lands ("Elfland") from the banal imitation which is really the outside world in disguise ("Poughkeepsie"). In *The Beginning Place* she brings Elfland into violent contiguity, as it were, with Poughkeepsie, both places rendered in a gray, gritty, realistic style which may annoy fans of the author's more colorful fantasies but which strikes me as an impressive Le Guinian advance.

About the inner landscape (which takes up most of the book) I think there can be no question: Le Guin is past-mistress here, from the too-simple wish-fulfillment of the beginning to the seeming lack of explanations to the sophisticated, conscious use of the Hero-Kills-Dragon myth to the final fading away of the protagonists' earlier loves as they enter a dream-perfect union and finally rejoin the real world. But back in Poughkeepsie the author has created a world so socially and politically abominable that to it the Inner Lands' classic, fairy-tale progression (from family of origin to reproductive family, a pattern that made sense in a stable, feudal society built on such progressions) is simply irrelevant.

In short, Elfland and Poughkeepsie are badly out of gear here, a situation which forces the author into inadvertent lies about the latter; that working-class people are inarticulate, that marriage is a mystical, once-for-all fusion (of the right people only, of course), that clumsy, shy Hugh is a possible real man (and not a woman's dream of one), that his gentleness will not vanish with his guilt over his mother (though Le Guin has previously connected the two), and that achieving his (carefully atypical) ambition will not lead to intense disillusionment.

Place falls flat at the end since the author can imagine no potential change in Poughkeepsie commensurate with the beauty and terror of the changes that have occurred in Elfland. The novel comes perilously close to recommending marriage for women and marriage-plus-upward-mobility for men as a victory over our system that produces exhausted, battered wives, embittered husbands, poverty, and a trashy life for almost everyone. But Le Guin's own socially conscious description of the real world in *Place* makes that solution totally inadequate. *The Beginning Place*, for all its beauties, remains hanging in the air; there is literally *no place* for the characters to return to save permanent residence in Elfland, a choice the author is far too sane and responsible to make.

Vonda N. McIntyre's apparently simple method of putting one foot carefully, rigorously and systematically in front of another leads her, at her worst, into merely intelligent and interesting stories and, at her best, into some very good ones. *Fireflood and Other Stories* contains the deservedly famous "Of Mist, and Grass, and Sand" (the story won a Nebula; the book *Dreamsnake*, which was a continuation of the story, a Nebula and a Hugo); a fine, early nightmare, "The Genius Freaks"; and to my mind the best piece in the collection, the magical novella "Aztecs," which blends a transfigured Seattle (most of the setting is underwater), sacrifice, biological technology and lost love in a way unique in McIntyre's work and rare in science fiction. (McIntyre's men, like Le Guin's Hugh, are the kind women wish for, but McIntyre's future worlds are also matter-of-factly sexual-egalitarian, which makes the existence of such men a good deal more plausible.)

The author's speculations are biological and solidly so, her work is compassionate, often incomplete (for example, the politics of the story "Screwtop" are vague although the landscape and the changed mores are – as usual – very good) and almost always concerned with rendering how it feels to be intelligent and nonhuman, from the exuberant flying carnivores of "The Mountains of Sunset, the Mountains of Dawn" and "Wings" to the earth-burrowing, volcano-tasting heroine of "Fireflood." Critics have noted McIntyre's feminism, but (at least in this collection) alienation – usually literal – is her real subject, and alien(ated) beings her heroes. As a dolphin, in "The End's Beginning," reflects tragically, "Humans have a terrible need to put things inside other things, to overcome the inevitable randomness of life. *People know better.*" (italics mine).

David Gerrold knows nothing of war, the psychology of command, or the behavior of men cooped up on a deteriorating spaceship – all the ostensible subjects of his *Yesterday's Children* – and yet his very human obsession with putting things inside things slowly creates something authentic and interesting. This reality may inhere in the exhaustively imagined ship itself, the only convincing element in the book, although its details are heavy going at first. Even the ending, extraordinarily silly in realistic terms (the characters are likewise impossible) works somehow as part of the grim, claustrophobic, tiring, ultimately worthwhile metaphor that the novel becomes.

The Demon of Scattery by Poul Anderson and Mildred Downey Broxon is a badly inflated publisher's package: big type, bigger margins, a small novella and lots of handsome off-key illustration by Alicia Austen. Within, one learns that a man may rape a woman repeatedly, murder her family and deprive her of her profession, but if he says he is sorry and satisfies her in bed, she will love him, forego revenge and live with him happily ever after.

"It was a brutal age," says Anderson defensively in his afterword about the ninth-century setting. Then why write about it except as protest (the Strugatskys) or nightmare warning (James Tiptree Jr.)? *Demon* does it for fun. There is much casual brutality and stiffly antiquarian detail, and one good sea-serpent which should have devoured the entire project, especially whoever thought up charging readers five times what the wordage would cost elsewhere. *Caveat emptor.*

The Magazine of Fantasy and Science Fiction, February 1980

On Wings of Song. Thomas M. Disch (St. Martin's Press, $10.00). *Painted Devils*. Robert Aickman (Charles Scribner's Sons, $8.95). *Kindred*. Octavia Butler (Doubleday & Company, $8.95). *Universe 9*. Ed. Terry Carr (Doubleday & Company, $7.95). *New Dimensions 9*. Ed. Robert Silverberg (Harper & Row, $10.95). *The Language of the Night: Essays on Fantasy and Science Fiction*. Ursula Le Guin, ed. Susan Wood (G.P. Putnam's Sons, $9.95)

Thomas Disch is a *sinister* writer. I mean by this that his work – most strikingly his latest novel, *On Wings of Song* – is an ominous attack on the morals and good customs of Middle America. I also mean that Disch, although an insider-turned-outsider (according to the flap copy of his story collection, *Fun With Your New Head,* he grew up in Minnesota, one of the repressive "Farm States" of *Song,* and "escaped" to New York), is not a direct revolutionary but a left-handed user of such methods as irony, parody, exaggeration, and other forms of oblique subversion. Bitterness lies under the surface of his wit, or rather is conveyed *via* his wit, and *Song* is sometimes chilly and disagreeable in its unremitting view of desolation. Although there is a revolution for the better, it takes place (typically for Disch) off-stage, and in comparison with the conventional treatment "sympathetic" characters receive in most fiction, *Song's* people may strike readers as abrasively unpleasant. In part *Song* compensates with comedy; in part Disch simply doesn't care to gum up his art with the karo syrup of conventional sympathy. When one's subject is the art of survival as practiced in extreme situations, auctorial button-pushings of readers' feelings are merely impertinent. For one thing, they assume that suffering matters only when it happens to nice people. And they neglect the indictment of a whole culture, which is *Song's* real subject. In place of the moral judgments which usually pass for characterization in literature, Disch gives us close attention to the *how* and *why* of behavior; even the mad Mrs. Norberg and the awful, elder Mueller are treated with analytical care and a kind of respect. When a prison-mate's family sends him not food at Christmas (the prisoners are deliberately starved by the authorities) but snapshots of their Thanksgiving dinner, the protagonist's reaction is fascination, not moral indignation – moral indignation is, after all, a luxury of the relatively secure; the truly powerless can't afford it. Except for a pervasive irony that is so much a part of Disch's oblique method that he probably can't drop it (though it's occasionally annoying), the book is unusually free of instructions to the reader about how the reader is supposed to feel. In fact the irony usually functions against the grain of the emotion: an asbestos-gloves method of handling difficult material. Some readers will feel cheated without a built-in instruction sheet; others may welcome the relative novelty of prose that keeps its eye on its object.

Song, a book about outsiderhood, is also about art and transcendence and the repression (and achievement) of both. There is the transcendence of "flying" (a kind of astral-travel-cum-psychedelic-trip) and the song – not necessarily art – which catalyzes it. There is the literarily traditional story of the young man who escapes from the provinces to achieve success in art in the big city. There is the linking of art and the urban milieu to the bizarreries of male homosexuality (a bel canto revival complete with *castrati* that Disch invents for the purpose). Only in this last area is the book less than clear, as if the author never decided whether to exploit the social myth of homosexuals-as-grotesques or to deny it; in the end he does both and – what is much worse – equivocates about his hero's relation to the whole subject so that on one page Daniel has been a hustler for years, on another he contemplates the possibility with distaste (p. 247), on yet another he's already actively homosexual (p. 274), and on yet another he seems to dismiss the possibility altogether (p. 254). I suspect Disch was novelistically tempted by the link popularly supposed to exist between homosexuality and artistic talent, although the linkage – art is *also* grotesque and crazy – is hardly one either side can want to support. At times the novel almost moves into the Anita Bryant-esque view of the flap copy (New York "peopled by grotesques and seething with corruption")[1] although the grotesques are only people, and the corruption much less than that of the Farm States.

That one cloudy area aside, *Song* is a brilliant, flamboyant, extraordinarily original work. And how he can write! There is the completely American penal colony of Spirit Lake (I hope the author's model was merely a summer camp), the descriptions of flying, the fuel shortage that coincides with a newspaper strike "as though winter had overtaken not only nature, but history as well" (p. 23). And here is a nine-year-old already so versed in family manipulation that he placates a mother who *might* return to live with him by the carefully politic, "Gee, Mom, I hope it works out so you can come and live with us." But it's stressful and he hasn't the resources of an adult; the fact that he's on the phone gives Disch a method of saying as much without instructions-to-the-reader and without judgment: "He put the phone on Hold before she could reply" (p. 7).

Science fiction writers and readers often talk about uniting science fiction with the mainstream; Disch has done it, not by hybridizing modes (a process someone tries in vain every now and again) but by pushing the possibilities of science fiction to the limit. *On Wings of Song* is a superb book.

In *Painted Devils* Robert Aickman has left out the parts of his horror stories which explain what is happening and why, thus achieving a mystifying noncompossibility (i.e. you can't put the damned thing together) which appeals to the *Literary Guild Newsletter* as "distinguished." Stories of his, isolated in other anthologies, can look appealing because his prose does have more literary polish than is usual in the genre, but in a collection the method becomes clear and quite exasperating. Despite the deliberately ambiguous surfaces of these tales, their basic ideas are banal, with the exception of "Marriage," an interesting satire that trails off into mystification.

1 Written, I suspect, by the author in a merry mood. Who else would perpetrate a phrase like "the lovely Boadicea Whiting"?

Octavia Butler's *Kindred* is more polished than her earlier work but still has the author's stubborn, idiosyncratic gift for realism. Butler makes new and eloquent use of a familiar science-fiction idea, protecting one's own past, to express the tangled interdependency of black and white in the United States; the black heroine's great-great-grandfather is a white man who can, half voluntarily, call her back into his time to help him in emergencies; Dana, drawn wholly involuntarily, must save him to preserve her own ancestry, at least until the conception of her great-grandmother – and Rufus is a Southern slave-owner, confused, spoiled, a rapist with a remarkable gift for self-destruction. *Kindred* is a family chronicle set in a small space; the limitations let Butler concentrate on the human relations and the surprising-but-logical interplay of past and present. (What other author would think of taking Excedrin to pre-Civil War Maryland?) Although characterizations in the past are detailed (Rufus as a little boy is especially good) Dana's present-day marriage is sketchy and her aunt and uncle, who disapprove of her white husband, are talked about, not shown. Past events may simply have crowded out the present or Butler may mean to indicate that Dana's present-day difficulties in being black are nothing to her past ones – she gets shut of the appalling Rufus only, finally, by killing him. *Kindred* is exciting and fast-moving and the past occurs without a break in style – a technique that makes it more real – even down to characters' speech (Butler describes their accents but wisely doesn't attempt to reproduce them). The end is crossed-fingers hopeful with some chance of sanity "now that the boy is dead" though Dana has assured her own birth at a price: her left arm, lost at "the exact spot Rufus's fingers had grasped it" (p. 261).

Terry Carr's *Universe 9*, the latest in his series of original anthologies, is a good collection, generally optimistic-social in tone, with only two wispies (Mary C. Pangborn's over-familiar "The Back Road" and Juleen Brantingham's over-arch "Chicken of the Tree") and one clunk, John Shirley's "Will the Chill," a tale of stylized, melodramatic, macho power-and-agony in which the beautiful, young heiress, committing suicide for love of the alienated, superduperman hero, does so not even in her own space-yacht but in her daddy's. Of Carr's other choices "Frost Animals" by Bob Shaw is an s.f. detective story with routine characters but a good, ingenious puzzle and a striking solution; Gregory Benford's "Time Shards" has a fine s.f. idea but a philosophical conclusion that would strike modern historians or sociologists as pretentiously false (it's precisely commonplace talk from the past they would find valuable); and Greg Bear's "The White Horse Child" is a pleasant story about imagination, not new in theme or manner but well detailed. Of the remaining three authors Marta Randall, by turning a cliché on its head (i.e. changing its personnel) produces a funny, shamelessly sentimental and to my mind irresistible mother–daughter story ("The Captain and the Kid" is both the story's title and a description of the cliché in question.) Novitski and Varley, occupying the same feminist territory as Randall but in more realistic fashion, portray the difficulties of future, sexually egalitarian societies. Novitski has, I think, the edge, since he concentrates (in the fine, solid detail of "Nuclear Fission," a story reminiscent of Marge Piercy's *Woman on the Edge of Time*) on male fears of abandonment: who will love men if women move into new territory with other women? The theme is tailor-made for bitterness, which Novitski avoids, though there is some unavoidable cheating; as in Varley's story, present-day characters inhabit a future world into which they don't quite fit (e.g. Novitski's Spider shuns male company for reasons which make sense in this world but not in his). Written about a woman's process of change (a doubtful business to begin with when a male author is attempting a feminist point) "Options" seems to maintain that even in a sexually egalitarian society the only people who can really treat the sexes equally are those who've experienced life as both – though at the same time the convincing, mildly drab lunar society Varley describes is clearly not egalitarian, a contradiction with which the author doesn't fully deal. Biology matters, or should, but it doesn't, or shouldn't – Varley's metaphor of androgyny brings with it hidden assumptions that the problem is a physical problem.[2] Varley has been admired for his female characters and "Options" is very well written (there are details that are a real tour-de-force for a male writer), yet the story is really the fearful husband's, not the serene and informative wife's, as its lack of emotional involvement and its summaries of what should be dramatized make clear. "Nuclear Fission" is less calm, less sophisticated, and the better story, though Varley is a more accomplished writer than Novitski.

Robert Silverberg, editor of *New Dimensions*, has always been as weighty, pessimistic, and experimental in editorial temperament as Terry Carr is genial, playful, and optimistic. *New Dimensions 9*, whether by accident, design, or the youth of the authors (four of the eleven pieces are first publications and two more are nearly so) is all this and more – it is a strikingly homogeneous collection in which almost all the stories deal with the alienation of white, well-to-do men from their own emotionality and from other

---

2 Androgyny is often used as a metaphor for psychic wholeness. Readers who like to tunnel about in libraries can try *Women's Studies* Vol. 2, No. 4 (1974) for a history and analysis of the concept in Western thinking. Four scholars, one of them male, argue that the idea is confused and made for cop-outs and that its history is at best mixed.

people, especially women, the authors employing for this purpose machine imagery that often goes beyond the informative into the obsessive. The hero of Timothy Arthur Sullivan's "The Rauncher Goes to Tinkertown" is a brutal, agonized, half-machine superman isolated on a desert planet; in Peter Alterman's "Binding Energy" a computer personality first fails, and then takes over the body of, a fifteen-year-old girl; "The Square Pony Express" by Felix Gotschalk is a world of machine adventure ("I made it. Yay!" p. 115) while in "Last" by Michael Conner, the last man alive on earth, more or less in league with the robots who are running things, betrays and then executes the last woman, who (unlike him) wants to live and fight back. In Tony Sarowitz's "A Passionate State of Mind" a scientist who's failed at human relationships (especially with his daughter) finds Nirvana *in* a machine (which stops time), while in Gregory Benford's "Calibrations or Exercises" the unhappy, alienated characters (Alpha, Beta, Delta) merely act mechanically and are talked about in terms of mechanism and calculation. In Jeff Hecht's "Crossing the Wasteland" a man coming out of ten centuries of "pseudocold" (as eloquent an unconscious symbol as John Shirley's Will the Chill in *Universe 9*) finds himself in a depopulated world run by machines and is at first mistaken for a computer malfunction. In Donnan Call Jeffer Jr.'s "The Sands of Libya Are Barren," a story not really in this group, the characters aren't machines but they *are* dead and existing in a desert, in an interesting, ghostly state Jeffers keeps spoiling with fascinated comments on his own paradoxical situation as the writer of the story, a new-writer phenomenon much like the discovery by new film-makers that they can turn the camera upside down, both groups being unaware that everyone except themselves long ago got bored with both techniques. (The female-preferred pronouns don't help, as they refer to nothing in the invented society and so merely look trendy.) Also dead, and in something like Hell, are the characters in Bruce Taylor's "The Attendant," a surreal situation that never becomes a story despite Taylor's attempt at a redemptive ending.

It's as if the authors (with the last two as possible exceptions) had woken up one morning in David Bunch's *Moderan* or in a Barry Malzberg novel. Yet without Bunch's loud ridicule (or Malzberg's agonized moral sense) the attempt to claim sympathy for the afflictions of privilege and power that neither the characters nor the writers show much inclination to give up strikes me as questionable. There is a lot of false fatality in these stories. Some, indeed, are having a good time: Gotschalk produces a plethora of machine details that would numb a human and Hecht's implicit cure for his wasteland is an old-fashioned, ambitious, *Analog* hero who rejects the only other human being in the story for not being beautiful, sexual, warm, and inspiring – no lovely, suicidal heiress, she. The stories also show a strange brutality of style, an incapacity for the simple, the slight, or the low-contrast, as if the authors were half anesthetized and could register nothing but the loudest and heaviest impressions – this may merely be a fault of youth but I find it too appropriate to their material for comfort.

And then there's Ursula Le Guin. Well! "The Pathways of Desire" is a splendidly middle-aged story with details that double back and bite you the second time round, from the fangless hotdog to the H. Rider Haggard cosmic constant that female names end in "a" (as the Indian Ramchandra says to the Russian-named Tamara). The heroine isn't quite old enough to be middle-aged (though that may be the point; it's a state of mind) and the love affair is a little too much idealized (people's babble in love is usually silly) but otherwise "Desire" is a dazzler which Le Guin has loaded with intellectual-fictional dissonance; the story barely holds together and almost self-destructs in mid-air, a virtuoso performance that exactly suits the writer's theme.

Perhaps the rest of the anthology ought to be sent to Le Guin's story to be psychoanalyzed, but "Desire" is really dealing with the masculine mystique in its historically earlier, ascendant (or Edgar Rice Burroughs) phase when hypertrophy of the chilly will brought other rewards than isolation and despair. (It's no coincidence that Marc Feigen-Fasteau's recent analysis of the destruction wrought upon men by sexism is called *The Male Machine*.)[3] Of the bunch, Gregory Benford exercises considerable technical skill on long-dead material and Peter Alterman captures some feeling, despite the compulsive overplus of machine detail. Peter Dillingham's poetry strikes me as too high-contrast, like a TV with the color control turned way up, but I'm no expert on poetry. (Could the Kindly Editor store it all and give it, once a year, to a real poet?)

Perhaps, instead of sending *New Dimensions 9* to "The Pathways of Desire" for help, one might send it to *The Language of the Night*, a collection of Le Guin's essays edited by Susan Wood, although Le Guin does not talk directly about sexism's depradations. Authors like Le Guin are perpetually being asked to "talk about their work," and since that is tantamount to recounting the cute things your cat did last week, authors respond – as Le Guin largely does here – with criticism. Of these intelligent and novelistically graceful essays, the weakest seem to me those in which the author tiredly repeats the obvious, usually at the prodding of a publisher, the best pieces written spontaneously and affectionately for fan magazines. At times Le Guin's teacherly generosity keeps her at too elementary a level; "From Elfland to Poughkeepsie," for example, is a model of how to do this sort of thing well,

3 Dell, New York, 1975.

but it's also something a fine mind ought not to do so often. There are some thoughtless or derivative remarks, as is inevitable in a collection of largely occasional pieces, e.g. Le Guin's traditional walloping of politicians (Shirley Chisholm?) and oddities like her condemnation of "sensualists" (p. 124) – do we still have them? What are they? Do you keep them in the refrigerator?

If there's an overall flaw in *Language* it's Le Guin's passion for morality and how that passion is likely to be misused by readers. She notes it herself (p. 128) and is flexible enough to avoid its dangers in pieces like "The Child and the Shadow" or the absolutely first-rate piece on Philip K. Dick, but many of her readers won't be. Much American youth, partly because of the movies, views moral decision as a choice between safety, comfort, happiness, and cowardice on the one hand and on the other misery, wretchedness, and the obedience to abstract rules. In such a scheme virtue amounts to self-destruction and nobody sane *can* choose it; thus the myth adds an all-dominating faculty called "conscience" which exists only in good people (that's how you know they're good). College sophomores, ignorant of their own limits and meager resources, go out into the world expecting to act on this romantic view of themselves; naturally they fold up at the first real crunch, and not having experienced the rush of conscious moral exaltation the myth tells them to expect, they turn either into guilt-ridden worms or baby cynics who think all they have to do to become rich and happy is to be immoral (they usually can't pull that off, either). Nobody ever told them that within the area of what is generally allowable in civilized life, most choices are purely prudential, or that severe moral choices are a signal of drastic social breakdown and hence abominably unpleasant double binds.[4] Le Guin's tendency to ethicize all issues feeds into this destructive mystique; I can only hope readers of *Language* also read "The Pathways of Desire," which is an argument along quite different lines.

One of the surprises of the collection is the author's delicious sense of comedy, from her "mad visions of founding a Hobbit Socialist Party" (p. 173) to a scene with a cat, a child, and a telephone cord that ought to be reproduced entire in fiction. Susan Wood, who comments and introduces too much, nonetheless deserves the thanks of all lovers of Le Guin's work for initiating and editing this volume.

---

4   Even these are choices between two values. If all the values are on one side, where's the choice?

Sinister Wisdom, 12, winter 1980

"Listen, There's a Story for you..."

Retreat As It Was! Donna J. Young (The Naiad Press, 7800 Westside Dr., Weatherby Lake, Missouri, 64152, 120pp., $5.00).

In *Literary Women* Ellen Moers notes that nineteenth-century women writers' insistent presentation of public acclaim for female genius in their fiction is due to "the impossibility of ever having [it] in real life" and that the embarrassingly "raw fantasy" of such scenes comes from having been "starved for centuries."[1]

Retreat: As It Was! by Donna J. Young is a heartbreaking non-book, although with training – especially someone to stand over her, yelling "Details!" every time she drifts into summary – she might eventually become some sort of writer. *Retreat* was written out of sheer starvation, published ditto (unless we're to believe that Naiad is simply being opportunistic), and will be read for no other reason, if it's read at all.

Ostensibly science fiction, *Retreat's* science comes from incoherently bad television; it's a mixture of faster-than-light communications and spacedrive, inexplicably endless sources of light and power, and no other method of transporting the wounded from a grounded spaceship to a provincial settlement than "pack animals" (with "spines" but otherwise undescribed), a grueling six-or-seven-day, hypothermia-inducing journey which looks bafflingly like a rather Darwinian version of triage. Since the wounded receive only psionic healing (the women disdaining such primitive devices as bandages, food, water, antibiotics, etc.), why not send the healers *to* the ship? But *Retreat* mystifies all its technology. Here are the book's only descriptions of technological activity, quoted entire:

> The room she entered contrasted to [sic] the rustic simplicity of the post. Instead of cave-like walls and fur-lined floors,[2] there were gadgets and square corners, levers and dials, hard stone underfoot.

---

1 Ellen Moers, *Literary Women,* Anchor Press/Doubleday, Garden City, N.Y., 1977, p. 278.
2 No one does any house-keeping in this book, even where details like furry floors suggest a lot of potential for mess.

> Lita, Tulla, Ain, and a few others were gathered around a console, making calculations. (p. 12)

> They turned and began the process of tuning the complicated machinery to the biological rhythms that were Ria's alone. First Lita placed her hand on a yellow, translucent square. She brushed her other hand over a series of colored plates to the left of the yellow square. Ria laid her hand down on the square next to Lita's and pressed the same plates in reverse order to Lita's. Lita then removed both hands from the console. (p. 14)

> The walls of the central room had been energized into multi-dimensional [sic] representations of various sectors of the known universe. Women were busy entering data, making changes in this diagram or that, running multitudes of machines and equipment. (p. 76)

And here is *Retreat*'s description of the cosmic disaster that ruins the women's sophisticated technology, leaves them vulnerable to the new crops of (mutation-induced) male children, transforms the fourth planet into the asteroid belt (I think) and proves that we've been on Earth all the time, thus validating that "jaguar" on page 1 (the book otherwise refers vaguely only to "large predatory beasts"):

> They were thrown to the ground. The earth shivered beneath them and roared in agony. The force of the vibrations rolled Ria and Mar across the open space, into each other and finally against another boulder. The buildings collapsed. The pyramid shook. Women inside the buildings screamed in panic.
>
> The quake died down, but another rolled in right behind it. Ria tried to regain her feet and fell again. The second shock ended soon, but the pyramid suffered more damage. Finally, only small vibrations rattled through the Post and Ria could stand. (pp. 90–91)

If I quote from *Retreat* at such length it's because I want to convey as forcefully as possible the absolute, limp, thinness of the book. Not only is there no science, no government, and no economics here, as well as barely any visualizable scenery or people characterologically distinguishable from one another, but Young's avoidance of concrete detail seems at times to amount to deliberate policy. Thus we have such annoying vagueness as "refreshments" (p. 73), "a steaming herb drink" (p. 71), "nutrient cubes" (p. 98), and "small portions of various foods" (p. 39), plus "a richly aromatic mug of liquid" (p. 87) – I suspect the author means that the liquid is aromatic, not the mug, but that still doesn't tell us what the stuff tastes like. Young's ear is so leaden that she can flood *Retreat* with said book-isms (like "'Ha-ha-ha-ha-ho', Ain laughed", p. 42) and barbarisms like "younglings" (children) and "the Mystery of Parthenogen" (pregnancy) or indicate one educated Sister's provinciality by having her say "I dunno" (p. 62) and the other's sophisticated ease by "I wouldn't want to enslave a sister to an unhealthy emotional attachment" (p. 63). But these remarks aren't characterizations since everybody in *Retreat* is like everyone else, totally good, harmonious, loving and non-erotic save for two who fall in love at first sight but don't get it on until they want to reproduce (or at all thereafter), a piece of Christian-fundamentalist prudery of which the author seems unaware.

What *is* the book about? Hugging, I think. Thirty-nine (non-erotic) hugs and seventeen incidents of weeping occur in one hundred and six pages, which averages out to one hug per 2.7 pages, one weep every 9.4 pages, and one of either (if you're not picky) every 1.9 pages. Unhappily visible under the surface of this story is an all-female commune in which everyone lives on welfare or child-support, in which there is a little child-care (but no messy diapers), a little herbal medicine, a little massage, a little yoga, no sex unless you are In Love, and a lot of that amorphous, judgment-less, uncritical, and ultimately meaningless "emotional support" which all too often passes among women for real love or real respect. And of course nobody shops, cooks, cleans, earns money, or has any idea of the enormous and complicated organism that is the modern industrial world, or ever quarrels, including the children, who always play "quietly and gently" (p. 19). Seldom have traditional female limitations been so painfully insisted upon in a piece of fiction. Naiad has done neither Young nor us a favor by printing *Retreat*. I can't imagine any positive reaction to the book from any reader whatever except a sobby-sentimental high followed by an equally slumpy anger against one's bedmates, housemates, and workmates for failing to live up to the book's saccharine ideality. Young (bemusedly, in her nightgown) has wandered out in the woods to toast endless, gluey marshmallows over the same fire that good-humored, shrewd Sally Gearhart, author of *Wanderground*[3] (in her L. L. Bean boots and down jacket) is using to heat her can of Trail Mix – supposed to be good for you but people really like it because it's full of sweet stuff like raisins and coconut. I am one of *Wanderground*'s godmothers and thus entitled to call Gearhart the Edgar Rice Burroughs of lesbian feminism (thus implying that she has both the defects and the considerable virtues of the creator of John

---

3 Sally Gearhart, *Wanderground: Stories of the Hill Women*, Persephone Press, Watertown, Mass., 1978.

Carter of Mars), but at least *Wanderground* has individualized characters and a sharp sense of the various kinds of hell nature can throw at you when she's in the mood.

But who is this on the third side of the fire – this noonday to Gearhart's sturdy Eveready flashlight and Young's druggy candle – this giant who is using the fire not to ruin our taste buds or distract our desperate minds with magical impossibilities but to hammer out tools for the future: ploughshares, hunting knives – and look, there's even a mold for a telescope mirror in the center of the ashes!

The Titan with the forge is *Motherlines*, by Suzy McKee Charnas, a book that sank like a stone in hardcover publication a year ago (where were you all! Asleep? On Mars? Oh woe!) and is now out in Berkley paperback with a cover as unjustly dull as Tee Corinne's cover for *Retreat* is unjustly seductive.[4] Charnas knows exactly what her characters eat and wear and use and what they have to do to get it and what happens to them if they don't, and that's rock-bottom political awareness if any ever existed. From the East Coast state of Holdfast (after World War Three) in which all women are the chattel slaves of all men, the runner Alldera escapes, to be rescued by the Free Amazons, the Riding Women of the plains. There are also the Free Fems, a community of other escaped slaves, and all Charnas's people are unforgettable, from pretty Daya (a "pet fem" until a master skewered her cheeks with a hot stick) who makes stories and trouble out of the same imaginative hunger, to wise, wealthy, tongueless Elnoa, boss of the Free Fems, too fat to leave the wicker wagons the fems pull, endlessly keeping "her accounts" (as they think) until she tells Daya in sign language – in one of the book's most moving scenes – *that she is writing history* because the world must never forget what they suffered, to the eccentric loner-artist Fedaka, healer and cloth-dyer, whose only lover is the Fems' god, Moonwoman. Among the parthenogenetic Riding Women are graceful, black, wise, quarrel-solving Nenisi Conor, who spends half her life in sullen fury because "My horse-farting teeth *hurt!*" and loud, crude, red-faced, dumb Barvaran, whose death is the great grief of the book, and crazy Grays Omelly who senses the collision of values the Free Fems bring before anyone else and so stands on one leg within strange rings of objects for hours "to keep things in their place."

Charnas doesn't tell you; she shows you – from the authentic eeriness of the Moonwoman legends to Alldera's becoming the reluctant George Washington of her people, capitulating to others' logic ("It [the Holdfast] was built on our backs"), leading sixty armed women back to the Holdfast, where men may still rule:

4 Suzy McKee Charnas, *Motherlines*, Berkeley, N.Y., 1979.

"Listen, here's a story for you:" [says Daya] "we are a small, grim army drawn up on some high path on the far side of the mountains, looking out in silence ... over our country, green to the horizon line of the sea..." (p. 251)

And here is the Fems' bitter "self-song":

> Wash all clean, black sea, roll stones,
> Break walls, salt sand, spare none ...
> We breathed earth all our generations.
> We can breathe an ocean of dead men and not care. (p. 233)

Listen, there's a story for you ... A *real one*.
Read it.

Frontiers, V:3, 1981

Woman's Creation: Sexual Evolution and the Shaping of Society. Elizabeth Fisher (McGraw-Hill, New York, 1980, 504pp., $4.95)

In her introduction Elizabeth Fisher writes of a "visionary" night in which she suddenly said to herself, "I've just rewritten Engels' *Origin of the Family, Private Property, and the State"* (p. xiii), but her clever publisher knew better than to call the book *Engels Supported by a Century of Other People's Scholarship and Rebutted by the Addition of Female Sexuality, a Subject With Which He Could Not Deal, Brilliant Victorian Though He Was, and No Wonder*. Not only would such a title have taken up the space devoted instead to one of the most visually appalling cover designs I have ever seen, it also would have given prospective readers some idea of what the book was about, thus enraging female separatists ("She's agreeing with a MAN!"), the non-feminist Left ("She's a FEMINIST!"), the feminist Left ("We know THAT!"), and the ordinary public ("A COMMIE WOMEN'S LIBBER, jeez!"). This way nobody is enraged because nobody is enlightened and most readers have so far dealt with the problem of another unpleasantly long, vaguely feminist tome by the serene expedient of not reading it.

When you think that the particular marsh you are stuck in is timeless (that is, ahistorical), you must look for timeless causes – or at least causes that have lasted as long as our existence as a species. This is exactly what Dorothy Dinnerstein does in *The Mermaid and the Minotaur*. Since her causes are so ingrained in "human nature" the only possible response is Dinnerstein's heroic despair: we're bound to lose but we'll go down fighting! An admirable position, but how much better (and what a relief) to be able to say with Fisher: Sexism, like a host of other evils, arose at a particular point in human history (that's the *historical* part) in response to the concrete, material ways in which people lived, that is, how they got their food, shelter, and so on (and that's the *materialism*), not out of some immutable biological essence imprinted on their genes or (this is Dinnerstein's version) pre-hominid social patterns *necessarily* transferred to a developing human species, with catastrophic results.

Fisher is a historical materialist. *Woman's Creation* is (as far as I know) the only thoroughly documented theory in existence that puts the origins of sexism on solidly scholarly ground. Fisher also provides the (to me) completely convincing evidence that female subjugation, the ownership of children, land as property, economic class, priesthood, characterological sadomasochism, war, the king-headed state, the transformation of sex from pleasure to profit, and slavery – usually of people from different populations who look different, that is, racism – does not just coincide with the establishment of civilization; this knot of horrors *is* civilization.

By contrast, the foraging-hunting life typical of the Paleolithic is leisurely; longer-lived; well-fed (foragers know their territory, as anthropologists have finally noticed); nonpossessive about children, whom they enjoy; freely and joyfully sexual, with a loose web of matrocentric authority; and sexually egalitarian. Furthermore they had some surprisingly effective means of birth control (another recent "discovery" that confutes earlier views), no private property save in utensils and clothing, a rich imaginative life, and one very plentiful possession: happiness.

Into the foraging-hunting way of life steps the villain: agriculture. Agriculture feeds more people per square mile than foraging-hunting, so once it's adopted, people gradually become locked into this technological advance. But agriculture also feeds people worse and demands immense amounts of gratification-deferring labor while gathering is immediately rewarding and can include the very immediate reward of eating. Where labor is valuable and private property possible (you can't carry land on your back and settled communities can store other forms of wealth, such as grain) children become valuable as future laborers and women as child-producers. Knowledge of impregnation, forced mating, and the castrating or killing of "unnecessary" male animals, a technology learned from animal-breeding (not merely animal-keeping), becomes a technology applicable to people: women and female sexuality are controlled by men in the service of profit (now that private profit exists), many men are controlled by few men for the profit of the few (ditto), and access to women or sexuality becomes a commodity which is then given by privileged men to less privileged men. The resultant frustration, anger, and displacement of sexual energy into "sadomasochism"[1] makes it even easier to keep people in their economic place, a place that comes to include slavery: Engels' "human cattle" (an exact analogy). Fisher traces this slow process as it is reflected in Sumerian/Akkadian written records both in law and myth. For example, here is "the birth of the phallarchy" in 2000 B.C., an official myth in which the mortal king of an Akkadian city-state is about to copulate with the daughter-goddess Inanna to produce plenty in the land: "With the exalted rising of the king's loins rose, at the same time, the flax, rose, at the same time, the barley ..." (p. 288). Much profit and much power but little pleasure, as Fisher points out. Perhaps a century and a half later appears a creation myth, in the same area, in which for the first time in human history the creation of the world occurs neither as birth (the earliest myths) nor as the result of copulation (the later ones) nor as the gods' artifactual making of human beings from clay, but *as murder*, with Marduk (the god associated with the Babylonian city-king) slaughtering the great mother-goddess Tiamat and *creating the world from her dead body*. Human beings are then fashioned from the blood of her slain consort.

There is much more in *Woman's Creation*, only some of which I can touch on here: Fisher's documenting the effect of the gun-and-horse technology on previously peaceful Americans of the nineteenth century – her classic example is the Comanches, who moved in one generation to a religion centered on cruelty, chastity, vengeance, and self-mutilation (p. 316) – the ghost of Engels can be heard applauding in the wings at this point – as well as her notes that Bronze Age life expectancy was half that of the Paleolithic or Neolithic (p. 320), that war is only five thousand years old (p. 320), and that the king-headed state precedes and is the model for the patriarchal family (p. 299).

Fisher's book ought to end once and for all the quarrels about which oppression came first and is therefore most important: *they all did*. They are, in fact, identical both in cause and in historical time, and they are

---

1 *Not* sexual sadomasochism but plain old cruelty.

furthermore *structurally dependent upon each other*. Fisher has not so much added feminism to socialism as put one over the other like transparent slides and – lo! – the two are one. That is, whatever Leftist and feminist people may think of one another (and most women's experience with most of the Left has been notorious), Marxist and feminist theory can no more quarrel than the physics of gravitation can quarrel with the physics of electromagnetism. I am not saying that feminism "needs allies" on the Left or that the Left ought to add to its body count by professing feminism – such sucking up has already happened and the kind of reaction it deserves is hardly speakable in the serene and dignified pages of this journal. What I do mean is that the women's movement needs more and better historical theory. And what a splendid time the last few years has been for feminist theory! On page 233 of *Woman's Creation* the reader can fit in Dorothy Dinnerstein's *The Mermaid and the Minotaur*, on page 303, Mary Daly's *Gyn/Ecology*, on page 323, Janice Raymond's *The Transsexual Empire*, on page 381, Susan Griffin's *Woman and Nature* – and Adrienne Rich's *Of Woman Born* almost anywhere after 1000 B.C. Then fit in everything else. Then look at Fisher's notes and bibliography and cheer. There she is, in the center, spinning it all together, like a wise spider.

What good news and what a good book!

"Book World," *The Washington Post*, May 10, 1981

Surpassing the Love of Men: Romantic Friendship and Love Between Women from the Renaissance to the Present. Lillian Faderman (Morrow, 496pp., $18.95, Quill paperback, $10.95)

This book is not about lesbians. According to Professor Lillian Faderman's quite thorough scholarship, the "Lesbian" did not even exist in Europe until the 1880s and in the United States until 1910. Not a natural phenomenon, she was invented by the medical profession to cope with women's entry into the professions and higher education and to insure that female economic independence would not allow women to avoid marriage. Love between women, which did exist, was unlike Lesbianism in being socially honored, not secretive, and extremely common, and here Faderman makes her most ambitious points and may lose some readers.

As late as 1929 a nationwide study of American women chosen as normal revealed that 50 percent had experienced "intense emotional relations with other women" while half of this group had experienced such relations as sexual. Earlier, in Faderman's words, "it was virtually impossible to study the correspondence of any nineteenth-century woman ... of America ... England, France and Germany, and not uncover a passionate commitment to another woman at some time in her life."

In short, the inventors of "Lesbianism" saw the bell curve of emotional and sensual experience as skewed towards one of its ends, the "normal," while the other end was declared a separate and "abnormal" phenomenon. Such an unnatural separation can be – and has been – used to make all close bonds between women suspect. In connection with the twentieth-century view that eroticism can be reduced to genital contact, this same artificial division functions to declare all passionate attachments between women either trivial (those without a genital element) or criminal (those with). This modern idea that genitality is the point of division in relationships between women (not a turn-of-the-century criterion, as Faderman points out) cannot – I think – survive Faderman's piling up of evidence. In an age when carnality with anyone was forbidden to ladies there is little written evidence of genital contact between women (though some exists) but erotically toned "romances," "love affairs," and "marriages" abound. The creators of Lesbianism got around the ubiquity of such behavior by declaring that their model Lesbian (who was hysterical, insane, promiscuous, congenitally defective, murderous, suicidal, and anatomically mannish) was the "real" one and all others somehow unreal. (Some contemporary feminist scholars persist in this confusion, stating that embraces, kisses, courtships, "losing one's heart," and wishing to "marry" another woman do not make their embarrassingly intimate subjects "really" Lesbian.)

Surpassing the Love of Men has its faults. The author's treatment of contemporary Lesbian feminism is very weak and at times she seems to say that sexism and the segregation of the sexes cause love between women, a confusingly negative view that contradicts her assertion of the normalcy (statistical and other) of such behavior. Nor does she place her subject in the context of the bourgeois invention of the family, another social artifact supposed to be eternal, which was also imposed on the vast majority of the population of industrialized countries little more than a century ago. Homosexuality – or rather, acknowledgment of the variety of human behavior – *is* a threat to the (compulsory) family. This is no surprise if the invention of homosexual identity is viewed as a last-ditch defense of "the family," which was already being threatened not only by the advent of feminist protests against it, but also by the necessity of imposing on most of the population a social artifact designed to insure the well-being of men of a relatively small owning class. The similarity of the tactics of the Right wing today and those of the nineteenth-century sexologists is probably not accidental, since both connect Lesbianism with feminism, invalidate "Lesbians" as "real" women, and attack "Lesbians" in order to defend "the family." The more liberal, then and today, stress that this (now) distinct minority "can't help it" – but both insist that homosexuals constitute a distinct and different group, an assertion that restricts any kind of deviant behavior to a supposed minority.

Since calling people's attention to something new is easier than telling them that something they've always believed in was invented with malice aforethought not very long ago, Lillian Faderman's book is certainly going to be controversial. Public policy on sexuality (in such issues as abortion, sterilization, sexuality, marriage, and the family) is so explosive precisely because it is located at the junction of the public and the private. That eternal division ("eternal ever since Wednesday" as Dylan Thomas once said of the Welsh snows) is beginning to disappear as various thinkers question elements of "family life": full-time motherhood, childhood conceived as crucial and with its own special psychology, the connection between romantic love and unpaid labor, the timelessness of the family, and the home as a private sphere distinct from the marketplace and the workshop, with its "natural" function of providing a haven for emotions and relations banished from the public world.

Surpassing the Love of Men is an important achievement in this process of demystifying social institutions. Of direct interest to all women, the book has implications which affect everyone. *Surpassing the Love of Men* is an important document in the use of scientific opinion as a form of social control and the creation of a social identity via the falsification of history.

Essays

Daydream Literature and Science Fiction

David Lindsay, in *Voyage to Arcturus*. It's a remarkable thing, because scientifically it's nonsense, the style is appalling, *and yet* this ghastly vision comes through.[1]

C. S. Lewis, "C. S. Lewis Discusses Science Fiction with Kingsley Amis," *S F Horizons* (Oxford, Spring 1964), p. 6

In spite of a prose which is occasionally rude and awkward, *in spite of* characters which appear and vanish before, in some instances, we can quite grasp their significance, *in spite of* a plethora of overdramatic names like Maskull and Nightspore, Lindsay has produced a book which it is difficult if not impossible to lay down ...

Loren Eiseley, "Introduction," *A Voyage to Arcturus* (Ballantine Books, 1968), p. vii

In general, Van Vogt seems to me to fail consistently as a writer in these elementary ways:

1. His plots do not bear examination.

2. His choice of words and his sentence-structure are fumbling and insensitive.

3. He is unable either to visualise a scene or to make a character seem real ...

The wonder is that, using such unlikely materials and adapting them without a grain of common sense ... the author should have produced a narrative on the whole so lively and readable. The references to atomics in the story [*Empire of the Atom*] are nonsense from beginning to end; so are those to strategy and tactics; even the multiplication is wrong; *and yet* Van Vogt's single-minded power maniacs exert their usual fascination.

Damon Knight, *In Search of Wonder* (Advent Publications, Chicago, 1967), pp. 61–62

All of us who are old enough have used Poe, but none of us has ever

---

1 All italics in these quotations are mine.

> got to be a better writer – a manager of words – by that use... [in Eliot's words] ... "If we examine his work in detail, we seem to find in it nothing but slipshod writing, puerile thinking unsupported by wide reading or profound scholarship, haphazard experiments in various types of writing ... without perfection in any detail." ... [Poe's] force works through, not with, the language. At his more ordinary levels, his force gains nothing and sometimes loses a good deal because of the language in which he deploys it. The words do not matter much but what does matter would not be there without them.
> R. P. Blackmur, "Afterword," *The Fall of the House of Usher and Other Tales* (New American Library, New York, 1960), p. 375

How often is one asked to applaud the quality of a story *in spite of* its appalling style, scientific nonsense, bad structure, unvisualized scenes, unreal characterization, melodrama, and lack of perfection "in any detail"?

Quite often.

There exists, in science fiction and fantasy literature, a category I would like to call Daydream Literature; *Voyage to Arcturus* is this kind of writing, Poe often falls into it, Van Vogt's appeal rests largely on it, and the work of David Redd, a new British writer, also exists mainly as Daydream Literature.[2] I suspect that most adolescent readers who specialize in fantasy of the adventure/romance type are transforming what they read into Daydream Literature, although the actual story read may be good in quite other ways (Tolkien's trilogy) or may aspire to Daydream Literature and achieve only cliché (any "Brak the Barbarian" story). One of the symptoms of the transformation is the insistence on the moral profundity of what is actually simple and obvious. One young reader of Herbert's *Dune*, a student of mine, insisted the book was *really* about the profound spiritual differences between men and women, and I have heard the Tolkien books praised for the "complexity" of their ethics – an astonishing opinion which must make George Bernard Shaw spin in his grave. Critics are generally baffled by writing which is clearly bad, but which (even in them) evokes some kind of response. (R. P. Blackmur is just as baffled as anyone else; he expresses his bafflement more elaborately.) They generally conclude that the book has some power ("mythopoeic power" or "imagination" are common terms) apart from the specific detail of characters, plot, language, scenery, situation, et patati et patata.

But if you take away the writing in the book (i.e. the plot, the language, the scenery, the characters, the diction) what is left?

2 David Redd, "Sundown," *The Magazine of Fantasy and Science Fiction* (December, 1967); "Sunbeam Caress", *If* (March, 1968).

Nothing.

I propose that Daydream Literature does, in fact, employ a specific technique of style, a specific technique of form, and in general a whole body of craft, and that any response the literature evokes is because of this style and form and not in spite of it. "The Assignation" and *The Narrative of A. Gordon Pym* are not simply bad stories. If they were, critics would have to give up on Poe once and for all.

Still, Daydream Literature is not good literature, for all that.

Specificity – or particularity – is the *sine qua non* of all literary art. This particularity may inhere in different elements of fiction; or rather, it may be created in different ways. (Forgive my being obvious for a few moments.) The commonest way, I would imagine, is the particularity of events or objects, often rendered visually:

> His wife had heavy black eyebrows.
> It wrinkled and was gone.

Specificity inheres in figures of speech:

> Zero at the Bone
> Lives like loose thread

Or sound:

> Unimaginable zero summer
> In spring time, in spring time, the only pretty ring time

Or the naive or sophisticated use of the inflections of voice:

> Didst thou not share? Hadst thou not fifteen pence?

Or in rhythm:

> Here was neither Physician to destroy my Body, nor Lawyer to ruin my Fortune; No Informer to watch my Words and Actions, or forge accusations against me for Hire: Here were no Gibers, Censurers, Backbiters, Pickpockets ...

> Hickory, dickory dock. The mouse ran up the clock.

Or in syntax and the emphasis of certain words:

After such knowledge, what forgiveness?

Strode from his tent – Ivan!

Him th' Almighty Power / Hurled headlong flaming from th'ethereal sky

Or in pacing – a kind of rhythm that uses longer units than the single line or sentence. Byron is expert at this, as is every good dramatist and novelist.

There are also the specificities of diction, or the switch from one diction to another (Cummings' "I sing of Olaf") and of course the specificities of character, situation, plot, what is emphasized and what is not, and so forth. There is no such thing as specificity of mood, since mood is an emanation of all of the above, not a separate element. Of course no piece of writing will be a pure embodiment of a simple element, or – probably – less than all. And I apologize for sloppily belaboring the obvious.

I do it because what is extraordinary about *Arcturus*, Redd's work, Van Vogt's (in large part) and, say, "The Assignation," is that all these specificities are consistently shunned. They are not merely disregarded, for then the author might hit upon one of them by accident, and this does not happen. Specificity, particularity – what might just as well be called concreteness, if the concept is extended to verbal concreteness – is banned altogether from Daydream Literature.

The most striking examples of this are to be found either in the fine texture of the work or in the overall structure. I suppose a prose narrative cannot do entirely without what one might call medium-sized events, but these are the easiest to fake for the impressionable or naive reader; the very small and the very large are more betraying. For example, it does not matter much that the Marchesa Aphrodite or Gordon Pym are not real characters, or even real figures, but notice, please, that they are not even *clear* figures. Nor is the Venice of "The Assignation" in any possible way a *clearly* imagined (though fantastic) city. As for the rhythm, Poe is famous for his *ondulation chez Edgar*[3] and one of the most striking features of the other stories I have mentioned is the monotony of the rhythm. *Arcturus* is an endless parade of medium-length declarative sentences varied by medium-length interrogative sentences. David Redd (whose prose is not nearly so wretched) goes in for an incredible flatness and evenness of tone and pacing, difficult to demonstrate without introducing lengthy excerpts

---

3 "Permanent wave at Edgar's place" (I forget who said this).

from his work. But here is one of the high points of "Sunbeam Caress," the reappearance of a woman killed early in the story:

> A swift mental probe at maximum sensitivity revealed no trace of her thoughts. That, and her curious shuffling tread, showed that she was dead. The Racemind could not regard this as certain because it had not recorded her death impulses, but there was little possibility of error.[4]

Neither David Lindsay nor David Redd has a real voice, and Poe's voice is often forced to the point of unreality. ("Illfated and mysterious man! bewildered in the brilliancy of thine own imagination" etc.) The sound follows suit. And figures of speech – when they occur – are extremely simple. In *Arcturus*, music issues "as from an unearthly orchestra" (p. 153), and "The huge stone hurtled through the air. Its flight looked like a dark shadow" (p. 147). There are two similes in "Sundown" (that I can find), one of which compares a lady to a column. In "Sunbeam Caress" complexes of cells are described as "resembling masses of sponge rubber or soap foam" (p. 18); there are "purple crags like fangs" (p. 20); crystals dart "like fish" (p. 27); a crystal watches some plants "like a benevolent child-guardian" (p. 15). There are about a dozen metaphors or similes in forty pages. The most evocative – and one that makes me suspect that Redd may become a writer in spite of himself[5] – is the following: "giving her the impression she was flying over a forest of living rocks that were breathing slowly in the hot sun" (p. 13). These are not – as Poe's figures of speech or comparisons are not – bad or stale or even silly, but there seems to be a maximum of complexity that is set very low by the author, as if allowing any more complicated ideas into his metaphors or similes would do violence to the story.

The syntax is invariably flat and simple – whatever the length of the sentences – flaccid after a while in *Arcturus*, over-rotund in Poe, and exasperatingly pedantic in Redd.

There is almost no use of sound (*l'ondulation* again).

The pacing is abominable. This elusive virtue is apparently one the Daydream story-teller does not want to use. I cannot, short of including whole chapters, give any impression of the trudging regularity of the events

---

4 "Sunbeam Caress," p. 32.
5 That is, a writer of other than Daydream Literature. His latest story for *Fantasy and Science Fiction*, "A Quiet Kind of Madness" (May, 1968) suggests that he has trouble with anything but description, and that this difficulty led him into starting his career with Daydream Literature.

in *Arcturus* or the grinding pedantry with which marvels and wonders are systematically reduced to diagrams in Redd's stories. Things *are not meant* to build to climaxes. Readers of *Pym* will recognize the same principle at work, though Poe is not nearly so bald about it and manages some variety. But the lack of drama is still absolute; this may be what made Henry James speak of the "would-be portentous climax ... where the indispensable history is absent ... There *are* no connections."[6]

To be brief, nothing develops from anything; nothing generates anything; the stories are entirely episodic, with consistent and apparently deliberate avoidance of emphasis, complexity, or change. The principle of structure is repetition. The intensively recomplicated plot of a book like *Slan* is – paradoxically – just as anti-dramatic. By constantly changing the direction of the plot, Van Vogt defeats any effort to make sense out of it, or any possibility that events may reasonably lead to other events. Furthermore, the situations presented in Van Vogt's 800-word scenes[7] are not developed but only revealed. The general rule is one event per scene, and the result is essentially a series of tableaux, not very different from the unvarying regularity of presentation of events in *Arcturus*.

Repetition.

No voice or a forced voice.

Simple figures of speech.

Evenness of pacing.

Thin characters.

Flat sentences, little variety of use of syntax.

No playing with sound, or mechanical sound.

What remains?

For one thing, a corresponding lack of visualization. The reader of *Arcturus* will note that although the scene is an alien planet, it is extremely difficult to remember what the planet looks like. This is, to put it quite bluntly, because David Lindsay does not know what it looks like, nor can Poe see the strange places of *Pym* or Venice, or the rooms and corridors of the House of Usher – I will not say as well as one can see one's own bathroom, but as well as Lovecraft (who is certainly given to mad, purple bombinations) can see a farm kitchen or an old house. Turning again to *Arcturus*, here is an example at random:

> Without losing time, Panawe led the way up the mountainside. The lower half was of bare rock, not difficult to climb. Halfway up,

---

6 Cited by Blackmur, *The Fall of the House of Usher*, p. 382.
7 A. E. Van Vogt, "Complication in the Science Fiction Story," *Of Worlds Beyond*, L. A. Eshbach ed., Advent Publications, Chicago, 1964, p. 54.

however, it grew steeper, and they began to meet bushes and small trees. The growth became thicker as they continued to ascend, and when they neared the summit, tall forest trees appeared.

These bushes and trees had pale, glassy trunks and branches, but the small twigs and the leaves were translucent and crystal. They cast no shadow from above, but still the shade was cool. Both leaves and branches were fantastically shaped. What surprised Maskull the most, however, was the fact that, as far as he could see, scarcely any two plants belonged to the same species. (p. 64)

Moreover, most of the really important things in *Arcturus* are of two colors that are *not describable in human terms*. This is unseeing with a vengeance. I would also invite readers of Poe's stories to draw maps of, or describe, or remember, or in any sense visualize the Bridge of Sighs in "The Assignation" or that cliff from which Pym falls. Even the "black" water in *Pym* is schematically black rather than sensuously black. And Redd, although he has a good pair of eyes, is capable of the following:

The circular central area, which Rrengyara had seen in the process of formation, was about four feet in diameter. The thirteen paths, curving from the center of the pattern out to the circumference, were each two feet wide and about nine feet long. The region where they overlapped enlarged the central area.

The huge colorless crystals were no longer at the outer rim of the circular pattern. Twelve of them were positioned at regular intervals along the grooved pathways leading to the center, and the thirteenth crystal was actually at the center. The twelve on the pathways were arranged in lines of four; in each group the innermost crystal was close to the center, the outermost was near the perimeter, and the two others occupied intermediate positions on their respective grooves. Each pathway was occupied by one crystal, except for the thirteenth which was empty. ("Sunbeam Caress", p. 23)

The persons in Lindsay's romance, although described in highly emotional terms ("wild, powerful, and exceedingly handsome", p. 81) or picturesquely ("She was clothed in a single, flowing, pale green garment, rather classically draped ... she was not beautiful ... Her skin ... was opalescent ... She had very long, loosely plaited flaxen hair", p. 46) do not exactly linger in the mind. One might expect not to be able to visualize Emma Bovary down to the last freckle, but these persons, who grow tentacles, extra eyes, and all sorts of strange organs apparently at will, certainly ought to be clearer *to the eye* than they are. Poe's heroines – much more elegantly – are famous for being compounded from a few stylized pictorial traits, among which large, brilliant, black eyes figure with somewhat tiresome regularity.

Without definition, an object loses itself in the region of the indeterminate. Why then do these stories possess any concrete existence at all?

Let me repeat that the lack of concreteness I have been sketching is not at all the same thing as the use of stereotypes or clichés. Both stereotypes and clichés are concrete – all too concrete – and what Daydream Literature seems to want to attain is not a state of specificity-gone-sour or specificity-overused, but no specificity at all. This is not easy. The particularity of both *Arcturus* and Redd's two works (although "Sunbeam Caress" does attain to a certain exoticism in some of its concrete descriptions) resides in two things: the names of people and places, and what I would like to call "notions": e.g. a country where sexual love is pain, the unsuitability of the hero's blood for Arcturus and the heroine's replacing it with her own by putting their arms together, two suns that affect the hero in spiritually contradictory ways, and so forth. I call these "notions" because they are not explained, elaborated on, or even described; they are merely noted down and followed by other notions. It is hard to believe, for example, that extra eyes and tentacles could be dull, but the unseeing applies here, too. Lindsay is not interested in what such things would really be like, or look like, or how they would affect a man of ordinary sensibility, or how they would feel. He takes them for granted. David Redd, similarly, packs centuries of history into the forty pages of "Sunbeam Caress" and offers all sorts of mentioned-but-not-realized poeticisms in "Sundown" – "slow time," telepathy as a feature of journeying together, giants paralyzed by sunlight, and so on.[8] Poe, who does indeed elaborate his notions, keeps them from clear realization by stereotyping and simplifying, and by over-describing them in language so feverish *and* so *general* that no more than Lindsay's can his nightmares enter the daylight world. Compare the entrance of Madeline Usher fresh from her coffin with Dracula's forcing the heroine to drink his blood in Bram Stoker's novel; the latter is melodramatic and silly, but it's *all there*, not dissolved in a mist of strange, twangling instruments, nerves, feverishness, and overblown rhetoric. Poe, I might add, often elaborates upon his notions schematically and mechanically – witness the black vegetation in *Pym* and the word "Tek-e-lili," about which Henry James complained. It pops up all over the place, not because this will lead to some discovery about the word, but simply because it is more

---

8   These are a good deal more evocative than Lindsay's notions, possibly because they are not original with Redd; to use them at all, he has to give them at least some elaboration or verbal, poetic realization.

horrible that way. Heroes of Daydream Novels, by the way, may be horrified (Poe's heroes are generally far more horrified than the adult reader) but *they are never surprised at anything.*

James Blish's comment about Van Vogt is apposite here:

> A writer like Van Vogt, for example, never really comes to grips with an idea, but just piles another one on top of it.[9]

The second concrete element in Daydream Literature is the names. Lindsay's names are brilliant. In their suggestiveness, their wit, their collapsing of many references and metaphors into one word, they gather into themselves the particularity so lacking in the rest of the book. It is through the ritualistic naming of things and people that Lindsay, Redd, Poe (at times) and even Van Vogt establish the reality of their worlds:[10] Maskull, Nightspore, Crystalman, Joiwind, Blodsombre, Alppain, Branchspell, jale, ulfire, Sullenbode (a special success), Lady Rowena Trevanion of Tremaine, Weir. And, of course, Usher itself. Poe is writer enough to extend the wild and thrilling naming to adjectives and sometimes the choice of common nouns, yet he is hardly alone in this. (When does a pond become a "tarn"?)

In general, "Sundown" sticks to established words like troll, oreade, gnome, sprite, The White Lady, Living Rock, and North Polar Continent. In "Sunbeam Caress": fireballs, glitterbells, the Bright Ways, sunbursts, rock hags, cave crystals, melters, streamerhags, wandercacti, zombie-snakes, cracklebushes, Rrengyara, titanomoles, gelatinous slumberers, struthominai.

If naming were doing, beggars would be kings.

I hope that by now it has become clear what the aesthetic and dramatic principles of Literature are. They are exclusion and unseeing. They are the principles of daydream: structureless, repetitive, either vague or schematic, undeveloped, ritualistically naming. For the Marchesa Aphrodite to be *called* the Marchesa Aphrodite is almost enough for Poe; stand her next to something called The Bridge of Sighs, and it *is* enough. Simply naming the strange organs grown by Arcturans (the poign, the sorb) is quite enough for Lindsay. Reality must be constantly kept out of these constructions, and to this end nothing concrete – not dramatic tension, or clear scene, or developed feeling – can be allowed to intrude. A breath of air and the story crumbles.

---

9   James Blish (William Atheling, Jr.), *The Issue at Hand*, Advent Publications, Chicago, 1964, p. 38.
10 E.g. the climax of *Slan*. Tentacle-less Slans are really "tentacle-less Slans". Well!

Real dreams are not at all like daydreams; they are witty, poetic, poignant, forceful, sometimes painfully vivid, often extremely clear, and they cover the whole range of human feeling. Just like art.

It is true that Daydream Literature has an effect, for it does exist; there is an irreducible minimum of actuality that must be put on paper or there will be no story at all. This minimum of reality, as it excludes the concreteness of good writing, must also exclude the concreteness of bad writing. The Daydream Writer must perform a difficult balancing act, neither perpetrating bad literature nor risking the dissolution of his daydream-world through good literature.

Daydream Literature is, in fact, anti-literary, and successes in it are few, if one may speak of success in a mode which is dead-set against any kind of art and which attempts to exclude as much of reality as possible. The formula writer uses pieces of concrete actuality to anesthetize the reader to the possibility of other pieces of concrete actuality. (It's true that some cops are Irish and are named O'Reilly, though if you use only Irish cops called O'Reilly, you thereby exclude the perception of the possibility that a cop might be a Jew called Feinbaum.) Possibly the formula writer, in repeating a public daydream, works with sturdier stuff than the Daydream Writer does; if the daydream is public, we all share it or at least give it limited credence. The formula writer can tolerate – even encourage – solidity, daylight, real feeling, people, events, even limited thought. The Daydream Writer cannot.

Ibsen said that "to be a poet is chiefly to see"[11] and Conrad wished "above all to make you see," but the Daydream Writer must, above all, prevent you from seeing. Lulled to sleep by the non-sentences (or as close as prose can get to them), pursuing the non-plots that involve non-characters who are only evocative names, distracted neither by the sound of real voices nor the shock of real perceptions, persuaded of the profundities of non-feelings and non-thoughts, it is possible to get to daydreaming all by yourself without shutting the book. It is one's own daydreams that provide the mythopoeic power, the "ghastly vision" of C. S. Lewis, the fascination, the glimpse of something that disappears every time one tries to look straight at it, the sense of "extremity and the sense of mystery" that Blackmur talks about. And as he also says, "It is the particularity the reader brings that fills out the form ... the authority is ours – almost the authorship."[12] What I have called "notions" are only the barest of pedagogic hints, to daydream more extensively and exotically than one could unassisted. That is why the hints must remain only hints – only single

---

11 Cited by Eric Bentley, *In Search of Theatre*, Vintage Books, New York, 1957, p. 228.
12 Blackmur, *The Fall of the House of Usher*, p. 379.

notions – never to be dramatically or poetically elaborated. Daydream Literature requires a lot of imagination – in the reader.

In fact, the Daydream Story bears an astonishing resemblance to pornography. One might call it the pornography of poetry. Just as there is a pornography of adventure (endless examples!) and one of tears (we call it "sentimentality") and one of love and domesticity (generally called "trash") so there is a pornography of poetry. There is probably a pornography of everything. Pornography is the attempt to bypass the medium and turn a work of art into vicarious experience – to arouse emotion or appetite directly without the inevitable alloy of reflection given by art and without any of the embarrassments of thought or the mixedness of real experience. In *The Other Victorians* Steven Marcus states that the pornography of sex is forced to exclude so much reality that eventually genuine eroticism is thrown out, too, and pornography itself becomes anti-erotic. Daydream Literature, no matter how skillful, is anti-poetic and anti-philosophic. Ideas, too, must be kept unrealized, lest the lotus-trance be disturbed, and emotions are all the better if you can't recognize them or pin them down. Daydream Literature inevitably falls into bathos and silliness; no Daydream Writer succeeds; he is forced to be self-contradictory. Writing that is not good *is* bad; characters that are not realized *are* bores; ideas that are inconceivable *are* inconceivable.

"You may be the stronger, but he is the mightier," says Maskull to Krag of Crystalman.[13]

Daydream Literature may be initially delicious, but there comes a time when – wish how one may – Daydream Stories, like the statement quoted above, become absurd and exasperating. To anyone with a feeling for language or dramatic construction, they are torture.

Adolescents, foreseeing a vague and glorious personal future which unaccountably has no connection with the real, dull present, turn to this stuff and find in it the exaltation and the sense of emotional and moral profundity – Blackmur's "mystery" and "extremity" (which he also ascribes to "permanent adolescents"[14]) – that such books seem to offer. Often adolescents make perfectly decent literature *into* Daydream Literature: witness the Tolkien cult, the cult of *Stranger in a Strange Land*, and the recent enshrinement of *Magister Ludi*. With time, the powerful emotions associated with the vague and glorious realm of the vague and glorious future begin, oddly enough, to "leak" into real life. They are not at all what one thought they'd be when they were still part of Cloud Cuckooland, but as they fix themselves in real things, real acts, and real people, the many-

---

13 Lindsay, *Arcturus*, after 286 mortal pages!
14 Blackmur, *The Fall of the House of Usher*, p. 379.

colored realm of escape slowly fades. One day you find that Dream Literature has turned into vile and exasperating slush, for it never dates (as bad literature does) and therefore never becomes an object of amusement or nostalgia. The emotion that once filled the pages has evaporated as if through the very covers of the book, for it was never fixed in words, and you try in vain to read between the lines, as you once did.

There was never anything there.

AFTERWORD

This article began after I had read four terms' worth of student writing and tried in vain to find a word that described its peculiar badness. The word is "schematic" and it is the key to Daydream Literature, too. Most student writing is either schematic or clichéd – in the latter case because the writer is inexperienced and in the former because the elementary transition from daydream to art has not taken place. That is what is wrong with Daydream Literature. Our own daydreams seem to us so vivid and colorful that only after extensive experience of other people's daydreams do we realize how thin and schematic all daydreams – including our own – are. It is the ineffable and inexpressible that makes daydreaming so exciting; but art must express the inexpressible or cease to exist.

Someone will object here that all art is vicarious experience and that there is no distinction between art and daydreaming; i.e. no artistic medium.

He is wrong.

Red Clay Reader, **No. 7, November 1970**

The Image of Women in Science Fiction

Science fiction is *What If* literature. All sorts of definitions have been proposed by people in the field, but they all contain both The What If and The Serious Explanation; that is, science fiction shows things not as they characteristically or habitually are but as they might be, and for this "might be" the author must offer a rational, serious, consistent explanation, one that does not (in Samuel Delany's phrase) offend against what is known to be known.[1] Science fiction writers can't be experts in all disciplines, but they ought at least to be up to the level of the *New York Times* Sunday science page. If the author offers marvels and does not explain them, or if he explains them playfully and not seriously, or if the explanation offends against what the author knows to be true, you are dealing with fantasy and not science fiction. True, the fields tend to blur into each other and the borderland is a pleasant and gleeful place, but generally you can tell where you are. Examples:

J. R. R. Tolkien writes fantasy. He offends against all sorts of archaeological, geological, paleontological, and linguistic evidence which he undoubtedly knows as well as anyone else does.

Edgar Rice Burroughs wrote science fiction. He explained his marvels seriously and he explained them as well as he could. At the time he wrote, his stories did in fact conflict with what was known to be known, but he didn't know that. He wrote *bad* science fiction.

Ray Bradbury writes both science fiction and fantasy, often in the same story. He doesn't seem to care.

Science fiction comprises a grand variety of common properties: the fourth dimension, hyperspace (whatever that is), the colonization of other worlds, nuclear catastrophe, time travel (now out of fashion), interstellar exploration, mutated supermen, alien races, and so on. The sciences treated range from the "hard" or exact sciences (astronomy, physics) through the life sciences (biology, biochemistry, neurology) through the "soft" or inexact sciences (ethology, ecology) to disciplines that are still in the descriptive or philosophical stage and may never become exact (history,

---

1 In conversation and in his discussion of "Speculative Fiction" given at the MLA Seminar on Science Fiction in New York City, December 27, 1968.

for example).[2] I would go beyond these last to include what some writers call "para-sciences" – extra-sensory perception, psionics, or even magic – as long as the "discipline" in question is treated as it would have to be if it were real, that is rigorously, logically, and in detail.[3]

Fantasy, says Samuel Delany, treats what cannot happen, science fiction what has not happened.[4] One would think science fiction the perfect literary mode in which to explore (and explode) our assumptions about "innate" values and "natural" social arrangements, in short our ideas about Human Nature, Which Never Changes. Some of this has been done. But speculation about the innate personality differences between men and women, about family structure, about sex, in short about gender roles, hardly exists. And why not?

What is the image of women in science fiction?

We can begin by dismissing fiction set in the very near future (such as *On the Beach*) for most science fiction is not like this; most science fiction is set far in the future, some of it *very* far in the future, hundreds of thousands of years sometimes. One would think that by then human society, family life, personal relations, child-rearing, in fact anything one can name, would have altered beyond recognition. This is not the case. The more intelligent, literate fiction carries today's values and standards into its future Galactic Empires. What may politely be called the less sophisticated fiction returns to the past – not even a real past, in most cases, but an idealized and exaggerated past.[5]

Intergalactic Suburbia

In general, the authors who write reasonably sophisticated and literate science fiction (Clarke, Asimov, for choice) see the relations between the sexes as those of present-day, white, middle-class suburbia. Mummy and Daddy may live inside a huge amoeba and Daddy's job may be to test

---

2 Basil Davenport, *Inquiry Into Science Fiction,* Longmans, Green and Co., New York, London, Toronto, 1955, pp. 39ff.
3 A recent novel by James Blish, *Black Easter,* published by Doubleday, Garden City, N.Y. in 1968, does exactly this. See in particular the Introduction, pp. 7–8.
4 Samuel Delany, "About Five Thousand One Hundred and Seventy Five Words," in *Extrapolation: the Newsletter of the Conference on Science Fiction of the MLA,* ed. Thomas D. Clareson, College of Wooster, Wooster, Ohio, Vol. X, No. 2, May 1969, pp. 61–63.
5 There have been exceptions, e.g. Olaf Stapledon, George Bernard Shaw. And of course Philip Wylie's *The Disappearance.* Wylie's novel really ranks as a near-future story, though.

psychedelic drugs or cultivate yeast-vats, but the world inside their heads is the world of Westport and Rahway *and that world is never questioned*. Not that the authors are obvious about it; Fred Pohl's recent satire, *The Age of the Pussyfoot*, is a good case in point.[6] In this witty and imaginative future world, death is reversible, production is completely automated, the world population is enormous, robots do most of the repetitive work, the pharmacopoeia of psychoactive drugs is very, very large, and society has become so complicated that people must carry personal computers to make their everyday decisions for them. I haven't even mentioned the change in people's clothing, in their jobs, their slang, their hobbies, and so on. But it you look more closely at this weird world you find that it practices a laissez-faire capitalism, one even freer than our own; that men make more money than women; that men have the better jobs (the book's heroine is the equivalent of a consumer-research guinea pig); and that children are raised at home by their mothers.

In short, the American middle class with a little window dressing.

In science fiction, speculation about social institutions and individual psychology has always lagged far behind speculation about technology, possibly because technology is easier to understand than people. But this is not the whole story.[7] I have been talking about intelligent, literate science fiction. Concerning this sort of work one might simply speak of a failure of imagination outside the exact sciences, but there are other kinds of science fiction, and when you look at them, something turns up that makes you wonder if failure of imagination is what is at fault.

I ought to make it clear here that American science fiction and British science fiction have evolved very differently and that what I am going to talk about is – in origin – an American phenomenon. In Britain science fiction not only was always respectable, it still is, and there is a continuity in the field that the American tradition does not have. British fiction is not, on the whole, better written than American science fiction but it continues to attract first-rate writers from outside the field (Kipling, Shaw, C. S. Lewis, Orwell, Golding) and it continues to be reviewed seriously and well.[8]

---

6 Frederik Pohl, *The Age of the Pussyfoot*, Trident Press, New York, 1968.
7 I don't want to adduce further examples, but most well-known science fiction is of this kind. It suffices to read *Childhood's End* for example (Arthur C. Clarke), and ask about the Utopian society of the middle: What do the men do? What do the women do? Who raises the children? And so on.
8 See William Atheling, Jr. (James Blish), *The Issue at Hand*, Advent Press, Chicago, 1964, pp. 117–19. I ought to make it clear that I am talking here of science fiction as a literary/cultural phenomenon, e.g., nobody can accuse George Bernard Shaw of suffering from the he-man ethos. But Shaw's ventures into science fiction have had little influence on the American tradition.

American science fiction developed out of the pulps and stayed outside the tradition of serious literature for at least three decades; it is still not really respectable.[9] American science fiction originated in the adventure-story-*cum*-fairy-tale which most people think of (erroneously) as "science fiction." It has been called a great many things, most of them uncomplimentary, but the usual name is "space opera". There are good writers working in this field who do not deserve the public notoriety bred by this kind of science fiction. But their values usually belong to the same imaginative world and they participate in many of the same assumptions.[10] I will not, therefore, name names, but will pick on something inoffensive – think of Flash Gordon and read on.

Down Among the He-Men

If most literate science fiction takes for its gender-role models the ones which actually exist (or are assumed as ideals) in middle-class America, space opera returns to the past for *its* models, and not even the real past, but an idealized and simplified one. These stories are not realistic. They are primitive, sometimes bizarre, and often magnificently bald in their fantasy. Some common themes:

A *feudal economic and social structure* – usually paired with advanced technology and inadequate to the complexities of a seventh-century European mud hut.

Women are important as prizes or motives – i.e. we must rescue the heroine or win the hand of the beautiful Princess. Many fairy-tale motifs turn up here.

Active or ambitious women are evil – this literature is chockfull of cruel dowager empresses, sadistic matriarchs, evil ladies maddened by jealousy, domineering villainesses, and so on.

Women are supernaturally beautiful – all of them.

Women are weak and/or kept off stage – this genre is full of scientists' beautiful daughters who know just enough to be brought along by Daddy as his research assistant, but not enough to be of any help to anyone.

---

9   The American pioneer was Hugo Gernsback, whose name adorns the "Hugo," the yearly fan awards for best novel of the year, best short story, etc. In 1908 Gernsback founded a magazine called *Modern Electrics*, the world's first radio magazine. In 1911 he published a serial of his own writing called "Ralph 124C41+". Gernsback founded *Amazing Stories* in 1926 and by common consent, real science entered the field with John W. Campbell, Jr., in the late 1930s.

10 Some of the better writers in this genre are Keith Laumer, Gordon Dickson, and Poul Anderson. Most magazine fiction is at least tainted with space opera.

THE IMAGE OF WOMEN IN SCIENCE FICTION

Women's powers are passive and involuntary – an odd idea that turns up again and again, not only in space opera. If female characters are given abilities, these are often innate abilities which cannot be developed or controlled, e.g. clairvoyance, telepathy, hysterical strength, unconscious psi power, eidetic memory, perfect pitch, lightning calculation, or (more baldly) magic. The power is somehow *in* the woman, but she does not really possess it. Often realistic science fiction employs the same device.[11]

The real focus of interest is not on women at all – but on the cosmic rivalries between strong, rugged, virile he-men. It is no accident that space opera and horse opera bear similar names.[12] Most of the readers of science fiction are male and most of them are young; people seem to quit reading the stuff in their middle twenties and the hard-core readers who form fan clubs and go to conventions are even younger and even more likely to be male.[13] Such readers as I have met (the addicts?) are overwhelmingly likely to be nervous, shy, pleasant boys, sensitive, intelligent, and very awkward with people. They also talk too much. It does not take a clairvoyant to see why such people would be attracted to space opera, with its absence of real women and its tremendous over-rating of the "real he-man." In the March 1969 issue of *Amazing* one James Koval wrote to the editor as follows:[14]

> Your October issue was superb; better than that, it was uniquely original ... Why do I think it so worthy of such compliments? Because of the short stories *Conqueror* and *Mu Panther*, mainly. They were, in every visual and emotional sense, stories about real men whose rugged actions and keen thinking bring back a genuine feeling of masculinity, a thing sorely missed by the long-haired and soft-eyed generation of my time, of which I am a part ... aiming entertainment at the virile and imaginative male of today is the best kind of business ... I sincerely hope you keep your man-versus-animal type format going, especially with stories like *Mu Panther*. That was exceptionally unique.

The editor's response was "GROAN!"

---

11 In *Age of the Pussyfoot* the heroine makes her living by trying out consumer products. She is so ordinary (or statistically extraordinary) that if she likes the products, the majority of the world's consumers will also like them. A prominent character in John Brunner's recent novel, *Stand on Zanzibar*, is a clairvoyant.
12 Also "soap opera" – the roles of the sexes are reversed.
13 I would put the ratio of male to female readers at about five to one. It might very well be higher.
14 I *think* March and I think it was *Amazing*; it is either *Amazing* or *Worlds of If* for 1968 or 1969. Sorry!

But even if readers are adolescents, the writers are not. I know quite a few grown-up men who should know better, but who nonetheless fall into what I would like to call the he-man ethic. And they do it over and over again. In November 1968, a speaker at the Philadelphia Science Fiction Convention[15] described the heroes such writers create:

> The only real He-Man is Master of the Universe ... The real He-Man is invulnerable. He has no weaknesses. Sexually he is super-potent. He does exactly what he pleases, everywhere and at all times. He is absolutely self-sufficient. He depends on nobody, for this would be a weakness. Toward women he is possessive, protective, and patronizing; to men he gives orders. He is never frightened by anything or for any reason; he is never indecisive and he always wins.

In short, masculinity equals power and femininity equals powerlessness. This is a cultural stereotype that can be found in much popular literature, but science fiction writers have no business employing stereotypes, let alone swallowing them goggle-eyed.

Equal Is as Equal Does

In the last decade or so, science fiction has begun to attempt the serious presentation of men and women as equals, usually by showing them at work together. Even a popular television show like *Star Trek* shows a spaceship with a mixed crew; fifteen years ago this was unthinkable.[16] *Forbidden Planet*, a witty and charming film made in the 1950s, takes it for granted that the crew of a spaceship will all be red-blooded, crew-cut, woman-hungry men, rather like the cast of *South Pacific* before the nurses arrive. And within the memory of living adolescent, John W. Campbell, Jr., the editor of *Analog*, proposed that "nice girls" be sent on spaceships as prostitutes because married women would only clutter everything up with washing and babies. But Campbell is a coelacanth.

At any rate, many recent stories do show a two-sexed world in which women as well as men work competently and well. But this is a reflection of present reality, not genuine speculation. And what is most striking about these stories is what they leave out: the characters' personal and erotic relations are not described; child-rearing arrangements (to my knowledge)

---

15 Me.
16 It is noteworthy, however, that the ladies of the crew spend their time as nurses, stewardesses and telephone operators.

are never described; and the women who appear in these stories are either young and childless or middle-aged, with their children safely grown up. That is, the real problems of a society without gender-role differentiation are not faced. It is my impression that most of these stories are colorless and schematic; the authors want to be progressive, God bless them, but they don't know how. Exceptions:

Mack Reynolds, who also presents a version of future socialism called "the Ultra-Welfare State." (Is there a connection?) He has written novels about two-sexed societies of which one is a kind of mild gynocracy. He does not describe child-rearing arrangements, though.

Samuel Delany, who often depicts group marriages and communal child-rearing, "triplet" marriages (not polygamy or polyandry, for each person is understood to have sexual relations with the other two) *und so weiter*, all with no differentiation of gender roles, all with an affectionate, East Village, Berkeley-Bohemian air to them, and all with the advanced technology that would make such things work. His people have the rare virtue of fitting the institutions under which they live. Robert Heinlein, who also goes in for odd arrangements (e.g the "line marriage" in *The Moon Is a Harsh Mistress* in which everybody is married to everybody, but there are seniority rights in sex), peoples his different societies with individualistic, possessive, competitive, pre-World War II Americans – just the people who could not live under the cooperative or communal arrangements he describes. Heinlein, for all his virtues, seems to me to exemplify science fiction's failure of imagination in the human sphere. He is superb at work but out of his element elsewhere. *Stranger in a Strange Land* seems to me a particular failure. I have heard Heinlein's women called "boy scouts with breasts" – but the subject takes more discussion than I can give it here. Alexei Panshin's critical study, *Heinlein in Dimension*, undertakes a thorough investigation of Heinlein vs. Sex. Heinlein loses.[17]

Matriarchy

The strangest and most fascinating oddities in science fiction occur not in the stories that try to abolish differences in gender roles but in those which attempt to reverse the roles themselves. Unfortunately, only a handful of writers have treated this theme seriously. Space opera abounds, but in space opera the reversal is always cut to the same pattern.

---

17 See Alexei Panshin's *Heinlein in Dimension*, Advent Press, Chicago, 1968, especially Chapter VI.

Into a world of cold, cruel, domineering women who are openly contemptuous of their cringing, servile men ("gutless" is a favorite word here) arrive(s) men (a man) from our present world. With a minimum of trouble, these normal men succeed in overthrowing the matriarchy, which although strong and warlike, is also completely inefficient. At this point the now dominant men experience a joyful return of victorious manhood and the women (after initial reluctance) declare that they too are much happier. Everything is (to quote S. J. Perelman) leeches and cream.[18] Two interesting themes occur:

(1) the women are far more vicious, sadistic, *and openly contemptuous* of men than comparable dominant men are of comparable subordinate women in the usual space opera.

(2) the women are dominant because they are taller and stronger than the men (!).

Sometimes the story is played out among the members of an alien species modeled on insects or microscopic sea-creatures, so that tiny males are eaten or engulfed by huge females. I remember one in which a tiny male was eaten by a female who was not only forty feet tall but maddened to boot.[19] There are times when science fiction leaves the domain of literature altogether. Least said, soonest mended.

I remember three British accounts of future matriarchies that could be called serious studies. In one the matriarchy is incidental. The society is presented as good because it embodies the traditionally feminine virtues of serenity, tolerance, love, and pacifism.[20] In John Wyndham's "Consider Her Ways" there are no men at all; the society is a static, hierarchical one which (like the first) is good because of its traditionally feminine virtues, which are taken as innate in the female character. There is something about matriarchy that makes science fiction writers think of two things: biological

---

18 Entertaining use can be made of this form. Keith Laumer's delightfully tongue-in-cheek "The War With the Yukks" is a case in point. You will now complain that I don't tell you where to find it, but trying to find uncollected stories or novellas is a dreadful task. I don't know where it is. I read it in a magazine publication; magazines vanish.

19 Again, vanished without a trace. It's an oldie and I suspect it appeared in one of Groff Conklin's fat anthologies of *The Best S.F.* for (fill in year). It was a lovely story.

20 This one may be American. A Russian (or American) and a Red Chinese, both from our present, are somehow transported into the future. They kill each other at a party in a xenophobic rage which their hostesses find tragic and obsolete. I remember that the ladies in the story shave their heads (that is, the ladies' own heads). Not exactly a matriarchy but a semi-reversal of gender roles occurs in Philip Wylie's *The Disappearance*, a brilliant argument to the effect that gender roles are learned and can be unlearned.

engineering and social insects; whether women are considered naturally chitinous or the softness of the female body is equated with the softness of the "soft" sciences I don't know, but the point is often made that "women are conservative by nature" and from there it seems an easy jump to bees or ants. Science fiction stories often make the point that a matriarchy will be static and hierarchical, like Byzantium or Egypt. (It should be remembered here that the absolute value of progress is one of the commonest shibboleths of science fiction.) The third story I remember – technically it's a "post-Bomb" story – was written by an author whose version of matriarchy sounds like Robert Graves's.[21] The story makes the explicit point that while what is needed is static endurance, the Mother rules; when exploration and initiative again become necessary, the Father will return. The Great Mother is a real, supernatural character in this tale and the people in it are very real people. The matriarchy – again, the women rule by supernatural knowledge – is vividly realized and there is genuine exploration of what personal relations would be like in such a society. There is a kind of uncompromising horror (the hero is hunted by "the hounds of the Mother" – women whose minds have been taken over by the Magna Mater) which expresses a man's fear of such a world much more effectively than all the maddened, forty-foot-tall male-gulpers ever invented.

So far I've been discussing fiction written by men and largely for men.[22] What about fiction written by women?

Women's Fiction: Potpourri

Most science fiction writers are men, but some are women, and there are more women writing the stuff than there used to be. The women's work falls into four rough categories:

(1) *Ladies' magazine fiction* – in which the sweet, gentle, intuitive little heroine solves an interstellar crisis by mending her slip or doing something equally domestic after her big, heroic husband has failed. Zenna Henderson sometimes writes like this. *Fantasy and Science Fiction*, which carries more of this kind of writing than any of the other magazines, once earned a

---

21 Again I find myself with distinct memories of the story and none of the author's name. I would appreciate any information. Science fiction is in a dreadful state bibliographically.
22 This is perhaps too sweeping a statement; Isaac Asimov certainly writes for everybody, to give one example only. But male readers do outnumber female readers, and there is a definite bias in the field toward what I have called the he-man ethos. I think the generalization can stand as a generalization.

deserved slap over the knuckles from reviewer James Blish.[23]

(2) *Galactic suburbia* – very often written by women. Sometimes the characters are all male, especially if the story is set at work. Most women writing in the field (like so many of the men) write this kind of fiction.

(3) *Space opera* – strange but true. Leigh Brackett is one example. Very rarely the protagonist turns out to be a sword-wielding, muscular, aggressive *woman* – but the he-man ethos of the world does not change, nor do the stereotyped personalities assigned to the secondary characters, particularly the female ones.

(4) *Avant-garde fiction* – part of the recent rapprochement between the most experimental of the science fiction community and the most avant-garde of what is called "the mainstream." This takes us out of the field of science fiction altogether.[24]

In general, stories by women tend to contain more active and lively female characters than do stories by men, and more often than men writers, women writers try to invent worlds in which men and women will be equals. But the usual faults show up just as often. The conventional idea that women are second-class people is a hard idea to shake; and while it is easy enough to show women doing men's work, or active in society, it is in the family scenes and the love scenes that one must look for the author's real freedom from our most destructive prejudices.

An Odd Equality

I would like to close with a few words about *The Left Hand of Darkness*, a fine book that won the Science Fiction Writers of American Nebula Award for 1969 as the best novel of that year.[25] The book was written by a woman and it is about sex – I don't mean copulation; I mean what sexual identity means to people and what human identity means to them, and what kind of love can cross the barriers of culture and custom. It's a beautifully written book. Ursula K. Le Guin, the author, has imagined a world of human hermaphrodites – an experimental colony abandoned by its creators long ago and rediscovered by other human beings. The adults of this glacial

---

23 See William Atheling, Jr. (James Blish), *The Issue at Hand*, Advent Press, Chicago, 1964, p. 112.
24 Carol Emshwiller is a good example, See the *Orbit* series of anthologies edited by Damon Knight (Putnam's in hardcover, Berkley in paperback).
25 Ursula K. Le Guin, *The Left Hand of Darkness*, Ace Books, New York, N.Y. 1969 (paperback). As of this writing it has also received the Hugo, a comparable fan award.

THE IMAGE OF WOMEN IN SCIENCE FICTION

world of Winter go through an oestrus cycle modeled on the human menstrual cycle: every four weeks the individual experiences a few days of sexual potency and obsessive interest in sex during which "he" becomes either male or female. The rest of the time "he" has no sex at all, or rather, only the potential of either. The cycle is involuntary, though it can be affected by drugs, and there is no choice of sex – except that the presence of someone already into the cycle and therefore of one sex will stimulate others in oestrus to become of the opposite sex. You would imagine that such a people's culture and institutions would be very different from ours and so they are; everything is finely realized, from their household implements to their customs to their creation myths. Again, however (and I'm very sorry to see it), family structure is not fully explained. Worse than that, child-rearing is left completely in the dark, although the human author herself is married and the mother of three children. Moreover, there is a human observer on Winter and he is male; and there is a native hero and *he is* male – at least "he" is *masculine in gender, if not in sex*. The native hero has a former spouse who is long-suffering, mild and gentle, while he himself is fiery, tough, self-sufficient, and proud. There is the Byronesque memory of a past incestuous affair; his lover and sibling is dead. There is an attempted seduction by a kind of Mata Hari *who is female* (so that the hero, of course, becomes male). It is, I must admit, a deficiency in the English language that these people must be called "he" throughout, but put that together with the native hero's personal encounters in the book, the absolute lack of interest in child-raising, the concentration on work, and what you have is a world of men. Thus the great love scene in the book is between two men: the human observer (who is a real man) and the native hero (who is a female man). The scene is nominally homosexual, but I think what lies at the bottom of it (and what has moved men and women readers alike) is that it is a love scene between a man and a woman, with the label "male: high status" pasted on the woman's forehead. Perhaps, with the straitjacket of our gender roles, with women automatically regarded as second-class, intelligent and active women *feel* as if they were female men or hermaphrodites. Or perhaps the only way a woman (even in a love scene) can be made a man's equal and the love scene therefore deeply moving, is to make her *nominally* male. That is, female in sex but male in gender. Here is the human narrator describing the alien hero:

> to ignore the abstraction, to hold fast to the thing. There was in this attitude something feminine, a refusal of the abstract ideal, a submissiveness to the given ...[26]

26 *Ibid.*, p. 201.

Very conventional, although the story is set far, far in the future and the narrator is supposed to be a trained observer, a kind of anthropologist. Here is the narrator again, describing human women (he has been asked if they are "like a different species"):

> No. Yes. No, of course not, not really. But the difference is very important, I suppose the most important thing, the heaviest single factor in one's life, is whether one's born male or female ... Even where women participate equally with men in the society, *they still after all do all the child-bearing and so most of the child-rearing* ...

And when asked "Are they mentally inferior?":

> I don't know. They don't often seem to turn up mathematicians, or composers of music, or inventors, or abstract thinkers. But it isn't that they're stupid ...[27]

Let me remind you that this is centuries in the future. And again:

> The boy ... had a girl's quick delicacy in his looks and movements, but no girl could keep so grim a silence as he did ...[28]

It's the whole difficulty of science fiction, of genuine speculation: how to get away from traditional assumptions which are nothing more than traditional straitjackets.[29] Miss Le Guin seems to be aiming at some kind of equality between the sexes, but she certainly goes the long way around to get it; a whole new biology has to be invented, a whole society, a whole imagined world, so that finally she may bring together two persons of different sexes who will nonetheless be equals.[30]

27 *Ibid.*, p. 223.
28 *Ibid.*, p. 281.
29 I am too hard on the book; the narrator isn't quite that positive and one could make out a good case that the author is trying to criticize his viewpoint. There is also a technical problem: we are led to equate the human narrator's world (which we never see) with our own, simply because handling *two* unknowns in one novel would present insuperable difficulties. Moreover, Le Guin wishes us to contrast Winter with our own world, not with some hypothetical, different society which would then have to be shown in detail. However, her earlier novel, *City of Illusions*, also published by Ace, is surprisingly close to the space opera, he-man ethos – either anti-feminism or resentment at being feminine, depending on how you look at it.
30 There is an old legend (or a new one – I heard it read several years ago on WBAI-FM) concerning Merlin and some sorceress who was his sworn enemy. Each had resolved to destroy the other utterly, but they met and – each not knowing

The title I chose for this essay was "The Image of Women in Science Fiction." I hesitated between that and "Women in Science Fiction" but if I had chosen the latter, there would have been very little to say.

There are plenty of images of women in science fiction.

There are hardly any women.

Bibliography

Fiction
James Blish, *Black Easter*, Doubleday, Garden City, New York, 1968
Ray Bradbury, *The Martian Chronicles*, Doubleday, New York, 1950 (available in Bantam paperback)
Edgar Rice Burroughs, *Thuvia, Maid of Mars*, Ace Books, New York, 1969 (others in the John Carter series are in Ace paperback)
Samuel Delany, *Babel-17*, Ace Books, New York, 1966
Robert Heinlein, *Stranger in a Strange Land*, Berkley, New York, 1969 (Many editions exist by now. The novel is copyrighted 1961)
Robert Heinlein, *The Moon Is a Harsh Mistress*, Berkley, New York, 1967
Ursula K. Le Guin, *The Left Hand of Darkness*, Ace Books, New York, 1969
Frederik Pohl, *Age of the Pussyfoot*, Trident, New York, 1968
J. R. R. Tolkien, *Lord of the Rings*, 3 volumes, Ballantine, New York, 1966
I suggest also the *Orbit* series for short stories:
Damon Knight, ed., *Orbit* (number whatever), Putnam's, New York (published in paperback by Berkley), semi-annual
Several years'-best anthologies are published:
Judith Merril, *The Year's Best Science Fiction*
Terry Carr, *World's Best Science Fiction*
Harry Harrison, *Best Science Fiction of*

Current magazines
Amazing and *Fantastic*, both ed. Ted White
Analog, ed. John W. Campbell, Jr.
Fantasy and Science Fiction, ed. Ed Ferman
Galaxy, ed. Ejler Jakobsson

Criticism
Kingsley Amis, *New Maps of Hell*, Ballantine, New York, 1960
William Atheling, Jr. (James Blish), *The Issue at Hand*, Advent Press, Chicago, 1964

who the other was – fell in love. The problem was solved by Merlin's transforming her into him and she transforming him into herself. Thus both destroyed and reconstituted in the other sex, they lived happily ever after (one assumes). Or as Shaw was supposed to have said, he conceived of his female characters as being himself in different circumstances.

Basil Davenport, *Inquiry Into Science Fiction*, Longmans, Green and Co., London, New York, Toronto, 1955

Samuel Delany, "About Five Thousand One Hundred and Seventy Five Words," in *Extrapolation: the Newsletter of the Conference on Science Fiction of the MLA*, ed. Thomas D. Clareson, College of Wooster, Wooster, Ohio, Vol. X, No. 2, May 1969

Damon Knight, *In Search of Wonder*, Advent Press, Chicago, 1967 (2nd ed. revised)

Alexei Panshin, *Heinlein in Dimension*, Advent Press, Chicago, 1968

Joanna Russ, "Dream Literature and Science Fiction," *Extrapolation* (see above), Vol. XI, No. 1, December 1969

SF Horizons, Nos. 1 and 2, eds. Harry Harrison, Brian Aldiss, available at 50¢ per copy from Tom Boardman, Jr., Pelham, Priory Road, Sunningdale, Berks., England. (No. 1 was published in 1964, No. 2 in 1965. The magazine then died.)

For those who wish to hunt it up:

James Blish, "On Science Fiction Criticism," *Riverside Quarterly*, August 1968, Vol. 3, No. 3, pp. 214–17

The Wearing Out of Genre Materials

Genre fiction, like all fiction, is a compromise.

Narrative fiction – unlike lyrical verse – cannot produce the big scene, or the rush of emotion, or the spectacular situation, or the emotional high point, in a chronological vacuum. Part of the story must be given over to rationalization, to chronological and/or dramatic development, to the background and explanation that make the emotional high point possible, let alone plausible, let alone reasonable, let alone humanly interesting.

That is, fiction is *a wish made plausible*. (I have developed this formula out of my own experience in writing and personal acquaintance with some two dozen living writers.) The written story is a compromise between the germinal, wished-for situation, action, or scene and the surrounding fictional circumstances which make the original X possible in a connected, chronological narrative. (Without a connected and chronological narrative, you have a lyrical treatment, not a story.) In good writing, the compromise between the wish and the forces of reason or conscience is in itself interesting and moving because it is in itself representative of human life. Our feelings, our actions, our perceptions and our decisions are a series of just such compromises between what we want, what we want to want, what we think we ought to want, and what we know (or believe) we can get. The process I have called making the wish plausible may in fact take over the work and itself become the work; then you have a story of disillusionment or self-deception. Bad writing is often called undisguised fantasy, but I would prefer to call it the wish insufficiently worked on by reason and conscience – good fantasy is often quite bald, and certainly no one could say of Sophocles' *Oedipus* that it is a "carefully disguised" fantasy. On the contrary, the Oedipal content of *Oedipus* (!) is hardly disguised at all, except by the character's denial that he knew what he was doing; what has been added to the wish (following Freud's notion of it) is the corollary: *What if this really happened?* That is, the original fantasy, again following Freud's idea of it, is combined with reason and conscience. I would add that to my mind the obligatory scene of Sophocles' play is the act of finding out about the past incest, not the act of incest itself, and that the finding-out scene is the emotional and dramatic high point of the play.

George Bernard Shaw has called great art the triumph of a great mind over a great imagination.[1] He has also described the process of producing a bad popular play as doing the most daring thing you can and then running away from the consequences.[2] To produce a good play, presumably, one does the most daring thing one can and then does *not* run away from the consequences. Both descriptions seem to me very like mine.

My thesis in this paper is that when writers work in the same genre, i.e. use the same big scenes or "gimmicks" or "elements" or "ideas" or "worlds" (similar locales and kinds of plots lead to similar high points), they are using the same fantasy. Once used in art, once brought to light, as it were, the effect of the fantasy begins to wane, and the scene embodying it begins to wear out. The question immediately arises: Which wears out? Does the underlying wish wear out or does the literary construct lose its power of embodying the wish, and do the two become disconnected from each other? There seems to be evidence for both hypotheses.

That art changes when society changes is one of the commonplaces of the history of art. That is, the old forms (as well as the old styles) do in fact disappear only when social conditions change, and a static society is apparently content to represent the same things over and over in the same way – at least in the plastic arts. It would be reasonable to assume that new forms are sought for new content, i.e. new embodiments of new wishes. As long as social conditions – and hence, presumably, what people want – remain the same, art remains the same and keeps its power over the reader or spectator. Moveover, old and forgotten artistic devices or obsessions do seem to reappear, i.e. they are either recreated or rediscovered when the wish behind them manifests itself again. For example, it has been suggested that modern ideas about drugs and the drug culture parallel early Romantic ideas about insanity – we are and they were looking for some kind of insight or vision beyond ordinary perception. The fact that this obsession has reappeared does not mean, however, that the wish was genuinely in abeyance in the intervening period; perhaps there was no means, or no ready artistic means, for embodying the wish. There is evidence in individual readers' and writers' careers that what really happens is that the wish persists but the artistic construct loses its connection with the wish – Auden has said that readers go from bad to good literature *looking for the same thing*. That is, in one person's lifetime the desire for a certain kind of fantasy persists, but the person is driven to a higher and higher quality of literary work. The bad work wears out.

---

[1] George Bernard Shaw, *Our Theatres in the Nineties*, Constable and Co., London, 1954, III, p. 16.
[2] *Ibid.*, p. 63.

Also suggestive of the idea that the wish and the construct become disconnected in the history of a genre is the surprising freshness and vitality of the best work within specific genres. A reader going back to H. G. Wells finds versions of many things now used in science fiction, but Wells' work isn't stale on that account. Often his imitators pall more quickly than he does.

Perhaps some motifs die a natural death over long periods – due to the effects of social change on the wish – while others are prematurely aged, especially in the last couple of centuries, by being used too much too fast by too many writers. (The Tristan myth seems to have really lost its power *as a wish* – the forbidden love/death theme repeated so often in Western literature. Some critics suggest that *Lolita* is the last Tristanesque novel and that Nabokov could only stay in the Tristan line by parodying it.)

Practically speaking and in the short run, motifs do wear out. Bela Lugosi, once the horrifier of thousands, now excites something much closer to laughter. It is not only the quaintness of the old *Dracula*, but its predictability, that amuses people. As a film genre the vampire movie has been done to death, perhaps even prematurely.

What does a writer do then?

The continuing success of what's old and good is heartening but although old work can please readers, this doesn't much help a writer. Most difficult of all is to be still interested in the buried wish but unable to use the scene or high point or action that embodies the wish because that scene or action has become ever more taken for granted, known, and expected, not only by the reader but (this is what really counts) also *by the writer*. You are suspended like Mahomet's coffin: you can't give up the wish, and yet you can't realize it.

I would like to suggest that there is a way out of this dilemma, that writers take it, and that their taking it accounts for the phenomenon of genre material wearing out (as all fictional narrative eventually may do). Not only that, the way out of the dilemma accounts for *the way* scenes or plots do in fact wear out: that is, not all at once but in three distinct stages. I have named these Innocence, Plausibility, and Decadence; they might just as well be called Primitivism, Realism, and Decadence (though "Realism" here has nothing to do with realism as a style or historical period).

In science fiction these three stages are usually very distinct, as science fiction themes or big scenes tend to be more than usually visible. Their intellectual and novelty content is high. There is, for example, the Revolt of the Robots. If you look into Damon Knight's collection, *A Century of Science Fiction*, you will find three robot stories: "Moxon's Master" by Ambrose Bierce, "Reason" by Isaac Asimov and "But Who Can Replace a Man?" by Brian W. Aldiss.[3] Mr. Knight has arranged them in chronological

---

3 Damon Knight, *A Century of Science Fiction*, Pan Books, London, 1966.

order, which turns out to be the order of degeneration as I've already described it, with Bierce's story at the stage of Innocence, Asimov's at the stage of Plausibility, and Aldiss's at the stage of Decadence (though I will have to qualify that last term).

Innocence is the simple and naive stage in the evolution of a genre construct. The progress of the story is merely that of drawing closer and closer to a marvel and the story's climax consists in a brief glimpse of the marvel, rather like pulling a rabbit out of a hat. I call the story "innocent" because the marvel in question here is – or rather was – a genuine novelty. "Moxon's Master" resembles those plays that Shaw could not stand because they were merely dramatic padding for some spectacular situation. (For example, Bernhardt's *Gismonda* ended with the Divine Sarah being burnt in the last act; the rest of the play was a clumsy and quite implausible leading-up-to the final debacle.)[4] From the moment Bierce's story finds its feet, it toddles toward the big scene – Machine Bites Man. The rest of the story is merely a set of devices to delay that final revelation and the creation of a sketchy world *into which* the final revelation can erupt. After explanations and preparations that probably strike modern readers as unnecessary, after a moody storm borrowed from the older genre of Gothic romance, the narrator finally witnesses the heart of the story – the invention turning on the inventor. And that is that. Bierce writes *as if* his readers had to be cajoled into accepting that last scene – one we can see coming from the fourth page of the story, if not before – although I would think (not upon any evidence, I admit) that Bierce's readers enjoyed the scene as much as he did. Multiplying the delays increases the anticipation; the scene itself, the idea itself, is still novel, that is, it is enough all by itself. We are still Innocent. "Moxon's Master" was written in 1893. Isaac Asimov's "Reason" was written in 1941. The situation is the same as that of "Moxon's Master" – the Rebelling Robot – although the outcome is happier. But with "Reason" we enter the stage of Plausibility and Asimov's story does a great deal more than pull a rabbit out of a hat.

Once you have managed to embody a wish (and I won't pretend yet to even know what wish that is) in the idea of a thinking machine that turns against its creators, and once the idea itself stops enrapturing you, the next step is to make it plausible. The wish (or situation) here is making many more concessions to logic. What we think of now as typically science-fictional questions are being asked: How would such a machine be constructed? At what level would technology have to be to make such a machine possible? What would such machines be used for? What would

---

4 Shaw, *Our Theatres in the Nineties*, III, p. 175.

people's attitude be toward such machines? And – most important – *what would such machines be like?* The question that's being asked in this second stage is "What, *if really?*" and the author isn't satisfied until he has constructed a whole society, a whole technology, and a set of rules for the operation of rebelling robots. You do not, as in the first story, see a marvel once and without any explanation. The treatment becomes complicated, plausible and (in that sense) realistic – I don't mean realism in style, as I said before, but realistic in the sense of making concessions to sense, actuality, and logic. It is at this stage, I think, that a great author may decide to treat the motif seriously – if it has unserious origins or pulp origins – as Henry James did with ladies' magazine fiction and Dickens with stage melodrama.

Shaw's dictum about great artists exhausting their material begins to apply here. I suggest that Asimov's "Reason" grew out of stories like "Moxon's Master" – this is a fine idea but we must treat it as if it were real and we must treat it in detail. In "Reason" (as in all of Asimov's robot stories) the focus of attention is on how robots would have to work – thus you have the Laws of Robotics and the explanation of malfunctions in terms of those laws. This is a far cry from the glimpse of the enraged machine in Bierce's story.

At the stage of Plausibility, the original inventor-writers' simplicity having gone stale, material can be used by good writers.

With the third stage, that of Decadence, we bifurcate or trifurcate; there are several ways in which a genre construct may become decadent:

1) Stories may become petrified into collections of rituals, with all freshness and conviction gone. Television Westerns are at this stage. This is the stage of foregone conclusions.
2) Stories may become part of a stylized convention – not to be confused with complete petrification. In a petrified genre, *the details are more important than the whole*, e.g. the cowboys' tight pants, while stylized fiction retains the sense of an aesthetic whole and a sub-ordination of parts to some sort of aesthetic order. Thus ballet is sometimes stylized and sometimes petrified; but vampire movies now seem to be petrified for good. Possibly stylization is just a way-station on the journey toward petrifaction. It's also possible that stylization agrees better with dance and music (the "purer" media) than with drama or fiction (the more impure media).
3) What once were the big scenes or *frissons* of the whole story may be shrunk, elided, compressed, or added to, that is, until only the original wish/scene is left as a metaphoric element among other metaphoric elements. For example, there are New York poets who make collages

of their favorite scenes from science fiction stories. This is not science fiction; this is using what originally was the point of some story or stories for a totally different artistic whole.

The motif or scene or thrilling action for whose sake whole stories were once written becomes a metaphorical or lyrical element *in something else*.

On the way toward this third kind of decadence is Brian Aldiss's "But Who Can Replace a Man?" which was written in 1958. Again robots turn on their creators, or try to, but the story is not about Revolting Robots: it is about something else. The situation that ends "Moxon's Master" and that informs "Reason" is here *assumed*, and the story does not go on to explore the supporting circumstances and consequences of the situation, as "Reason" does. The robots' capitulation at the end is not victorious because the human race has won; nor is it interesting because you are told *how* the human race has won (as Asimov does in "Instinct").

The end is strangely moving and very complex: the animalism of the man, the eerie childishness of the robots, the homeliness of Aldiss's comparisons ("like a pincushion," "like a dull man at a bar," "no bigger than a toaster"), the exhaustion of the land, the oddly parodic journey in which one traveler after another falls by the wayside and is left keening among the barren rocks – all these compose a kind of lyrical image. The story is really about what it is to be human – it shows you this by creating the oddly human incompleteness of the machines. "But who Can Replace a Man?" makes us experience some of the less attractive qualities of humanity by reproducing old adventure-story incidents for its own purposes and by dwelling on apparently irrelevant detail. The story is not about robots rebelling, or why robots rebel, or what robots are; it uses these common science fiction elements for another purpose: showing us what *we* are. In fact, many of the explanations which would make up the bulk of a second-stage story are completely missing: for example, how has humanity survived long enough to wear trace elements out of the soil? Why didn't we blow ourselves up first? And so on. Other details, like the classes of brains, are only referred to obliquely and fleetingly.

"But Who Can Replace a Man?" shows us a science-fictional element on the verge of death – i.e. on the way to continued existence *only* as a metaphor. A "straight" story about Revolting Robots written this late in the day can only be a stylized story – for example, a parody – or a petrified story. The Revolting Robots must be there for some other reason besides themselves. We've come a long way from "Moxon's Master". One might even argue that in "But Who Can Replace a Man?" we witness the emergence of a new big scene – the last scene. The emotional weight of the story is in that scene. But perhaps the process can only go one way.

The three stages of Innocence, Plausibility, and Decadence may present a paradigm of the history of every aesthetic element in art – if you look at the prelude to the big scene in Bierce's story, you will see that it is a potpourri of once-fresh, then-decadent materials: the stormy night, the glimpse of horror, and so on. Old fiction provides the leaf-drift out of which rises the new. And I wonder if metaphor is not the ultimate destination of every narrative element. At first it is the wish itself, the big scene, the fascinating part presented almost bare; then it become plausible, complicated and an occasion for realistic thought; finally it dies as narrative and, entering the general culture, becomes matter for lyric poetry or metaphoric material for new fiction.

Of course this process has been very much hastened in the last few centuries by the increase of social change and in the last few decades by the instant dissemination of every novelty through television, radio, and movies. Motifs begin to rot before they have got out of the first stage. The mass media seem to have got stuck at a level of ritual repetition, what passes for "new ideas" on TV being mostly a desperate addiction to quirks and the trimming with cheap gimmickry of very stale stuff indeed. Maybe the real process then goes underground.

Can the process be reversed? May someone, noticing a glancing allusion, a figure of speech, a metaphor, all that's left of a once-sprawling empire of fiction, be inspired to flesh out that hint and make it fiction once again? I think not, but I cannot substantiate my suspicion. Self-conscious reconstructions of the old can lead to something new but not usually what the imitator thinks he's after. Renaissance Italy wished to copy Greek drama; it ended up inventing opera. But this is not reversing the process; it's happenstance.

Where do the new elements come from? I really don't know. I suspect that genuine novelty is usually crude and/or silly, and that it occurs in bad or undistinguished work. Far from being original or truly revolutionary, great work – even good work – is apt to be the last or next-to-last of something, the use of collective creations as a sort of jumping-off place. Critics are apt to hail second- or third-stage work as "new" – Dickens' novels, for example, or Ibsen's plays, although in retrospect it is clear that nobody could imitate either of them without being instantly smothered by their example.

Of course, different parts of one author's work will be on different levels of evolution (so will elements within one story) and the whole process is usually quite complex. Tracing origins is a tricky business.

Let me use vampire stories and films as an example. Where is the real origin of our modern genre – in Gothic romance? Did writers like Monk Lewis and Mrs. Radcliffe get the vampire from real folk-tales? How much was invented and by whom? Did the reporters or translators of the folktales color and change them (as Andrew Lang is supposed to have done)? Sheridan Lefanu's "Carmilla" is clearly already at the stage of Plausibility; yet much of Bram Stoker's *Dracula* is back in the rabbit-out-of-the-hat stage. Not only that, but their vampirish conventions are different. Did Stoker not read "Carmilla"? That hardly seems likely. Why, then, didn't he adopt Lefanu's convention that vampires can live in daylight? Did he draw his ideas from some other source? It seems to have been Dracula that stuck for the genre; why? "Carmilla" is a much better story. Did subsequent writers avoid imitating "Carmilla" *because* it was a better story? Even if you assume that the modern genre comes from Bram Stoker, is it via the book or the film? And which film – the 1931 film with Bela Lugosi or Hammer's reincarnation of the early 1960s which makes explicit the sexuality only implicit in the former? By the time you get to the movie *Blood and Roses* you are in the period of decadence in both the bad and the good sense; *haute couture*, incest, neurosis, lesbianism, and high society are icing on a pretty stale cake. These frills, however, resonate very interestingly with the basic story, and the film's hallucinatory sequences are pure third-stage: vampirism for the sake of something else. Bergman's *Hour of the Wolf* goes further still, into the purely metaphoric stage; it appropriates the whole tradition in one or two glancing incidents (e.g. the gentleman who walks up the wall and the last scene). Certainly there is no future for the genre except as a metaphor within some other work. By now the whole complex of ideas has passed so into the general culture that it is conceivable in art only as lyric imagery or as affectionate reminiscence. In fact, the vampire tradition has hardly been used in lyric verse – I can only remember one poem in *Fantasy and Science Fiction*. I always thought Italian directors would do very well with vampires as cultural symbols for the rotten rich – many of the traditions about the vampire are close to the atmosphere of films like *La Notte* or *La Dolce Vita*.

Lyric writing (verse or other) is *a graveyard of dead narrative* – events, dramas, personages once used in narrative in their own right. Certainly lyric verse is generally in advance of prose fiction, both in style and matter. It is the first to adapt to shifts of sensibility because it has already digested everything the general cultural context has to offer, while fiction and drama lag behind, their sources being everything that is produced as reportage, chronicle, history, sociological analysis, etc. The lyric mode must, I think, work with well-digested material, since the central organizing impulse of the lyric is a collecting of imagery around some emotional or other center. The combination is therefore what counts – fresh material would prove too centrifugal, too distracting.

The emotional or other center of the lyric, however, may very well turn out to be new itself – thus the stage gets to Samuel Beckett's *Endgame* long after the publication of Eliot's *Waste Land*. The emotional center of the poem becomes the big scene/high point/emotional weight of the play. But the poem can produce the X without surrounding material, without chronology, without explanation, without plausibility, without leading-up-to. The play – even Beckett's play – must wait until the central image can somehow be set in chronology, in dramatic progression, in some kind of plausibility, in some kind of explanation.

As theatre and fiction become more and more lyrical, one would expect the time-lag to become narrower and perhaps to disappear. This is happening. Brian Aldiss is now no more a writer of narrative fiction than is Donald Barthelme.

Of course, when I speak of genre constructs wearing out, I'm speaking of writers, not readers – what matters is what *writers* find stale. Unfortunately, the commercial possibilities of a totally petrified genre are enormous, as the eternal life of Western films testifies. But even here the very oldest genres sink to the bottom and finally drop out of existence.

Some genres tucked away in odd corners: nurse novels, spy stories, detective stories (a: sordid American, and b: English village), modern Gothics, Westerns, much science fiction, pornography, avant-garde fiction, etc.

We do seem to insist on specialization in our fiction.

Some genres have hardly been touched – pornography, for example, seems never to have passed the first stage. Some are dead: Westerns, detective stories, spy stories. Some are beginning to lose their bloom: avant-garde novels. Some, like science fiction, are entering the third stage.

Now a writer can do much worse than rummage among "trash," that is, genres like the nurse novel. Trash is one of the sources of art. The crude, stupid, obvious novelties can begin a whole cycle.

In fact artists usually pay a great deal of attention to "low" culture, and when they find low culture that interests them they pay it the supreme compliment of stealing it. The demand for originality from good writers is a rather late development in the history of literature. Everyone knows that Chaucer's plots were not his, nor were Shakespeare's, but even in the recent past many great artists can be shown to have stolen all sorts of things from bad art. Ibsen, for example, owes a considerable debt to Scribe, Shaw to all sorts of melodrama (see his preface to "The Devil's Disciple," for example, or that to "Captain Brassbound's Conversion"), Henry James to ladies'-magazine fiction.

One of the reasons science fiction is reaching a wider audience now than ever before may be that many of its concepts have reached the stage of being digested (if I can call it that) – they can be picked up by writers outside the field. That is, science fiction is becoming decadent in both the good and the bad sense. I find that my students read and admire Asimov and Clarke in greater numbers than students ever have before, but when they write they steal fantasies from A. E. Van Vogt, who is unmistakably in the first stage, that of pure invention. They don't write A. E. Van Vogt stories; they use him for poems or for strange works that aren't, properly speaking, science fiction at all, or for science fiction which owes nothing directly to Van Vogt but an eerie kind of glamor. When artists are given a choice between imitating crude originals and second-hand, polished literary versions thereof, most bad artists will choose the literary version and most good artists the bad original. My good writing students don't imitate Asimov because one can't imitate Asimov; he is good enough to have exhausted his subject matter. A. E. Van Vogt (to put the matter as politely as I can) is a very inventive and yet very bad artist – in Shaw's words, the victory of an enormously fertile imagination over a commonplace mind. (He said this about Marie Corelli.)[5]

Of course not all new science fiction writers are third-stage writers. Larry Niven, for example, is a second-stage writer and a very good one. But "new wave" science fiction is third-stage science fiction, or rather it exists on the border between the second and third stages. I think the time of petrification and ritual is still far away; it may never come or may not come until our whole Western idea of science and our Western idea of change themselves go the way of all social constructs. Science fiction is the only genre I know that is theoretically open-ended; that is, new science fiction is possible as long as there is new science. Not only are there new scienc*es* – mostly life sciences like neuro-biology – there are also a multitude of infant sciences like ethology and psychology. More important than that, all of science – indeed, all philosophical (or "descriptive") disciplines – are beginning to be thought of as part of one over-arching discipline. Thus physics is continuous with chemistry, chemistry with biology, biology with ecology, ecology with sociology, sociology with psychology, psychology with philosophy, and philosophy with the arts. And so on. This opens the whole world and every single extant discipline to science fiction.

Science fiction, therefore, need not limit itself to certain kinds of characters, certain locales, certain emotions, or certain plot devices. Whoever writes fiction about how things might be if they were not as they are, writes this seriously, and does not offend against what is known to be known (as Samuel Delany puts it), is writing science fiction.

---

5 *Ibid.*, p. 16.

Even now much science fiction is not genre writing – the only element that makes many stories science fiction is that they are not about things as they are. We may end up dividing writing into two parts: fiction about things as they characteristically are or were (contemporary fiction and historical fiction) and fiction about things as they may be or might have been (science fiction).

No particular artistic element in fiction can survive forever, but the speculation, the free-wheeling free thinking we prize in science fiction, may turn out to be too general a principle to be tied to particular scenes or particular emotional high points or particular plot devices. Only a change in the most basic of our social assumptions will make science fiction non-viable, as only a change in extremely basic assumptions can cause people to stop writing satire or fantasy, both of which assume that the status quo is not all there is, and that things might be different. Put "things might be different" together with any kind of scientific method and you have science fiction. Surely such a compound will survive mere changes in fashion.

It may – and I think it will – become as widely read and as important as fantasy, the tradition of which is several thousand years old.

I will be very glad to see that happen.

***Turning Points*, ed. Damon Knight (Harper and Row, New York, 1977)**[1]

Alien Monsters

Good morning – or rather, good afternoon, everybody. I'm very glad to be here and very glad to be speaking to you. In asking me here to speak, you know, Tom Purdom really paid me a tremendous compliment. After all sorts of things about how intelligent I was, and how he was sure I'd be so interesting and give such an interesting talk on a fascinating subject, he paid the ultimate compliment: He said, "And most of all we want you to be first on the program because you're a teacher." (I thought he was going to say, you know how to talk, you'll be fascinating, fluent and so on, but this wasn't it.) No, he said, "You're a teacher and you have a regular job and you're the only one we can depend on to get up early enough in the morning." Little does he know!

I am glad to see, looking around, that this is not true. I'm not the only one. Thank you all. It was heroic. It was heroic for me, anyway.

Now I'm going to try, today, to talk about something that people will disagree with – some people, anyway – and some of you may get pretty mad at me before I am finished. But I think it's worth it, anyway. I'm trying to operate on the old Leninist principle of presenting a united front to outsiders but being perfectly free to quarrel among ourselves. I think this is something science fiction ought to do – I mean the quarreling among ourselves. And if we're going to indulge in it, we had better do so pretty quickly; there isn't much time left. The days of our privacy are numbered. Really, the academicians are after us, and there is going to be an invasion of outside people into this field of the kind none of us has ever seen before – all sorts of goggle-eyed, clump-footed types who will be bringing in all sorts of outside standards (good or bad), outside experience, outside contexts, outside remarks, naïveté in some things, great sophistication in other things, all sorts of oddities, all sorts of irrelevancies – well, Heaven only knows what. I don't even know if it'll be good or bad or how good or how bad. But it is going to happen. The academicians are after us.

Now, if you don't already know it, literary academicians – and, by the way, I want to include what you might call semi-professional types, like

1 Speech delivered at the Philadelphia Science Fiction Conference, November 9, 1968.

the sorts of writers and critics who write for magazines like the *Atlantic*, even though they may not be actually connected with universities – anyway, literary academicians are always looking for something new to criticize or some new way to criticize something old, and they are just beginning to realize that right under their noses is a whole new, absolutely virgin field of literature that nobody has even had a go at yet. What's going to happen when they realize this fully will be a sort of literary California gold rush with what we have always considered our own private property trampled under mobs and mobs of people who haven't the slightest respect for our uniqueness, or the things we like about ourselves, or the pet grievances we've been nursing for years, and so on. Some of these people are fools, but some of them – and I know some of them – are a lot more sophisticated than anybody in this room. I know that they are certainly much more sophisticated than I am. I think when they get into the field of science fiction, as critics of course, that they will find s.f. is an antidote for a lot of nonsense that *they* are subject to, but I am afraid it's going to work the other way round, too.

Actually, I want to get my own licks in before the crowd arrives.

All this was brought home to me in a very personal way a couple of weeks ago. I teach at Cornell, and when Cornell University people find out that I write science fiction, there's this sort of wary and cautious couple of steps back – "Oh, you write science fiction?" – and then, with a kind of glaze over the eyes, they say, "Ah – that's H. G. Wells and all that, isn't it?" and I say, "Right!" And then they run away. This is how it happens. Well, this is no longer so. Just two weeks ago today I found in my office mailbox a note asking me to teach a course in Science Fiction this summer: ENGLISH 305; SCIENCE FICTION – *Open to Graduate Students*.

And that started me thinking about all the things I've just been saying here this afternoon. And it made me feel very strongly that instead of trying to please both other people and myself, I had better be as nasty as possible. After all, *we* know we're good. *We* know we're on to something. I knew it ever since I was fourteen, when I found out that science fiction was more exciting than vampire stories. And it is, too. I've been reading the stuff for about sixteen years now – I'm addicted to it, like everyone else here – but lately what you might call the Long-Term Fan Syndrome has been happening to me. This is the disease that everybody gets sooner or later and the symptoms are always the same. "Oh, they used to write it better. Oh, it was better in the old days." Of course, when you talk to people, you find out that they never have quite the same old days in mind – some will pick the thirties, some the early fifties, some the late fifties, etc., etc. Then there is this student of mine – "Oh, they used to write it better. Oh, it was better in the old days." I asked him how old he was – seventeen – and what the old days were. It turned out that by the old days he meant *last year*. When people start differing like that, it is obvious that what they mean is the days of their own youth, that is, the days when they first started reading s.f.

Now, I don't like this. I want to keep on reading the stuff. I want to enjoy it. So I started thinking, and out of all the things I could complain about, all the things I could kvetch about and criticize, *one* story and *one* picture somehow stuck in my mind.

I'm not going to tell you what magazine the story was in, or who wrote it, or who did the picture, because those things really aren't important. You can find many, many other stories like it, and quite a few other pictures like it. And I want to make clear at the very beginning that I am *not* talking about the individual defects of individual writers or individual editors – this is not the point at all. What I am trying to do is get at something that is in the air, and that affects science fiction as a whole. It's not a question of there being a multitude of coincidental decisions as to what to write, just by happenstance. Because a lot of these writers are very different from each other personally. I know many of them. But something in the field is affecting all of them and making people who are not alike write alike.

Anyway, the story itself was a very clear, simple little story – very delicately and carefully told. It was about homosexuality on Mars. Why Mars I don't know, except that wherever you are as a reader, you're not *there* at any rate. The point of the story was that men who are isolated for a long time without women will attempt to get their sexual satisfaction from each other – and this is quite true; this is the sort of thing that any warden of any prison in the United States can tell you, not to mention the people who know perfectly well that such things happen – although not of course, to everyone – in places like the Army. Anyway, the story was perfectly unsensational and even decent to the point of reticence. There wasn't even any sex in it. Instead – and this is typically American – one man killed another. It was really an all-right story, very rational, very reasonable, and not in the least shocking. I read it. I had to sort of prop my eyes open, you know, because actually it was pretty dull, but I read it.

Then I came to that picture.

It was a picture of the murderer – this one guy who had killed the man who had made advances to him. Out of horror and disgust, you see. And the story made the point that such exaggerated horror was a product of unconscious, latent homosexuality. Well, apparently the artist had taken alarm even at *latent, unconscious* homosexuality, and had decided that, by God, he was going to show you that this character was no effeminate sissy – he was a *man* – so what he did was put layer on layer of muscles on this character, and give him beetling eyebrows and a snarl – I simply cannot describe the effect. He would've made an adult male gorilla look fragile. It was absolutely wild.

I was reading my magazine in the student cafeteria and as I reached this picture, and I think I made some sort of extraordinary noise, like "Eeyah," which attracted the attention of a student who was nearby.

"What are you reading?" "Science fiction." "Can I see?" – he was very interested – "Oh, that's an alien."

Well, he was right, of course. He was absolutely right. In the anxiety to show you a real he-man, the artist who did the picture had created a megalith, a monster, an armored tank, something that had only the faintest resemblance to a human being. I loved that picture. It was so awful that it was wonderful. I wanted to keep it but it fell in my orange juice and got sort of messed up. Still, every once in a while I think of that picture – and then I think of one of those megaliths trying to rape another megalith – and it makes me feel good. In its own way, it's perfectly inimitable.

Of course, the trouble is that the science fiction illustrator who did the picture was *not* trying to be funny. And therein lies the whole point of my speech today.

It is a scandal, a real scandal, that in a field like ours, which is supposed to be so unconventional, so free, free to extrapolate into the future, free of prejudice, of popular nonsense, so rational and so daring, it is an especial scandal that in *our* field so many readers and so many writers – or so many stories, anyhow – cling to this Palaeolithic illusion, this freak, this myth of what a real man is. And it's a scandal that he ruins so many stories. Because he does, you know, he ruins everything he touches. He has only to make one appearance and at once the story he is in coughs, kicks up its heels and dies dead. He has only to look at a woman to turn her into pure cardboard.

Let me put it more generally, and I hope more clearly.

Science fiction is still – very strangely and very unfortunately – subject to a whole constellation or group of values which do not have any really necessary connection with science fiction. I would call them conventional or traditional masculine values except that they are really more than that; they are a kind of wild exaggeration of such values. Of course, everything becomes exaggerated in s.f. because we don't show things in the here-and-now, but as they might be. It's a kind of fantasy and dramatic high relief. By the way, I think what I'm talking about is particularly American; I don't think American s.f. has in the past owed very much to British s.f. or that they spring from the same roots at all. American science fiction began in the pulps – I'm not downgrading this, I think it's a very good thing, although I can't go into the reason why – now – because I don't have time. But this origin in trash – real, popular trash – may have something to do with the persistence of this really strange kind of image. If I wanted to put it in one sentence, it would be something like this:

The only real He-Man is the Master of the Universe.

Which, of course, leaves out a great many people.

If you believe this but are a little less extreme about stating it, it comes out something like this:

> The real He-Man is invulnerable. He has no weaknesses. Sexually, he is super-potent. He does exactly what he pleases, everywhere and at all times. He is absolutely self-sufficient. He depends on nobody, for this would be a weakness. Toward women he is possessive, protective and patronizing; to men he gives orders. He is never frightened by anything or for any reason; he is never indecisive, and he always wins.

In short, he is an alien monster, just as I said.

The trouble with this creature – the megalith with the beetling eyebrows – is the trouble with all mythologies. It's not that he doesn't exist, because everybody *knows* that he doesn't exist. I don't think there's a single sane man on earth who could seriously and honestly say: Yes, I am all that. I am like that. I am never frightened of anything. I have no weaknesses whatsoever. I am a sexual dynamo. I always have my own way. Everybody obeys me – and so forth. We all know that such a person is impossible. We don't really believe that he exists.

But we do believe that somehow – despite what we actually know about other people and ourselves – that he *ought* to exist, or that he's in some sense ideal, or that there's something wrong with people who are *not* like that. Or, at the very least, that it would be a hell of a lot of fun pretending you really are like that, even though you know you aren't and you couldn't possibly be.

Now I don't like this – part of the reason is obvious. This is an ideal that is *by definition* absolutely closed to me. I can pretend to be Cleopatra but I can't very well pretend to be Antony. And for various reasons, Cleopatra doesn't appear in science fiction much. I like to think that because I'm a woman I can stand outside this whole business and be somewhat more objective than if I were caught up in it, as I think a man has to be, to some degree.

I also don't like this strange myth that is set up as a person, because he kills every story he touches, or almost every story – they're usually stone dead before the first word comes out of the typewriter. If the stories are alive, they live through the other characters, or through the alien characters, or through incidental comedy or through other interesting things that come in as sort of sidelines. But this turns the story into a grab bag, with no center. The story cannot live through its central character, its central conflict, or its central system of values.

The third reason I don't like this kind of thing – and this is the most important of all – is that this ultramasculine scheme of values messes up one of the most important and fascinating subjects science fiction is dealing with today. Also, *was* dealing with, by the way, although I will stand corrected about this – but I think it's been a preoccupation of s.f. from way back.

I am talking about the subject of power. Now this is a serious business. What you and I think about power, and what we expect powerful people to do, what we are willing to let them do, the kinds of people we give power to, whether *we* have any power, and how much – these are really important. And for some reason, s.f. seems to have gone right to questions like this from the beginning. How should power be used? What does power justify? How can power be overcome? All this sort of thing. For a contemporary novel – only one among many – *Bug Jack Barron*. It's practically about nothing else.

I think again that this may be a particularly American thing, the flavor(?), well, the quality, the particular kind of concern we have with power. Europeans tend to concentrate on the ethical side, and you get things like Albert Camus writing about suicide being the supremely moral act, things that tend to seem pretty bizarre to an American. Europeans – would you believe European movies? after all, I haven't read *everything* – seem to take it for granted that people are pretty powerless, pretty helpless, everybody has weaknesses, everybody is limited by society – and that's just the way it is. For us, power seems to be a problem *per se*, just because it exists. And vulnerability, too – the opposite side of power – this, too, is a problem just because it exists. We aren't just concerned with power; we're downright obsessed with it. And we tend to link up the idea of power with that old, beetling-browed he-man I was talking about. We insist that power – mind you, *absolute* power, too, power of all kinds – is equivalent to masculinity.

This leads to trouble. The trouble with making masculinity equal to power – especially the sort of absolute, ultimate power that s.f. writers like to write about – is that you can't look at either power or masculinity clearly. This is bad enough when you can't think clearly about masculinity, but when you can't think clearly about power, it's god-awful. In politics, for instance, power is simply real – it exists – it's like the electricity in the lights of this room; and if you look at a real political situation or a real moral situation, and instead of seeing what's really there, you see Virility – Manhood at Stake – goodness knows what – everything gets all mucked up. Of course, this sort of problem isn't confined to science fiction: you can see it happening all over the place. But science fiction has a unique chance to deal with these things in the chemically pure form, so to speak, to really speculate about them. But so often we don't.

One of the strangest things in s.f., when you meet this concern with power, is that s.f. writers seem pretty much to insist on an either/or situation. That is, people in stories tend to be either all-powerful (this the Ruler of the Universe again) or absolutely powerless. Either the hero is conquering the world or the world is returning the compliment by conquering *him*. In any case, it's a completely black-and-white situation with nothing in between. Alexei Panshin once complained about characters who are strangled by their vacuum cleaners. Well, I think this idea of megalithic, absolute power has a lot to do with being strangled by your vacuum cleaner. If the real man is absolutely invulnerable, then if you're not absolutely invulnerable, you're not a real man, and if you're not a real man, you're absolutely weak and absolutely vulnerable, so even a vacuum cleaner can get you. You even sometimes get this weird hybrid, who is at the same time a superman (utterly powerful) and is being persecuted by the whole world (i.e. he is utterly powerless). In fact, he's being persecuted *because* he's a superman, that is, because he's powerful. But if he is persecuted, he's powerless. That is, he's powerless because he's powerful. Or vice versa. Sometimes the brain just reels.

Also, you get something else very bad in science fiction from the confusion of maleness – masculinity – with power. You get what's been called pornoviolence, that is, violence for the sake of violence. ("Pornography of violence" – pornoviolence. An elegant word.) I certainly think that science fiction is less of an offender here, if you want to call it a offense, than what's called "mainstream" writing. But we do get a lot of this. I am also getting tired of characters who are tortured or flayed or impaled alive in various ways, or who have to drag themselves along corridors "in a blaze of pain" (it's always a *blaze* of pain in these stories – nobody ever feels just *bleh*) or they climb mountains while their lungs are bursting just so the author can enjoy himself masochistically by showing what strong stuff his heroes are made of. "Every nerve screamed with the pain that was coursing through him." We've all read this dozens of time. Sometimes it's pain and sometimes it's rapture, but it's always bullshit. Bullshit is nice for fun and games, but when you adopt the attitude behind the bullshit and try somehow to apply it or believe in it in real life that's not good. What I mean is, power is a real thing. It exists. To have power over other people, to control other people, is a real thing which produces real emotions, real problems, real anxieties, real pleasures – a writer can depict these. But if he is all hung up on the masculinity-equals-power bit or the heroes-must-be-all-powerful-or-they're-not-heroes then he is going to thrash around in a sort of void. At the worst, he will simply produce stuff that is too dull to read. At best, he will produce a kind of pornography.

But he won't get beyond that. I wish I could bring in here a book by Stephen Marcus called *The Other Victorians*. It has one of the best definitions of pornography that I've ever seen. Mr. Marcus's point is that what makes something pornographic is not simply that it excites you sexually. After all, even a book like *Madame Bovary*, which we consider very reticent, should excite you sexually, among all the other things it does. What pornography does is exclude everything else, and – in the process, ironically enough – it ends up excluding real sex, too. Pornoviolence is pornographic because it excludes real violence, and the real experience of what violence is and means and feels like. It excludes real power, and the real experience of what power is and means and feels like. In their place, it puts myths, fantasies – in a word, nonsense.

Let me return now to my beetle-browed, lumpy-muscled friend. I've complained about the bad effects of a system of values that make being Ruler of the Universe the only decent position in life for a red-blooded American boy. But there is another objection to this system of values besides the way it messes up people's heads when it comes to thinking about power. I mentioned before that although nobody actually sets up as the Invulnerable Superman, still there's this kind of omnipresent, vague feeling that it would be pretty nice if you *could* be an invulnerable superman, though, alas, one can't be in real life. Let me run down the list again: No weaknesses. Super-potent. Absolutely uncontrolled by others. Absolutely self-sufficient. Depends on nobody. Gives everybody orders. Never afraid. Never indecisive. He always wins.

Ah! if only one could be like this.

But is it so attractive, really?

It seems to me that for the one quality – being invulnerable – every other quality has been given up. The super He-Man is super-potent (he has to be, this is an expression of strength) but does he have super-pleasure? Not in the stories I've read. Pleasure involves a kind of letting-go, a kind of loss of self, and he can't afford this. This would be weakness. Is he super-happy? Usually not. He does exactly what he wants – that is, nobody controls him – but is he therefore super-spontaneous? Super-impulsive? No. Being spontaneous would be dangerous; it would expose him to weakness, and he must not be weak. He can be fond of other people, in a sort of parental or protective way, and he can behave tenderly toward them – although he doesn't usually – but no one can be tender to *him* because that would mean he depended on someone, and depending on someone would mean he was weak. People admire him but they can't love him, and if you think for a minute, you'll see that he can't love anyone else, because love is possible only between equals and by definition he has no equals. He is a very lonely man. There is a kind of sadness that runs through stories about the superman, and the rugged he-man, too – sometimes the author is aware of it and sometimes he is not – but there is often (underground, sometimes) this profound, despairing sadness. I'm thinking now of Gordon Dickinson's Dorsai, the warrior people, where the sadness is quite explicit. You see, the price you have to pay for absolute mastery of every situation is awful. It's the whole rest of life.

Well, if you don't have traditional masculine values, then what? Traditional feminine values? I can't answer this vehemently enough. No, no, a thousand times no. There *are* stories like that in s.f. and I hate them. If I opened *Analog* tomorrow and found that by divine fiat it had suddenly turned into *The Ladies' Home Journal*, I think I would drop dead. And not just from shock, either.

If anything gets me madder than the strong, laconic individual who defeats Ming the Merciless by killing sixteen million billion aliens with his bare hands in four pages, it's the sweet, gentle, compassionate *intuitive* little woman who solves some international crisis by mending her slip or something, when her big, strong, brilliant husband has failed to do so for twenty-three chapters.

I find conventional masculine heroics funny, but conventional feminine heroics are nauseating without being funny. To me, anyway.

Well, what I want – I can't describe it really, because it would be different for every writer, but maybe I can give a sort of general impression.

I would like to see science fiction keep the daring, the wildness, the extravagant imagination that we got from starting out in the pulps – but I would like to see us shed the kind of oversimplified values and attitudes it got from the same place – this business about the He-Man is only one of them. So many science fiction stories operate on assumptions about people and assumptions about values that would hardly be adequate to describe the social relations of a bunch of flatworms. There are science fiction novels – whole big fat novels – built around moral problems that would be instantly solvable by a year-old chimpanzee. I have also, by the way, seen first-rate adventure stories ruined by people who insisted on reading them as if they contained profound moral problems, though the story itself clearly had not such intentions. There is no reason on earth why a story *has* to be didactic, *has* to teach an explicit moral. But if you are going to moralize, you had better make sure it's above the Kindergarten level.

Anyway, as I said, the barbarian hordes are knocking at the gate. And these people are *sharp*. I think we're going to open their eyes to an awful lot, but I think the converse is going to happen, too, and sometimes I don't like the idea at all. They're very sneaky and they're very erudite. Unfortunately, the academic critics are going to bring along their own brand of nonsense, but not all these people are bad critics, or academics, or even critics at all. There are writers, too, people from other fields – movie-makers and painters and all sorts of people. And what is important is not what they will like or dislike about science fiction. After all, nobody has to be bound by what *any* critic says, inside the field or outside it – what matters is that once you've let an outsider into your private preserve, your own personal backyard, the place never looks the same to *you* again. It's like letting a stranger into your house – it's not what the stranger thinks, but that suddenly you find yourself looking at your own domain with a difference.

You turn into a stranger yourself. You know, "Oh, lovely rug. Oh, beautiful chairs. Nice picture ... What, no storm windows?" Things are never quite the same again. This is what's been happening to me, ever since I learned I was going to have to teach science fiction this summer. Everybody knows that you don't *teach* science fiction; you just do it. But you do teach it.

So, I picked on one thing for today. There are dozens of others. There are good things, wonderful things, too, of course. And I'm not complaining about things I don't like *just* because there are going to be outsiders analyzing s.f. and watching what we do and criticizing what we do and so forth. It's the kind of thing I would complain about anyway. I want the stuff to be better. I enjoy reading it even more than I enjoy writing it. I want it to be thrilling, and real, and alive, and about real people. I want it to be complicated and various and difficult like life – not smooth and predigested and simpleminded, the way nothing is but bad stories. I want my sense of wonder back again.

And I have it all figured out for the summer, what I'm going to do in the class, I mean. When this keen, studious, frightening brilliant graduate student comes up to me and says, "You know – I've been reading *Savage Orbit*. Now of course I understand the peripety in the last chapter, but I can't quite place the mythic resonance of the objective correlative." Then I will look at him – and smile, just a little, knowingly – a sort of Ellisonian smile – and say, "Read it again. Page seventy-eight. *Lithium hydroxide?*" And he will be flattened for life!

From *Twentieth-Century Science Fiction Authors*, ed. Curtis Smith (St Martin's Press, New York, 1981)

H. P. Lovecraft

That horror stories are externalized psychology is a commonplace of literary criticism, but readings based on sex and aggression (the two themes literary critics have tended to pick up from Freudian psychology) do not quite fit H. P. Lovecraft. Lovecraft himself warns readers away from interpretations of his work based on the fear of retribution for specific acts or impulses. His horrors are (as he says again and again) "cosmic"; he declares the worst human fears to be displacement in space and time (as in "The Shadow Out of Time"); and in a letter quoted on p. 388 of L. Sprague de Camp's *Lovecraft: a Biography* (Doubleday, New York, 1975) he speaks of "the maddening rigidity of cosmic law," and his insistence on creating a non-fantastic and materialistic fiction world – i.e. science fiction – all imply a concern with the conditions of being, not with particular acts or situations. When the conditions of existence are themselves fearful, when such basic ontological categories as space and time break down (as does the geometry of space in so many stories, for example "The Call of Cthulhu"), we are dealing with what the psychiatrist R. D. Laing calls *ontological insecurity* (*The Divided Self*, Penguin Books, 1965, Chapter 3). If one fears that one doesn't exist securely, or that one is made of "bad stuff," any contact with another becomes potentially catastrophic.

Everyone shares, to some degree, doubts about the psychological solidity or reliability of the self and the possibly devastating effects of others on that self. Lovecraft, although certainly not psychotic, did, according to de Camp, have a lifelong sense of marked isolation from others, an intense emotional dependency on things and not people, and the kind of overpossessive bringing up which makes it reasonable to expect that such issues would appear in his work. They do – strongly enough to make him an innovator in weird fiction – for they take precedence over either the beastliness of aggression (embodied, for example, in werewolves) or the lethal possibilities of sexual abandon (e.g. the figure of the vampire), both of which themes figured largely in nineteenth-century supernatural fiction. Sex and aggression presuppose a self existing securely enough to have desires and a relatively non-threatening (or at least limited) Other toward whom such desires can be directed. Neither an unproblematic sense of self nor a non-catastrophic other exist in Lovecraft's work. In his early

Dunsanian fiction he can frolic – but with ghouls! – in the charming (but, alas, never rewritten or polished) *Dream-Quest of Unknown Kadath* or write pleasing, optimistic fantasies like "The Strange High House in the Mist," but much of his earlier and most of his later fiction are preoccupied with the foreseen, yet unavoidable, engulfment of a passive, victimized self. If the narrator is a lucky spectator who escapes with his life, or even sanity, intact, his peace of mind has been shattered forever. The real point of these stories is revelation – if the engulfment does not actually happen, nonetheless it will or it can – and this revelation becomes the central truth of a universe thus rendered uninhabitable. The cannibalistic other takes several forms, but the commonest, strongest image, and the one readers seem to remember best, is the shapeless, monstrous, indescribable "entity," (a favorite word of Lovecraft's) whose most terrifying characteristic is its structurelessness. ("The Unnameable," "The Call of Cthulhu," "Dragon," "The Dunwich Horror," et al.). The obsession with psychic cannibalism (expressed as physical in one of the flatter stories, "The Picture in the House"), and the insistence on the indescribableness of the threat all seem to point to experience so personally archaic it is felt almost as pre-verbal, as does Lovecraft's characteristic straining after adjectives. In one of his best tales, "The Color Out of Space," the threat is most abstract, its cannibalism is reported third-hand (through *two* narrators) and the relatively low-keyed, realistic setting gets most of the author's attention.

In only two stories does Lovecraft focus fully on the alternative to engulfment: loneliness. Selves exist and survive in both tales; they even – after a fashion – blossom into initiative. But both are figures that appear in other stories as monsters: in the poetically melancholy "The Outsider," a ghoulish walking corpse, and in the very interesting end of *The Weird Shadow Over Innsmouth*, a degenerate animal/monster. Both stories suggest that the menace is in the narrator, a suggestion not only psychologically truer than the image of the engulfing other that Lovecraft uses elsewhere, but also one dramatically more interesting.

The view that human relations exist only as engulfment is a serious limitation on a narrative artist. Toward the end of his life Lovecraft seems to have been unhappily aware of this; unfortunately he also underrated his own work and died before it began to be popular. His originality and his undoubted talent (the eerily parodic autobiography of "The Outsider," details like the "gelatinous" voice in "Randolph Carter" or "a warmth that may have been sardonic" of *Innsmouth*) is best at its quietest, worst in its bravely direct but often inadequate attacks on a theme that requires (at the very least) poetic genius. The very rarity of literary treatments of Lovecraft's main theme give his work added interest, however, and his work will probably always appeal to readers who find his theme compelling.

If he had not died young, he might have moved beyond the kind of horror story that says *This is what it feels like* to the kind that adds *And this is what is really happening*. The latter moves into tragedy and implied social criticism (as does, for example, Shirley Jackson's *The Haunting of Hill House*). Lovecraft concludes "the spectral in literature ... is ... a narrow though essential branch of human expression" (p. 106), a comment that might well describe his work: narrow, not appealing to wide tastes and even considerably flawed, yet authentic, and by those who find it congenial, securely loved.

Author's Note

"Schizophrenia" is not the right word here. I would still maintain, nonetheless, that Lovecraft's work is about solitude and alienation from others. I still love the best of it, like "The Color out of Space" which gains much from its (relative) understatement, and the dreamlike ritualism that informs stories like *Innsmouth* and "The Outsider" (read very effectively in a recording by Roddy MacDowell).

Writers Comment on Their Own Work

Fiction is always a joy, always an obsession and always hard (and gets harder as I get older). I write first drafts on a typewriter and so am placebound. I love to see the words and letters sprat down on the page. That is, when I begin to write. When I continue and get faster, that stops being important.

Writing has to be fitted around everything, everything. Teaching, friends, business correspondence, love, laundry, food, shopping. I have at least one or two medical appointments a week, sometimes three or four. And one marathon week it was five. I have constantly to ration my sitting and my standing and switch from one pain to another. It's always a matter for calculating: shall I continue and know I'll hurt for a week or two? Or stop? Or try handwriting? (How bad is my arthritis and will it get worse?) There are sieges of other illnesses, usually the result of medications, and then sometimes I can't write for months. (Two years recently.) So I'm always juggling illnesses, energies and time. Having to live with disabilities is like running a small business.

Fiction (sometimes non-fiction) begins with a first sentence or a smell or someone's gait or speech. Something inexplicably loaded with meaning. Sometimes from other books; either I want to do them better or present an anti-thesis to their thesis. Another s.f. writer[1] wrote a book about a spaceship crashing on an uninhabited planet and the people on it colonizing the planet. *I* think this American-imperialist sort of business is morally dubious. In yet another book an unpleasant message ("There is nothing left to be done and we must die gracefully") is given by an old, white-bearded, saintly patriarch. And my telling my writing class they couldn't write a first-person story which ended with the writer reporting her/his own death. These all came together and I had the beginning of *We Who Are About To*, in which the narrator does almost say "And then I died" at the end of the book. And I gave the message to the most unpopular, unappealing, unpleasant character I could, the point being that the truth or falsity of the message does not depend on the attractiveness of the messenger – but people act as if it did. And then I simply had each character have at least one confrontation with each other character. And I ended it with *almost* the equivalent of "And then I died."

1 Marion Zimmer Bradley.

If no one published things I wrote, I'd like to think I'd keep on writing fiction. It does matter to me that the work be published and read. But the motives for these two things are different motives. I want to get my work widely distributed and have it kept in print – oblivion is terribly discouraging – but that's not the motive for *doing* it. The publish/distribute/review/vanity stuff comes into being after something is completed. I don't write with readers in mind exactly (except for some technical habits that are now more habits than anything else) but rather a sort of ideal shape for the piece itself. In a way I am my own reader, or rather one part is the reader, who checks the work against some ideal standard.

Success is knowing in my bones that the statement is true and good if non-fiction, and if fiction is the proper shape and alive, the right taste, the right squiggles here and the right stretches out there. That's the kind of success that makes me high.

I don't think of an audience except for things like: translate quotations, check spelling, check intelligibility of sentences. Non-fiction I write to educate or persuade, usually, and I cut it ruthlessly. Fiction is different. I am not (except in the most trivial sense) responsible for anybody's response to fiction. The fiction is the way it is, period. I tend to like the most intellectually complex or challenging of my pieces, like "Bodies" and "What Did You Do During the Revolution, Grandma?" (my favorite) and not like much emotional, obvious stuff like "Souls." (All these are from *Extra (Ordinary) People*.)

I very much dislike theorists who talk about "women's" writing. They invent too much theory too soon on too few examples. We don't yet know the tradition of women's writing in English and far too much remains to be discovered and understood.[2] I also think that these theories about how different and unique women are move into essentialism and focus on the one thing we ought to be taking for granted. We are who we are and the hell with it. They fall into the mythology (the same one) we were trying to get out of twenty years ago. Critics who talk about this too often are not writers themselves and don't know nearly enough how public writing is and how very grounded in public constructions.

What I am aware of in my own writing, since about 1970, is what Sarah LeFanu (in a forthcoming book about women's s.f.) calls "creating the reader as female." This reader (implicit, usually) is almost always male in the world of fiction written in English. I have been sharply aware of that ever since 1969 when feminism burst over all of us across campus after campus in the U.S. I want to rewrite the world not *in* female (as a language)

---

2 Susan Koppelman's work is a must here.

but *to* females (women, that is). This project is as dependent on the public, social agreements about fiction and how to do it as is any other way of writing. I twist it; I hammer at it. Every artist whose aim is not to say the usual thing better or more intensely or broadly, but to say something else than the usual thing (the culturally dominant thing) must do this, from Herman Melville to Virginia Woolf. Literary critics are far too often simple-minded about this, particularly those critics I look to for most – feminist critics – no, actually they're better (book-reviewing language ran away with me above, see?) but I want more from them.

Theories about women or women's whatever being Different from men's often back into the very femininity we were justifiedly trying to get rid of fifteen years ago. Throwing established methods away doesn't usually work; there has to be some acknowledgment that they do exist – and many of them are important and useful techniques – what I do, anyway, is a kind of isometrics – pulling against the tradition *and* pillaging it – but wearing one's pillaged clothes askew – I like that. Of course, no one theory can ever be applied to every piece of literature, although many literary critics seem to think so. And, by the way, creating the female reader *in the work itself* is not quite the same as writing "for women," although I try to do both. (Never mind; this theory is as restricted as all the others, too.)

Writing against obstacles? I'm no judge. I begin to understand why so many women who've made some kind of name for themselves in field X, Y or Z talk as if they'd experienced no discrimination. It's because they are measuring their success against nothing instead of against more success! They have lived with such solid expectations of lack of success that they take these for granted; it never occurs to them to call what has happened "obstacles." I had a mother who read poetry to me and told me stories from my infancy on up. She was delighted when I scribbled, and by the time I learned that I was *not* ready for a Nobel Prize at age twenty, I was old enough not be discouraged. I owe her much. My father was fond of popular science. From him I learned how marvelous the universe was and how to work.

My life's been hard and painfully discouraging in all sorts of ways but the writing itself was always a plus. I got modest recognition from 1959 on (and earlier, in writing classes in college). I have had several good editors but no colleagues with whom I could constitute a sort of group like the ones in *The New York Review of Books*, etc. No colleague of mine could take me with her or him (mostly her) to fame and fortune nor could I do much for them. I had a lot of trouble publishing some of my s.f. (more as I got older) – but again, I look at my male colleagues and see mostly commercial success, which I've never had. Or expected. Of course there are obstacles for women that men never have to face! Let's have no more confusion, Joanna (but you see where the confusion comes from).

A young woman s.f. writer, a housewife, wrote me, saying that at her first convention an established male writer (and some fans) told her not to tell everyone she was a housewife. It created "such a bad impression." If I wrote about heterosexual love and created admirable (that is, "nice" and important) men I bet my writing income would be tripled. Networking with women only – which I try hard to do – brings little in fame or money.

I don't believe I have political obligations *as a novelist*. I certainly have them as a human being, a woman and a citizen. Nor are the identities detachable; but I do not write fiction *in order to* forward the women's liberation movement. Of course what I feel strongly about and think important gets into my fiction, but I have always censored myself as little as I can – I'm not always aware I'm doing so, of course – and I don't write fiction to improve anyone or create feminist models; the whole thing is much less controllable than that. I fight through, feel through, enword, imagine, clothe in verbal body (or essay) whatever is fascinating me or driving me mad at the moment.

The motive for fiction is aesthetic and personal, if those words mean anything. Non-fiction I sometimes just hack out as well as I can, but fiction is different. It sometimes feels dangerous – "Oh God, now they'll know about me," or "Uh-oh, they won't like this one" – and then I know I've got a good one. Often things come to me as technical puzzles which I feel, thrillingly, I can solve, like "And then I died" in *We Who Are About To*. I don't plan for anything to be feminist at all. (E.g. *Kittatinny* never began as a lesbian feminist bildungsroman but merely as an attempt to think up the most exciting and magical things that I could.) Sometimes the judgments of readers or critics are too narrowly, too simplistically "feminist" – but even then they usually call attention to something that *is* a problem in my writing and I've learned a lot that way.

I also spend a lot of time doing feminist criticism and social commentary and of course this eventually gets into the fiction. And I try more and more to put even more pressure on the process of writing, the feeling through and thinking through. It's hard to describe the process although I'm intensely familiar with it. One critic called it "piezo-electric" – putting strains on the usual form and usual style in order that the stress/crack/straining can loosen meanings. The visible surfaces of life are not enough; that's probably why I write so much fantasy, which can provide analysis as well as meaning and can do laboratory experiments with themes and people – imaginary ones, of course.

Author's Note
This piece was written in reply to a request of *The Women's Review of Books*. I was one of many writers they asked to write about writing.

Letters

Sinister Wisdom, 11, fall 1970

The following letter is in response to two articles in *Sinister Wisdom,* 9: Bertha Harris's "Melancholia, and Why It Feels Good" and Irena Klepfisz's "Lesbian Literature and Criticism."

Dear *Sinister Wisdom*

Someone ought to step between Irena Klepfisz and Bertha Harris. Bertha is being outrageous, as usual, and she rather deserves the Response, but Bertha is – in her indirect, dramatized way – right too, especially in one throwaway line: "the onerous inhibitions lesbian-feminist politics seek to place on the writer of genuine talent."

Bertha Harris is the author of a very fine book, the best Lesbian novel I've ever read and possibly the best novel of the last thirty years. *Lover. Lover* has been mostly ignored in the women's press and when it hasn't, it's been called politically incorrect (to my knowledge) though a *Feminist Review of Books* reviewer recently rediscovered it.

Why?

Most artistic and literary criticism in the women's press is very bad. It reacts to having its P.C. buttons pushed. Much of it is practiced by refugees from the misuse of the high culture tradition in high schools and colleges to bully and stupidify the young – this is largely class warfare, owing most of its virulence to the teachers' own insecure class position and their defensiveness about it, teaching having become (since high schools and colleges lost their elite character some time in this century) a road to upward mobility for children of the lower middle class. There is also the problem of the compensatory Instant Junk Food commercial culture which pretends to be a popular alternative to the poisoned (and often poisonous) high culture, and the consequent false split between "art" and "entertainment." And of course there is the priggishness of certain revolutionaries who really wish to escape from individual personality, individual voice, idiosyncrasy, and any interpretation of life that demands all three. Women (as Phyllis Chesler once said) have a real terror of difference.

What Bertha is trying to defend, in her exasperated, flamboyantly offensive, Southern Gothic fashion is (I think) her right to her own artistic obsessions and her own sense of fantasy – that is, she's defending in a deliberately nasty way (because attacked and exasperated) what every artist must defend: the absolutely inescapable, crucial fact that *expression is logically and chronologically absolutely prior to analysis.*

Bertha Harris has given much of her life to feminist publishing, has finally cut her ties to a self-sacrificing job in women's studies which was extremely harassing and energy draining, has been either ignored or belittled by the very women's community she's been trying so hard to serve, and has had to watch the stupidest sort of mediocrity praised above her own work. (I'm *not* talking about Irena Klepfisz.) I'm not surprised that she exploded – and knowing Bertha, that she did so elliptically, cryptically, and as angrily as possible.

Every few weeks someone sends me some incredibly clunky artifact of women's culture which falls helplessly on my desk and instantly expires of sheer unworthiness to live. In between the lousy poems and the excruciatingly dull fairy tales, some singer who can't stay on key and whose untrained voice can't sustain a note for more than two seconds arises and proclaims: *Wooh-mun/will be far-ree-hee-hee!* wrenching her diction, choosing the wrong vowels for her words, letting air escape uncontrollably past her glottis, and radiantly telling interviewers she is "self-taught" and therefore innocent of sexism. This isn't a new, woman's style, it's not a blues style, it's not any style. It's simply incompetent.

Incompetence – praised incompetence, revered incompetence – has (I suspect) driven Bertha Harris mad.

It drives *me* mad.

Do I want therefore to suppress such efforts? Not at all. They're absolutely necessary. (Irena Klepfisz is not talking from the point of view of incompetence, of course. She's talking as someone who's absorbed everything The Boys teach as "art" and is busy throwing much of it out, in an extremely sophisticated and analytical fashion.)

But The Boys are still, by and large, custodians of the most technically rich and adroit literary culture that exists in English, even though it isn't the only literary culture (they pretend it is) and it has no monopoly on all the other virtues. (They pretend it does.)

Books aren't bad because they include long words and subtle literary devices. (Surely a classless world will include education in *all* literary traditions, even the one now called "high culture.") They also aren't – quite obviously – bad because they don't.

I'm speaking from Harris's corner and to Klepfisz because the latter is being rationally persuasive. I agree with her, and Bertha, instead of arguing, simply went Stomp Smash Crash Blonk and walked out.

We must try to exercise some sense of where people are coming from and what they really mean instead of fastening on each individual statement and walloping it. The latter leads to nothing but aggravated temper, hurt feeling and increased insecurity for everyone. I'm not suggesting a meaningless "toleration" – only that language is a very imprecise medium and that 85 percent of most statements are in a code that really means *I want, I need, I feel, my situation is* ... To consider these as positive, precise statements of a considered political position is male-style linear thinking. (And how much more politically incorrect than that can you get?)

Different needs aren't betrayals. Incompleteness (Mary Daly's lack of awareness of economics, Ellen Moers' white solipsism) is not *deliberate* betrayal, either. Though if we handle these that way long enough, we may produce plenty of real betrayals. And a large lack of women left to demonstrate any kind of solidarity with.

Bertha, come home. We love you. A dozen long-stemmed American Beauty roses await you. The intelligent, rationally persuasive, brilliantly talented Irena Klepfisz is favorably reviewing *Lover*. The entire membership of The Oppressed Lesbian Mothers' Grim Denim Bikeathon and Deprivation Society has donned elegant riding habits and mounted chestnut mares and is exquisitely dashing about the *bois*, calling your romantic name. Come home!

All is forgiven.

Author's Note
It took the American Right wing twenty-five years to pick up the phrase, "politically correct" – they're slow learners. I first heard the phrase in the mid-1970s. It was used by feminists I know in Boulder, Colorado, as a wry way of saying "Yeah, I know you may not like this but, dammit, that's what I think!" We would chuckle. There were, of course, some real arguments (if you think that feminism or the Left have a monopoly on faction, think again) and one of them is spoken to in the letter printed above. I still think most statements are in code and when people don't have a direct stake in a conflict (which they obviously do in some conflicts, like class) this kind of fake conflict is an important way of finding out what people want and need and what their situation really is. It was in Boulder that I attended a Women's Studies meeting in which everyone was asked to tell why they'd come into it and (briefly) what issues were important to them *in their lives*. What followed this discussion was a lot of clarification: "So that's why you always emphasize ..." "So that's why you don't believe in ... " We need more of that and by "we" I don't mean only feminists. (Don't tell the Right; if they did this, they'd get much more effective and, Heavens, we don't want that!)

Village Voice, October 1972

Dear Sirs

I could not help agreeing with the recent review of Phyllis Chesler's *Women and Madness* (*Voice*, October 11). After all, you can't have all these unlicensed prophetic visionaries running about saying nasty things about Herod or standing in wells yelling "Alas, Babylon!" As every liberal knows about every radical, that is going *too* far.

But then just for a teeny moment, the good doctor blew his objective, liberal cool sky-high – and in addition unwittingly substantiated what may be a reason for Ms. Chesler's radical, lesbian stance (if such it is) – i.e. that men, when frightened, threatened, or flustered, can be pretty much depended upon to pull rank *and that rank is sexist rank.*

I refer to the reviewer's comment about Ms. Chesler's supposed lack of sexual experience outside the clinical situation. Didja ever hear such a fancy version of the old chestnut,
"All she needs is a good –"
book reviewer?

Author's Note
Yeah, the reviewer really said what I said he said. Yeah, guys did a lot of that then. Later Shere Hite published her books and they did it to *her*. Feh.

Signs, winter 1977

Comment on Helene E. Roberts' "The Exquisite Slave: The Role of Clothes in the Making of the Victorian Woman" and David Kunzle's "Dress Reform as Antifeminism" (vol. 2, no. 3)

"The Exquisite Slave: The Role of Clothes in the Making of Victorian

Woman" and "Dress Reform as Antifeminism: A Response" are not only interesting in themselves but also typical of a certain kind of current debate about feminist issues.[1] It usually involves three positions: (1) A common feminist position is to identify an erotic perversion or other bizarre behavior[2] with ordinary social behavior in order to damn the ordinary social behavior; this is Helene Roberts' identification of tight-lacing with the ordinary wearing of corsets in order to damn the wearing of corsets. (2) The counterposition (often antifeminist, "common sense," and useful in supporting the status quo) is to separate the two, calling one "normal" and the other "abnormal" in order to prove that the ordinary social behavior is innocent or even trivial. This seems to be David Kunzle's position: the ordinary wearing of corsets is entirely different from tight-lacing, and therefore the corset is not important. In fact, denouncing it was "the obsession of small minds." (3) A third position, not present in this debate, is the identification of an erotic perversion (or other bizarre behavior) with ordinary social behavior in order to clear both. This is the strategy of would-be liberals, who wish to indicate that they aren't judging anybody as long as they don't have to talk about the revolting business, whatever it is. It is sometimes the strategy of erotic minorities prior to the solidarity of liberation movements, in which case it usually doesn't work. All of these positions mystify the subject.

I believe Kunzle to be right in insisting that tight-lacing was a genuine erotic specialization and that the ordinary wearing of corsets was not. But he seems also to imply that therefore the wearing of corsets was unimportant. If it was, was dress reform therefore trivial? Did Louisa May Alcott and Amelia Bloomer have small minds? I would say that nothing which reifies women is trivial, and that most of Roberts' statement applies

1 The issues are still with us, I think, but the material discussed in the two essays (Roberts' and Kunzle's) was nineteenth century.
2 I wish here to indicate my own uneasiness with those words and our relative lack of vocabulary in this area. The words "perversion" or bizarre" seem to me to gloss over many differences in behavior and attitudes toward behavior. First, there are erotic specializations, which I do believe to be distinct from more general likings and dislikings. I would like to speak of specializations without indicating either value judgment or beliefs about etiology (both of which are indicated by the word "perversion"). But to speak of specializations alone does not indicate the social dis-esteem in which such behavior is held. To speak of "perversions" in quotation marks indicates that I don't believe such behavior to be different from non-specialized erotic behavior, which is not the case. To speak of extreme or bizarre behavior puts us in the same difficulties. Behavior is "bizarre" or "extreme" because it is considered so by somebody; but such behavior may not only be considered (in another age or by another group) to be the acme of health and reason; it may also have nothing at all to do with erotic specialization.

to ordinary social behavior, not to the erotic perversion of tight-lacing. Kunzle's paper seems to me to show insensitivity to what a feminist issue is; his impatience with the subject suggests that once we have separated the abnormal from the normal nothing remains to be said. I agree with his separation, but the rest of his paper seems to me suspect, that is, his argument that dress reform was often antifeminist (and, by implication, that feminism was not concerned with dress reform). One could construct a parallel argument about modern feminism and the subject of cosmetics that would look just as reasonable and be just as wrong. It's not surprising that feminists *and* sexist conservatives may appear to unite in opposing something, especially something intended to eroticize women's bodies. One cannot conclude from this that the eroticizing of women's bodies is not (or was not) a feminist issue.

Kunzle is right to insist that we must stop confusing erotic specialization with ordinary social behavior. Roberts is muddying the waters when she uses "exhibitionism" for showing off and "masochism" when she means self-hatred. I do, however, believe that insisting on a massive fusion of the two is (in the long run) more productive than saying there is no relationship at all. For example: Is tight-lacing identical with wearing corsets? If not, how does tight-lacing relate to the submissiveness, docility, fragility, delicacy, ladylikeness, etc. that were part of the Victorian ideal of ladies? Was it an erotic ideal and not a domestic ideal? What traits appear in both ideals? What were their functions? (Perhaps the erotic ideal was supposed to prevail until the woman married, when the domestic ideal was supposed to take over. Both Mary Wollstonecraft and Kate Millett suggest that this improbable transformation was *de rigueur* for middle-class brides.) Is the relationship between sexual specialization and ordinary behavior merely fortuitous? Or is behavior transformed when fused with eroticism? Or was tight-lacing a form of self-assertiveness in women (as Kunzle suggests)? Are the "delicious sensations" enjoyed by some women identical with the "profoundly unhappy ... [who] courted severe injury"?

The relation of extreme behavior to ordinary behavior is not trivial. A comparable subject in feminist thought today is rape. The conventional, "common-sense" attitude toward rape is like Kunzle's toward tight-lacing: rape is "crazy" and therefore totally distinct from ordinary heterosexual behavior. Early feminist statements about rape tend to assimilate it to ordinary heterosexual behavior, but as far as I know nobody has decided what relation exists between rape, rape fantasies, sexual masochism and ordinary behavior. And what are we to understand by "ordinary behavior"?

Signs, II:4, 1977

Comment on "Prostitution in Medieval Canon Law," by James Brundage

James Brundage's article, "Prostitution in Medieval Canon Law" (Summer 1976), was interesting, but Brundage's definition of prostitution makes odd reading in *Signs*.

He speaks of promiscuity as central to the medieval definition of prostitution and adds his own agreement: "There is much sense in this" (p. 827). He adds, "It may be possible to be promiscuous without being a prostitute" (why the tentativeness? – of course it is possible), but "it is hardly possible to be a prostitute without being sexually promiscuous." Prostitution thus becomes a subcategory of promiscuity.

Brundage seems entirely unaware of a feminist definition of prostitution (by no means a new one) that sees as central to it the exchange of sexual availability for considerations other than erotic ones. In this view, which was, for example, Emma Goldman's, marriage is a subcategory of prostitution. Women who trade sexual availability for financial security are prostitutes even if they do so with only one man and within institutions socially defined as respectable.

The patriarchal view makes indiscriminateness the test of whoredom. The inconsistencies of this view (which engage Brundage's comment in his article) are perfectly consistent with its central tenet: that a woman's sexual availability must be owned by one man, whether an earthly husband or polygamously by God. (Nuns, who are "brides of Christ," have no counterpart in monks, who are not thought of as husbands of the Virgin Mary.) The real issue here is female independence; hence it is the unowned woman – the "promiscuous" one – who is at fault, whether she has sexual intercourse with many men for her own gain or does so for her own pleasure. Both are equated with the woman who has sexual intercourse with one man, but outside marriage. All are unchaste.

In the feminist view, trading in sexual availability is prostitution, whether the customers are human or divine, singular or plural. Female independence is again the issue, but feminists are for it; thus the statement "Marriage *is* prostitution" becomes a parallel to Proudhon's "Property *is* theft," and thus we have frequent praise of the prostitute (in the patriarchal sense) as more independent and more honest than the conventionally married woman.

By the way, I do not want to bring up the issue of emotional commitment, which is a separate issue. The fact that a scholar in *Signs* can confuse emotional commitment, affection, or love with the plurality or singularity of a woman's sexual partners is testimony to the persistence of the patriarchal view that an unowned woman is as immoral and socially dangerous as a masterless man used to be.

The inconsistencies Brundage finds in the medieval view of prostitution, including the sexual double standard of behavior, make perfect sense in the light of the feminist analysis. Patriarchal sexual morality for women is "object" morality; only if women are considered to be owned by men does it make sense to cure a woman of selling herself partially and with her own control to many men by insisting that she sell herself totally and with no control over the bargain to one man. The issue is social control of female behavior; I would add that the social opprobrium attached to prostitution is (among other things) a way of cancelling out the *relative* freedom it gives to some women in a patriarchal society.

In a nonpatriarchal society, the sale of sex would be a possible but not particularly attractive way of making a living: about on par with being a yes-man for a business magnate. Neither is personally pleasant. Until we reach that happy state, let us at least not confuse the issue, which I am afraid Brundage does.

Author's Note
I was too hard on Professor Brundage here. He protested in his Reply that he had meant only to depict the medieval opinion of the matter and not his own. He did, too, but the subject was too important (and interesting theoretically) to ignore.

Frontiers, **IV:2, 1979**

Dear Editors,

Judith Schwarz's article and Lee Chambers-Schiller's review in Vol. IV, No. 1 of *Frontiers* are both excellent, yet I find myself in paradoxical agreement with Anna Mary Wells. Of course Wells' attitude is nonsense – it resembles Norman Mailer's contention that a man who by sheer willpower has managed to keep his hands off other men's bodies "has earned" the right not to be called homosexual. But something is crucially absent from both article and review, something certainly central to the subject of lesbianism, and that is erotic intensity between women. Or, in the vernacular, lust. Schwarz and Chambers-Schiller both de-emphasize it, Schwarz in clear reaction against the homophobic myth that homosexuals are sex-obsessed degenerates, and Chambers-Schiller (I think) because she is uncomfortably aware of possible homophobia in her readers.

Thus we have caring, commitment, affection, couples, emotional satisfaction (I'm quoting from both), alternative lifestyles, love, devotion, primary affectional ties, romantic attachments, fulfillment, a life together, partnership, shared lives, companionship, dyads, relationship, one "physical love," one "attraction", one "sexual intimacy," one "sexual expression" (as if sex were always the adjective and never the noun!), and Carroll Smith-Rosenberg's "sensual." It is the prudish Wells who is quoted as saying "ardent"! How saintly and Victorian it all sounds.

I believe that all women, heterosexual and homosexual, still labor under a real terror of perceiving or honoring female appetite in a culture which denies it and punishes us for it. Our heritage, our anti-genital conditioning, and our adult experience all make it plain that women have no choice but asexuality or reactive heterosexuality. We are also aware that the latter is dangerous and dishonorable without love. Even feminists still find it hard to admit that women are sexual outside of "relationships" – not affectionate, not romantic, not loving, but impersonally and biologically appetitive. The very idea is terrifying. We don't even do it in talking about heterosexual behavior, but *homosexual* behavior? Two steps backwards and three to the right!

What's at stake is not lesbian history; it's the whole traditional double standard of sexuality, with its concomitant unfreedom, with its fear of parts of experience and the consequent fragmenting of identity, and all those bad things we're trying to get away from.

Let's not perpetuate that! Even lesbians (who do not have the same reasons to be afraid of one another that woman have vis-à-vis men) often talk as if sex uncontrolled by "love" or "commitment" automatically precludes decent, civil, or kind behavior. This may be true in sexist situations (it often is) but surely it's no longer necessarily true.

The fear is a hangover; let's do away with it.

Author's Note
I think this issue is still a live one. The Great Lesbian Sex Wars are one expression of it, but it's a heterosexual issue too. The Good Girls versus Bad Girls split has been commented on by many feminist writers as well as the historical roots of the split. When a split seems as absolute as this (for example, the feminist/anti-pornography movement versus the pro-sex feminists) I don't think anyone can find out anything by simply attending to what both sides think are their "issues." What has to be done is to become aware of the whole situation and of what particular experiences people are talking from. I don't think the two sides are actually in conflict at all, I think that each is demonizing the other, and that nobody has done the hard work of relating ideas to experiences, i.e. what we used to call "consciousness raising." That the trees on a windswept slope lean in different directions doesn't tell you a lot about which trees are "right" and which trees are "wrong," but if you notice where the giant boulders are in this region and what eddies of the wind they produce – then you have a hope of understanding why some lean this way (pornography is all the same and all evil) and some lean that way (sex is good and you're all prudes).

Chrysalis, No. 9, fall 1979

Author's Note
In *Chrysalis* No. 8 Nancy Sahli had published "Smashing: Women's Relationships Before the Fall," an essay in which she made the important point that during the last two decades of the nineteenth century a good many women's close relationships were damned by the label "lesbian" as a way of defusing the feminism that was then extremely active in Europe and the United States. (Neither feminism nor this particular tactic used against it has disappeared, obviously.) Unfortunately she also claimed that her examples were "not lesbian" when it seemed pretty clear to me that some of them were. It seemed to me then (and seems to me now) that the worst possible way of countering such accusations was to insist that the women in question were *not* lesbians, a tactic that left the "charge" of being lesbian unchallenged, as if a woman's "lesbianism" somehow invalidated her feminism. Hence this letter.

Dear Editors,

Nancy Sahli's essay was delightful. And yet there are things in it that present a real problem, one that has appeared recently in other women's publications: Judith Schwarz's article on Katharine Lee Bates and Katharine Coman, and Lee Chambers-Schiller's review of *Miss Marks and Miss Woolley*, both in *Frontiers* IV:1; and Judith Hallett's very peculiar essay on Sappho in *Signs* IV:3. To varying degrees all these pieces present the appearance of uneasily backing into a subject that all of them are either soft-pedalling or (in the case of Hallett) denying outright.

Here is Sahli, insisting that "the" point is not "whether these relationships were sexual, even on an unconscious level" and protesting Krafft-Ebing's identification of a woman who dressed in men's clothing (in 1884), wrote "tender love-letters" to another woman, and disliked the idea of relationships with men, as a lesbian. Why? Because her affair was "platonic." And again, Sahli protests the identification of Olive Chancellor, in *The Bostonians*, as a lesbian since "nowhere in the novel can one find evidence of any variant sexual behavior."

Explicit sexual activity seems some kind of Rubicon for Sahli, on the other side of which lies Heaven knows what. I'm reminded of the heterosexual teenage code of the 1950s in which petting above the waist was

O.K. but petting below the waist imperiled one's respectability – as if both activities weren't erotic! There is, in Sahli's essay, an obvious and very appealing delight in the all-female space she describes, a space that's innocent, emotional, free, and romantic. And yet it is perfectly clear that the motivational fuel for all this activity is erotic. Without genuinely erotic intensity between the women Sahli speaks of, there would be no motive, no *point*, to all the courtship except as play-acting, i.e. a substitute or rehearsal for "real" sex, which is ("of course") heterosexual. This was not only the nineteenth-century attitude, the "girl friendship" stage of Josiah Holland; it persisted into the twentieth century, although the age at which this state of attachment was supposed to end got earlier and earlier (from college age to puberty itself) as female solidarity was perceived as more and more threatening.

Why is genital activity such an absolute dividing line for Sahli, as well as the other writers I've mentioned, all of whom – to some degree – betray uneasiness with the subject? To apply Sahli's reasoning to heterosexual activity would lead to some strange results; are we *not* to call a nineteenth-century young woman heterosexual because although she has experienced passionate attachments to young men, writes them "tender love-letters," and does not wish for close relationships with women, she nonetheless does not engage in specific sexual activity with these men? Surely not.

I'm not sure what the taboo really is here. Is "lesbian" still so loaded a word that its very presence impugns the innocence, the emotionality, even the human decency of the relationships Sahli describes? Is sexual activity itself so guilty or so base or so frightening (heterosexual activity can certainly be all three for women in patriarchy) that it can't be allowed – even as a motive – into Sahli's paradise of freedom and innocence? (The title of the essay, "Before the Fall," is suggestive!)

The sexuality underlying these relationships is not "the" point, but it certainly is an important point. Some conclusions that can be drawn one this point, for example, are that people are more erotically various than they are supposed to be, that sexuality is more complex than it is supposed to be, and that splitting of erotic feeling into "sexual" and "emotional" is a product of male training, not female. (What we get is a general anti-genital training, which men don't.)

Trying to insist that women are not explicitly sexual or that our relationships with both sexes are "emotional" and not genital does not counter the exploitation and abuse of women's heterosexuality by patriarchy, and it certainly will not prevent the kind of labeling Sahli deplores in her article. There is no sense in colluding with the patriarchy in this area; our sexuality ought to be named for what it is, as it is our very great resource. Nor must we follow implicitly masculine definitions of what sex is (which is what

Sahli may be doing) and refuse to acknowledge as sexual any motive or action that isn't explicitly physical. Acknowledging lesbian sexuality (one's own or other women's) puts one into direct confrontation with the patriarchy and subjects one to dangers and discomforts that the college girls of Sahli's essay didn't have to face.

Personal or not, the issue of lesbianism, of erotic feeling between women, is a kind of Rubicon for feminism. It's not just that the issue can be used to divide women or that "lesbian" is a code-word for female solidarity (as used by anti-feminists, that is). There is something more at stake here, namely the fashion in which sexuality itself is controlled by patriarchy and the particular mystifications it undergoes in our contemporary form of patriarchy: from binding women to the family and the economy to the repressive desublimation that occurs more subtly under late industrial capitalism – the reduction of sex to "only" sex, to a consumer good, to something mechanical, simple, and manipulable. And the lack of real choice and autonomy for women in both situations.

What is crucial about woman/woman eroticism is that it (much more than man/man eroticism) stands completely outside both the heterosexual institution and the way human sexuality itself has been viewed and controlled by patriarchal societies. Historically, lesbianism has been totally "wild," not only taboo but impossible, non-existent, in the West in a way that male homosexuality has not. Nowadays male homosexuality seems to be fairly easily culturally assimilable to a reductive consumer-goods view of sex. (Read some of the male gay publications on sale at your neighborhood newsstand!) Lesbian sexuality, because it is neither male nor heterosexually institutionalized, resists such treatment.

One of the things this means is that we are forced to talk about female sexuality in general in an alien vocabulary. Stress the physical eroticism of woman/woman ties, and one is "progressing" into the reductive view of "only" sex (as well as the presumed ugliness and nastiness that accompany that view in this very anti-sexual society). Stress the emotional bond, and one is "regressing" into the view of women as asexual creatures who have plenty of emotions but no independent, real appetite.

It is striking that even in a work intending to demonstrate that women's love for women is called names only when it's perceived as a threat to the system, Nancy Sahli herself shies away from what seem to me the obvious erotic components of what she's describing. If you want examples of women's autonomy being slandered by being declared lesbian, Krafft-Ebing's German lady and Henry James' Olive Chancellor are extraordinarily bad examples. (James' own homosexual temperament is something of an open secret, by the way.) What is so awful about recognizing the erotic intensity in such women's behavior?

Here is Harriet Desmoines in the latest issue of *Sinister Wisdom* (#9): "The partition of the body that patriarchy tries to effect does not work very well with [women] ... it's not so easy to isolate the sexual from the nonsexual [with] ... women. The word Lesbian points to the erotic tone of everything that happens between women ... mothers and daughters ... sisters ... students and teachers ... girl friends. And if ... that makes you feel as nervous as it makes me feel, then I think we can agree that the energies we generate between ourselves ... are tabooed in patriarchy because those energies are powerful – and scary – and it's about time we tapped into them."

"Feminist Review," *The New Women's Times,* February 29–March 13 1980

Dear Editors,

Mary Sojourner's review of Phyllis Chesler's *With Child* is a lovely piece, and yet – oh dear! It's not just that Mary Sojourner knows so little about the realities of publishing (or seems to), the difference between fame and success and what female "really" means (some of this latter information can be found in Chesler and Goodman's *Women, Money, and Power*, Bantam, 1977); it's that her ignorance (?) is shared by so many, and is so American and so very female.

E.g. "Had this writing appeared in soft-cover, for a fair price, we might have admired her courage ..." "We have ... access to publication" "I resent paying $9.95 to male publishers" and "WOMEN are hot stuff right now."

1. The real (media-created) "stars" of feminism must make their livings via commercial publishers because they are otherwise *unemployable*. Fame is absolutely distinct from (and often detrimental to) success. *People* magazine recently informed us that Germaine Greer was teaching permanently in Oklahoma at a relatively low-ranking and unknown university at $15,000 a year (the same salary a young woman in her middle twenties

recently got here in Seattle for her first full-time job). Better then welfare? Sure, but what is Greer doing in Nowheresville at a salary not enough to put her financially into the middle class? (A male colleague of mine recently commented about his own $20,000 a year, "Well, it's O.K. if you're single.") Eating, I suspect. For example:

2. Writer Star A, teaching for a year in order to save money to live on for the next one (at a salary like Greer's) found out simultaneously that she had a serious illness and no medical insurance (oddly enough) though medical insurance is standard in academic contracts.

3. Academic Star B, whose honors in the profession are dazzling, dislikes her tenured location but has never moved. Why? "Too radical," I was told; "No one else will employ her."

4. Writer Star C, having sold the paperback rights to a now published and well-known book on condition that there be a previous hardcover sale, spent three years trying to find a hardcover publisher. One after another refused the book, despite the large guaranteed income (half the paperback advance) such a sale would automatically bring in.

5. The income from internationally famous Writer D's paperback sales are still going to her hardcover publishers after five years to earn back the hardcover advances; meanwhile D is getting nothing from two of her books and is trying to make a living farming.

6. The independent film company that wants to make *Rubyfruit Jungle* into a (relatively inexpensive) film still can't raise enough money to do so.

7. Star E, bringing out a monumental feminist non-fiction work, speaks bitterly of spending three solid years "rescuing" the book from its publisher.

"WOMEN" may be hot stuff, but feminism isn't and anything lesbian is practically unpublishable.

Most publishers will not publish a book in paperback without a previous hardcover sale; not only are original paperbacks not reviewed in the trade and have no guaranteed sale to libraries, but also most publishing houses survive on that 50 percent of the paperback income (advance and royalties forever and ever amen) that is standard in the trade.

Most commercial publishers have, in the last ten or so years, been bought by giant conglomerates. If you resent paying $9.95 for a book (a low price; look around!) note that you are not even paying it to "male publishers;" you're paying it to Gulf and Western, American Express, CBS, RCA, Xerox, Raytheon, or whatever other giant has just gobbled up the publisher in question. The gory details are in *Chrysalis 8* (Summer 1979), Celeste West's "The Literary Industrial Complex."

Indeed we do need our own publishing and distributing businesses, but are they growing? Diana Press no longer publishes. Women in Distribution (distribution is the real problem, financially) has just vanished.

If feminist writers are not to depend on other jobs (as I do) – and some of them can't since they are now infamous – they must earn a living by writing. Women's presses do not provide a living wage. And I know of no feminist writer who, after an initial best-seller (like *Women and Madness* or *Small Changes*), found publishers lining up to beg for her next book, although that sort of thing is commonplace enough when non-feminist writers produce best-sellers. (I would bet that Marilyn French, whose *The Women's Room* was a real word-of-mouth success, will find the same thing happening to her.) The "star" pattern is really more and more publicity, more and more criticism (both inside and outside the women's community) and more and more trouble finding publishers or jobs, with all the publicity never, somehow, "paying off." That adrenaline rush is really insecurity.

But then feminists are not supposed to succeed. Neither are women, period. Neither is feminism. Audre Lorde told us all so at the Modern Language Association annual meeting in San Francisco three (?) years ago. In fact, what she said was, if I remember, that we were not even supposed to survive. Publicity, glamor, visibility, the big American shuck, is not success. It isn't even money. (By the way, the college lecture/performance market, once the mainstay of feminists, has all but vanished.)

If we are to reach each other, one of the things that must go is the illusion that some women have "made it." What looks from afar like Manhattan myopia and TV adrenaline is really the knowledge that one has worked and worked only to acquire a few more insecure privileges, an exhausting toe-and-fingerhold on a cliff-face with large numbers of men (including one's publisher) throwing rocks on one's head from above. Having sand thrown at you from below while female voices yell "Cop-out!" doesn't improve the balance.

I am talking, of course, about real feminists and mean this as an addition to Mary Sojourner's piece not as a quarrel. Writing, like acting, is an unbelievably badly paid profession for all but the very few – and those few are not Phyllis Chesler but Rosemary Rogers. The glamor of publicity disguises that nasty fact.

If anything, I suspect that Mary Sojourner feels guilty because as a white woman and a middle-aged one (why middle-aged? that I don't get) she is not really oppressed enough.

Hollow laugh from Stars A through E. And me. And Chesler too. Heh. Ho. Huh. Ha. We all are, quite enough. Which, I should think, is the whole point, unless one wants (as I do not think Sojourner does) to sternly send Chesler et al. back to welfare or Woolworth's, in which case there will be no books from anyone past the age of, say, thirty-odd. And soon no books from anyone, period.

I understand the psychology of "I'm different" which Sojourner is deploring, and yet Phyllis Chesler is extraordinary. Extraordinarily tenacious, for one thing. Extraordinarily unkillable. Extraordinarily hardworking and extraordinarily underpaid.

Aren't we all?

Author's Note
Writing pays very badly. *Writing pays very badly.* Writing pays worse now than it did then. If you do it, do it for love of it. You may even make a living at it and you may not. (If you do what Danielle Steel does, you probably will.) This issue is very American, i.e. the idea that celebrities have real lives and the rest of us don't. Publicity doesn't necessarily mean power *or* money and unfortunately believing that the "real" news is about celebrities leaves us all totally ignorant of the forces that are truly hurting us, and truly shaping our lives.

Gay Community Center Newsletter, July 1980

Dear GCC,

Your *Pick a Color* essay in Vol. II No. 6 was a fine idea. My only objection is that "stylish and masculine" as it is, it doesn't go far enough. I'd like therefore to pass on an additional signal system. It works with band-aids worn in various places and coloured with laundry-marking pens. (These are not only cheaper than handkerchiefs but can be changed to suit the wearer's mood.)

> Yellow, right knuckle: in closet at work, terrified of losing job
> Yellow, left knuckle: out at work, terrified of never getting job
> Yellow, across nose: has just lost job, plain terrified
> Black, right knuckle: aspiring bank executive, &c., doesn't understand why America hates queers
> Red, left knuckle: does understand why but is sick of explaining it to aspiring bank executives, &c.

Green, forehead: wants to be held and comforted non-sexually but would rather die than let anyone know

Green, chin: wants to hold and comfort another non-sexually but what sort of pervert would get off on something that ridiculous, anyway?

Orange, earlobe: enjoys conversation but can have that with straights, so why go to a bar for it?

Orange, across mouth: likes conversation too, but feels shy and silly and wishes someone else would start it

White, nose: is afraid of getting old and ugly

Pink, chin: resents gay community's sexism

Gray, chin: resents gay community's consumption and classism

Brown, chin (white person): resents gay community's racism

None, chin (person of color): resents gay community's racism

Rainbow, across both eyes: wants to be "apolitical"

Is afraid of not being popular, feels lonely, knows he's really not good-looking, and secretly suspects his penis is too small: no band-aid necessary (condition assumed).

I realize the above is not exhaustive. I am afraid I cannot provide a lesbian code as the other lesbians I know seem never to have developed an efficient signal system and rely almost entirely on an archaic method of communication called "talking". I hear they are also into something called "touching". But such accounts are hardly credible, being neither modern, efficient, masculine, nor stylish.

Science-fiction Studies, #2 = 7:2, July 1980

Women and SF : Three Letters

Author's Note
First, Susan Gubar wrote a good essay about women's science fiction. It was published in *Science-fiction Studies*. Then I wrote to the journal saying

Good-oh and added stuff (letter one). Then Linda Leith wrote back and said things about *my* letter (you want to make men secondary, men and women are opposites which need to be reconciled, etc.). So I wrote another letter (academics enjoy this sort of thing). The "Flasher" books to which I refer in letter two was part of an essay I wrote, published in *Science-fiction Studies* in 1980. It is available (if you want to find it) in *To Write Like a Woman: Essays in Feminism and Science Fiction*, a collection of my essays published by Indiana University Press in 1995. The title of the essay was "*Amor Vincit Foeminam*: The Battle of the Sexes in Science Fiction."

* * * *

Susan Gubar's essay was so good that I'd like to add a few details which would enrich Gubar's case. (1) Rockets are seen by fans not as "womblike" (p. 17) but phallic. Vonnegut thinks so, too, in his bitter satire "The Great Space Fuck." (2) In *Juniper Time* Wilhelm is more explicit and political than Moore: the heroine pretends to decipher an "alien" code which is, in truth a human (male) fake. Her real "alien" allies are those complete outsiders in the white, male, technological world: native Americans. (3) The ultimate, conscious use of woman-as-alien is of course Tiptree's "Houston, Houston. Do you Read?" in which the "alien" women, asked "What do you call yourselves?" by the male narrator, answer matter-of-factly, "mankind." It's a pity the focus and length of Gubar's article precluded exploring these examples.

But Gubar is thoughtless in using the word "tradition," which implies that the writers in question have read and been influenced by each other. One would have to prove such connections, which in some cases (e.g. Lessing) might be difficult. I suspect that until the late 1960s we had not a tradition, but scattered cases of parallel evolution. One must not assume a purely literary ancestry for phenomena.

Especially not in SF, where the traditions are derived primarily from science itself and only secondarily from literature, especially literature before Verne and Wells. Gubar's feminism alerts her to the use of "alien" = woman in women's SF, but there is another reason why women are not as innocently gleeful about technology as so many men in the field. Samuel Delany's "gravitic" metaphor (which he calls the central metaphor of SF in his *The American Shore* [Dragon Press, Elizabethtown, N.Y., 1978], p. 184) may be unusable by women – or other outsiders. In this "gravitic" metaphor a story typically progresses via machinery or other means (in *The Star Maker* a form of astral travel) from the Earth's gravitic field (metaphorically: realities, values, possibilities) into space (weightlessness, hence an absence of a system of values or expectations about reality) and from there to a different gravitic field and a different world (reality, value, possibility). We have here Darko Suvin's "cognitive estrangement" made concrete. We have also, by the by, the origin of SF's horror at life underground (remember the fuss about fallout shelters in the 1950s?) To live under the surface of the Earth is to capitulate completely to gravity. In Forster's "The Machine Stops" the metaphor is a direct descendant of Plato's Fable of the Cave, given Forster's classical education and fascination with ancient Greece: the emergence onto the surface of the Earth is an emergence into static, timeless truth. But in SF emergence from underground leads typically not to a timeless union with nature and truth but to a leap upward into a night sky filled with stars. Plato's tale represents truth as static; the SF metaphor reminds us that the Sun is only one star among many. Truth is plural.

But what if the original gravitic field is not "ours" at all, just as the status of "human" is not "ours"? Tiptree's use of technology is always ironic, and her use of the gravitic metaphor sometimes hideously so (as in "A Momentary Taste of Being"). Why go looking for cognitive estrangement when we live it out every day on what is supposedly our home planet?

Uncomplicated, unironic use of either the alien or the gravitic metaphor may be the mark of the Insider author: Heinlein, Asimov, Clarke (it does not matter that the aliens are "good," as in Clarke: they are still Other). Perhaps a similar use of the End of the World story may also betray the Insider; when the post-Holocaust society of *Walk to the End of the World* starts to crumble, the heroine (unlike Aldiss) does not grieve, but flees in relief. The world is ending. Ah, but whose?

* * * *

Adrienne Rich writes that when women turn their faces to each other, they are often perceived as turning their backs on men. It is a commonplace of feminism that women must make women their first priority: Linda Leith instantly makes the leap (common to anti-feminist polemic also) to a role-reversal. Why should Susan Gubar's reversing "the degradation of women's secondariness" mean the degradation of men? It is Leith who insists on this.

She also seems to equate the men in my Flasher books with all men, which I do not. If I had, would I have quoted Philip Slater and Michael Korda or discussed pro-feminists like Frederik Pohl, Theodore Sturgeon, and Mack Reynolds, or included in my list of feminist Utopias Samuel Delany's *Triton*? My contempt is for the Flasher books themselves. (One may measure the damage done by the Flasher myth by noting that some of the authors cited in my paper have done good work elsewhere.) The weakness that underlies the myth is not something I wish to gloat over, but rather the only aspect of those vile fictions that in the least redeems them. If "vile" sounds strong, read them. Or read the April 1980 issue of *Mother Jones*, devoted to articles on the pornography whose pervasive theme is male conquest of powerless women; there is even a sequence that corresponds exactly to the Flasher stories: men in Star Trek uniforms meet naked "women's libbers," overawe them with the size of their penises, and then set them to performing docile services like ironing clothes and fellatio. Consumers of such fantasies obviously don't believe in the power of the penis; if they did, they would not pay to be reassured.

If none of the Flasher books envisions a womanless world, that may be because much great literature has already done so, for example *Moby Dick*. It may also be that such a vision would now be seen as homosexual by authors and readers alike, a phenomenon taboo in the sexist terms of the myth itself. The feminist Utopias, having broken the cultural imperative of male dominance, have no qualms about breaking others; thus the Lesbianism of the separatist stories and the sexual permissiveness of the rest. I am not a separatist in the sense that I envision the perfect future for our planet as a manless one – such an eventuality seems to me undesirable, immoral, and totally impossible – but I do believe that crucial to the process of women becoming primary to themselves is the possibility of becoming able to imagine such a state. (The two most intransigent stories in the feminist group, *Motherlines* and "Houston, Houston, Do You Read?," are written by happily married women, and Charlotte Perkins Gilman's *Herland* fits right into this group.) Far from reveling in a role-reversal, none of the feminist Utopias show women as dominant over men (such situations are confined to the Flasher books, all written by men). And the all-female feminist Utopias provide explicit and clearly stated reasons for keeping men out: rape, battery, the threats thereof that restrict women's freedom and safety, and the male monopoly of activity in the public world. (The resemblance to our world is not coincidental.) It is, of course, up to particular men in the real world whether they will continue to permit or practice such atrocities or whether they will fight them.

Leith's comment strikes me as apolitical and hence confused. In what way can the members of a big-brained, weakly dimorphic, and highly plastic species be considered "opposites"? If men and women constitute a polarity, like day and night, how can such utterly different creatures be "reconciled" and to what? To being so different? But they already *are* different!

Unlike Leith, I assume – and I think Gubar does – that the sexes constitute classes whose relation is political. This means that before "integration" can occur there must be conflict – a prospect Leith is, I suspect, trying to short-circuit. Talk about polarities and integration when the issues are exploitation and abuse, physical, economic, and psychological, is a way of avoiding conflict. Unfortunately such tactics also avoid change, which can occur (and has occurred) only through conflict. I am impatient with Leith's talk of biological determinism for the same reason. It resembles the old questions (which are being revived, by the way) as to whether blacks are stupid or the poor shiftless, and if so, is it right to give school-children hot lunches and prevent the survival of the fittest? Such talk can prevent change for years – centuries, if we're persistent enough.

The relation between women and Capitalism is the subject of a good book, *For Her Own Good* by Barbara Ehrenreich and Deirdre English (Anchor, 1979). As for the relation between women's SF and technology, I was attempting in my earlier essay to distinguish between the attitudes of those who imagine they own the world (in some sense) and those who don't, but there may be more to the matter; Marc Feigen Fasteau's *The Male Machine* (Dell, 1976) is a good book with some insights on this point.

I do apologize for inadvertently implying that Darkover is a feminist utopia in *The Shattered Chain*; I meant, of course, the Guild of Free Amazons, which shares the characteristics of the other feminist utopias (classlessness, concern with children, sexual permissiveness, etc.).

Written to *Venom*, November 27 1981

Author's Note
Venom: the Magazine of Killer Reviews appeared in 1981, a sportive little publication perpetrated by science fiction writers who remained anonymous somewhere in San Francisco. To be published in *Venom*, an author had to write a pseudonymous and nasty review of one of her or his own works. Then one was allowed to submit killer reviews of others' work. Unfortunately, by that fall, the magazine editors, overburdened with work, had quit publishing it and so this letter was never printed. I still think Elizabeth Lynn was involved. She won't say.

Dear Vipers,

Another of those forced marriages of brutality, gynecology, and Raymond Chandler came my way only two days before *Venom* appeared, one "Dark Angel" by Edward Bryant. In this one a witch (get that? *that's* what all this talk about Women's Lib comes to; give a woman any power at all and [a] she'll be irrational and dangerous and [b] up to no good) makes pregnant the man who got *her* pregnant twenty years before and then abandoned her. In Myrna Lamb's play "What Have You Done For Me Lately?," which uses the same plot device, the man is a U.S. Senator who's led a public campaign against women's right to abortion (after abandoning the woman – a *doctor*, Edward, not a witch – who nearly died in labor with his child). But everybody knows what Women's Lib really wants – brutality, viciousness, and a prose style stolen from a Bogart flick, a bad one. "He hurried. I was dry and it hurt. I made him use spittle" (p. 163). "Everybody can have one mistake, I told myself. One only. I suddenly wanted to leave the elevator, the hotel, Phoenix. I didn't want to go back to Denver. I wanted to go anywhere else" (p. 171). Myrna Lamb provides her male character with an abortion, after an elaborate discussion of the ethics of abortion; Ed knows that's sentimentality and provides *his* with no birth canal and a pregnancy nobody but he and the witch can see. Yeah, I guess they get some weird kick out of it, but this one's got me so mad I can't even be witty about it. He's got our number all right; what we really want is to stop wearing dresses, take out other kids' eyes when we're a kid (this is put in to show you how evil the witch is – and it's her *father* who reproves her), and act out Guess Who's worst impulses. At least I assume they're his worst impulses. When not giving us such dazzlingly verisimilar glimpses of the liberated future, Bryant can write reasonably decent stories.

But not about us.

About *Venom*: re A.D.'s *Afterlife*'s (too many s's?) review. In the midst of this elegant tour-de-force there is one small mote: Russ has never attained the pinnacle of academic success; no Dr., she. This fact rather pleases me.

I look forward to future issues.

Who Goes Where
(not "There" dammit)

Sojourner, 10:8, June 1985

Dear Editors

Time and time again, feminist talk about sex betrays the influence of homophobic and sexist assumptions that cling to us and of which we're not aware. Ruth Hubbard's "There Is No 'Natural' Human Sexuality" (April, 1985) betrays this process. After quite accurately describing the biases of contemporary "sex" education, she proceeds to a surprisingly destructive series of inaccuracies and illogic.

First, to erase any distinction between sexual desire and affection serves nothing but an anti-sexual attitude already far too prevalent. In our cultural tradition women have been taught for centuries (or have retreated into the idea as an illusory protection against male sexual exploitation) that sex is love – or ought to be – and that sexual appetite uncontrolled by love is, *by its very nature*, exploitative, cruel, mechanical, or debased. In such a situation the simple observation that sexual arousal is a basic biological appetite, varying in strength in people and varying in what can evoke it but still not interchangeable with affection, emotional intimacy or "sensuality" like having one's back rubbed or hair stroked, still seems to send many of us into a flurry of defense. Some women insist that emotional intimacy is the only permissible cue for desire, some argue that "long-term relationships" are morally privileged, and some – like Ruth Hubbard – simply use the terms "love", "sexuality," and "affectional relationship" as if they were interchangeable.

Those who can honor both desire and affection may satisfy their sexual appetites inside a love relationship or outside, or do both, but they know that the different hungers, sometimes mingling (in some people, at some time) and sometimes separate (in some people, at some time) are capable of all sorts of combinations, and are not identical or necessarily fused. Nor, excluding coercion and violence, is one form of sexual satisfaction morally privileged over others.

And what on earth is so wrong with that?

It seems that for many of us it's so wrong it still mustn't be perceived even when it falsifies the facts. For example, Hubbard's citation of Kinsey is totally incorrect. Kinsey never said, in his research, that we can love people of either sex. In fact, his restricting his research to genital acts leading to orgasm (not "love") was used by many critics of the day to pronounce his statistics invalid. To go further, he didn't even show that most Americans were capable of same-sex contact leading to orgasm. What he did find was that a surprisingly large number of American men had had at least one homosexual contact leading to orgasm. (These findings were so shocking at the time that they were used to cast doubt on his methodology and on the sheer possibility of studying sexual behavior.) Those who were substantially homosexual in their behavior were a minority (in both women and men), those predominantly homosexual a still smaller minority, and those exclusively homosexual in their behavior an even smaller minority.

Defending a minority by assimilating them with the majority is no defense, yet Hubbard's view of homosexual people at once insists that everyone is homosexual (sort of) and simultaneously that nobody is really exclusively homosexual at all – in short, that there is no minority.

This may look "liberal" at first glance, and yet Hubbard's logic leaves a lot to be desired. For one thing, when some people risk extreme social punishment (ranging from continual harassment to jail to incarceration in the back ward of a mental hospital to the risk of losing job, family, housing, and even life), it seems rather peculiar to call their behavior a "choice" in any ordinary sense. And when *some* people report that they had different feelings and desires from others at a very early age, and felt "different" because of this, Hubbard flatly dismisses their account of their own experiences with absolutely no justification except that she just doesn't believe them. Why? Apparently because *most* people are capable of desiring partners of both sexes! She then goes on to talk about theories of the genesis (I think she means the channeling) of sexuality in "men" and "women," ignoring the applicability of these theories to the minority of people, who don't exist anyway *because* the theories she talks about as applying to the majority don't fit this minority.

What a muddle!

Alas, we're just as far as ever from accepting genuine human diversity. I'm reminded of the liberals of the 1930s onward who tried to advocate an end to "discrimination" (as the phrase was then) by insisting that "Negroes" were just like "us," or the fighters against anti-Semitism who have argued that Jews are "just like everybody else." To defend the rights of a minority by asserting that it doesn't exist is – to put it mildly – self-defeating. It also makes the minority in question wonder if friends like that are not worse than enemies. Within minorities there are people who share almost nothing more than that they are hated by the same bigots; there are those who share more; and there are those who hate each other's guts for in-group reasons that outsiders can't even understand. To go even further, arguing that because a Jewish person could have (in infancy) been raised as a Gentile and then would have exhibited Gentile cultural traits and Gentile beliefs, that an adult Jewish person is in some sense a Gentile, or is just like a Gentile, or ought not to be persecuted because she or he could have been a Gentile, is to talk nonsense. Yet Hubbard seems to be making the exact same argument about homosexual people. Because sexuality is plastic does not mean that once sexual cues and preferences have been established they can then automatically be treated as still plastic, and yet this is exactly what Hubbard's non-logic implies.

If I go on at such length about Hubbard's essay, that's because in feminism (and politics) in general an awful lot of us are "progressing" backwards. "Feminism" now means anything you want it to mean. It's announced in quite a few places that equality between women really means that everybody's opinion is equally valuable and equally descriptive of the world as it is, which is grotesque (is Phyllis Schlafly's opinion as valuable as, say, Adrienne Rich's?); that women's sexuality is loving and personal while men's is violent and exploitative; that everybody's sexuality is (or ought to be) fused with love or really is love; that pornography is the rootcause of patriarchy; or, worst of all, that feminism is a lifestyle instead of being an activity in the public world – and so on.

Hubbard looks so wise, compassionate, and white-haired in her picture that I felt guilty about writing this letter, but I looked in the mirror, noted my own wrinkles and gray hair (the wisdom you'll have to decide for yourselves) and hardened my heart. The economic and political reasons for the scramble to retreat from feminism are pretty obvious – but must we simply give up during a period of reaction, or can we do something about it?

The Women's Review of Books, II:9, June 1995

Dear Editors

Bless us, another Sadistic Lesbian novel! Ildiko de Papp Carrington doesn't seem to recognize the genre to which Joyce Carol Oates' *Solstice* belongs. This may be fortunate as far as she's concerned (not having read all the other ones has kept her from a very bad taste in the mouth after reading this one) but it's also unfortunate, since her lack of familiarity with the tradition keeps her from spotting a newly malignant member of this very nasty and ultimately anti-feminist tribe and so warning the rest of us.

Lousy Lesbian Novels are the one kind that commercial publishers will readily buy and handle, the other being the Ridiculously Awful sort (like the unreal silliness of *Kinflicks*, that strange combination of falsely comic sex and real mother/daughter suffering).

The Loathsome Lez began in the United States in the 1920s (Lillian Faderman traces the genre's development in her *Surpassing the Love of Men*), usually converging with the Older Woman Has Mysterious Power Over Younger plot. What de Papp Carrington describes in her review is yet another cautionary tale about how awful the whole repulsive business is. Women who love women really hate women. Trust another woman, especially if your feelings towards her are sexual, and she will do ghastly things to you. Desire as betrayal. Love is abjection. And so on.

Oates has been long obsessed with this kind of unreal violence. I would protest against it as a novelist, and as a feminist I detest it. Oates often seems to have accepted the patriarchal view of the world as one in love with victimization and violence. As a lesbian woman, I'm afraid I see *Solstice* as just another piece of anti-woman and anti-lesbian propaganda. If I had not read all those other books and plays (and recognized them in Faderman's description in Carrington's review) I might even have accepted its view of relations between women as, if not realistic, at least imaginatively original. But when something is the fiftieth or eightieth or hundredth of its kind, one becomes skeptical.

Women are not angels. Even lesbians aren't, believe it or not! There are *some* women who are sadistic toward other women, *some* lesbian women who are also. But what Carrington describes isn't like any possible human being I've ever met or even heard about in my fifty years of experience in this world, though it does bear a suspicious resemblance to literary fantasies of a certain florid and awful kind.

De Papp Carrington's review concretizes, for me, a disturbing tendency in *The Women's Review of Books*. To have a publication "not restricted to any one conception of feminism" is to have no clear standards for feminism and hence no clear standards at all. There is a lot of this eclecticism lately in "feminist" quarters. If the *Review* did have its own definition of feminism, it *might* have rejected Carrington's review as one that did not take enough cognizance of any kind of feminist, or economic, or historical, or social-analytical context. In fact, as far as I can tell, Carrington's review of Oates' new book might appear in many non-feminist literary/academic journals without a word being altered. Why was it published in *The Women's Review* at all?

I'm not calling for anger in such reviews, or platitudes about how rotten men are, or anything that illogical or fruitless. But if there is no broader context (as Linda Gordon's "When Biology Became Destiny" does so admirably have) why print something in a journal *expressly designed to be feminist?* Criticisms like the Oates review are in very long supply in academia, and, to my mind, do not place Oates' symbolic activity, or her claim that feminist novels are narrow, in any kind of broader view.

There is enormous counter-activity going on right now in feminism; "anything goes" means that anything vaguely about women is given the same priority as anything by women, and that anything vaguely "for" women (or maybe not – isn't that what "objectivity" means?) is fine.

May your editorial board acquire some flaming radicals, bomb-toting crazies, "sadistic" lesbians, and iconoclastic marxists. It'd be the making of the *Review*!

Author's Note
Here we go again. Women are worse than men. Lesbianism as torture. Lesbianism as a Strange Power Exercised by a Sophisticated Older Woman Over an Impressionable Girl – something I would dearly love to have if only I could find out where to get it, but unfortunately the demand seems to exceed the supply, if there's any supply at all besides the homophobia of seventy years ago. (I'm thinking of the Broadway play, "The Captive," presented in 1926.) As I recall, the reviewer (above) found the book baffling; unfortunately I didn't. Anglo-Saxon nations are crazy about sexual matters; it's so sacred that anything but the One True Way to Do It is unspeakably vile and awful. Even I believed enough of this not to notice that I'd used the word "sadistic" above to describe what is *not* a certain kind of sex or sexual fantasy. What I meant was cruelty and treating other people badly (which is *not* negotiable, I think).

Why are heterosexuals so *weird?*

The Women's Review of Books, III:6, March 1986

Author's Note
The mystification of money and power issues in the United States (and elsewhere, of course) seems to me often to take the form of complicated, even hair-splitting analyses of abstractions like "justice," "fairness," and so on, which are discussed as if they were extremely difficult to define and so abstruse that the discussion is elevated into a Heaven of ideas where such ordinary things as human beings and concrete events in their lives don't exist. As I recall it, *Gender Justice* was a Right-wing attempt to confuse all of us by insisting that the most minimally nominal "freedom" was identical with real freedom. Nope.

Dear Editors

The concept of "liberty" over which Rosemary Tong spends so much time in her review of *Gender Justice* (January 1986) is a fake; it doesn't exist today except for a very small minority of the rich and powerful (virtually all of whom are white men) *and it never did*.

The liberty of the free market, which is what the book's authors are talking about (it's enjoying an ideological revival today, for obvious political and economic reasons), never applied to the peasants who endured appalling conditions in the factories of the early Industrial Revolution because they'd been kicked off their land. Nor does it apply today to giant corporations, multinational banking, massive advertising, and a situation in which, of the largest 100 economic powers in the world, 57 are countries and *43 are multinational companies. (One-third of world trade now consists of each multinational company trading with itself.)*

We live today in a world in which oligopolies (a few giant corporations which control the majority of the market) raise prices in good times and bad, prefer large per-item profits on a low volume of sales to smaller unit profits on many more sales, and shift the social costs of pollution, ecological disaster, poverty, unemployment, aging and disability to everyone else – anyone else – in the name of "liberty."

This isn't liberty. It's piracy. *Private* piracy. In such a situation groups are created onto whom the social costs of big business can be shifted, especially the cost of overwork, unemployment, poverty and consequent popular anger: racism, sexism, *compulsory* heterosexuality (which ensures enforcement of the marriage contract, which – as French feminist Christine Delphy writes – is a *labor* contract), what we now call age-ism, able-ism, the persecution of fat people, especially fat women, and so on.

The liberty of the marketplace is, and historically has been, an excuse for the worst kind of vampirism. Despite the enormous inequities between men sanctioned by this (very self-interested) version of "liberty," the inequities between men and women are worse: globally, women do two-thirds of the world's work and receive 10 percent of the world's pay.

Gender Justice lies about *civitas*: women in the labor force in the U.S. are paid (on the average) one-third less than men for anywhere from twenty to forty hours *more* work – the famous double job, of which the authors of *Gender Justice seem* totally ignorant. In 1976 60 percent of working women (52 percent in 1962) were in just four occupations: clerks, saleswomen, waitresses and hairdressers.

This isn't liberty. This is force and fraud. Private force and private fraud. That most of us are taken in by it to some extent isn't surprising when it bombards us daily, but I still wish Ms. Tong had either spent her review time on something more fruitful or given the silly book the trouncing it deserves.

If she (and I) sometimes act like "liberals" I'm afraid the reason isn't far to seek: we're located in the top layer of the relatively well-paid slice of the working class and in a profession (the idea business) whose economic function is, in part, to keep the rest of the working class (those who don't live off their property but their work, mental or physical) in line. We're split – and it shows.

The Seattle Source, **April 11 1986**

Dear Editors

Kathy Walmer's editorial is a little confused about the difference between separatism and segregation.

Segregation is imposed by the more powerful on the less powerful (or the minority, on the minority). It amounts to the powerful forbidding the less powerful to have access to the more powerful's desirable territory: well-paying jobs, pleasant places to live, leisure, money, community status as "important" or "normal" and so on.

Separatism is the attempt of the less powerful to deny the more powerful access to themselves and their spaces, few and meager as these are, while also claiming equal access to those good jobs, nice places to live, leisure, community status as "normal" and "important," space to have their news reported in community papers and so on. Getting angry because straight people invade a gay bar is separatism; making it impossible for gay people to be ourselves in straight places without feeling uncomfortable or being afraid of violence is segregation.

To claim half a page out of a sixteen-page paper isn't separatism; it's segregation. "Womensource" is that old, condescending newspaper tradition, The Woman's Page, under a new name. Many of us campaigned to get the big dailies to drop that sexist stuff for years. *The Source* oughtn't to start off by doing the same nerdish nonsense. A woman's page WILL cause dissension between the lesbian and gay male communities – and we have enough of that as it is, right?

Author's Note
The Seattle Source was a gay community newspaper, begun in Seattle, Washington, in 1986 (when I was living there). Complaints about women and women's doings going unrepresented in the paper led to the editorial mentioned above: one page out of 32 was proposed to be devoted to "women's" news. The editorial also condemned a strictly all-female newspaper (which possibility had been mentioned as a solution to the lack of women's news in *The Source*) as segregation.

The Women's Review of Books, III:12, September 1986

Dear Editors,

The bias Carolyn Heilbrun finds in Janice Raymond's *A Passion for Friends* (*Women's Review*, Vol. III, No. 9, June 1986) is all too clearly Lesbian "bias" – as opposed to the heterosexist (not heterosexual) bias of readers Heilbrun believes might be alienated by Raymond's book. Feminism is not limited to lesbians but we certainly have less of a personal stake than heterosexual feminists in staying within the bounds of prescribed female behavior and a much, much more personal stake in examining all ramifications of the assumption that "woman is for man."

It's hard to be heterosexual and a feminist. For one thing, heterosexuality is for the vast majority of women so much a matter of taken-for-granted social pressures that the possibility of not associating with men in some kind of sexual-familial arrangement never even arises. Second, unless a heterosexual feminist's male partner fights the patriarchy to a degree that puts him in continual economic or personal danger, he is in very important ways *not her ally*. To remain with any other kind of man (they are in very long supply) requires a woman to distort her thinking, to take customary behavior as moral behavior and restrain from pushing her own feminist requirements "too hard," like the prisoner who learns to avoid painful contact with an electrified fence by stopping just short of its limits and who then learns to forget the original process of learning so that the fence becomes psychologically invisible and she can pretend she's free.

For the majority of women, avoiding personal sexual association with men simply isn't possible; the price is too high. In trying to become aware of the social forces that limit our behavior as women, public patriarchy is easier to face than the private kind. Ideally all feminists should face both, but as least a lesbian can become aware of the sexism that is trying to kill her without having to face profound personal ambivalence about her partner. For heterosexual women this ambivalence can become tragically intense – which is often why it remains in the clouded area of the not-clearly-felt and never-examined.

I have great respect for Carolyn Heilbrun but the attitudes implied in her review strike me as dangerous to the entire feminist movement. To assume that heterosexuality and homosexuality are somehow equivalent personal choices, that Lesbianism is a civil rights issue only, and that any comments by Lesbians on the limits imposed on feminist insights and behavior by heterosexuality reveal Lesbian bias, is to abandon the radical analysis that made the Women's Liberation Movement possible. To assume (as Heilbrun also seems to do) that friendship and erotic intensity are entirely distinct from one another is unrealistic. Surely their interrelationships are multiform.

Carolyn Heilbrun might answer this letter by saying that my interpretation of her review is inaccurate. I hope she does! I will be glad to be mistaken, as I have seen a cluster of such attitudes far too often in the last few years: a denial of the compulsory nature of the heterosexual institution, praise of psychotherapy (especially psychoanalysis), increased attention to the valorization of women's behavior along with decreased attention to what we used to call the oppression of women, an "encouragement" of men to broaden their "roles" – fancy anybody talking about racial roles or class roles! – and (among many literary feminists) an emphasis on language rather than those gritty and much more intractable realities, money and power. Such practice adds up to a "liberal" abandonment of the insights of the Women's Liberation Movement of the late 1960s and early 1970s that made feminism possible at all.

Such beliefs are worth exposing, whether Heilbrun shares them or not. I hope this letter can begin such a discussion. As I said, I hope that I have misconstrued Heilbrun's review. I will be more than happy if I have.

Author's Note
Like the punished-via-sexuality/punished for having a (forbidden) sexuality split in experience, the lesbian/straight split in experience is an annoying one. Each side knows what the other doesn't. As usual, I tried to speak to the issue involved and not to attack the individual piece of work that, to my mind, raised the issue. What is crucial about putting together everyone's necessarily varying experience (this is where ideas of "oppression" and "values" come *from*) is that only such a joining together can possibly furnish accurate political/social/economic/aesthetic/you-name-it theory. The set of attitudes and beliefs called "homophobia," like that other crucial set of attitudes and beliefs which we call "racism," can vary from outright bigotry and hatred to the subtlest assumptions that "women" means only certain kinds of women to an ignorance not even aware of itself. As the radicalism of the 1960s and 1970s wanes – inevitable now that some of the pressures that drove white women to it are somewhat relieved – early ideas like "compulsory heterosexuality" are getting lost. My point above (which was misunderstood by some) is NOT that lesbians make better feminists than heterosexual women, but that in order to know a subject it is necessary to know all of it and nobody can claim to know all of it or be the norm for knowing it.

The Women's Review of Books, IV:10–11, July/August 1987

Old Maids: Short Stories by Nineteenth Century U.S. Women Writers. Ed. Susan Koppelman (Routledge and Kegan Paul/Pandora Press, New York/London, 1984, $9.95 paper). *The Other Woman: Stories of Two Women and a Man.* Ed. Susan Koppelman (The Feminist Press, New York, 1984, $8.95 paper). *Between Mothers and Daughters: Stories Across a Generation.* Ed. Susan Koppelman (The Feminist Press, New York, 1984, $8.95 paper). *Close to Home: A Materialist Analysis of Women's Oppression.* Christine Delphy, trans. Diana Leonard (University of Massachusetts Press, Amherst. MA, 1984, $10.95 paper).

There's a whole body of women's writing in English that is at once relatively unknown and superbly good *if* one reads the works in the contexts of their own literary tradition, which is not that of the masculinist canon we all know. Even critics who have created new analytic tools we can apply to women's literature have worked on the relatively narrow base of those (atypical) works that have made it into the masculinist canon. Susan Koppelman has spent fifteen years searching for American women's short stories from 1826 to the present (she found, incidentally, that the short story form was pioneered and developed by women) and from the more than two thousand "minor" or unknown stories she unearthed, most from single-author collections and women's magazines, she has fashioned these three volumes. (Five more have been accepted for publication and fifteen are planned at this time, including a "big book" of 150 stories from 1826 to 1980.)

To my mind, what is so very exciting about Koppelman's research is seeing the characteristic themes of women's writing emerge from the body of the work – they are still characteristic today – and finding how stories that first seem pale or puzzling gather extraordinarily vivid, suggestive force once one reads them in the context of all the works. More, there are geniuses here – Mary E. Wilkins Freeman is only one of them – and subject-matter never mentioned in traditionally masculinist criticism but whose power we know in our women's bones. For me the map of literature has been altered forever by Koppelman's anthologies.

The books may have been ignored partly because reading the stories without attending to Koppelman's interpretations can be a puzzling business. (The whole point of the books is the enhancing power on individual works of a knowledge of the entire tradition.) There's also the matter of Koppelman's introductions and notes – they look simple but aren't. They illuminate nothing less than the whole conjunction of sexual politics, literature and history, and with a grand sweep. These are wonderful books.

I include Christine Delphy's witty collection of essays here (it's translated from the French) because it, too, has received less attention from American feminists than it deserves. The *Psych et Po* current of thought in French feminism has become an American academic favorite recently, which may have contributed to the silence about Delphy's quite different work. What she does is to demonstrate (in the very same argument) both the limits and the necessity of Marxist class analysis. That is, *women are a class in Marxist terms*. American consciousness of Marxist class analysis, including far too much feminist consciousness, is frankly non-existent. In fact the kind of attention most American feminists give to class issues scares me silly; either they assume it's men's nastiness which somehow doesn't apply to women and which feminism will automatically fix, or they insist that there's nothing wrong with capitalism that a little good will and changing sexist "attitudes" can't remedy.

That the capitalist wage economy is parasitic on the "female" economy of domestic work, reproduction and the social/emotional work that holds communities together is a feminist insight and one which Marx, I think, refused to see. But that doesn't mean that his insights about the exploitative mess of the wage economy (which grew out of and in turn enforced the socially created split between the "private" world, which was dumped on women, and the "public" one, not a bargain for most, which was enforced on men) can't let women in *as a class*, despite the propaganda about women's gains in the last twenty years (mostly illusory). We are far too expensive, whether attitudes change or not. Without knowing this, too many professional and academic women will go on trying for the respectability that perpetually somehow evades all but a few and in the process limiting and falsifying the very feminism that matters so much to them. Me, too.

It's a painful subject but a fine book.

Author's Note
The Women's Review of Books asked many writers for their choice of reading and the resultant material was published under the title "What Writers Read." The books described above are still my favorites – and Susan Koppelman has since published more of her fine anthologies.

Lesbian Ethics, 2:3, summer 1987

Dear *LE*,

Thank you, Julia, for your essay ("Heteropatriarchal Semantics," *LE* 2:2) which untangles the confusion I've always felt in *LE* (and elsewhere) about butch/femme, masculine/feminine talk.

My own experiences: I was a child during World War II and absorbed all those posters and movies of heroic women – remember? I also grew up a third-generation Ashkenazy (Eastern European Jew) in a similar community in New York City. Much later, after I came out a second time at 33, I was very puzzled by the definitions of butch I heard around me. I was also embarrassed and ashamed because I hadn't the slightest desire to fix cars, play softball, fight, be "physical" and all the other things I saw/heard were "truly lesbian" or "truly butch." I was usually characterized as a "butchy femme" because, although I liked clothes and sewing (which I learned from my *father*, originally, and later taught myself; he had learned it from his *mother*) and didn't fix cars, etc., I was articulate, "bossy," pushed everyone around, insisted on doing so, got openly angry and passionately bitter about sexism, and so forth.

I have just realized that when I was called "male-identified" (by other lesbians) *or* "femme," what the lesbians around me were perceiving wasn't the same split *I* made between "masculine" and "feminine" because theirs was Gentile. Mine was Jewish.

No man fixed cars or was athletic in my neighborhood; no man I knew ever fought physically with another. To the first- and second-generation *shtetl* descendants around me, what was reserved to men, and what made them superior to women, was not the qualities Julia lists but intellectuality, scholarship, and religion, all activities denied women. The third-generation Jewish boys I knew at college were quite viciously sexist, but it never would have occurred to them to claim a monopoly on cars or athletics; what they claimed for their own was poetry, philosophy, science and fiction, all the things I loved the most.

They were the *rabbis*, the *melameds* (teachers) I wanted so passionately to be.

As for clothes and jewelry, first- and second-generation Ashkenazy women wore them much the way their ancestors did: not so much as badges of "beauty" or "weakness" but as loudly competitive signs of wealth. They are not so far from being twelfth-century small-town ghetto dwellers, after all.

To have weakness or fragility or gentleness as ideals for women would have struck them as crazy; a *shaine maedel* (lovely girl) was "beautiful," true, but she abounded with health, she knew how to run the family finances, she could work, she would be fertile, and she would form part of the practical network of community services Jessie Bernard has called the "integry."

And of course there were *no spinsters* in the Ashkenazy community, not even devalued ones. Family was all. Which drove me more batshit than anything, even then.

It's a heteropatriarchal system, all right, but not the *same* one!

Of course, by the third generation we were also being assimilated into the American Gentile ideals, so that what Julia calls the HP system was superimposed over our own Yiddish system.

It's second nature to me to believe (underneath the assimilated values) that the ideal human being is a combination of *balabusteh* (crackerjack housekeeper), community leader/organizer, businesswoman, needle trades worker (all female excellences) AND a spiritual leader, poet, historian, philosopher, counselor, political analyst, story-teller and teacher, in short a *rabbi* and a *melamed* (the excellences reserved for males).

This combination is perplexing to women who have grown up in a different tradition, it seems.

Our ethnic differences must make many differences like this. I think CR is necessary to discover and untangle them; your Reader's forum *is* CR, to my mind, i.e. specific. Let's have more.

Author's Note
The United States is a nation made up of many very different sub-cultures (this is not even mentioning class differences). I have heard talk – largely from middle-aged white men – to the effect that everything used to be so harmonious and people so happy and what happened? – but they don't really want to know. Differences that used to be firmly suppressed in a hierarchy that was sold to all of us as "natural" are now busting out all over. When they take the forms of theory or morals (and even when they don't) it's impossible to argue them away. They exist. The Left (to which I belong) must learn them. We must all learn them. It's time and it's hard to do. I'm trying.

Gay Community News, January 22–28 1989

Dear *GCN*

There must be New Age believers who make more sense than Chris Griscom (author of *Ecstasy Is a New Frequency: Teachings of the Life*), but those I know are all too like her, at least in what they are willing to believe. In order to believe that the universe is just and kindly, people will tolerate any sort of silliness and confusion. The New Age believers I meet have come from some form of white American Protestantism and I – like Duncan Mitchel (see *GCN*, Nov. 6–12, 1988) – see Griscom and Shirley Maclaine's beliefs as a disguised form of Christianity: obsessed with individual salvation, unaware of history, justifying its own contradictions, appealing to mystery and faith, and lacking in community and social conscience.

Don't understand it? Have faith! Don't believe it? Have faith! Or as one young woman said to me when she found out I didn't believe in God, "But you ought to *try*," as if belief were an athletic feat like running a four-minute mile.

I'm an atheist. I had an entirely secular upbringing, but with the emphasis on ethics and social action typical of the secular Jews of my parents' generation, in whom Messianic fervor had been transformed into a passionate determination to understand the world and an equally passionate commitment to changing it for the better. I'm also someone who's had many experiences of what I can only call mysticism during my teens and twenties: a feeling of unity with the natural world and even moments in which I "knew" (in ways I could never recall afterwards or describe) that space and time were – I use such language for lack of a better – illusions. This sort of experience turns up in the literary records of all sorts of religions and while the experience is remarkably the same in all accounts (or almost all) it is used by particular mystics to "prove" the truth of their own particular religious belief. In short, it has no necessary connection with the facts of that creed nor does it – in my experience – have any connection with morality of the ordinary kind. I never made the jump from such experiences to any kind of creed; I merely assumed that everybody felt like that sometimes and let it go at that.

It's those who get religion in childhood who need religion later.

If my mysticism is or was connected with anything, the connection is with some sort of feeling I can only call aesthetic, the same sort of thing I feel for music or mathematics.

Ecstatic, wonderful experiences happen and are a part of life. There are also experiences that are terrifying or bleak. These are part of life also. The world's religions have bent logic into pretzels trying to erase the pain of life and all of them have had to mystify it. Thus we are told simply that pain is a mystery or that life is an illusion anyway or that the afterlife will make up to us for it or that we are being tested or that our perceptions of pain as pain are at fault, and lately that victims choose their fate and it doesn't really hurt anyway.

Mitchel thinks such beliefs are contemptible. I agree.

In fact there seems to be something very U.S.A.-style imperialistic about such stuff; i.e. that the agony and death of others exists *for us*, either to add to our wealth and self-congratulation in the ordinary economic/political way of thinking such things or – in Griscom's view – to teach us that the suffering of others doesn't matter and that it exists *for us* too.

I had to write and add my voice to Mitchel's. And thank him.

The Women's Review of Books, VI:7, April 1989

Dear Editors,

Claudia Koonz is too polite about Joan Wallach Scott's *Gender and the Politics of History* (January 1989). I'm strongly reminded of the politically ghastly 1950s in which abuses of the New Criticism likewise served to "push reality into the wings" and give all agency to language.

Is it surprising, in the politically reactionary 1980s, to find a parallel attempt to turn academic attention to "the process of signification" and away from the human actors who create it, continue it and often suffer from it in this bad real world?

To say that language influences reality and helps create or stabilize it and that events do not occur unmediated by human beliefs and social systems is one thing. To say that nothing else exists or that we can legitimately know only language is another thing entirely. The *reductio ad absurdum* here is so obvious that I feel silly merely pointing it out: signification is all we can talk about, signification is produced by human subjectivity and human experience which (a) do not exist or (b) are to be ignored as unknowable – therefore we are discussing a subject, signification, *which we cannot know and which cannot exist* because it can be judged by nobody because we cannot talk about human subjectivity.

I'm not accusing Scott of participating in a conspiracy, nor do I want to imply anything about her motives. But one of the advantages of aging is that when you see the same damn nonsense coming round again you can spot it in one-tenth the time it took you to recognize it the first time. The 1950s' literary emphasis on the autonomy of texts was an escape into a realm divorced from the nasty world in which professors were being kicked out of jobs for being "subversive" and witch hunts against homosexuals were a regular feature of public life. Current reality is also mighty unpleasant; how nice it would be if it *were* only language and we could control it by controlling language, or if attempts to do anything else were impossible or useless. (And look how important that would make us.)

There are other ways of abandoning or gutting feminism and they are happening: attempts to amalgamate it to the anti-feminist intellectual tradition it used to criticize; focusing on issues even non-feminists can deplore (like individual violent acts against women) and turning away from the apparently more refractory issues, like money; attempts to create a "women's culture" or even a women's religion unconnected to economics or politics; or labeling "feminist" everything one judges to be good, like peace, ecology or vegetarianism. Meanwhile my undergraduate students assure me that feminism is no longer necessary because we've solved all that and various female colleagues and graduate students derive it from two white gentlemen, ignoring twenty years of extra-academic and other academic feminist work and writing.

I would say that we've been betrayed, were not such a remark one of the banalities of history. And so heartbreaking.

Author's Note
This one doesn't need a note!

SFRA Newsletter, No. 172, November 1989

The Other Side

Dear Editors,

Sarah Lefanu's *Feminism and Science Fiction* may not be the kind of book Rob Latham wants Lefanu to write but I believe it is, nonetheless, a good and important book. Lefanu has written a book not about feminism but a search for the possibilities of feminism in science fiction. The book *is* feminism. Perhaps Latham's hostility to the work springs from his lack of acquaintance with the last twenty years of feminist theory in the U.S. and elsewhere. This is knowledge rarely found in the academy. Acceptance there of the French school of Psychoanalyse et Politique and associated work oriented toward Freud and Lacan omits most of French feminism (which is quite different from the kind popularized here in the academy) and almost all of the rich tradition originating outside the academy in the last two decades of U.S. and British writing. Some other questions Latham's review suggests:

What's wrong with eclecticism? Criticism isn't a science, nor does it proceed by everyone's accepting certain basic principles and reasoning deductively therefrom.

Why demand a definition of "science fiction"? Genres always have clear, pointable-at centers and fuzzy boundaries.

In the absence of any kind of comprehensive account of women's writing in English of the last two centuries – all we have had is pounds of criticism applied to a penn'orth of canon – should we trust anything besides the kind of particular readings Lefanu does so well? There is such a long tradition of women's work and there are some pioneers – see, for example, Susan Koppelman's work.

Although Latham praises Lefanu for her particular readings, he also accuses her of "unsubstantiated claims," "accusations," "sneering," and "smugness." It is true that Lefanu does not soothe or flatter – she is angry at men as a privileged *class* and makes no bones about it – but her anger does not necessarily impugn the truth of her generalizations. That science fiction has been a male preserve since the 1920s is hardly a debatable statement. And I join Lefanu in much of her anger, and her cynicism about the sudden popularity of female heroes in male writers' science fiction.

Why is *The Handmaid's Tale* a "major" work? Despite my admiration for Atwood's other work, I find this novel thin and evasive, lacking in economic plausibility and without any of the political history we have every right to demand of a dystopla. *Swastika Night* is much better science fiction and hence a much better book, but it certainly isn't part of the U.S. tradition of science fiction, which grew out of the pulps, and which was joined by British science fiction only after World War II.

Why include Margaret St Clair, Shirley Jackson or Miriam Allen de Ford as feminist writers? One might make a case for Shirley Jackson as a writer who depicts the female situation but feminism is surely more self-conscious and politically explicit than this.

Why not include "minor" fiction, like Marion Zimmer Bradley's if it suits one's critical purpose? Bradley is a very popular writer whose work has certainly influenced readers.[1] She has written at least one explicitly feminist statement, *The Shattered Chain*, which was part of the mini-explosion of explicitly feminist science fiction in the U.S. during the 1970s. Other books include Suzy Charnas's *Walk to the End of the World* and *Motherlines*, my own *The Female Man*, Alice Sheldon's "Houston, Houston, Do You Read?" and "The Women Men Don't See" (and possibly a few others like "Mama Come Home"), Le Guin's *The Left Hand of Darkness*, Sally Gearhart's *The Wanderground*, Delany's *Triton*, and Marge Piercy's *Woman on the Edge of Time*. Piercy and I and Charnas and I have corresponded, as have I and Delany; Bradley named one of the characters in her book after one of the characters in mine; Alice Sheldon and I also corresponded (until her death); Piercy read all the other books, and everybody read everybody. Both by her intention – we all, as far as I know, made our intentions very clear – Bradley belongs in this group. (I think she and I did write a few letters to each other but I can't find them.) I was one of the people who read Gearhart's early stories and urged her to write more. (I even sent a *geschrei* to Le Guin, about which she was remarkably patient.)

I hope Lathan's review will not keep anyone who is teaching women's studies, science fiction or women's literature from getting and using Lefanu's very good book.

---

1 A fan fiction has grown up about her invented world, Darkover, which has produced some originally-fan, now-professional, writers.

Extrapolation, 31:1, spring 1990

To the Editors:

Veronica Hollinger's essay in 30:2 [on "James Tiptree, Jr."] (1989) sent me back to Alice Sheldon's letters. The relevant passage is from a letter dated the twenty-fifth of September, 1980, "0400 hours."

> Just been reading the Coming-Out stories ed by Stanley & Wolfe (with a lot of Adrienne Rich) and it occurred to me to wonder if I ever told you in so many words that I am a Lesbian – or at least as close as one can come to being one never having had a successful love with any of the women I've loved, and being now too old & ugly to dare try. Oh, had 65 years been different! I *like* some men a lot, but from the start, before I knew anything it was always girls and women who lit me up. (Oh, the sad, foolish, lovely tales I'm going to have to put down some day!)
>
> I just thought I'd mention it, since you seem to have found yourself. (Possibly my reward for years of stasis & misery is to be the ideal confidante!)

Pre-Stonewall life was hard on homosexual people; our response to the hostility and bigotry around us has often been to associate love with death – or at least love with disaster, which is still a possibility today despite some of the advances of the last two decades. Unrequited love is a way of protecting oneself against the fear that the desire brings and yet expressing that desire. Hence the "stasis & misery."

I'm sending the letters Tiptree wrote me to the Lesbian Herstory Archives in New York. The address is: Lesbian Herstory Archives, P.O. Box 1258, New York, N.Y. 10116.

Author's Note
"James Tiptree, Jr." was a science fiction writer whose very fine work began appearing in the 1960s. No one had ever met "Tiptree" and theories about "him" were rife. Finally "James Tiptree, Jr." was revealed to be a sixty-year-old biologist called Alice Sheldon. We corresponded extensively, both before this revelation and afterwards. I loved James and was sad to lose him but I loved Alice too (she sent postcards typed in blue ink with blue-ink octopi drawn on them) and was much sadder to lose her because her

loss (her death) was permanent. Straight people, however sympathetic they may be, don't know the texture or the difficulties of gay lives. When I heard of her death I determined that she wouldn't go down in history as another happy, heterosexual woman (like Virginia Woolf) whose life was edited because her real desires were held to be somehow an "attack" on her character. Sheldon, like Woolf, was married and happily so but she was a lesbian. Therefore I wrote the above note to *Extrapolation* and donated her letters to what I considered the appropriate place.

Publication of the Modern Language Association, March 1992

Author's Note
If academic intellectuals have a besetting vice it's abstraction. It's so easy to lose awareness of people's concrete situations in studying their rhetoric or the structures of their situations. I don't know if Rita Felski has incorporated a down-to-earth knowledge of gay lives in the late 1890s into her book, but I *do* know about being gay in the 1950s and 1960s (I was there) and it seemed to me that she didn't. Where does the money come from? Who gets it? What do they have to do to get it? What happens if they don't do it? Questions like these tend to slip silently out of many academic theories. Some years ago I read a poem by Oscar Wilde, a flamboyant exotic-erotic affair written when he was an undergraduate of nineteen. It seemed to me rather overblown in its purple and sensuous imagery – until I realized that he was writing about his own kind of sexuality and suddenly I could see the conflict *in the poem itself* between wanting to say it straight out and knowing that he couldn't. Saying it could put you in jail. You could be stuck in a mental hospital. Your career could be ruined, your family could desert you, your job could disappear. In Wilde's time these were not possibilities but dead certain. In fact, they happened. It's things like this that most academics tend to leave out of their theorizing when the people in question are not like them. And that is a very, very bad thing for everyone.

To the Editors:

In "The Counterdiscourse of the Feminine in Three Texts by Wilde, Huysmans, and Sacher-Masoch" (*PMLA*, 106 [1991]: 1094–105), Rita Felski doesn't emphasize the writers' conscious motives for the fin-de-siècle "cult of art and artifice" (p. 1094) she otherwise treats so well. Of course, her forthcoming book may do just this, but I think her article scants the extent to which the writers involved knew what they were doing.

First – and I don't think this can be emphasized too much – careers and lives could easily be smashed by any openness at all [about homosexuality], and everyone knew it.

Second – and Felski seems to me to have de-emphasized this too – there is the formidable difficulty of describing or envisioning oneself at all, given the cultural counters available. How to describe – or even be – this man-who-is-not-a-man? How to do so especially at the particular time Felski notes? As Jonathan Ned Katz demonstrates (*Gay/Lesbian Almanac: A New Documentary*, Harper, New York, 1983), the crucial business of inventing "heterosexuality" – that new identity the European medical profession was so insistent about – required for real success "homosexuality": its bad and deviant twin, to which certain qualities were attributed. Unnatural? Fine; we'll make a value of artifice. Immoral? We'll make a virtue of heartlessness. Feminine? We'll scorn women. Defective? We'll be aristocrats, either by birth or by taste.

Without more emphasis on the reactive nature of the "cult," readers of Felski's article may misinterpret such phrases as "a subtext of anxiety and repressed violence" (p. 1102) and "deeper anxieties about sexuality and the body" (p. 1101) and conclude that such anxieties resulted from homosexuality or that they caused it. When oppression is soft-pedaled, the connection between anxiety and oppression gets lost, as does the link between anxiety and outright persecution.

When actual gay politics becomes active rather than reactive, so do cultural politics, of course. Some of this happened in the period Felski describes. I look forward to her book, but I hope it will embrace more of the historicity of the phenomenon she studies and will face more squarely the problem of how conscious a strategy the decadent sensibility was and what sort of strategies were practical for writers whose earning a living depended directly or indirectly on their work. Along with Katz, Sheila Jeffreys (*The Spinster and Her Enemies: Feminism and Sexuality, 1880–1930*, Routledge, London, 1985) and Lilian Faderman (*Surpassing the Love of Men: Romantic Friendship and Love Between Women from the Renaissance to the Present*, Morrow, New York, 1981) are important sources for this period; that Felski doesn't use them here is a mistake, I think.

A note on Huysmans's character Miss Urania: her name is a joke clearly aimed at those in the know. A German term, originating in the 1860s, *uranism* was used throughout the 1880s and 1890s (especially in the United States, says Katz) to mean homosexuality. Huysmans' brutal strong man at the fair reappears in Quentin Crisp's *Naked Civil Servant* as the tall dark man and throughout Jean Genet's novels as just about everybody.

Sojourner: The Women's Forum, **September 1993**

Rewind After Viewing

Ishtar, written and directed by Elaine May. RCA/Columbia Pictures (1987)

Is a feminist buddy picture about men possible? Yes – when the director's Elaine May, with her brand of gentle lunacy/common sense. In *Ishtar*, Dustin Hoffman and Warren Beatty are lousy songwriter wannabes – unheroic, generous, unsuspicious, openhearted and more than a teensy bit slow (in short, sheltered white American men as May and I would like to see them). Isabelle Adjani, revolutionary heroine, is the real hero of the picture, so disguised during most of the movie that we see only the tip of her nose and her upper lip. (She flashes one breast for a millisecond in a crowded airport in a scene so utterly anti-erotic that it probably explains much of the critics' venom toward the picture.) At the end we get to see her *whole face* – briefly – in a very demure dress with a lace collar.

May doesn't set up her laughs and pile-drive them home. The picture's pacing is gentle and respectful, in a way I associate with women's pictures; i.e. things *ripple* and you get to smile at them. I found it all excruciatingly, deliciously funny, from Beatty's knitted cap with its pom-pom and his overstuffed quilted jacket with waddle to match (they make him look like a five-year-old in a snowsuit) to a wonderfully awful camel that personifies sheer animal self-will; it goes when you want it to stop, sits when you want it to go, wanders in circles no matter what you do, and groans horribly at all the wrong moments, like a distressed basso trombone. There's one impulsive kiss just as clumsily uncomfortable as such things really are, and the actors are obviously delighted to be playing real people and not Hollywood glitz.

Given the outline of the kind of film feminists cringe at, May has produced – by some major miracle – a woman's film. There's not a trace of the patriarchal adulation of male heroics; Adjani's smarts (and compassion) save the day, and there's a wonderful portrayal of a C.I.A. man so oily your fingertips cringe – you know if you touched him, they'd come away greasy. If Indiana Jones (and all the others) make you snarl, *Ishtar* is the perfect antidote. The critics disliked it, and it bombed at the box office, but it's a gem.

The Lesbian Review of Books, I:3, 1995

In her essay in *The Persistent Desire*, Lyndall MacCowan says something that seems to shed a lot of light on the ongoing lesbian debates on sexuality, the latest manifestation of which occurred in I:2 of *The Lesbian Review of Books*.

MacCowan says that "women's" sexual pain comes from being punished by means of their sexuality for being female, while "lesbians'" sexual pain comes from being punished *for* being sexual (p. 32). These groups are not mutually exclusive, obviously, and many of us have been punished in both ways. Nonetheless, depending on which kind of punishment has been dominant in one's life (and perhaps depending on which happened earlier), it's probable that a particular lesbian will be found on either one side or the other of the debate.

Those punished in the area of their sexuality are probably those who have lived a heterosexual life or (like me) tried to, and they will be keenly aware of the ways in which abusive and domineering behavior can be confused with sexuality, forced on them under the pretext of sexuality, or excused because it is "sexual." Those punished for their lesbian sexuality will be vividly aware of how "improper" sexual desires can be the reason for hatred, cruelty and exclusion. Both will have low flash points for anything that resembles (or even simply reminds them of) what they have been put through. Thus one group will see plastique explosive in what another regards as Play-doh, and the latter will perceive any request for analysis as another raid by the police.

What the two sides are arguing about is a *difference in experience*. Both are right. Both are wrong. When one speaks of sexual freedom, the other will react as if the first were advocating violence; when one attacks violence, the other will react as if the attack were against freedom. In this spiraling of perceived threat, one faction will talk about the other's "sex phobia" and the second faction about the first's "violence against women." Thus in 1982 Kathleen Barry insisted (in *Trivia*) that Gayle Rubin's wish to repeal age-of-consent laws meant condoning rape in which the rapist used threats of murder (p. 90). I have heard some young lesbians similarly dismiss feminism as a conspiracy of evil witches (like me) who had "desexualized" lesbianism – without any awareness that it was feminism that had in large part secured for them the relative freedom they have today.

As MacCowan says, the feminism of the 1970s did indeed originate in the experience of white women attached to middle-class white men. I was one of them. I know that our experiences and assumptions were heterosexual, *no matter what our orientation may have been*. This is not a crime. It was hard enough, at that time and in that context, to trust our own experience at all, and that we succeeded in doing so to any degree at all was an immense achievement. Nonetheless, our analysis was incomplete.

On the other hand, I agree emphatically with Jeffreys that changes in style do not in themselves cause social change and neither does sexual pleasure. Style changes are perfectly O.K. things, but insisting that everything you happen to like is "subversive" is the overreaction of persecuted people.

Every oppressed group desperately needs coalitions. These won't happen if people continue to talk past each other. I think the only way to make our positions intelligible to each other is not by arguing in abstractions, but by *recounting experiences* and connecting them to our particular ideas, i.e. by consciousness raising. That is what the fine anthology *The Persistent Desire*, and Kathleen Barry's fine biography of Susan B. Anthony both do.

Once we know about each other's experiences and the ideas which come from them, we can avoid the kind of thing Halberstam inadvertently does at the end of her review of *The Lesbian Heresy*. For over a century many men have used derisive references to women's "prudery" and "frigidity," as well as pleased accounts of how sexually liberated they themselves are, as a way of insulting women, feminists and feminism. I endured this more times than I care to remember in the years spanning 1950 to 1980. It was (and is) sexism of a particularly nasty kind. It doesn't belong in a book review and I don't like it, even though I agree with much in Halberstam's review, especially her comments on the erotic DMZ and something ghastly "skittering" across it. We must stop making jokes that are not jokes to the other side. We must stop making totalizing statements, employing a double standard of behavior (if one of Us does it, it's a human flaw; if one of Them does, it's a sign of Their evil), and demonizing each other (no matter what They say, I know what They really mean and it's bad). What folks value, what they do, what they know, what they accept and reject, all come from what has happened to them. I am talking about knowledge, and understanding other people's knowledge is what it's all about.

Author's Note
The Great Lesbian/Feminist Sex Wars continue. I would like to lock one of the less sensible of each camp in a room until they either come to some agreement or meet the fate of the Gingham Dog and the Calico Cat.

Index of Books and Authors Reviewed

7 Conquests. Poul Anderson (Macmillan) 26
Abyss. Kate Wilhelm (Doubleday) 64
Age of the Pussyfoot, The. Frederik Pohl (Trident) 18
Aickman, Robert, *Painted Devils* (Charles Scribner's Sons) 175
Aldiss, Brian, *Frankenstein Unbound* (Random House) 108
— *Report on Probability A* (Doubleday) 44
Allen, L. David, *Cliffs Notes: Science Fiction, An Introduction* (Cliffs Notes Inc., Lincoln, Nebraska) 114
Anderson, Poul, *7 Conquests* (Macmillan) 26
— *Satan's World* (Doubleday) 41
Anderson, Poul, ed., *Best SF Stories from New Worlds #2, The* (Berkley) 25
Anderson, Poul, and Mildred Downey Broxon, *Demon of Scattery, The* (Ace) 173
Anticipations: Eight New Stories. Ed. Christopher Priest (Scribner's, New York) 147
Anvil, Christopher, *Pandora's Planet* (Doubleday) 80
As Tomorrow Becomes Today. Ed. Charles Wm. Sullivan, III (Prentice-Hall) 117
Ashes, Ashes. René Barjavel, trans. Damon Knight (Doubleday) 9
Asimov, Isaac, *In Memory Yet Green: The Autobiography of Isaac Asimov, 1920–1954* (Doubleday) 141
— *Opus 200* (Houghton Mifflin) 142
Bad Moon Rising. Ed. Thomas Disch (Harper & Row) 97

Barjavel, René, trans. Damon Knight, *Ashes, Ashes* (Doubleday) 9
Bed Sitting Room, The. Richard Lester (movie) 52
Beginning Place, The. Ursula K. Le Guin (Harper & Row) 171
Bernard, Jessie, *Future of Marriage, The* (World) 86
Best of the Best, The. Ed. Judith Merril (Delacorte) 8
Best SF Stories from New Worlds #2, The. Ed. Poul Anderson (Berkley) 25
Best SF: 1968. Eds. Harry Harrison and Brian Aldiss (Putnam's) 37
Beyond Apollo. Barry Malzberg (Random House) 83
Biggle, Lloyd, *Light That Never Was, The* (Doubleday) 81
— *Still Small Voice of Trumpets, The* (Doubleday) 15
Black Easter. James Blish (Doubleday) 11
Blish, James, *Black Easter* (Doubleday) 11
— *Day After Judgment, The* (Doubleday) 67
— *Midsummer Century* (Doubleday) 82
— *Warriors of the Day, The* (Lancer) 4
Blish, James, and Norman L. Knight, *Torrent of Faces, A* (Doubleday) 10
Blum, Ralph, *Simultaneous Man, The* (Atlantic–Little Brown) 49
Blunt, Wilfrid, *Omar* (Doubleday) 21
Born With the Dead. Robert Silverberg (Random House) 102
Boswell, Harriet A., *Master Guide to Psychism* (Lancer) 61
Bova, Ben, *Millennium* (Random House) 125

Boyd, John, *Last Starship from Earth, The* (Berkley) 31
Bradbury, Ray, *I Sing the Body Electric* (Knopf) 44
Brown, Frederic, *Paradox Lost* (Random House) 100
Brunner, John, *Total Eclipse* (Doubleday) 106
Buckland, Raymond, *Practical Candle Burning* (Llewellyn) 60
Bug Jack Barron. Norman Spinrad (Avon) 34
Bulmer, Kenneth, *Doomsday Men, The* (Doubleday) 15
Bunch, David R., *Moderan* (Avon) 74
Butler, Octavia, *Kindred* (Doubleday & Company) 176

Can You Feel Anything When I Do This? Robert Shackley (Doubleday) 79
Carr, Terry, ed., *Year's Finest Fantasy, The* (Berkley Putnam, New York, 1978) 136
— *Universe 9* (Doubleday & Company) 176
Chant, Joy, *Grey Mane of Morning, The* (George Allen & Unwin, London, 1977) 138
Clement, Hal, *Small Changes* (Doubleday) 24
Clement, Hal, ed., *First Flights to the Moon* (Doubleday) 53
Clewiston Test, The. Kate Wilhelm (Farrar, Straus and Giroux) 122
Cliffs Notes: Science Fiction, An Introduction. L. David Allen (Cliffs Notes Inc., Lincoln, Nebraska) 114
Cloned Lives. Pamela Sargent (Fawcett Gold Medal) 127
Comet. Jane White (Harper) 126
Committed Men, The. M. John Harrison (Doubleday) 78
Complete Book of Magic and Witchcraft, The. Kathryn Paulsen (Signet) 59
Complex Man. Marie Farca (Doubleday) 102
Conrad, Earl, *Da Vinci Machine, The* (Fleet Press) 32
Cooper, Edmund, *Sea Horse in the Sky* (Putnam's) 51

Cube Root of Uncertainty, The. Robert Silverberg (Macmillan) 54

Da Vinci Machine, The. Earl Conrad (Fleet Press) 32
Daly, Mary, *Gyn/Ecology: The Metaethics of Radical Feminism* (Boston: Beacon Press, 1979) 155
Dann, Jack, ed., *Immortal: Short Novels of the Transhuman Future* (Harper & Row, New York) 145
Dark Symphony, The. Dean R. Koontz (Lancer) 51
Davidson, Avram, *Phoenix and the Mirror, The* (Doubleday) 22
Day After Judgment, The. James Blish (Doubleday) 67
Day of the Dolphin, The. Robert Merle (Simon and Schuster) 33
Del Rey, Judy Lynn, ed., *Stellar 1* (Ballantine) 114
Demon of Scattery, The. Poul Anderson and Mildred Downey Broxon (Ace) 173
Dialectic of Sex, The. Shulamith Firestone (Bantam) 62
Diary of a Witch. Sybil Leek (Signet) 60
Dick, Philip K., *Flow My Tears, The Policeman Said*. (Doubleday) 106
Dickson, Gordon, *Star Road, The* (Doubleday) 100
Dinnerstein, Dorothy, *Mermaid and the Minotaur, The: Sexual Arrangements and Human Malaise* (Harper & Row, New York, 1976) 160
Disch, Thomas M., *On Wings of Song* (St. Martin's Press) 173
Disch, Thomas, ed., *Bad Moon Rising* (Harper & Row) 97
Dispossessed, The. Ursula K. Le Guin (Harper & Row) 110
Donaldson, Stephen, *Lord Foul's Bane* (Holt, Rinehart and Winston, New York, 1977, Ballantine, 1978) 138
Doomsday Men, The. Kenneth Bulmer (Doubleday) 15
Dying Inside. Robert Silverberg (Scribner's) 96

Effinger, George Alec, *What Entropy Means To Me* (Doubleday) 85

INDEX OF BOOKS AND AUTHORS REVIEWED

Elder, Joseph, ed., *Eros In Orbit: A Collection of All New Science Fiction Stories About Sex* (Trident Press) 91

Elliott, Robert C., *Shape of Utopia, The: Studies in a Literary Genre* (University of Chicago Press, 1970) 68

Ellison, Harlan (collaborations with various authors), *Partners in Wonder* (Walker) 66

Elwood, Roger, and Sam Moskowitz, eds., *Strange Signposts, An Anthology of the Fantastic* (Holt Rinehart and Winston, 1966) 3

Emphyrio. Jack Vance (Doubleday) 36

Empty People, The. K. M. O'Donnell (Lancer) 38

Emshwiller, Carol, *Joy in Our Cause* (Harper & Row) 112

English Assassin, The. Michael Moorcock (Harper & Row) 120

Eros In Orbit: A Collection of All New Science Fiction Stories About Sex. Ed. Joseph Elder (Trident Press) 91

Faderman, Lillian, *Surpassing the Love of Men: Romantic Friendship and Love Between Women from the Renaissance to the Present* (Morrow, Quill paperback) 188

Falling Astronauts, The. Barry N. Malzberg (Ace) 76

Farca, Marie, *Complex Man* (Doubleday) 102

Farmer, Philip José, *Flesh* (Doubleday) 16

Feinberg, Gerald, *Prometheus Project, The: Mankind's Search for Long-Range Goals* (Doubleday) 28

Final Programme, The. Michael Moorcock (Avon) 14

Fireflood and Other Stories. Vonda N. McIntyre (Houghton Mifflin) 172

Firestone, Shulamith, *Dialectic of Sex, The* (Bantam) 62

First Flights to the Moon. Ed. Hal Clement (Doubleday) 53

Fisher, Elizabeth, *Woman's Creation: Sexual Evolution and the Shaping of Society* (McGraw-Hill, New York, 1980) 185

Flesh. Philip José Farmer (Doubleday) 16

Flow My Tears, The Policeman Said. Philip. K. Dick (Doubleday) 106

Frankenstein Unbound. Brian Aldiss (Random House) 108

Friend, Beverly, *Science Fiction: The Classroom in Orbit* (Educational Impact, Inc., Glassboro, N.J., 1974) 120

Future of Marriage, The. Jessie Bernard (World) 86

Gerrold, David, *Yesterday's Children* (Fawcett Popular Library) 172

Gilman, Charlotte Perkins, *Herland: A Lost Feminist Utopian Novel* (Pantheon, New York, 1979) 152

Goulart, Ron, *Sword Swallower, The* (Doubleday) 21

Greenberg, Martin Harry, and Patricia S. Warrick, eds., *Political Science Fiction: An Introductory Reader* (Prentice-Hall) 116

Grey Mane of Morning, The. Joy Chant (George Allen & Unwin, London, 1977) 138

Gunn, James, *Listeners, The* (Scribner's) 95

— *Some Dreams Are Nightmares* (Scribner's) 105

Gyn/Ecology: The Metaethics of Radical Feminism. Mary Daly (Boston: Beacon Press, 1979) 155

Haining, Peter, ed., *Satanists, The* (Taplinger) 58

Harding, Lee, ed., *Ursula K. Le Guin's Science Fiction Writing Workshop: The Altered I* (Berkley, New York) 148

Harrison, Harry, *One Step from Earth* (Macmillan) 54

Harrison, Harry, ed., *Light Fantastic, The* (Scribner's) 65

— *SF: Author's Choice 2* (Berkley) 54

Harrison, Harry, and Brian Aldiss, eds., *Best SF: 1968* (Putnam's) 37

Harrison, M. John, *Committed Men, The* (Doubleday) 78

Hart, Harold H., ed., *Marriage: For and Against* (Hart) 86

Herbert, Frank, *Santaroga Barrier, The* (Berkley) 19

Here, Mr. Splitfoot. Robert Somerlott (Viking) 62

Herland: A Lost Feminist Utopian Novel. Charlotte Perkins Gilman (Pantheon, New York, 1979) 152

High Cost of Living, The. Marge Piercy (New York, Harper and Row, 1978) 129

Humanity Prime. Bruce McAllister (Ace) 77

I Sing the Body Electric. Ray Bradbury (Knopf) 44

Immortal: Short Novels of the Transhuman Future. Ed. Jack Dann (Harper & Row, New York) 145

In Memory Yet Green: The Autobiography of Isaac Asimov, 1920–1954 (Doubleday) 141

In the Pocket and Other SF Stories and *Gather in the Hall of the Planets.* K. M. O'Donnell (Ace double) 77

Into the Unknown: The Evolution of Science Fiction from Francis Godwin to H. G. Wells. Robert M. Philmus (University of California Press, 1970) 71

Iron Dream, The. Norman Spinrad (Avon) 94

Jones, Margaret, *Transplant* (Stein and Day) 20

Joy in Our Cause. Carol Emshwiller (Harper & Row) 112

Kelley, Leo P., *Time Rogue* (Lancer) 55

Kindred. Octavia Butler (Doubleday & Company) 176

Koontz, Dean R., *Dark Symphony, The* (Lancer) 51

Language of the Night, The: Essays on Fantasy and Science Fiction. Ursula Le Guin, ed. Susan Wood (G.P. Putnam's Sons) 179

Last Starship from Earth, The. John Boyd (Berkley) 31

Le Guin, Ursula K., *Beginning Place, The* (Harper & Row) 171

— *Dispossessed, The* (Harper & Row) 110

Le Guin, Ursula, ed. Susan Wood, *Language of the Night, The: Essays on Fantasy and Science Fiction* (G.P. Putnam's Sons) 179

Leek, Sybil, *Diary of a Witch* (Signet) 60

Leiber, Fritz, *Rime Isle* (Whispers Press, Chapel Hill, N.C., 1977) 135

Lester, Richard, dir., *Bed Sitting Room, The* (movie) 52

Let the Fire Fall. Kate Wilhelm (Doubleday) 29

Levin, Ira, *This Perfect Day* (Random House) 46

Light Fantastic, The. Ed. Harry Harrison (Scribner's) 65

Light That Never Was, The. Lloyd Biggle (Doubleday) 81

Listeners, The. James Gunn (Scribner's) 95

Lord Foul's Bane. Stephen Donaldson (Holt, Rinehart and Winston, New York, 1977, Ballantine, 1978) 138

Lord of Light. Roger Zelazny (Doubleday) 6

Malzberg, Barry, *Beyond Apollo* (Random House) 83

— *Falling Astronauts, The* (Ace) 76

Marriage: For and Against. Ed. Harold H. Hart (Hart) 86

Marshak, Sondra, and Myrna Culbreath, eds., *Star Trek: The New Voyages* (Bantam) 127

Master Guide to Psychism. Harriet A. Boswell (Lancer) 61

McAllister, Bruce, *Humanity Prime* (Ace) 77

McCaffrey, Anne, *Ship Who Sang, The* (Walker) 39

McIntyre, Vonda N., *Fireflood and Other Stories* (Houghton Mifflin) 172

Merle, Robert, *Day of the Dolphin, The* (Simon and Schuster) 33

Mermaid and the Minotaur, The: Sexual

INDEX OF BOOKS AND AUTHORS REVIEWED

Arrangements and Human Malaise. Dorothy Dinnerstein (Harper & Row, New York, 1976) 160

Merril, Judith, ed., *Best of the Best, The* (Delacorte) 8

Midsummer Century. James Blish (Doubleday) 82

Millennium. Ben Bova (Random House) 125

Mind Parasites, The. Colin Wilson (Arkham House) 7

Moderan. David R. Bunch (Avon) 74

Modern Science Fiction. Ed. Norman Spinrad (Anchor Press, New York) 119

Moorcock, Michael, *English Assassin, The* (Harper & Row) 120

— *Final Programme, The* (Avon) 14

— *Stealer of Souls* and *Stormbringer* (Lancer) 5

Moore, Raylyn, *What Happened to Emily Goode After the Great Exhibition* (Donning [Scarblaze], Norfolk, Va., 1978) 133

Neeper, Cary, *Place Beyond Man, A* (Dell, New York) 150

New Dimensions 9. Ed. Robert Silverberg (Harper & Row) 177

O'Donnell, K. M., *Empty People, The* (Lancer) 38

— *In the Pocket and Other SF Stories* and *Gather in the Hall of the Planets* (Ace double) 77

Omar. Wilfrid Blunt (Doubleday) 21

On Lies, Secrets, and Silence: Selected Prose, 1966–1978. Adrienne Rich (Norton) 143

On Wings of Song. Thomas M. Disch (St. Martin's Press) 173

One Step from Earth. Harry Harrison (Macmillan) 54

Operation Ares. Gene Wolfe (Berkley) 57

Opus 200. Isaac Asimov (Houghton Mifflin) 142

Painted Devils. Robert Aickman (Charles Scribner's Sons) 175

Pandora's Planet. Christopher Anvil (Doubleday) 80

Paradox Lost. Frederic Brown (Random House) 100

Partners in Wonder. Harlan Ellison (collaborations with various authors) (Walker) 66

Paulsen, Kathryn, *Complete Book of Magic and Witchcraft, The* (Signet) 59

Pavane. Keith Roberts (Doubleday) 17

Philmus, Robert M., *Into the Unknown: The Evolution of Science Fiction from Francis Godwin to H. G. Wells* (University of California Press, 1970) 71

Phoenix and the Mirror, The. Avram Davidson (Doubleday) 22

Piercy, Marge, *High Cost of Living, The* (New York, Harper and Row, 1978) 129

Pig World. Charles W. Runyon (Doubleday) 78

Place Beyond Man, A. Cary Neeper (Dell, New York) 150

Pohl, Frederik, *Age of the Pussyfoot, The* (Trident) 18

Political Science Fiction: An Introductory Reader. Eds. Martin Harry Greenberg, Patricia S. Warrick (Prentice-Hall) 116

Practical Candle Burning. Raymond Buckland (Llewellyn) 60

Priest, Christopher, ed., *Anticipations: Eight New Stories* (Scribner's, New York) 147

Prometheus Project, The: Mankind's Search for Long-Range Goals. Gerald Feinberg (Doubleday) 28

Report on Probability A. Brian W. Aldiss (Doubleday) 44

Retreat As It Was! Donna J. Young (The Naiad Press, 7800 Westside Dr., Weatherby Lake, Missouri, 64152) 181

Rich, Adrienne, *On Lies, Secrets, and Silence: Selected Prose, 1966–1978* (Norton) 143

Rime Isle. Fritz Leiber (Whispers Press, Chapel Hill, N.C., 1977) 135

Roberts, Keith, *Pavane* (Doubleday) 17
Runyon, Charles W., *Pig World* (Doubleday) 78

Sanders, Thomas E., ed., *Speculations: An Introduction to Literature Through Fantasy and Science Fiction* (Glencoe Press, Beverly Hills, California) 117
Santaroga Barrier, The. Frank Herbert (Berkley) 19
Sargent, Pamela, *Cloned Lives* (Fawcett Gold Medal) 127
Satan's World. Poul Anderson (Doubleday) 41
Satanists, The. Ed. Peter Haining (Taplinger) 58
Science Fiction: The Classroom in Orbit. Beverly Friend (Educational Impact, Inc., Glassboro, N.J., 1974) 120
Scortia, Thomas N., *Strange Bedfellows: Sex and Science Fiction* (Random House) 91
Sea Horse in the Sky. Edmund Cooper (Putnam's) 51
SF: Author's Choice 2. Ed. Harry Harrison. (Berkley) 54
Shackley, Robert, *Can You Feel Anything When I Do This?* (Doubleday) 79
Shape of Utopia, The: Studies in a Literary Genre. Robert C. Elliott (University of Chicago Press, 1970) 68
Ship Who Sang, The. Anne McCaffrey (Walker) 39
Silverberg, Robert, *Born With the Dead* (Random House) 102
— *Cube Root of Uncertainty, The* (Macmillan) 54
— *Dying Inside* (Scribner's) 96
Silverberg, Robert, ed., *New Dimensions 9* (Harper & Row) 177
Simultaneous Man, The. Ralph Blum (Atlantic–Little Brown) 49
Small Changes. Hal Clement (Doubleday) 24
Some Dreams Are Nightmares. James Gunn (Scribner's) 105
Somerlott, Robert, *Here, Mr. Splitfoot* (Viking) 62

Speculations: An Introduction to Literature Through Fantasy and Science Fiction. Ed. Thomas E. Sanders (Glencoe Press, Beverly Hills, California) 117
Spinrad, Norman, *Bug Jack Barron* (Avon) 34
— *Iron Dream, The* (Avon) 94
Spinrad, Norman, ed., *Modern Science Fiction* (Anchor Press, New York) 119
Star Mother. Sydney J. Van Scyoc (Berkley Putnam) 126
Star Road, The. Gordon Dickson (Doubleday) 100
Star Trek: The New Voyages. Eds. Sondra Marshak and Myrna Culbreath (Bantam) 127
Stealer of Souls and *Stormbringer*. Michael Moorcock (Lancer) 5
Stellar 1. Ed. Judy Lynn del Rey (Ballantine) 114
Still Small Voice of Trumpets, The. Lloyd Biggle (Doubleday) 15
Strange Bedfellows: Sex and Science Fiction. Ed. Thomas N. Scortia (Random House) 91
Strange Signposts, An Anthology of the Fantastic. Ed. Roger Elwood and Sam Moskowitz (Holt Rinehart and Winston, 1966) 3
Sullivan, Charles Wm., III, ed., *As Tomorrow Becomes Today* (Prentice-Hall) 117
Surpassing the Love of Men: Romantic Friendship and Love Between Women from the Renaissance to the Present Lillian Faderman (Morrow, Quill paperback) 188
Sword Swallower, The. Ron Goulart (Doubleday) 21

Texas–Israeli War, The: 1999. Howard Waldrop and Jake Saunders (Ballantine) 108
This Perfect Day. Ira Levin (Random House) 46
Time Rogue. Leo P. Kelley (Lancer) 55
Torrent of Faces, A. James Blish and Norman L. Knight (Doubleday) 10
Total Eclipse. John Brunner (Doubleday) 106

Transplant. Margaret Jones (Stein and Day) 20

Universe 9. Ed. Terry Carr (Doubleday & Company) 176

Ursula K. Le Guin's Science Fiction Writing Workshop: The Altered I. Ed. Lee Harding (Berkley, New York) 148

Van Scyoc, Sydney J., *Star Mother* (Berkley Putnam) 126

Vance, Jack, *Emphyrio* (Doubleday) 36

Waldrop, Howard, and Jake Saunders, *Texas–Israeli War, The: 1999* (Ballantine) 108

Warriors of the Day, The. James Blish (Lancer) 4

What Entropy Means To Me. George Alec Effinger (Doubleday) 85

What Happened to Emily Goode After the Great Exhibition. Raylyn Moore (Donning [Scarblaze], Norfolk, Va., 1978) 133

White, Jane, *Comet* (Harper) 126

Wilhelm, Kate, *Abyss* (Doubleday) 64
— *Clewiston Test, The* (Farrar, Straus and Giroux) 122
— *Let the Fire Fall* (Doubleday) 29

Wilson, Colin, *Mind Parasites, The* (Arkham House) 7

Wolfe, Gene, *Operation Ares* (Berkley) 57

Woman's Creation: Sexual Evolution and the Shaping of Society. Elizabeth Fisher (McGraw-Hill, New York, 1980) 185

World's Best Science Fiction: 1968 (Ace) 31

Year's Finest Fantasy, The. Ed. Terry Carr (Berkley Putnam, New York, 1978) 136

Yesterday's Children. David Gerrold (Fawcett Popular Library) 172

Young, Donna J., *Retreat As It Was!* (The Naiad Press, 7800 Westside Dr., Weatherby Lake, Missouri, 64152) 181

Zelazny, Rogert, *Lord of Light* (Doubleday) 6